PRAISE FOR
LAUREN SMITH

"*The Gilded Cuff* is a dark, sensual tale that teases and tantalizes the senses. It's all about anticipation, seduction, and surrender. You will be every bit as enthralled with the story as Sophie is with Emery."

—Give Me Books Blog

"From the very first page I was lost to the suspense, romance, thrills, and chills of this intriguing story. In fact, I was so engrossed in the dramatic plot that I stayed up all night to finish the story. There was no way that I would be able to sleep without knowing how everything played out."

—SizzlingHotBooks.com

"If you love a great mystery with a giant dose of steam and a beautiful love story, you will swoon over this novel!"

—The Reading Cafe

The Gilded Chain

ALSO BY LAUREN SMITH

The Gilded Chain

Book 3 in the Surrender series

LAUREN SMITH

FOREVER
YOURS

New York Boston

Copyright © 2015 by Lauren Smith
Excerpt from *The Gilded Cuff* copyright © 2015 by Lauren Smith
Cover design by Elizabeth Turner
Cover copyright © 2015 by Hachette Book Group, Inc.

Forever Yours
Hachette Book Group
1290 Avenue of the Americas
New York, NY 10104

hachettebookgroup.com
twitter.com/foreverromance

First ebook and print on demand edition: December 2015

Forever Yours is an imprint of Grand Central Publishing.
The Forever Yours name and logo are trademarks of Hachette Book Group, Inc.

The publisher is not responsible for websites (or their content) that are not owned by the publisher.

The Hachette Speakers Bureau provides a wide range of authors for speaking events. To find out more, go to www.hachettespeakersbureau.com or call (866) 376-6591.

ISBN 978-1-4555-3282-7

The Gilded Chain

Chapter 1

*Someday after we have mastered the air, the winds,
the tides and gravity, we will harness for god the
energies of love. And then for the second time in the
history of the world, man will have discovered fire.*

—Teilhard de Chardin

*Y*ou are cordially invited to the engagement party of Hayden Thorne
and Fenn Lockwood—"

With a pained gasp, Callie Taylor ripped the expensive cream
card and blinked hard against the thick tears that started to drip
down her cheeks. Fenn, the man she'd loved her entire life, was getting married to her friend Hayden. It was too much to process over
the sudden and shattering pain inside her chest. With a little ragged
gasp of breath, she glanced about her small bedroom, her last refuge
on the wide open expanse of her father's land. The only place she
could really call her own on Broken Spur ranch.

Her room was covered with painting canvases, sketchbooks, and
palettes with half-dried paint smears. For years she'd painted her
dreams, and those dreams had always included Fenn. But a month
ago her entire world in the little Colorado town of Walnut Springs

had been flung on its head when Fenn's real identity was discovered. He was the long-lost twin to Emery Lockwood, heir to the vast technology-based fortune, who lived on Long Island. Once Fenn had learned who he really was, Callie had known she would lose him forever, but standing there holding his engagement announcement in her hand was the first time she'd had cold hard proof of that fact.

The moment Wes Thorne, Fenn's childhood friend and Hayden's brother, had placed the engagement announcement card in her hands, her dream was dead. The man she was in love with was going to marry someone else. And not just anyone, but Hayden Thorne. When she'd first met Hayden, she'd instantly liked the other woman as a friend. A pang of envy rippled through her, casting a green tint to her heart.

I'm happy for them…but…

Disgust came after, weighing her chest down like invisible stones. She shouldn't be jealous of Hayden, not when she cared so much about her friend. But the thought of watching her get married to Fenn? She couldn't think. It was too awful…She let the torn pieces drop from her hands and float slowly to the floor of her bedroom. Little fingerprint smudges coated the pieces of the card where her paint-covered hands had rubbed on the expensive paper as she'd ripped it to shreds. Those vibrant colored pieces lay at her feet in a mocking collage that only made fresh tears burn in the corners of her eyes.

Footsteps on the stairs drew her attention. Had her father come up to check on her or was it Wes? When Wes had shown up at the Broken Spur a few minutes ago with a letter from Fenn, Callie hadn't been able to help herself. Having no idea of the damning information the letter contained, she'd gone straight to her room to read it. Too excited to have one scrap of affection from Fenn or any sign that he might be missing her while he spent time on Long Island with his family, she'd blown right past her father and Wes as if they'd ceased to exist.

God, I'm such a fool. How could she have been so blind as to not see that while Fenn was learning who he really was, he was also falling in love with Hayden? God, they even *looked* good together, both of them beautiful and perfect: Fenn with height and muscled build and gold hair, Hayden with her bold red locks and stunning body. A wave of nausea rolled through her stomach. *I'm just the sad little hanger-on sister to him. I never even had a chance.* She'd opened her heart to him, given him everything that she was, and never held back. And what had that gotten her? A broken heart. And it was entirely her own fault.

Whoever had come up the stairs now knocked on her bedroom door. *Pull yourself together*, she told herself, and using the back of her hands, she wiped away any evidence of her tears.

"Who is it?" she called out, desperate to hide the way she was crumbling to pieces.

Her dad couldn't see her like this. He'd only just gotten home from the hospital after his heart attack a month ago, and seeing her hurting wouldn't do him any good. He was supposed to be resting, letting the new ranch hands and construction workers handle all the heavy lifting and major work. Not that Jim Taylor ever understood the idea of resting.

"Callie, it's me, Wes." Wes Thorne's voice was soft on the other side of the door, as though he was trying to be nice. He wasn't nice. He was a wolf, a predator. She'd figured that out the moment she had first laid eyes on him when he and his sister, Hayden, had shown up at the ranch to tell Fenn who he really was and to take him home, away from her. Wes was the last person she wanted to see right now.

"Go away," she called out. When there was no sound of retreating footsteps, she crept over to her bedroom door and opened it just a crack. She came face to face with an expensive suit shirt and an immaculately tied silk tie. The man always looked like he'd walked out of a *Vanity Fair* magazine ad. Raising her gaze up his chest, she saw his throat, then his full lips, and finally his cobalt blue eyes.

Wes, the harbinger of her own personal doom, stood there, worry knitting his brows as he gazed down at her.

"Are you all right? I thought I heard…" He studied her, probably seeing her red eyes. The last thing she needed was his pity.

"I'm sorry." She shoved past him, escaping her bedroom and his assessing gaze as she ran down the stairs, tears almost blinding her vision. She had to get out of here, get away from him, from her father. She wanted to find a quiet dark place and curl up in a ball to lick her wounds, not handle twenty questions from men who didn't have a clue what she was going through. *Have to be alone. Have to.*

She hit the bottom of the stairs and passed through the living room just as her father appeared in the doorway of the kitchen.

"Callie, honey, you okay, sweetheart? You look like you've been crying." Jim started toward her, but she held up a hand.

"I'm fine, Dad. I just need to go for a ride, okay? I'll be back in a few hours." And without another word to him, she rushed out onto the small porch of their ranch house.

Even as the fresh Colorado mountain air hit her lungs, it wasn't enough. She still couldn't breathe…She needed space, distance, to clear her head. She hoped both Wes and her father would leave her alone. Wes would hopefully focus on what he always did. Business. If he stayed close to the new cabins being constructed she could avoid him.

Something about him unnerved her. He was so damn quiet and intense. She didn't like that intensity. It made her pulse beat faster and her palms sweaty. Not like Fenn. Fenn was safe, didn't make her edgy or her breath quicken with a queasy anticipation. It was too confusing. Wes made her feel like a skittish barn cat.

Shoving thoughts of him away, she sprinted to the barn where her quarter horse, Volt, was in his stall, happily munching on oats. This is what she needed. To get outside and ride away from everything that left her hurt and confused. Volt was fast and he'd help her escape. Ever since she'd been a child, riding had been her outlet, a way to get free of everything. It was her father's fault really. When her mother had died, Callie had been only four, and her father had bought her a small pony to give her something to care for and to learn to ride. From then on, riding had been her go-to cure for a broken heart.

Callie threw a bridle over Volt's head and then put a blanket and saddle on him. Volt huffed and bumped his nose affectionately against her shoulder as she cinched the girth strap and then led him from his stall. She didn't even wait to get out of the barn before she mounted up.

Once she was astride the horse, she kicked his sides, clicking her tongue, and Volt jolted forward. She broke him into a canter to warm him up. He didn't need much to get into the rhythm. Another swift kick and he was shooting across the back field, straight toward the mountains. The wind lashed her hair in stinging slaps across her face, but the pain felt good. It was a pain she'd rather focus on instead of the searing agony in her chest.

Volt seemed to sense her need to flee, and he ran like wild lightning from a summer storm. Ahead of them, the wooded mountains were carved with trails of bright green grass. Callie urged Volt to gallop parallel to the grove of Aspen trees that bordered the farthest edge of her family's property. The white trunks looked like slender ghosts weaving through the dappled sunlight. The brilliant gold leaves reminded her of the cadmium paint color she'd been mixing on her palette this morning. *This morning.* So much had changed since then.

A few hours ago she had been experimenting with acrylic paints, dabbling really, since she had no clue how to use that particular medium. A half-painted canvas, one depicting the Aspen leaves falling, was supposed to be a gift for Fenn Lockwood, to remind him of the home he'd had at Broken Spur. And even though he now had a new life on Long Island, Broken Spur would always be a part of him. At least, that's what she'd hoped as she lost herself in creating the painting. It had been twenty-five years since Fenn had come to Walnut Springs. Twenty-five years since Jim and Maggie had taken Fenn in as a surrogate son. An entire quarter of a century where Fenn had been unaware of the family looking for him thousands of miles away. Roots like that didn't just disappear, did they? Even if she couldn't be Fenn's future, she was certainly a part of his past and she clung to that thought like a lifeline.

Everything about Fenn had been perfect. Tall, muscled, blond-haired, and hazel-eyed, he'd been her dream in Wranglers and a fitted plaid shirt, like a god born to rule the wild lands from centuries ago before man trespassed here. A strong, quiet, intense man who cared for everyone around him with such a depth of emotion that it scared her sometimes. But she couldn't stay away.

She had followed him wherever he went, to every bull-riding competition he participated in, and he'd even been her date to her senior prom since she'd been eighteen and allowed to bring an older date. All of her friends had been so jealous, but that night, she'd hoped more than anything he'd kiss her. He hadn't, except for a brotherly kiss on the cheek before sending her upstairs to bed. Never once had she dared to tell him how she loved him, but she'd shown him in every breath, every look, every action she could. And it hadn't been enough to even turn his head. Would it have mattered if she'd told him how she felt? *No. It wouldn't. Because he looks at Hayden in a way he's never looked at me.* Some truths hurt. Bad. Bad enough that she suddenly had trouble breathing again past the burst of a sob.

And now he was getting married. To Hayden.

Tears dripped down her face. She wasn't even sure if it was the wind or from her broken heart. Tugging on the reins, she slowed Volt down. He dropped back into a canter and then to a walk.

"Easy boy," she crooned and patted his muscular neck. "You always want to push too hard for too long." It was something she sometimes felt inside herself. A wild need to push herself beyond her own limits until she broke free.

Volt tossed his head, his black mane flaring in a ripple over his skin as though to protest her words but kept their leisurely pace as they moved along the line of Aspen trees, his hooves churning the blanket of vivid yellow leaves. They were a few months away from heavy snow, but there was no mistaking the distant aroma of winter. Something about that scent calmed her. Snow buried. Snow covered. It hid away things that needed to be erased or at least temporarily forgotten.

Could she forget her broken heart if it lay beneath an early snowfall? Perhaps, but it didn't erase the fact that she would have to go to the engagement party. See them smiling, together, posing for pictures, holding each other close. Things she'd never get to do with Fenn.

The winding gold trail that Volt climbed soon led to a small hill where large gray rocks littered the slope. She tugged back on his reins, and he halted. Callie slid off his back and led him to a copse of trees. After looping his reins around a sturdy low branch of a nearby tree, she walked over to the outcropping of rocks and climbed up a particularly thick, waist-high rock half covered in pale wintergreen moss. She let one leg dangle down the front of the rock while she tucked her other leg up and rested her chin on her knee.

Clouds swept across the skies, their shadows playing a game of chase upon the rolling hills and tree-strewn valleys below. Her father had shown her this spot after her mother had died. The two of them had been lost without her. Nature had become the mother she'd lost. Her father had taught her that a person could find peace here, under the brilliant skies and in the changing winds.

A few stray tears escaped her eyes, but she didn't wipe them away. There was no one here to witness her breaking apart in a thousand pieces, just the wind, skies, and mountains, and they'd hold her secret heartache for as long as she needed them to.

She knew she was a fool to think that Fenn could ever return her feelings, but she hadn't been able to stop herself from hoping. But now it was certain; there would be no Cinderella moment for her, no grand transformation. Just life on the ranch and perhaps a job in the town, if she didn't need to work with her father.

What I need to do is find a way to move on. Learn to live without him.

A flood of memories engulfed her, the way Fenn used to hug her and ruffle a hand through her hair, the way he'd carried her up to bed when she'd been ten years old after she'd fallen asleep on the couch. How his natural scent would cling to his coats and she'd used to wear them when he wasn't around, just to feel close to him.

Such a fool…to love so much and lose so much.

She couldn't let this happen again. No more falling in love. No more exposing her soul in hopes someone would see her for who she was. There could be no half measures here—she couldn't stand this kind of pain again.

I'm done with men, done with love, done with all of that romantic nonsense. It's not worth the pain. Callie was never going to let her heart dupe her into falling for a man ever again.

Her composure back in place, Callie rubbed her palms on her jeans and then slid off the boulder. She walked back to Volt, who was waiting patiently for her. She unwound the reins from the branch.

"Time to go back." She didn't want to, but she was a big girl and had to face this, even if it killed her piece by piece.

* * *

Wes Thorne stood on the porch of one of the brand-new, nearly completed luxury cabins that was being constructed on the backside of the Broken Spur ranch lands facing the mountains. The wood of the porch railing was slightly rough but would be smoothed out with a sander soon. The oak was solid and firm and a rich color of brown that was pleasing to the eye. These cabins would be incredibly lucrative for Jim and Callie.

The scheme had been his sister Hayden's idea when she realized Jim was in danger of losing the ranch because they'd defaulted on their high mortgage payments. Hayden had suggested to Wes that they build cabins on the property and use them as a destination for high-stress workaholics who needed a vacation from 24/7 e-mail and super-powered cell service. It was brilliant of course, but he wasn't surprised. Hayden was a better businesswoman than he was a businessman when it came down to it. He loved art more than business, but he thankfully had a great amount of success in his own business as an art expert.

While his sister was preoccupied with her wedding plans, he'd agreed to come out and check the progress of the cabins. He'd known telling Callie about Fenn and Hayden's engagement wasn't going to end well. From the moment he'd met the wild, free-spirited

Callie, he'd known she was in love with Fenn. Her heart was pinned on her sleeve for the world to see, and he'd hated having to be the person to deliver the news that would cut her sweet, innocent little heart to shreds.

She'd taken it worse than he'd expected. He'd gone up to check on her, and when she'd answered her door her eyes were red and her cheeks were still stained with shiny tears. There was a wildness to her anguish that was breathtakingly gorgeous and something in him had rumbled, like a deep quake beneath the earth. Her pain had unsettled him, and few things *ever* unsettled him. So he'd decided to stay a few days to make sure she was going to be all right. Of course, if anyone asked, he was only staying to check on the cabins. That was his story and he was sticking to it. He shook his head. He couldn't leave her when she…Wes stopped himself. She didn't need him. Hell, he doubted she even liked him. She was always running off, hiding, avoiding eye contact as though she was nervous around him.

None of that changed the fact that he *wanted* her. For the last several weeks he'd been caught up in fantasies of having her in his bed, wrists and legs bound, body completely bare and ready for him to explore every inch of her with his mouth and hands as he introduced her to his darker world of pleasure. The things he wanted to do…*craved* to do to her were driving him slowly mad.

He'd never lusted after a woman like he did Callie and he couldn't figure out why that was. She was young, innocent, not his usual type. So why then did his hands twitch with the urge to touch her whenever she was close, and the hint of her scent after she'd freshly showered and walked past his room seemed to carve itself into his bones? While he'd been away from her, he'd attempted to convince himself it was a silly obsession. When he bolted up in the middle of the night in his empty bed and he was hard and frustrated because she wasn't there beside him he'd told himself it was nothing but an itch he needed to scratch to get out of his system. But now that he was here with her, so close that he could see all those unhidden emotions on her face, especially the pain he'd caused by coming here…leaving was impossible. And the itch…it wasn't temporary.

He was going to have her. It was only a matter of time. He'd vowed the moment he set eyes on her that she was going to be his. He needed to tame her, to bring her into his world. It would take a long, slow seduction, but Callie would be his. She had to be. Her innocence mixed with her natural sensuality was about to kill him. If he could just get her to forget about Fenn and show her all the wicked pleasures life could bring, then he'd have her, body and soul.

As he stepped off the porch, dusting his hands over his jeans, he saw Callie leave the ranch house and walk toward the barn. Her steps were firm, her face held high, and she had a look of determination on her features. Whatever heartbreak she was suffering, she'd masked it and taken a firm hold of herself.

That's my girl. The thought slipped out before he could take it back. She wasn't his. But she would be. Soon. With a low chuckle, he continued to linger near the cabins and waved to some contractors who had just arrived, but he kept a watchful eye on the barn. They would talk, soon, and he'd set in motion his plans to have her.

* * *

Callie couldn't help but watch Wes as he worked with the contractors. She fed the chickens in the coops, worked with a new foal that had been born a few weeks ago, and checked on the cattle feeding and water troughs over several hours and all of those tasks kept her in plain sight of Wes.

He wasn't in that suit he usually wore, the one that made him

Lauren Smith

look expensive and mysterious. No, he was in jeans, a t-shirt, and boots and...Her mouth ran dry as she realized that rather than make him look more normal, more approachable, the casual attire gave him a dangerous edge that seemed to say, *I'm not afraid of getting down and dirty and taking you with me, sweetheart.* The thought made her blush. That was ridiculous. He was just another handsome man in jeans, one she was currently avoiding. That was the whole point of swearing off men, which she definitely had. No sexy, rugged, dangerous men for her. She'd locked her heart in a steel box and sealed it shut forever. There wasn't going to be any man getting through to it so he could smash it. Not ever again.

Despite her promise though, she couldn't keep her eyes off Wes. It had to be harmless just to watch him, right? Lust and love were two totally different things after all...Weren't they?

She watched him crouch by the porch of one of the cabins, a pair of contractors with him, gesturing at something. Even from where she stood, she could see the flex of the muscles on his forearm and the glint of his expensive watch on his wrist. She licked her dry lips and glanced away, only to find herself turning back his way. The light breeze carried just enough of their conversation that she realized they were discussing the wood trimming against the stone base of the cabins. Of course, Wes seemed to know all about the subject. Was there a subject Wes Thorne wasn't an expert on? His seemingly limitless knowledge was wildly intimidating under the best circumstances, but after he'd seen her meltdown yesterday, well, Callie wasn't challenging him to Trivial Pursuit anytime soon.

Callie hadn't been able to afford college. And if she could have, there was no way she would have been able to leave her father, not when he was shorthanded and the ranch was in jeopardy. Now here she was at age twenty, stuck in the same town she'd lived her whole life.

Half of her loved ranch life, but the other half of her wanted to get out into the world, test her limits, and live her life.

Wes suddenly stood and shook hands with the two men he'd been speaking with and then walked away, out of her sight. It was just as well. She really needed to get back to work. With a little sigh, she turned around to go back into the barn and smacked right into a solid, warm male chest.

"Oomph!" She made an unlady-like sound as their bodies collided and she stumbled back.

Firm hands gripped her waist. "What were you doing? Hiding behind this truck?" His tone was full of dark amusement, as though he was fully aware she'd been spying on him.

She sniffed, raised her chin, and tried to dislodge his hands from her waist. He allowed it, and she was fully aware of that fact more than anything else.

"I was checking on the hay." *I was not watching you in those snug jeans.*

"Mmm." He made a little throaty noise as though he were agreeing with her, but she heard the disbelief in the sound.

"If you'll excuse me, I still have chores to take care of in the barn." She stalked around him and headed straight for the open doors of her sanctuary. He wouldn't come after her. He had things to take care of, too. This would be over soon. She'd go back to being alone, left in peace and free of strangely intense men. Thank heavens for that, she thought.

Heading straight for Volt's stall she decided to give him a quick brushing; that would make her look and feel busy. She slid the stall door open on its sliding rails and grabbed her brush bucket. Then she settled in for a good combing. Volt didn't pay much attention to her as he buried his nose in his oat bucket, munching loudly.

The sound of footsteps behind her had her spinning. Wes stood in the open stall doorway, watching her.

"Are you all right?"

She barely contained a bitter laugh. "All right? Of course I am. Why wouldn't I be?"

From the corner of her eye, she saw him drift a step closer, and she heard the soft shuffle of his boots on the hay-strewn floor. Wes was too intense for the quiet life on a ranch.

"Here, let me." Suddenly he was right behind her, the heat of his body searing her skin through the thin layer of her jeans and shirt. His right hand settled over hers gently, grasping the brush and sliding it off her palm. Her hands settled on Volt's coat as Wes kept her caged while he continued to brush the horse. She watched the way his hand moved the brush swiftly over the horse's flanks. Did he know much about horses?

Funny, she hadn't thought to ask. When she'd last been around him, he'd seemed more a dark shadow, a presence just out of sight while she'd been focused on Fenn and the threat on his life. Now, though, she had to admit she was curious, even if he scared her a little. He patted the horse's back and then turned to her, handing her the brush.

"You seem to know what you're doing," she finally said, peering over her shoulder at his face.

Observing his profile, she noticed the twist of his sensual lips in a bare hint of a smile.

"I own six of them. I should hope I know what I'm doing." His words lit a strange fire deep within her belly, and she knew she'd bump into him if she leaned back even an inch.

Callie took the brush from him and set it in the grooming kit outside Volt's stall. She dusted her hands off on her jeans as she waited for Wes to leave the stall.

"You really have horses? Why didn't you say anything before?" She could have made him muck out the stalls…the image of him, hay fork in his hands, shoveling manure made her bite back a little smile.

He actually laughed. The rich sound of it did funny things to her stomach. It quivered and a slow wave of heat moved across her face.

"You seem surprised," he noted as he closed the stall door and then latched it.

Callie retreated a few steps, the barn suddenly feeling much warmer than it had a minute ago.

"Well, you never said anything before about horses. And you don't look like you do a lot of riding." She swept her gaze down his black t-shirt, which did nothing to disguise the lean cut muscles of the abs beneath it. *You're not checking him out, Callie. Stop it,* she warned herself. She dragged her eyes upward and noticed his powerful forearms and she couldn't forget that the feel of his hands on her skin always seemed to burn her in those brief times he'd touched her. Oh yes, Wes Thorne unsettled her, and she didn't like it. If she kept getting swept away by how attractive his abs and arms were there was no way she was going to be able to keep her vow. She had to get out of there and fast. She grabbed the saddle and headed for the tack room, hoping he would take the hint and not follow her.

That silent prayer went unheard because he filled the space of the tack room doorway, as though to stop her from escaping him again. She focused on putting her saddle away.

"You and I haven't talked much, and certainly not about horses. I'd be happy to talk now…about horses. I play polo. A man has to be very good on a horse." He paused and that caught her attention. When her eyes met his, he continued. "I enjoy riding, and not just the horses."

For a second, she had no clue what he meant. Riding…Then

it hit her and she flushed with mortification. He was implying that—*oh!*

"Well, sorry to disappoint you, Mr. Thorne, but I'm not up to being ridden today, or ever. I'm not interested, period."

Rather than anger him enough to send him away, he sidled closer.

"No, you're not up to it, not yet."

Turning to face him, she shot him the fiercest look she could manage. "I don't think you get it. I want to be left alone. No more men, no more romance, no more anything..." Suddenly her words came out a little choked, as though she couldn't breathe. Here she was confessing her heartache to him, the last man on earth who'd understand what she was going through. His sister had told Callie all about Wes. The women he dated, how he never fell for anyone. He was nothing like Fenn. Wes wasn't a man for loving, but for lusting, and she didn't want to be around that either.

Wes tilted his left wrist to study the face of his expensive watch, checking the time.

"That sounds a bit like a challenge to me. Do you want to *challenge* me?" It wasn't a threat, no, but something about the way he said the word "challenge" made her insides squirm.

"Challenge? I don't know what you're talking about."

Wes's lips twitched. "So you've decided you won't fall in love? Is that it? No more men for you because *one* man broke your heart?"

Rather than answer him, she just swallowed hard and drew in a much needed breath.

"A friendly little wager wouldn't put you at any risk then, would it? What if I said that in thirty days I could change your mind? Make you want a man again, not just any man, but *me*."

Callie focused on the doorway, debating if she could escape him, but it didn't seem likely. What if she just let him play his little game? It wouldn't hurt her; he couldn't get to her.

I'm safe. He won't get to my heart. She was sure of that. Sure enough that she finally met his gaze and nodded.

"You think you can seduce me in thirty days? Fine. You're on. Good luck with that, Mr. Thorne."

"Thank you, but I've never needed luck." When she started to dart around him, he stayed her with an outstretched arm. "Now, just a minute, we've terms to discuss. If I lose I'll have one of my connections at art school on Long Island write you a recommendation for entry to their program."

"Art school?" How could he offer that? She wouldn't ever be able to afford that.

"Yes, they have a scholarship program you'd qualify for and my friend's recommendation would seal your acceptance."

Callie let all of that sink in. If she resisted the temptation to sleep with him, he'd help her get into art school? The one thing she wanted more than anything? There had to be a catch.

"And if you win?" She couldn't quite say the words "if I lost."

"If I win you'll get passion beyond your wildest dreams. I know how to please a woman, Callie. Every trick, every toy, every little fantasy you've ever had, they can all be yours. I can promise that while we're together your life will never be the same. Anything you want, I can give it to you. *Anything.*" He was so confident, so bold, she almost believed him.

But there was one thing he couldn't give her and thankfully it was the one thing she never wanted to experience again. Love.

"That doesn't sound like a hard bet to win," she replied. Why she felt the need to taunt him, she wasn't sure.

He chuckled, not at all upset. "If you think this will be so easy a challenge to win, you won't refuse anything I suggest?"

Suggest? Just what did he think he could suggest? "What do you mean?"

"I've got to make a trip to Paris in the next week and I think it's only fair to take you with me. I've seen your artwork. I know you'd enjoy taking in the museums and the sights. It's the perfect place for an artist to visit."

Paris…What he offered her, the world she'd always dreamed of, as though it were an easy thing to give her…it was impossible. She could never afford that trip.

A shameful heat filled her cheeks and she ducked her head. "I'm sorry, but I can't afford to—"

With a low growl he forced her chin up so she had to look him in the eyes again. "I may not be a man with honorable intentions toward you, but if nothing else, I'm still a gentleman. The trip and anything on it will be at my expense. All you need do is join me."

"A free trip to Paris?" She couldn't help but look this handsome gift horse in the mouth. He answered with a nod.

Paris. How could she refuse? He'd chosen the one place in the entire world she couldn't say no to.

"All I have to do is go with you?" Her heart was beating so fast that she had to force herself to calm down.

"Yes, come with me. Give me my thirty days to court you as you deserve." He sounded so solemn, so serious about a silly wager, but the heat simmering in his eyes was full of promise and it scared her a little.

He won't get in, she promised. *He won't. I'm safe.*

"Okay. I'll go with you." The words came out and she felt as though she were living in a strange sort of dream. She was going to Paris with Wes Thorne. Was this all really happening?

"Good. I can stay with you, help you with Volt if you like." He didn't move away from her when she tried to get past him again.

Callie needed to get away from him. Just because she'd agreed to go to Paris with him didn't mean she wanted him to follow her around all day. She wanted to be left alone, left in peace. Not being intimidated by a man who was the personification of sin when she'd just sworn yesterday to avoid men like him. This bet was likely just a way for him to amuse himself. He had to be playing with her. Nothing more. There was no way a man like him would have any interest in her, and she didn't want him to. Wes would want a tall, polished model, a thin society beauty, not a short, curvy girl in jeans with calloused hands. It just didn't make any sense for him to be interested in her. He had to be really bored out here if he was paying attention to her. *I must be the only female for miles if he's paying attention to me.* It was a depressing thought.

"I'm sorry. I'm not in the best mood. You should probably just go." *Please go away,* she prayed. If she had to ask again, she feared her plan to avoid men like him wouldn't last. She'd be a sucker all over again and throw her heart into something only to get hurt. *No more Ms. Nice Guy. I have to protect myself, don't I?*

The intense wolfish gleam in his eyes softened and he inched toward her. Before she could move, he trapped her against one of the posts bearing an old saddle she'd been oiling earlier that day. The thick scent of the hay, the tang of the oil, and the exhale of Wes's breath consumed her, shrinking her universe into this one infinite yet enclosed span of time. He rested one hand on the saddle by her waist, so close, but not quite touching her hip. His other hand curled under her chin and gently lifted it up so she had to tilt her head back to look him in the eye. His gentle but firm touch made that newly built brick wall around her heart quake.

No, I can't let him get inside my head. She had to control her emotions and her response to him.

"Shed your tears for him, Callie. You are allowed that much," he whispered. His warm breath fanned across her lips as his face inched closer to hers.

"Allowed?" She bristled and flattened her hands on his chest, pushing hard. He didn't budge.

"Yes." He smiled, almost coldly. "You're allowed to cry when your heart is broken, but just know that when you're ready the entire world awaits you."

Wes cupped her cheek, closed the distance between them, and pressed his lips to hers. It was no chaste kiss. His tongue slid inside, stroking hers, and she jolted against him. He assaulted her senses, his hands suddenly everywhere, sliding slowly over her back, tracing her hips, caressing the sensitive skin at the nape of her neck. Her blood thundered in her ears, like the resounding beats of a mustang's hooves upon the fields on the other side of the mountains.

His teeth sank into her bottom lip, the little sting making her gasp in shock and a traitorous zing of awareness and pleasure rippled through her. He coaxed, teased, and played with her mouth and seemed to be memorizing her body with the way his palms shaped her curves and slopes. She couldn't think, couldn't breathe. She had to stop this. She needed to… When she started to tremble he suddenly stepped back and rested his forehead against hers, their shared breaths an equal measure of soft pants.

"You aren't ready. Not yet." He brushed a lock of her hair back from her face and tucked it behind one of her ears. The gesture was intimate and tender. She trembled.

"Ready for what?" she demanded, but her tone was breathless.

"For me. But you will be. I have thirty days to prove it to you. Unfortunately I have to return to Weston for a few days but I'll come back and pick you up." He withdrew from her personal space, gazing for one minute longer at her before he strode out of the tack room and away from her.

Callie lifted her fingertips to her lips, her hand shaking. What had she done? Wes had kissed her. *Kissed her.* Her first kiss. It was not the way she had planned it, and it was not from the man she wanted, the man she loved. Her heart shuddered in her chest. It felt as if she had betrayed Fenn, but she hadn't. A person couldn't betray someone they had never been in a relationship with. That was the biting reality she had to accept. She may have loved Fenn, but he didn't love her back, not romantically. She would only ever be a little sister to him. And that had shattered her heart into a thousand pieces. What would being around Wes do to her if she couldn't stay cold and unmoved by his passion?

What am I going to do?

The phantom press of his lips still lingered against her own, as though he'd branded her with that single sensual kiss. She hated herself for the way her body had melted into his, and the crawling need just beneath her skin that craved his touch, his caress. But she didn't want it, didn't want him. And she shouldn't.

Wes Thorne was dangerous. Frighteningly intense and too much of everything. There was still that unspoken word humming in the air around her. He'd never said it, but she'd felt it in his kiss.

Soon. It was only after she'd started back to the house that she realized if she went to Paris with Wes, she might miss Fenn and Hayden's engagement party. Had he done that on purpose? Given her a distraction to keep her from facing something that would grind her heart to dust? Maybe Wes wasn't so heartless after all…or he was cunning beyond her wildest dreams.

Chapter 2

The Gulfstream G150 slid into the air, climbing high into the late afternoon sky. The clouds above the Colorado mountains were thick and painted in a range of tangerine and pomegranate reds. Wes leaned back into the soft white leather seat of his family's private jet and watched the wings of the plane slice through the heavens.

He could still taste Callie, addictive, sweet, so breathless and innocent. Until he'd sat down in the plane, his entire body had been rigid with pent-up passion. He shouldn't have kissed her, not so soon, not when he'd have to leave for a few days before seeing her again.

Fuck, he wanted her. It actually hurt not to have her near him. Had that ever happened to him before? Not that he was aware of. He dropped his head back against the headrest and tried to collect his thoughts. He only had to last a month without getting what he wanted right away.

Thirty days.

Thirty days was enough time to seduce her and make her forget

Fenn. Her father had assured him she had an up-to-date passport. She would need a new wardrobe and so many other things. He would fill her days with adventure, passion, and art. He would offer her the world, and in return, he'd take her to bed and finally conquer this strange obsession with her.

He touched his lips yet again, having done it several times on the drive back to the airport. Kissing her had made him *feel* again. For too long he had not felt much of anything. He had gone to great lengths just to regain even the smallest bit of pleasure in his life. Callie had changed everything.

One month ago he had flown out to Colorado to rescue his long-lost childhood friend Fenn Lockwood, only to find Fenn in bed with his sister. The initial meeting between them after twenty-five years of thinking Fenn was dead hadn't gone well. He and Fenn had gotten into a fistfight over Hayden. They had been fighting in the dirt outside an old trailer, and Jim Taylor had driven up and fired a shotgun over their heads. And then Wes looked up and saw *her*.

Honey-blonde hair tugged playfully by a mountain breeze to form a golden halo around a face so lovely he'd forgotten to breathe. She was not like any of the models on the runways in Milan or Paris. She was a head shorter than him, with killer curves and a classically beautiful face. A slightly upturned nose, gold lashes, hazel green eyes, and pale pink lips. Lips he'd finally tasted, and his imagination hadn't been able to compare to reality. Yes, he had taken one look at Callie Taylor and knew that he would have to have her, possess her in every way because she had made him feel. His blood still hummed in his veins and his heart beat wildly at the thought of the chase, the seduction, and finally the months he planned to spend learning the secret ways of her body and soul so that she would be fully his.

His phone vibrated in his pocket and he pulled it out, wondering who'd be calling. *Corrine Vanderholt.*

That was a problem he needed to deal with before he initiated Callie into his world. As one of the premier members of the exclusive BDSM club, the Gilded Cuff, one of the perks was the luxury of having almost any female submissive at his beck and call. Nearly all of the club members were outwardly polite society girls he chatted and danced with at fund-raisers and galas under the unsuspecting eyes of the crowds. But at the Gilded Cuff, these women stripped down to bare skin and knelt at his feet, begging to be dominated. He had always been happy to comply. Corrine, however, was not like the others. The rest knew that any relationship in the club ended outside the doors, and that was the way everyone liked it. For Corrine, the club was a stepping stone to marriage, and Wes knew she had set her sights on him. She was a fool to think she could control him. *He* was the dominant.

With a little smile, he answered his phone. "Thorne here." Not acknowledging he'd seen her name on the screen.

"Wes, sweetheart, it's me," Corrine murmured huskily.

He almost rolled his eyes. "I have many sweethearts, which one in particular are you?"

He bit back a laugh at her angry little hiss through the other end of the phone.

"It's Corrine." Her tone was curt.

"Oh, Corrine, of course. What is it?" He settled back in his chair and kicked his feet up on the leather seat opposite him.

"I thought you might want to top me at the club tonight." She was forcing that huskiness in her voice now, and he tried not to smile.

"I'm afraid that's not possible. I'm leaving for Paris in a few days and have to make travel arrangements." The last thing he wanted to do was top Corrine. That meant being her dom and conducting a sexual scene with her. The only woman he wanted was Callie.

"When you get back then," she insisted.

"No. I'm not going to be topping anyone at the club for a while."

"What?" Her voice was hard and cold. He'd ruined her plans.

"There are plenty of doms who will be happy to scene with you. Now if you'll excuse me, I've got to go." He didn't wait for a response, but simply hung up. Pocketing the phone, he resumed his study of the clouds.

Everything in his life would be changing soon. It was one thing to conduct a simple scene with a submissive at a club, but training one and doing it at his home was an entirely different matter. Callie had innate submissive qualities in her, but she was not weak, nor easily tamed. It would be a complicated process of seducing her and introducing her to his world without frightening her. He wanted everything to be perfect, for himself, but also for her.

She deserved a sweet, slow seduction. He had already moved too fast, taken a risk with that kiss in the tack room. She wasn't ready for him or his lifestyle. If he came at her too hard and fast, she'd bolt, just like an unbroken filly. Not that he wished to break her. No, never that, but Callie needed taming, and he planned to soothe her with little touches, tiny caresses, soft whispers, all the things a masterful lover knows how to employ. And he was the best. Out of all of the dominants at the club, he was the one who understood the art of BDSM the best. He could read a female submissive and know immediately what she needed and give it to her. It was the single most rewarding and arousing thing about being a dom, knowing he had the power to give a woman what she needed and satisfy her every desire and fantasy. It would be a lie to say he didn't get off on the idea. He loved wielding such a power, knowing he could bring such pleasure to a woman.

Callie was young and innocent, and as much as his body wanted to rush headlong into bed with her, the rest of him sensed slow was the best pace. She'd had her heart broken and that would take time to heal. He would coax the woman out of her chrysalis and glimpse the transformation at its own natural pace.

When his phone buzzed again, he answered in a low growl of displeasure.

"What is it, Corrine?"

A masculine chuckle made him blink and stare at the phone screen.

"Yeah, I'm definitely not Corrine," Royce Devereaux said.

"Royce, what is it?" Wes snapped.

Royce was one of his close friends from childhood, a dominant at the Gilded Cuff as well and a paleontology professor at a local university in Weston, Long Island.

"Guess you haven't heard the news?"

Wes sat up in his seat. "What is it? Has something happened to the twins? My sister?" His blood started to pound in his ears as old fears resurfaced.

"No—God no. Everyone is fine. Christ, Wes, you've only been gone a few days. What do you think could have happened in seventy-two hours?" Royce asked with a low chuckle.

Wes exhaled in obvious relief. After everything they'd been through recently, he needed rest, relaxation. No more assassins, explosions, or villains.

"As long as no one is dead or dying, I don't really care," Wes said. "I'm on vacation from all drama and life-threatening incidences."

His friend laughed. "Getting boring on me, are you?"

"You know I'm never that boring," he reminded Royce. They'd spent too many nights at the Gilded Cuff together for Royce to ever say otherwise.

"I just thought you'd be interested to know that the Mortons were robbed last night."

Wes didn't see the significance of this. "And this is of interest to me because?"

Royce sighed dramatically. "It wasn't a typical robbery. Only one thing was taken. A painting."

He straightened in his seat. "A painting? Which one?"

He was intimately familiar with the Mortons' private art collection. He had a hand in procuring most of the pieces in their collection. The Mortons were old money, like his own family, but unlike his parents, the Mortons valued art and it had been a pleasure to work with them.

"I think I heard it was a Goya," Royce said.

The Goya? Wes growled softly. The most expensive piece, valued at 450,000 dollars. He'd done the bidding for the Mortons at Sotheby's. And now it was gone. Something tightened in his chest, a sliver of pain, swiftly followed by fury.

"How was it taken? The Mortons have an advanced security system and their private collection was fairly unknown to the general public. It's not easy to walk away with something like a painting."

"Yeah, I know." Royce paused. "It looks like a professional job. The FBI is checking into it. I told them to come see you if they had any questions about the painting."

Wes scrubbed a hand over his jaw, scowling. The last thing he needed was the FBI crawling all over him, not when he wanted to focus completely on Callie. Feds were always a mood killer.

"What time are you due back on the island?" Royce asked.

Wes checked his watch. "About five hours, why?"

"We could go to the club. There's a sweet little sub I would love to tag team—"

"No thanks." Wes chuckled. "I've got to take care of a few things, and besides, I may not be coming to the club for a while."

"Oh?"

Wes couldn't miss the interest in his friend's tone.

"Yes." He didn't elaborate. Callie was his little secret. He didn't want to share her with anyone else, especially not a charmer like Royce. There couldn't be any risk that she would find another man more attractive than him.

Royce's tone turned serious. "Does this have something to do with Callie Taylor?"

How did he know about Callie? Wes didn't answer. He knew responding would reveal more. It was best to play the game as if he had no information.

"I was checking on Jim and his daughter for Fenn. He worries about them, since he and Hayden won't be moving back to Colorado for a month or two, at least not until after the engagement party."

"Checking, huh? Is that what the kids call it these days?" His friend sniggered. "I bet you checked on that sweet little cowgirl all night."

"I spent all my time working on the cabins for Hayden. There was no night, Royce. Make a comment like that again and you'll regret it," he promised darkly.

"Admit it. You want that girl. I heard Hayden talking about her. She's young and sweet. Everything your usual bed partners aren't. Are you having a midlife crisis or something?"

Fuck. His friend just didn't know when to shut the hell up.

"I'm thirty-three. A man does not have a midlife crisis until he is actually in the middle of his life," he shot back.

"Uh-huh," Royce answered, almost placating him. "Does your sister know you have a black room?"

"My sister does not know and will never know about that particular part of my house. The more important question is, how did you get inside it?" He and Royce had shared women at the club, even at Royce's house, but the black room at Wes's home…that was his secret, his private place no one was supposed to know about. A room containing his most treasured paintings and other things too valuable to share with the rest of the world. It also had a bed and a dresser with some rather fun sex toys, but he'd never met a woman yet who he'd trusted enough to show the room to. It was called the black room because it wasn't on the floor plans of the mansion and unless someone knew where it was, it could never be found. Royce had seen him leaving it once, but hadn't questioned him about it. Apparently the bastard had been biding his time until he could get in to check it out.

There was a faint clinking noise as though something metallic hit wood on the other end of the phone line.

"I knew you were out of town so Hans is showing me how to pick locks. Can you believe I didn't know how to listen for tumblers? We're using your place as practice, by the way."

Wes muttered a few choice curse words under his breath.

"You and Emery Lockwood's bodyguard are at my place picking my locks?" He knew it shouldn't have surprised him.

Royce was wild and unpredictable at best, and this was by far one of his tamer pranks. What amused him, despite his anger at his black room being infiltrated, was that Royce was with Hans Brummer. The bodyguard was in his early fifties, and one of the most dangerous men Wes knew. Hans had spent the last twenty-five years protecting Emery Lockwood after he and his twin, Fenn, were kidnapped at age eight. Now that the men trying to kill the twins were dead, Hans must have been bored enough to freelance his talents and was apparently training Royce in all manner of illegal activities.

"You never know when picking a lock will come in handy," Royce replied once the clicking noise returned.

"Why would a professor of paleontology need to know how to

pick locks?" Wes asked as he slipped his Breitling watch off his wrist and then reset the time from mountain to eastern. He still had a few hours left in the flight, but he liked to get his watch set.

Royce snorted. "Well, let's see. Emery and Fenn were kidnapped. Emery was almost blown to bits, Cody the hacker wonder boy was tortured by an assassin, Hans was shot in the chest, you were nearly incinerated in a car bomb. I'm just getting in some survival 101 with my old buddy Hans here."

There was a deep laugh in the background, and Wes knew it was Hans.

"How did you bypass my security system?"

"Child's play. We just rewired it."

Wes sighed. That meant he'd have to have someone come out and fix it. "Don't you have some term papers to grade?"

"That's what my teacher's assistant is for," Royce announced proudly, and Wes could only shake his head. "Kenzie's going to be busy over the next month reading everything and preparing the final exams I sent her."

"I thought you butted heads with your TA."

"Yeah, well, Kenzie is too smart for her own good. She's lucky she's my TA or I'd take her to the Cuff and strap her to a spanking bench and give it to her good." Royce's tone was suddenly husky, and Wes knew what the other man was thinking about.

"So why don't you?" Wes taunted his friend.

"Oh no, there's no way I'm getting involved with a student. I like my job."

"But she's over eighteen, right? She's a graduate student. It's legal."

Royce growled softly. "Legal maybe, but it doesn't look good if I go against school policy. I don't want to be *that professor*. My students already know about my club habits, and the bouncers at the club have to check IDs carefully to make sure no one slips inside who isn't a genuine member. I feel like a damn animal in a zoo sometimes."

His friend paused, then added, "Maybe I need a black room, too."

"Get out of there right now, Royce," he warned. That space was his, only his, and even his best friend was not allowed in there.

"Fine. Spoil our fun," Royce returned. "Call me tomorrow morning. We need to visit the Mortons."

"Right, thanks." He definitely had to see the Mortons and assure himself the other pieces in their collection were still safe. He would mourn the loss of the Goya.

He slid his cell phone back into his pocket and closed his eyes, picturing himself in the black room. His refuge, his comfort. Maybe soon he'd be able to show Callie, to let her inside his sanctuary.

Thirty days.

He had to make it. It was crucial that she had her time to accept Fenn's engagement and move on. And once she had, he would move in and claim her.

Chapter 3

At precisely ten the following morning, Wes climbed into Royce's Porsche Spyder, and a few short minutes later they were pulling into the front driveway of the Morton mansion. Wes wore his favorite suit, a light gray Burberry classic-cut light wool suit, while Royce had gone more casual in jeans and a black sweater beneath a leather coat.

"Is the FBI still in town?" Wes asked his friend.

"Probably, but I haven't heard. I'm sure the Mortons will know."

They drove through the black gates tipped with gold spires and stopped in a circular drive before a massive Mediterranean-style stucco mansion. It was a grand palisade that always impressed Wes each time he visited. The real attraction was the Roman statuary that filled the gardens and the limestone gazebo where rich amethyst-colored blooms of wisteria draped over the stone every spring, filling the air with its thick scent. It was a beautiful sight during the late spring and early summer.

Wes reached the door first and pressed a finger on the small white doorbell incased in a gold frame. A few seconds later, a man appeared, dressed all in black. The butler, Mr. Clancy, nodded in greeting.

"Mr. Thorne, Mr. Devereaux, this way please." He led them to one of the sitting rooms off the main hall.

The Mortons, Jill and her husband Daniel, were seated on a sateen loveseat speaking quietly, their faces strained. They were in their sixties, but both still trim and almost ageless in looks. They were a favorite family among the island's elite, and they deserved the attention. The Mortons, while rich, were not ostentatious, and as patrons of the arts, they put much of their wealth back into the artistic community. More than once, Wes had flown with them to New York to see an opera or ballet. They also offered up the pieces of their private collection to the Met for temporary exhibits. Wes admired them, and he admired few people in this world. He only wished his parents had taken lessons from the Mortons, rather than lose themselves in their obsessions with social power and elitism.

"Wes, my dear boy," Jill stood and greeted him, taking his hands in hers, shaking them gently. Her light blue eyes, though somewhat dimmed with worry, still managed a small twinkle. *Dear boy.* He was a grown man, but she'd known him since he was a child. The endearment would have angered him coming from anyone else, but from her it made him smile.

"I'm sorry, Mrs. Morton. Royce called me with the news about the Goya."

Daniel stepped forward and shook his and Royce's hands.

"We've had a devil of a time coping with it," Daniel admitted, his faint British accent coming through. He'd moved to America as a young man and had made his fortune here, married Jill, and became a U.S. citizen, but the Brit was just underneath his skin.

"One minute the Goya was there; the next it was gone. We were hosting a party and in the span of two hours, it was removed right under our noses."

Wes thought this over carefully. "Do you have a guest list I can see?"

"Yes," Jill said. "The FBI took a copy and is interviewing all of the guests, but you know how these parties can be…"

Wes knew only too well how easily things could go wrong at parties on the North Shore of Long Island. Twenty-five years ago, eight-year-old twins had been kidnapped out of their own kitchen in the midst of a summer party their parents were hosting. The kidnappers had seemed to have no trouble vanishing into the night without being seen or discovered. Not much had changed in the way of security.

"How did you know it was gone? Royce said there was a forgery left in its place?"

"Oh." Jill blushed. "It was the frame. That was the only way I could have known. The wood had a hairline fracture, from when Daniel dropped it a few weeks ago. You could feel it, but not see the crack."

Jill retrieved a wood frame from the coffee table by the loveseat.

"The FBI returned this to us after they swept it for prints. It was clean. But it's not our frame." Daniel ran an index finger over the edge of one of the corners. "There was a crack, just here. I only noticed it was wrong because the painting was slightly crooked and I touched it to readjust it. It was then I saw the lack of the break."

He ran a hand through his gray-streaked hair and sighed.

Royce examined the frame and passed it to Wes. The frame was eight-by-ten in size, incredibly small by most art standards. Rather like the *Mona Lisa*. Many famous paintings were tiny in comparison to the general public's expectations, but this particular Goya was even smaller.

The Goya was a small painting of a woman overlooking a cliff from a terrace. It was not in the form of his dark period, which was his most famous style, but more along the lines of the years he painted portraits of high-society members. The image of the woman was strangely personal, as though Goya had seemed to know the woman intimately, the way the wind teased her hair and her skirts fluttered about her legs, showing her fine figure. Wes knew the woman in the painting had a story to tell, and when it came up for auction, he contacted the Mortons immediately. They'd wanted to buy it and he'd helped arrange it.

He continued to study the frame.

"What do you think, Wes?" Jill took the frame back from him and set it down on the table.

Wes pursed his lips, thinking. He wasn't an agent, or a police officer, and had no real skills in investigation, but he knew art. And more important, he knew the seedier side of the art world.

"Whoever took this will have to hire someone to fence it, and then it will be put up on the black market, unless they already have a buyer arranged. I will put my feelers out, but I also want a copy of your guest list and copies of the video footage of the collection gallery."

Daniel nodded. "Of course, we can get that for you. We're waiting on the FBI to finish with the tapes and then we'll send them to you."

"Good." Wes thanked the couple and then he and Royce headed for the door.

Wes stared at the car. He'd been too lost in thought earlier when Royce had picked him up to notice the state of the Spyder. It was dirty and covered in splashes of mud.

"What the hell have you been up to while I was gone?"

Royce threw back his head and laughed. "You have no idea, and I'm definitely not telling."

"Right." Wes chuckled and got into the passenger seat. His phone buzzed and when he pulled it out he saw there was a text from Lilly Hargrave, a woman who owned an expensive clothing and lingerie shop in town.

"Back to your place?" Royce raked a hand through his hair before he buckled his seat belt.

"Actually, take me into town. Lilly has something for me." Wes buckled himself in and couldn't resist the smile. The day had started out grim, but things were looking up.

"Lilly? What do you want with her? I thought you and she were over ages ago?" Royce, the paleontologist, said, digging up Wes's fossilized romantic history trying to find answers.

"We are done," he assured his friend. "But Lilly is still a friend. She's ordered something for me from Paris, and I want to pick it up immediately."

"Well, aren't you Mr. Mysterious today." Royce spun the wheel and the Spyder shot out of the Morton's gravel drive and onto the road toward town.

Wes ignored his friend's subtle taunt. "What do you make of this painting situation?"

"Me?" Royce was quiet for a moment. "Depending on the level of access of the guests, we might be looking at one of our own on the North Shore as a potential thief. Of course, a stranger may have gotten into the house during the party, but I'll hold off on guessing until I see the footage and the guest list. What about you?"

Wes drummed his fingers on the windowsill of the passenger side. He didn't want to think about one of their own being responsible, but the sad truth was it could be very possible.

"I think we may have a fox in our hen house, Royce." It was time for hunting.

* * *

Callie stared at the Gulfstream G150 on the tarmac, her knuckles white on the little duffel bag containing her clothes.

Jim let out a low whistle.

"That boy sure knows how to travel in style. Good thing, too, because you deserve the best, sweetheart." Her father hugged her with one arm and kissed her cheek.

"Thanks, Dad," she whispered. It was weird to think she was leaving Colorado for the first time in her life and she'd have to say good-bye to her father, at least for a month.

"You'll be fine," Jim said softly. "He'll take good care of you. If he doesn't, I'll put some buckshot into that boy's behind."

She hugged her father back, torn between fighting off tears and laughing.

Jim grinned at her and then waved to the distant figure who appeared at the top of the plane's steps.

Wes Thorne, in a black suit, looking every inch as intimidating as ever, waved back at Jim. Callie glanced away, her entire body heating up with embarrassment. She knew her face had to be beet red. The last time she'd seen him, he'd been ruthlessly kissing her in the tack room of the barn. It was not an experience she could ever forget. In fact, it was branded in her mind, like a flaming beacon, both alluring and frightening. She hadn't been able to make it one day without thinking about that kiss and how it had changed her. It *had* changed her; she couldn't argue that. She hadn't been able to get him out of her mind. The way his lips felt against hers, the heat of his body, and the secret longing to know more of what could be between them. And at the same time, she hated herself for that curiosity and desire.

"Come on, Callie." Her father's rumbling baritone made her jolt as she realized he was already disappearing into the plane, no doubt to get a good look at what was inside.

Wes strode down the steps, meeting her at the bottom. She nearly stumbled back because he towered over her, making her feel instantly vulnerable.

"Hello, Callie." Her name was exotic and beautiful when he said it, and he made it sound like saying her name tasted good on his tongue. When she thought of his name it escaped her lips in a breathless sigh so easily.

With a little shake she forced herself to regain control. "Mr. Thorne, nice to see you again. You really didn't need to fly me to New York like this. I could have flown commercial just fine."

Wes's cobalt eyes narrowed. "Callie, everything I do has a distinct purpose." His tone was almost cold, and she swore she could feel its icy burn. For some reason that infuriated her.

"Everything you do has a distinct purpose? Is that what you call kissing me in the barn? What purpose did that serve? Was it all part of your plan to seduce me?" She dropped her bag at her feet and jabbed him in the chest with one finger. Rather than retreat from her, he leaned in even more.

"It did indeed have a purpose, and when you're ready, I shall tell you," he explained in a silky tone that seemed more dangerous than sensual.

"You can't use me, Mr. Thorne. I'm not that kind of girl," she warned him, not really sure how she'd be able to prevent him from doing anything to her. If he dared to touch her again, she might lose her senses.

"Someday you will *beg* me to use you, Callie, and when that day comes, I will concede to your wishes and satisfy us both." He brushed the back of his knuckles over her cheek and she shivered, not backing down. He wouldn't dare do anything like kiss her again, not while her father was close by.

"That will never happen," she reminded him.

A flash of something dark and wild shadowed his eyes for the briefest instant before he masked his reaction with cool indifference.

"We'll see. I do have thirty days to change your mind, after all."

She bit her bottom lip and bent to grab her bag.

"Don't be silly," Wes murmured and beat her to it. He wrapped his long elegant fingers around the straps of her duffel and hoisted it up. Then he turned his back on her and marched up the plane stairs, where he handed the bag to one of the attendants. Wes turned and held out a hand to her as she ascended the steps.

She reacted without thinking and placed her hand in his. As his fingers closed around hers, she couldn't help but wonder if she'd accepted a devil's bargain. The gleam of approval in his eyes warmed her to the tips of her toes.

"Pick any seat you like."

She had to squeeze past him to get into the cabin. He always did that, got into her space and made her aware of his physical dominance and strength, and how small and delicate she felt in comparison to him.

Her father was at the back of the plane stroking one of the leather seats and shaking his head with a smile.

"This is quite a plane, Wes," Jim announced with obvious approval.

"Thank you, Mr. Taylor. I agree. Make yourself comfortable, Callie. We have drinks and food at your request. Just ask Lindsay, the attendant." He nodded at the middle-aged blonde-haired woman who was seeing to their luggage.

"Do you mind if I have a word with you, Wes?" Jim moved to stand in the doorway of the plane and with a subtle jerk of his head indicated Wes to come outside with him. Wes glanced at Callie before following her father down the steps and out of view.

Uh-oh, I hope Dad doesn't threaten to shoot him. Callie smirked. Maybe putting some buckshot in Wes's ass was what the man needed.

* * *

Wes followed Jim down the steps of the small ladder leading to the tarmac. When they both were standing away from the open plane door Jim shoved his hands into his pockets and studied Wes.

"My baby girl is hurting," Jim noted.

"Yes," Wes agreed. The image of her standing in her bedroom, her face contorted with pain, her body trembling as she unraveled before him…It was a punch to his gut. The anger at thinking of her loving Fenn, a man who didn't want her, had vanished in an instant and the need to hold her, comfort her, had overridden his other thoughts. She brought out the strangest urges in him, and it was damn uncomfortable, but if he had to put up with feeling unbalanced just to have Callie in his arms, in his bed, he'd take it.

"I like you, Wes." Jim's compliment sounded more like a warning. He took a step closer to Wes.

"The feeling is mutual," he replied, uncertain how to respond. The old rancher had won him over, which was not an easy thing to do.

"Good. Now, since we like each other so much, it would be a good idea not to do anything to jeopardize our budding friendship, right?" The rancher's eyes were twinkling with mischief.

The question sounded rhetorical and Wes didn't answer.

"I know you want her, boy. And I'll say this. She's a grown woman, free to live her life, and I want her to do that." Jim rolled back on his heels, in a casual manner, hands still tucked into his pockets.

"That's why I'm taking her to Paris. It's the best place for her to live, to try a life of adventure and discover who she really is." He hadn't meant to let that last part slip out, but it did. Maybe Jim wouldn't think him a romantic, because he certainly wasn't, but he knew this was what Callie needed more than anything else.

Jim's eyes narrowed but only slightly. "Paris is the city of love."

"And art. Callie is talented. Gifted. I want her to see what she could become if she applies herself and gets the best instruction." He had the strange need to justify why he wanted to take Callie to France. It wasn't all about seduction. He wasn't a villain intent on ravishing an innocent maiden. Well, he did want to ravish her, but he wanted her to see where her talent could lead if she was willing to explore her passion for it.

"Fine. Sounds like a trip she'd enjoy. My baby girl's never left the state of Colorado before now and she needs to see the world." He reached into his pocket and pulled out a small leather box and handed it to Wes.

"What's this?" Wes asked. He opened the box to find a small seashell bracelet and a folded piece of paper.

"I meant to give it to Callie on her twenty-first birthday but now's a better time than any. I knew she'd be upset about Fenn. This bracelet was her mother's. I made it for her from shells we picked up on Venice Beach, where we went for our honeymoon. It was the only trip we could afford when we got married. It's Callie's. Give it to her when you feel the time is right."

"Thank you." Wes tucked the leather box into his pocket.

Jim suddenly smiled. "Oh, just one more thing." He leaned in, a menacing feral gleam in his eyes. "It doesn't matter where you are, if my baby gets hurt and it's your fault, a Winchester rifle works just as well in France as it does in Colorado and I have an up-to-date passport."

Wes grinned, returning the warning in his own expression. "Understood."

Jim nodded and waved a hand at the plane. "Now, go on, you don't want to miss your flight out of New York. And remember, take care of my baby girl."

"She'll want for nothing," he promised. It was a promise he intended to keep.

Wes tugged at his necktie, a bittersweet smile on his lips as he nodded and turned back to the plane and climbed the steps.

* * *

Callie briefly considered sitting down against one of the window seats and using her purse and backpack to put distance between her and Wes, then decided not to. She was a big girl and could handle him. Besides, there wasn't much he could do to seduce a woman on a plane.

There was a large TV at the front of the cabin next to the space that led to the cockpit and the stewardess area. Callie set her purse and backpack next to the row of leather chairs and sat down. The leather gave against her weight, and she had to stifle the satisfied sigh at the feeling of sitting in such a luscious seat. She studied the TV for a minute before she saw a small shiny wooden cabinet beneath it that looked more like a part of the wall. Callie leaned forward and pressed against one corner of the door and the pressure latch clicked and the door opened. Inside, a wall of movies was revealed, along with a Blu-ray player and a couple of remotes.

Movies. She loved movies. Her father had called her a movie buff when teasing her, but it was true. There was something magical about the way a story was presented on the screen. She supposed film appealed to her because she was so visual, and it was like moving paintings, or dancing art, to her way of thinking.

Tilting her head to the right to better read the titles on the spines of the cases, she paused when she came to one. *Laura*. A 1940s film noir classic about a street-smart detective who falls for a beautiful woman whose murder he is investigating. It was one of her favorites. She started to pull the case out, then stopped and slid it back into place. This wasn't her plane and she should ask Wes before using the player.

Surely Wes wouldn't mind, and watching one of her favorite movies would help her relax. Besides, what was the point of riding in a plane decked out with the best of everything if you weren't going to use it? Then again, Wes struck her as a workaholic, and maybe that intensity didn't allow for sacking out and watching a movie on your private plane.

Callie felt a pang of envy remembering why exactly Wes had this private plane. He was an art specialist and traveled to Europe frequently to consult with museums, auction houses, and private collectors on pieces. That wouldn't be work to her. To have a job like that would be a dream come true. A dream she'd certainly never get to live. At twenty, she knew she could still start college, but she hadn't saved up and wouldn't know where to begin the process of getting enrolled in a decent art school. The idea of figuring it all out and knowing she'd leave her father and the ranch behind was scary. She admitted that, and she hated herself just a little for feeling so scared of something she wanted. Even if she won this bet between her and Wes, and she was able to go to art school on a scholarship, what if she wasn't good enough to stay?

The wave of depression that hit her made her sink back into the leather chair, her shoulders sagging. What was she going to do? She couldn't stay on the ranch forever, not when she knew Fenn and

Hayden would be returning there to live permanently. She'd over-heard her father and Fenn talking about it one night on the phone. The luxury cabins were Hayden and Fenn's plan to save the ranch and create a business to run while living out there. And when they came home, the ranch was going to feel awfully crowded with her as a third wheel. She wasn't stupid. There was no reason to torture her-self or pour salt on her heart's wounds.

"Your father said he has to get back to the ranch but to call him when we reach New York."

She tensed and looked up to find him leaning in the doorway of the cabin, watching her. His red hair had grown a little in the month since she'd seen him. It was longer, almost touching the tips of his ears. She had the sudden urge to slide her fingers into his hair and see if it was as soft as it looked. Instead, she walked over to the small window on the opposite side of the plane and saw her father stand-ing on the tarmac. He must have seen her because he suddenly lifted a hand and waved. She waved back, a lump forming in her throat as she tried not to bolt for the door and run back down to him. It was the first time she was really leaving her home and him and it was scary as hell.

"He'll be fine. I told him he better take it easy while you're gone otherwise he'll ruin your trip by making you worry." Wes's hand set-tled on her shoulder in a gentle touch.

Scrubbing at her burning eyes, she moved back from the window and he allowed her to brush past him to return to her seat. She flinched when she realized she'd left the cabinet door open with all the movies displayed.

"You're welcome to watch a movie." Wes's voice was gentle, amused, the almost sweet tone surprising to her. He slid out of his suit coat as he talked, then removed his cuff links and rolled up his sleeves. Aside from the ranch, it was the most relaxed she'd ever seen him.

"Oh no, I couldn't—"

"Nonsense." He turned to his left, knelt in front of her as he faced the TV cabinet, and picked out a movie. *Laura*. He popped it into the disc player.

She stared at him. How in the hell had he known that movie was the one she wanted to watch? He hit play and powered on the flat-screen TV. He stood and walked into the attendant area, where he retrieved a briefcase and then, without so much as an invitation, sat down directly beside her, not looking at her. He buckled in and then dug around in his briefcase for some papers before he set the case on the floor and leaned back again, his lap covered in documents. He set his pair of cuff links down on the armrest and she reached for them, worried they'd fall to the floor. Their flat surfaces were etched with a letter T and a thorny branch entwined around the base of the letter. Elegant and edgy. Like him.

Did he have to do that? Sit right next to her when there were other seats? She blinked owlishly at him, almost disbelieving that he'd do that. It was to ruffle her, she was sure.

"You don't have to sit there," she almost whispered.

A devilish look came over him as he glanced at her, then leaned toward her conspiratorially. She leaned close automatically, wanting to hear whatever he planned to say.

"I have to sit here, darling. You're cornered, just the way I like. That nervous edge makes your breath a little quick and I like knowing you're thinking about how close I am to you."

When he leaned back into his seat, she knew her jaw was scraping the floor as she gaped at him. Then irritation flared under her skin. He was toying with her! With a frustrated little growl, she turned away from him and focused back on the TV screen.

The sound of the movie momentarily distracted her and when she looked in his direction again, he seemed to be deep in his work.

She could feel his body heat radiating off him. She half watched the film, and half watched him, fascinated and irritated. He was doing this on purpose, to rile her. The question was why? She couldn't even guess. Even that kiss in the barn hadn't been because he was attracted to her. Was this part of his attempt to win the bet? That was the only explanation and she still didn't understand why he was so determined to sleep with her.

Men like him didn't go for the little small-town girls like her. She would have bet everything that he liked girls who were stunning, sophisticated, women who wore tight dresses and strappy heels and knew how to politely laugh at anything he said. She wasn't that girl. She liked running wild, feeling the rain on her bare skin, cuddling down in her PJs on the couch and watching old movies. Her eyes darted to the screen, where the detective was exploring the dead woman's home and had stopped before a painting of the lovely woman.

Thoughts of Wes and his ulterior motives momentarily vanished as she lost herself in the story. A man falling in love with a dead woman simply by seeing an oil painting…She sighed. The best part of the movie was when the detective discovered that the woman wasn't dead, but that a friend of hers had been killed when the murderer mistook her for the heroine of the story. It was a love story disguised as a harsh film noir.

As the detective on the screen started interviewing suspects, Callie lifted the armrest to her right and used the two empty chairs next to the window to stretch her legs out and then she rested her head in one hand. The weight of a gaze settled on her, and she tried not to look to her left. He was staring at her. Finally she couldn't stand it anymore and glanced his way. He was in the most relaxed pose she'd ever seen him in. His legs were stretched out, his papers put away, and he was leaning his left elbow on the armrest. He rested his chin in his hand as he continued to gaze at her. Much like she knew a lion watched a grazing gazelle. Content for now to observe. It was only a matter of time before he struck. Her heart fluttered wildly and her blood began to pound in her ears. She was in serious trouble.

Chapter 4

She couldn't think straight with him staring at her like that, all brooding and quiet intensity.

Clearing her throat, she attempted to start a conversation, even though the movie played softly in the background.

"Is Wes short for Wesley?" Where she found the courage to ask him that she wasn't sure. She assumed it had to be, but it was like he'd said, they hadn't really talked before, not unless it was about his sister or Fenn.

He held out a hand palm up, and she set the cuff links into his hand. "Yes. Wesley. It's a family name. My grandfather's."

"Really? Did you know him?" She'd been too young to remember either set of her grandparents before they'd passed away.

Wes pocketed his cuff links and smiled. It was a small smile, but very warm and almost sweet. In the short span of time she'd known Wes, she'd never seen him look so affectionate. He ran a hand through his hair, tousling it, seeming unaware that he'd made a delightful mess of his normally combed-back hair. Callie liked it. It made him more approachable, less perfect. He was way too perfect.

"My grandfather is an old bear. I mean that in a good way. He is big and gruff, but a good man. He used to smoke Cuban cigars and drink cognac every Friday night, and I would sneak out of bed and go to his study. We'd sit in two wingback chairs by the fire, and he would tell me about the old days. He served in the navy during World War II. His stories kept me spellbound."

Callie loved seeing Wes's eyes soften and his lips move as he talked.

"He sounds wonderful," she replied.

"He was. He was the one who taught me to love art." Wes leaned forward in his seat and rested his elbows on his knees. "How did you come to love art so much? When Hayden first showed me your paintings at the ranch, I was astounded at the talent."

She swallowed and heat flooded her face. He thought she was talented? Was he really serious about the bet they'd made? About getting her into art school? He had to be. She didn't think Wes was a man who didn't keep his promises.

"I don't know how it started," she admitted. "When I was little, after my mother died when I was four, I just kept thinking I wished I knew what she looked like because I couldn't remember. So I started finding my father's photographs and drawing her as much as I could. I didn't want to forget her face." She'd never told anyone that before. It was a secret she'd kept hidden even from her father because it felt too sad and yet important at the same time and she didn't want to remind him of what he'd lost. Some loves hurt too much. She'd learned that the hard way.

"There can be no real art without pain." Wes's voice was low and gentle, and the intensity of his gaze had softened. "Someone who has never lived their life will never know what the depth of colors can evoke on a canvas or how to paint a scene that would move even the hardest of hearts."

"Even yours?" she teased without thinking and then clamped her mouth shut in embarrassment.

He only laughed. "Even mine."

Wes seemed to catch himself and he looked at his watch. "We have another couple of hours. The movie is almost over. Would you like to watch another?"

Almost over? She blinked. She missed her favorite movie because she'd been in a tortured state of distraction. Each time he'd shifted his body, or talked to her, she'd been so aware of her own body. It was strange, the way she couldn't stop watching him, the way he positioned his body, stretched his legs out, or folded his arms.

"Well? What do you say? Another one?"

"Sure, but you pick this time since you seemed to know I wanted to watch *Laura*." She had to admit, she was dying of curiosity, wondering what he would choose. The array of movies in the cabinet either indicated a wide variety of Wes's interests, or it might be that they were his sister's movies, since Callie knew Hayden loved movies.

Wes steepled his fingers, watching her for a long moment, as though the choice in movie would be found on her face. Then he got up and knelt by the cabinet and selected one. Because he was using his body to shield the case from her, she had to wait for him to hit play before she'd know what he picked. Wes sat back in his chair, but reached underneath the seat and pulled out a small pillow.

"Here, take this. If you want to stretch out, it works well on the armrest."

She took the pillow hesitantly, measuring the row of seats they were on. If she lay down, she'd end up close to his lap. The idea sparked a wave of longing inside her. What would it be like to be so intimate with someone that you could do that? To rest comfortably against them and sleep. She couldn't imagine. That was the price of being a virgin. And it sucked. Once, when she'd been fifteen, she'd been out late in town with Fenn, and he'd driven them home in his truck. She'd fallen asleep, her head resting on his shoulder. A deep sense of peace and warmth filled her. She trusted him, loved him, and it had been wonderful, except it had only mattered to her. Not to Fenn.

"What's the matter?" Wes's voice broke through the creeping gray ache in her chest.

"What?" she asked, voice a little husky as she sought to hide her pain and the way it choked her.

"You seem…upset. I didn't mean to…" Wes trailed off, his blue eyes so dark they seemed almost onyx. It was clear, by the tic working in his jaw, that he was uncomfortable with the idea of upsetting her. Something softened in her chest toward this brooding, intense man. Maybe he didn't know he was arrogant and rude and that he ran roughshod over people. He was probably used to people scrambling out of the way when he strode past. Well, he wasn't going to make her cower, whether he meant to or not, nor would he frighten her.

She fluffed the pillow and set it on the armrest between her and Wes and then settled in, getting comfy. The credits appeared on the screen and the swell of a familiar love song gave her goose bumps. When the title appeared, her entire body went still and for a second she couldn't breathe.

An Affair to Remember.

He'd picked that movie on purpose. He was sending her a message about the bet. The man was too cocky, but for some reason it made her want to laugh.

The idea of having an affair with him, well, she admitted it would be memorable. The certainty of it made her tremble. As much as she wanted to believe she was going to win this wager, she knew it was going to get harder and harder to fight her fascination and attraction to him. Could she sleep with him and not let her heart get involved? That was what worried her more than any bet. A little shiver rippled through her.

"Cold?" His voice was low, a baritone rumble that awakened strange sensations in her body that she didn't want to feel, not with him.

"I'm fine," she muttered, curling her arms against her chest and rubbing her cheek against the pillow. It felt good to lay here. She could almost fall asleep like this. Because Wes was only six inches away, and she was attuned to his every move.

He remained uncommonly still, as though trying not to frighten her, but it still rattled her to be that close. That predatory stillness she'd seen so often in nature, like a hawk perched on a fence post, watching the grass below, holding very still as a field mouse made the foolish mistake of trusting that its silence and stillness meant it was safe.

* * *

Wes held his breath for several long seconds as he watched Callie drift to sleep. The movie continued to play, and he smiled at the little joke. Perhaps it was a tad dramatic, but he knew she'd gotten the message. They were going to be together and it would be an affair to remember for both of them.

His blood had heated when she'd taken the pillow from him and cuddled down on the seats as he'd suggested. It pleased him that she'd obeyed his wishes. He had no desire to break her, but to teach her that he could lead her, and she would enjoy it. He did not want to control every facet of her life. His goal lay only in control of her in bed, but in order for her to trust him there, she would need to learn to trust him outside the bedroom first.

His body tensed as Callie shifted, nuzzling the pillow and then exhaled a soft little sigh. Lust exploded through him like a flash bang. He loved the sound of that sigh, craved to hear it again and again as he possessed her and gave her such pleasure she thought she might die.

Wes forced a breath out and checked his watch, counting the seconds and minutes before he deemed it was safe to move. He slid a hand beneath her pillow and carefully eased the armrest down so that he could settle her pillow in his lap, buying her a few more inches to stretch out. And he got what he wanted. Her. Closer. His hand hovered about the tumbling waves of honey-gold locks, his skin tingling with the need to touch.

Just one little touch, he promised.

Her hair felt even softer than it looked and he marveled at the way it slid like silk beneath his hand. He stroked her hair. The urge to connect to her, even in such a small way, was a bone-deep need he couldn't ignore. Thirty days of taking it slow to win her over was going to be hell on his control. Her claiming would not be easy, but then again, anything worth having was never easy to obtain.

He'd accomplished much more than he thought he'd be able to in so short a time. Of course, there was the knowledge that once they got off the plane things could revert back to how they'd been a few days ago, and she would be thinking of his friend Fenn with those lovely eyes full of tears. She had put that man on a pedestal, and it infuriated Wes. He was friends with Fenn, but it didn't mean he couldn't be angry at his own jealous response to the way Callie thought of him with hurt and longing. The problem was she was young and didn't know her own heart or how to love and she was under the illusion that she loved Fenn.

I'll change her mind and enlighten her to everything she's been missing out on while she moons over that bull rider.

Wes threaded his fingers through Callie's hair, the gentle strokes soothing more to him than to her. He let out a soft sigh of his own. For the moment he was in control. She was close and he was content. He watched the movie a few more minutes, not quite paying attention before he leaned back against the headrest. His eyelids fell shut, and he found that for the first time in years he could relax. So long as he touched Callie, the restless beast inside him ceased to prowl.

* * *

One day later she was exiting the Charles de Gaulle airport, one duffel bag in tow, following Wes through the maze of travelers. At least a dozen languages could be heard within earshot and the signs were all in French. She'd taken one year of French and now, being in France, she couldn't remember a single word. Wes reached out and grasped her hand, keeping her close. She clung to him, relieved by the connection. He was the only person she knew here, the only thing familiar, and given that he was still mostly a mystery, that wasn't comforting.

People bumped into them and she kept muttering apologies. When they reached the outside of the airport, drivers were waiting for guests, little dry-erase boards in their hands with names scrawled on them. Wes bypassed all of them and met a man standing at the back, who didn't have a sign. He grinned as Wes shook his hand.

"Monsieur Wes, I'm glad to have you back so soon." The driver, a man in his early forties, and fairly attractive, shot a glance at her and then spoke to Wes. *"Qui est la femme? Elle est très jolie, mais non?"*

Wes smiled at the man and turned to Callie. "This is Monsieur Michel Lavoie. Michel, this is Callie Taylor."

Michel's brown eyes twinkled and he bent over her offered hand, kissing the backs of her knuckles.

"Enchanté, mademoiselle."

Callie blushed and nodded. "Nice to meet you."

Michel straightened and took the bag from her hands. "This way, mademoiselle. The car is waiting."

She and Wes followed Michel to the temporary parking area outside of the airport where private taxis waited. Michel led them to a black Porsche SUV and quickly loaded their luggage into the back. Callie was too distracted to notice much about the car as she climbed into the backseat with Wes. The distant city skyline of Paris held her captivated. The thin needlepoint of the Eiffel Tower was beautiful and she blinked several times, expecting it to vanish.

"We're really here," she exclaimed in wonder.

Wes brushed a lock of her hair back from her face. "Yes, we are." The smile on his lips was indulgent and sweet, making her insides warm.

"Ahh, the mademoiselle, it's her first time in Paris?" Michel's eyes met hers through the rearview mirror, his gaze mischievous.

"Yes," she answered.

"Then *bienvenue*, Mademoiselle Callie." He pronounced her name "cahl-ee" and it made her grin.

"Merci." She remembered that much from her year of French. Michel laughed merrily and she couldn't help but laugh, too.

The traffic was overwhelming, along with the sights and sounds. Callie nearly had her nose pressed to the glass of her window as Michel took them over a bridge and into the right bank of the Seine. Large riverboats with multiple decks cruised the scenic river, tourists' cameras snapping wildly at the views around them. Callie sighed. She had no camera or even a cell phone with a camera and wouldn't be able to get any snapshots. She and her father hadn't been able to afford anything but the landline.

Wes's hand settled on her arm, and she turned back to him. "Here, this is for you. It has an international plan with unlimited minutes. I gave your father one before I left. You can call him whenever you like." He offered a slim shiny smartphone, the latest and most expensive model on the market. Her eyes widened and she hesitated. Wes pressed it into her hands.

"But—"

He pressed a finger to her lips. "No, no protesting, or I'll be tempted to put you over my knee. This is a gift. You can't refuse it. You can…however, repay me in pictures. There is a twelve-megapixel camera on this model and it's supposed to be excellent." His lips quirked into a crooked grin.

Callie shivered inside. This man was so different from other men. He gave her expensive things, yet his idea of repayment was unexpected. And she didn't let herself dwell on his other comment, the part about him putting her over his knee. He meant a spanking. The mere idea made her lower half throb with a sudden pulse of awareness. She'd never been spanked in her life, not by her father, or another man, in punishment. So why did Wes's subtle, almost teasing threat stir her body to life? Surely she couldn't be aroused by the idea of—

"What on earth are you thinking about?" Wes asked, still smiling.

"Huh?"

He leaned closer to her, slightly crowding against her side of the car. "Your face is an enchanting shade of pink. I'm dying to know what you're thinking about," he mused. "Was it something I said?"

He drew the tip of one finger down the bridge of her nose, then over her lips, his gaze intense as he stared at her mouth.

"Was it…the part about putting you over my knee?"

A new rush of heat flooded her, no matter how hard she wanted not to react to him.

"Ahh, that *was* it." The dark triumphant light in his eyes would have scared a rational woman. But, as Callie was discovering, she was not rational when it came to Wes.

"You like the idea?" he asked in a soft tone, too quiet for Michel to overhear. "I love a woman who likes a little spanking. Her bare bottom open for my touch, the light sting, the gentle stroke that follows. Oh, Callie darling." His breath roughened slightly and his pupils dilated. He was on the edge of his control and they both knew it.

"Wes." She uttered his name in a panicked warning.

She sensed an animal just beneath his skin, a primal creature ruled only by desire and it frightened her, not that she feared he would hurt her, but more that she would surrender to him and that darkness. The need to offer herself, like a sacrifice to a lusty god, was so strong that she feared her own control, or the loss of it. When he looked at her like that, eyes so heavy with sinful intent…a side of herself threatened to emerge, a side she never knew existed, probably shouldn't exist. She wasn't ready to be that woman.

His lashes lowered to half-mast and he remained close to her, their noses almost touching, letting the intimacy, the closeness of their bodies almost drug her with a need to be touched, held…and so much more. Then he shifted back to his side of the car.

"Michel, have you notified Françoise that my kitchen needs to be stocked? Callie and I have not had breakfast yet."

"Oui, Monsieur Wes, it is full of food. She went to the market early this morning and is ready to prepare your meals."

"Thank you," Wes replied, his focus on the view outside his window, away from her.

The foot of space separating them seemed so wide, a gulf now, as though a galaxy could drift in the space between them. *Worlds apart.* And she didn't like it.

I'm addicted to him. To his touch, his arms around me. How had that happened? She loved Fenn, but already the memories felt dusty, faded, and she knew they were beyond saving. Her heart could never resurrect that love. It had died the day before and all that was left behind were the slow healing wounds. What a strange thing to wake up one day and have become a completely different person.

Michel stopped the Porsche in front of a tall stately apartment building. It was a grand-looking street, too, with tall old trees and dozens of little colorful produce stands dotting the street's landscape between the apartment buildings. There were quite a few little stores with awnings that had words like "Charcuterie" and "Patisserie" on them. From the contents of the windows it looked like Charcuteries sold meat products and Patisseries sold pastries.

"Welcome to the Rue Cler," Michel announced as he got out and walked around to the trunk to fetch their bags. Callie opened her door, which faced the curb. Wes walked around and joined her, watching the pedestrians on the street.

"Rue Cler?" Callie asked.

"It's a little neighborhood tucked between the government district and Les Invalides."

Callie felt silly, but she had no clue what any of that meant. "What's Les Invalides?" There was so much about this place she didn't know. It made her feel very small and a little overwhelmed. Not like at home. She could navigate her way through mountains and forests and never feel lost. Here in this land of monuments and stately old buildings she was lost.

"Les Invalides is a set of buildings containing museums and monuments relating to the military history of France. I'll point it out when we pass it. It has a gold dome at the top of one of the main buildings." Wes took their bags from Michel and gestured for Callie to head into the apartment building.

"We're staying here?" She tilted her head back and admired the stone building with its dark green roof.

"Yes. My apartment is on the top floor."

She and Wes left Michel. The lobby was a beautiful old-world style blended with modern touches. Marble floors, rich carpets, but sleek leather furniture and crisp, bright light fixtures. A man sat at a welcome desk and waved to Wes.

"Welcome back, Monsieur Thorne." The way he said Thorne left the "h" almost silent due to his heavy accent.

"Bonjour, Paul," Wes greeted and then pointed out a set of silver elevators down a corridor. "We'll go over there." He nudged her in that direction.

Callie led the way, trying to stem the nervous flutter of butterflies in her stomach. She was really here. After a seven-hour flight from New York, she was in Paris.

The elevator doors opened and Wes hit the sixth-floor button. When the doors slid apart again they revealed a long hall and only three sets of doors. One on each side and one at the end of the hall.

"We're at the end," Wes said. Callie reached the door first and Wes pulled out a set of keys and let her unlock the door. When she pushed it open, she gaped.

There were no words for it. It was too beautiful. A warm walnut wood floor was a striking contrast against the entryway's white-painted walls. There was a set of doors on the left that opened to a dining room and on the right were two rooms: a family room with a billiard table, couch, and huge TV, and a room next to it that had a fireplace and a cushy-looking loveseat ringed with two plush armchairs. A study with a large oak desk covered in folders, papers, and a laptop at the end of the hall was the last room before the space opened up to the library. Callie's feet moved, guiding her through the endless wonder of surprises this apartment held. Off the library was a kitchen with a small nook. Granite countertops and sleek stainless-steel appliances were pricey and state of the art. At the back of the library there was a curved staircase, which hinted to more rooms upstairs.

"This way." Wes headed for the stairs and Callie snagged her duffel bag off his shoulder so he wouldn't have trouble in the small curved passage.

"There are two bedrooms, one for you and one for me. We'll share the bathroom." He led her through the first room, which had a large four-poster bed with a red coverlet. The room was masculine and yet…strangely inviting, like Wes's embrace. Callie touched her face with the back of her hand, sensing the heat flare in her cheeks. She prayed he wouldn't notice.

A large Jacuzzi-like tub sat in the middle of the bathroom, with a pair of French doors opening out onto a large balcony facing the Eiffel Tower. Callie doubted there was a better view of the tower in the world than this. No wonder Wes owned this apartment. If he wanted the best, he would have it. In so many ways he was predictable, except when it came to why he wanted her. She wasn't the best and she wasn't perfect. Perhaps that was her allure. She was a novelty he'd acquire and then grow tired of. It was a chilling thought.

"This is your room." The expectant look on Wes's face drew her attention to the new room as they entered.

The walls were a soft gold color and a king-size bed sat against one wall. The headboard had a tapestry on it of a rococo-dressed woman in a flowing blue gown, who sat swinging on a large garden swing. Her lover leaned against a marble column in the midst of the background foliage, watching the woman gaily swinging. Like a moment trapped in time, a world nearly forgotten, yet here it was, woven in threads. Callie's gazed transfixed, aching to paint the piece. Her hands vibrated with energy, needing to expel the rush of creative juices suddenly flowing through her. Her father had often teased her and said she was possessed when she felt like that.

"Do you like it?" Wes's smooth, seductive voice teased her left ear.

Smack! The duffel bag slipped from her fingers and hit the wood floor as she was jolted out of her artistic daze.

"It's amazing," she admitted, a little breathless. The bed's coverlet was a rich blue, with gold embroidery of fleur-de-lis across it that glinted and sparkled in the morning sunlight that filled the room. A pair of French doors opened onto the balcony, giving her another view of the Eiffel Tower. But rather than look at the tower, she was looking at Wes. The faint streaks of gold amid the red of his hair were distracting. She hadn't noticed the depth of colors there before, the subtle blend of many colors to make one. He ran a hand through it, slightly tousling it, and Callie's insides quivered. She had the urge to touch his hair, to grasp its strands and feel them between her fingers. To touch him was to risk herself and she couldn't do that. At least not yet.

He turned, a look of satisfaction or perhaps more relaxation on his face. He seemed to be a different man than the hard brooding soul she'd known from Long Island. There was a softness to his mouth, a warmth to his eyes as he gazed at her, as though Paris had lightened whatever burdens rested upon his shoulders.

"Are you happy to be here?" He moved slowly, cautiously toward her as though approaching a skittish colt. She didn't move, didn't want to move, if it meant he might caress her. For some reason, she needed human touch, knowing it would ease the homesickness she felt.

When he was standing right in front of her, he cupped her face, his large palms shockingly gentle on her skin.

"Happy?" she asked dreamily as his blue eyes, that arresting shade, seemed lit by an inner fire of desire that robbed her of rational thought.

"Yes," he murmured, his head slowly lowering to hers. "I want to make you happy." There was a faint note of pleading in his tone and then he was kissing her.

A melding of mouths, tender and exploring. Callie responded easily, naturally, learning how to move her lips with his. A dizzy sense of delight made her purr when he parted her lips with his tongue. The playful thrusting motion of his tongue stimulated a deeper need her body had now. Before she was aware of it, she was rocking against him, trying to rub herself along the lean lines of his body. Wes groaned against her mouth, his hands almost shaking as they kept her face framed, as though he was doing everything in his power to restrain himself.

Was she happy? The question seemed to float through her desire-fogged mind like a single feather caught upon the breeze. Here…in this moment, half a world away from the man who broke her heart, she felt something. If not happiness, then it was close to it. And she was with a man who seemed to want her. Her, not anyone else, as hard to believe as that was. The bet be damned, she wanted to enjoy Wes's kiss.

When their lips parted, Wes's heavy-lidded gaze sent shivers through her.

"Let me show you everything Paris can offer," he said, with a little grin. "Starting with a Parisian breakfast." His eyes twinkled as he stepped back. "Get settled in. I'm going down to one of the patisseries and will select something for us to eat."

Callie nodded, shocked by the boylike look of excitement on his face. Who was this man? It certainly wasn't the Wes Thorne with dark secrets and threats of seduction she'd grown used to over the last few months. He was someone else. She couldn't seem to reconcile the two men and yet strangely she was drawn to both sides of him, like a moth to fire. She would fly closer and closer to the sputtering flame until her wings were lit with fire and she burned.

Chapter 5

Wes inhaled the Parisian air, loving the smells of the city as he stepped onto the Rue Cler. With all of the produce stands and patisseries as well as delis, the street itself seemed to have a taste. Sugar and butter coated the air, mixing with the subtle tang of meats. It made him feel alive to be here. After kissing Callie, his entire body was as active as a live wire. She would love it here. He'd prove to her this was a place she belonged, like he did. He wished he had an excuse to come to Paris more. With Callie, he might just have the chance.

Everything had to be perfect. Showing her Paris would create the romantic ambience that would woo Callie to his bed and inspire her to pursue her art. She should be a happy woman in his bed and giving her everything would be the best way to do it.

A small patisserie on the corner caught his eye. The window displayed a wide variety of sweet breakfast items bathed in the gold light of the shop. Wes strode inside and studied the numerous racks stocked with every sinful sugary delight. There were croissants filled with dark chocolate, and brioche bread baked with chocolate chips. The tortes were succulent fruit arranged symmetrically in tiny pie crusts that fit in the palm of his hand, covered in a honey glaze to make them shimmer. Wes's mouth watered at the thought of kissing Callie after she'd tasted a torte, the way the sugar would mix with her own natural sweetness. He shifted uncomfortably as an instant erection stretched his trousers.

Damn.

He focused back on the crème-filled éclairs. He could only think of Callie, on her back, his head buried between her thighs, her crème on his tongue…

Fuck.

He would never look at éclairs the same way again.

"*Bonjour, monsieur. Que voulez-vous commander?*" the plump female baker asked. Her apron was splashed with chocolate stains and flour as though she'd just come from crafting an edible masterpiece.

"*Bonjour, madame. Je voudrais deux éclairs, deux tartes aux fruits, et deux brioches au chocolat, s'il vous plait.*"

"*Oui, monsieur.*" The woman collected the items and tucked them into a white box with care and Wes slid his credit card across the glass countertop.

He took the box and headed back to the apartment building. He knew Callie would be tired after the long flight. She had barely slept on the flight and had spent hours watching movies. He had hoped she would trust him enough to use his shoulder to rest on but she hadn't. She'd seemed almost too quiet, whether from nerves or worries he didn't know. It was a big step for her to leave her father and the ranch behind. It had driven home the fact that she really had seen nothing of the world and was so young and innocent.

As he reached his front door and unlocked it, he noticed the apartment was quiet. Wes set his keys down and headed for the kitchen. He set out the brioche and put the éclairs and tarts in the fridge. Françoise had fully stocked up on fruit, eggs, butter, meat, juice, and freshly ground coffee for his coffeemaker.

"Callie?" he called out. No answer.

Wes shrugged out of his coat and headed for the stairs. He passed through his room and the bathroom and then halted in the doorway to her room. Her bag was open and half of it was unpacked. Callie lay on the bed, her face pressed against a pillow, deep asleep. Wes's heart gave an uneven thump in his chest. She looked so perfect, lying there in the bed he had chosen just for her. It was an antique frame that had once belonged to a French princess who had lived in the 1700s. He hadn't missed the way her eyes had immediately focused on the tapestry of the headboard. A look of longing and hunger, not sensual but creative, took hold of her.

She was an artist, not a small-time hobbyist, and had the makings to be a modern master. Wes would do everything in his power to provide her the training and the opportunities to make that possible. But right now, she was a beautiful young woman in a bed and that was all he could think about. Her golden hair caught the slanting sunlight and it reflected like a halo around her face.

"Mine," he whispered. *You are mine.* The need to possess her, to know her every thought, to fulfill her every desire was overwhelming. Wes didn't believe in love, let alone love at first sight, but he believed in obsession at first sight. And he was obsessed with Callie.

He took a few more steps to the side of the bed. A small pattern of goose bumps on the flesh of her arms and a little shiver caused him to frown. The open windows let in a chilly breeze and she'd probably been too tired to notice. Wes retrieved a thin afghan blanket from the closet and gently draped it over her. She didn't stir even when he caressed her cheek with his knuckles. He was satisfied she would be all right to rest a few more hours, before he woke her. The trick with international travel was to sleep only a short time to recover from jetlag.

He paused in the doorway, gazing at her. *"Le monde vous attend, mon petit chef-d'oeuvre."* *The world awaits you my little masterpiece.*

While she slept, he would see to a few things in his office. Wes went back downstairs to his study and took a seat behind his desk. The old gallows writing table was fashioned from myrtle burr veneers with herringbone and a black leather inlay top, turned legs, and brass drawer pulls and castors. It was a solid antique he had found hidden away in the dusty storage room of an old antique shop in Montmartre, the artist district. The seller hadn't known the desk's value but Wes had. It had required a fair amount of restoration work, but now it was a fine desk. He smoothed his fingertips over the polished wood. How many great men had lived their lives at this desk?

As his laptop buzzed to life, Wes leaned back in the leather desk chair and checked his phone. A few texts from Royce, most of it unimportant, except for the last text.

Royce: Mortons have FBI video footage back. Sent it to your secure e-mail.

Finally. He had been waiting for the FBI to return the footage on the robbery of the Goya and now he had a chance to see it for himself. Royce would have informed him of any arrests or progress in the case if the FBI or the Mortons were aware of anything.

Keying in his password, he accessed the secured private e-mail he used and found Royce's e-mail with a zip file. As it downloaded, Wes waited, oddly a little nervous. Stealing a painting was dangerous and hard. Whoever had achieved this was not a low-level smash-and-grab-type thief. The man was methodical and precise. His only mistake was the slight damage to the original frame. A detail overlooked because it was so small and the thief's focus had no doubt been primarily on the Goya.

The video opened and began to play. The white-and-black screen contained a shot of the hallway of the main collection. Many of the guests weren't in that portion of the gallery. It was a secluded area. Suddenly a woman appeared on the screen, leading a man by the hand. The man laughed, stumbled, and caught the woman about the waist. He pressed her against the wall, far too close to the Goya as he kissed her. The Goya's small frame was to the far right, just at the edge of the camera's view. The Mortons had a lapse in complete viewing of their gallery on camera. That was a risk that would have to be rectified immediately.

The man in the video moved his face away as he bent to put his mouth on the woman's neck. Her face turned toward the camera, the light illuminating her clearly.

Corrine Vanderholt.

What a naughty girl. He almost smiled, distracted by her ruthless seduction of some poor partygoer. The man had no idea what a viper Corrine was. Forcing his attention away from Corrine's indiscretions he looked back to the right, searching for the edge of the Goya.

His heart beat hard and he blinked rapidly. A flash of movement. Like the picture frame tilted slightly.

The Goya was gone. In that brief moment, the switch had been cunningly and quickly made. Wes rewound the frames and slowed down the speed. To the left, Corrine was throwing her head back as the man thrust a hand up her dress and kissed the top of her breasts. It was distracting. Damn distracting, but not in a good way. He used a notepad from his desk and covered the left side of the screen, and then he studied the edge of the Goya's frame. It moved, slower this time as the frames relayed the picture on the screen. The thief removed the piece and put the forgery in its place. The Mortons security system didn't have wall sensors, only cameras. The Goya was small. It could be removed and rolled and put in a small bag. Plenty of women had brought handbags to the party.

"Fuck," Wes muttered. The Mortons didn't have any other camera angles. There was no way to tell who had pinched the painting. He spent the next hour watching the guests leave through the front door, eyes trained on the ladies' bags. None of them were big enough to carry the Goya.

Another dead end.

He e-mailed Royce, telling him to get the security at the Morton house reassessed and pointed out several other key weaknesses. Royce could cover and walk the Mortons through the needed changes.

The rest of his inbox was full of e-mails from clients and industry contacts. An avid art buyer and close friend, Dimitri Razin, was going to be at the Louvre tonight and wanted to meet Wes for dinner before they took a look at the piece Dimitri was considering purchasing. For security reasons, it was being analyzed and stored at the museum rather than at an auction house. Razin always used Wes to consult on pieces and examine their provenances. Wes replied to the e-mail, letting Razin know he'd meet him at Fouquet's on the Champs-Élysées at seven thirty and then they could go to the Louvre.

A smile curved his lips. It would be fun to take Callie to the Louvre at night. The lighting of the glass pyramid after sunset was stunning. And she could get a good taste of the Louvre in a very private, exclusive way.

After a quick glance at his watch, he realized it was nearly lunch time. Callie should be getting up soon. If she slept too long her internal body clock would never adjust. He shut his computer down and went back to the kitchen, to brew some coffee, a Parisian blend

Françoise knew he favored. When he heard soft footfalls on the stairs he grinned.

* * *

Coffee.

Callie could smell it. Warm, dark, sinfully good. Like the taste of Wes, exotic, wild, and a promise of dark eroticism. The scent of the delicious brew pulled her out of a heavy sleep. Bleary-eyed she peered down at the light blanket covering her. She didn't remember that on her bed when she'd decided to take a quick nap. Had Wes found her napping and put it over her? The thought of someone caring for her made her entire body warm up and it felt fuzzy in a strange and pleasing sort of way. She lifted her left wrist and checked the time.

Noon.

She'd slept for two hours. Callie tossed the blanket aside and got out of the bed. She moved to the bathroom and then through Wes's room. When she reached the top of the stairs, the coffee scent hit her with full force. She followed the tantalizing aroma into the kitchen. Wes was resting against the granite-topped island, a mug in his hand. When she drew closer, he held out the mug for her.

"Here, this will wake you up." He pressed the cup into her hands and then reached behind his back and retrieved a white plate with what looked like soft baguettes flicked with dark spots.

"What is that?" She took the plate and eyed it curiously.

He chuckled. "I promise you'll like it. I ran to a patisserie while you slept. It's brioche au chocolat. Basically it's sweetbread with chocolate baked into it."

Callie's mouth watered at the description and she set her coffee down on the counter. She took a nibble of the bread, and its sweetness hit her with an explosion of taste. The dark chocolate added to the flavor but tamed the sugary bread to perfection.

"Well?" Wes asked, eyes alight with anticipation.

"I think"—she paused and licked chocolate off one of her fingers—"that if this is how the French always eat breakfast, I'm never going home." She was teasing as she found another finger covered in chocolate and she started to move it toward her mouth.

Wes caught her wrist with one of his hands, keeping her from moving, and then he dipped his head, sucking her index finger into his mouth. Callie's lips parted in silent inhalation. A sharp stab of arousal shot through her still-sluggish body. His tongue stroked her finger and then he nipped the pad before releasing it. Callie stared at him, shock, excitement, and confusion rippling through her in dizzying waves. How could he turn her on her head and make her feel so hot and alive? She didn't want to feel like that, not after Fenn, but Wes was forcing her to experience it despite her every intention to not feel that way ever again.

He wound a lock of her hair around one of his fingers and played with it, a dark, intent look in his eyes that made her nervous.

"I know you feel it, Callie."

Attraction. He didn't have to say the word. She turned her face away, knowing a blush betrayed her as always.

"I'll wait, but soon you'll have to embrace it or you'll drive us both crazy." He stepped back. "Now," he said calmly, like the Wes she knew, a man in control. "Finish your breakfast. We have some errands to run before tonight." He began to prepare another mug of coffee and motioned for her to sit at the table.

Callie tried not to think about him and the attraction she felt. It wasn't something she was ready to deal with, so she kept her focus on his last sentence.

"What's happening tonight?"

"We're meeting a friend and client of mine at a restaurant on the Champs-Élysées and then we're going to the Louvre for a quick inspection of a painting after-hours." The way he said "we" did something funny inside her chest and she almost smiled.

"The Louvre?" She knew he was going to take her, but she hadn't thought it would be this soon, or at night, after-hours. The man really was well connected.

"We can go after it closes?"

Wes nodded. "I can get us in. I knew a few people. I'll explain tonight on the way to dinner. For now, finish your brioche. There's fruit juice in the fridge. Then shower and change. We'll go out for a few hours."

"Okay." Callie didn't usually like to be bossed around, but she was way out of her depth. She didn't remember much from her one year of high school French and she had no idea of what to do, what to see, or where to go in Paris. She had to trust Wes. The man came here often enough that he owned an apartment. It was logical to put her fate in his hands, but she couldn't feel that it was symbolic of something more.

Callie went up to the large bathroom between their two rooms and explored the shower. It was expensive looking with quite a few jets that aimed at her lower back. A set of towels was on the counter, ready for use, and Callie quickly retrieved her toiletries from her duffel bag. An expensive-looking bottle of French shampoo and conditioner were already in the shower. When she used them they filled the room with the scent of peppermint.

After showering and changing, she was ready to leave and tucked her wallet, passport, and money into her purse. She had some money saved, not a lot, but she figured she could visit a few discount stores, assuming there were any around here.

Wes was waiting for her in the library, a thick book in his hands as he reclined in a wine-colored leather chair.

"There you are." He smiled as he set the book aside and rose to his feet. When he held out his hand, she took it. "It's time we buy you something decent to wear."

* * *

"It's too much…" she whispered fretfully, eyeing the massive stack of clothes.

Wes had dragged her through the entire Galeries Lafayette with its multiple levels and hundreds of shops. She'd refused to enter the store when she viewed price tags that made her eyes pop out of her head. The evening gowns, the jewelry, and the shoes…She tried them all on at Wes's insistence and had twirled in front of him more than once while he sat on a sofa and watched like a king of an ancient land, waiting to be entertained.

More than once his eyes lit up when she'd worn certain things. Like the red evening gown that had a tight shell-cupped bodice but flared out at the waist in folds. It looked like something Grace Kelly would have worn. Classy, yet still sensual. Wes's eyes had heated up enough that she could almost feel the burn on her bare skin. He'd waved over one of the eager store attendants and she'd bent down to listen as he whispered something in her ear, and then she straightened and rushed away.

Callie touched the smooth red satin of the dress. It was lovely. All of the things she'd tried on today had been. So far she'd purchased only one blouse, and she'd held out her euros with a shaky hand, trying not to think how much that one item set her back. The exchange rate was not strong for the dollar and she winced as she paid for it.

"Come here, Callie." Wes pointed at a spot on the floor in front of him.

She moved, the gown's train whispering over the crème carpet as she came to a stop in front of him. He parted his knees and reached out to hold her hips as he straightened on the couch. His face was level with her breasts as he gazed up at her. It was a strange sensation to be looking down at him. She did not feel any more power over him than before, but the position made her body hum with awareness.

"Do not worry about the expense. I've been buying everything that looks good on you."

"What?" She tried to pull away but he held on to her hips.

"No, no, no, my little Callie. You are exactly where I wish you to be. Now listen carefully. I brought you here, and I will pay for everything because it's part of my end of the bet we made. I expect nothing for these gifts, so do not even think about telling me I'm trying to buy you. I'm not. It simply pleases me to give you what you deserve. Do not argue with me or that spanking I promised will happen. And if I spank you…" His eyes churned with inner storms. "Then I won't be able to control myself and I'll take you to bed. Do you understand?"

Callie nodded frantically, trying to escape his hold again and he let her.

"The dress is perfect. Go and change. I think we've bought half the clothes in the Galeries Lafayette today." He grinned, the traces of that dark side nearly gone. There was still a shadow, just at the edge of her vision, one that reminded her that the part of himself he fought to control wasn't far from the surface.

The store clerks packaged up the purchases and would have them delivered. Callie tried not to think of how overwhelming it all was. Or how young and foolish she felt compared to the tall, skinny, young women with perfect hair and makeup who attended to Wes all day. He hadn't looked at them, not really, but Callie still felt that at any moment he'd decide his interest in her had been a passing fancy. A crazy one at that and he'd ship her back to Colorado on the first available flight.

Wes handed the cashier a black credit card and the woman's eyes grew round. He didn't seem to notice the woman's reaction.

"There's a champagne and coffee bar here if you'd like something," Wes suggested.

Callie shook her head. She felt a little…light-headed.

"Can we do something outside? I think I need some fresh air and would like to walk."

Wes touched the back of his hand to her forehead. "Are you all right? You feel fine."

"I am." She brushed his hand away.

"Very well, a walk it is."

He led her out of the huge mall and back onto the streets. The tourists were out, crowding the streets and crosswalks. Wes wrapped an arm around her shoulder. At any other time she would have pulled away, resisted the touch, but people in the crowds seemed to part when Wes walked, and if he was touching her, she was afforded the same rite of passage. She knew what held them in awe. Wes was incredibly attractive with his chiseled features and brooding stares. He looked like he stepped out of the pages of a fashion magazine. But it was more than that. It was the way he moved with a panther-like grace and a sense of innate authority. And she was with him. That little fact never ceased to puzzle her.

He took her to a place called La Grand Épicerie de Paris and when she saw all of the rows of walnut shelves covered with rare, exotic chocolate brands she actually giggled.

"Choose as many as you like," he encouraged and gave a little push on her lower back.

After several long minutes, she selected two bars of milk chocolate. One had a beautiful pen-and-ink drawing of Notre Dame on it and the other had a red man and woman silhouette as they leaned in to kiss.

"Why those two?" Wes whispered, his voice right in her ear. She jumped and his hands settled on her hips.

"I, well, I like the art." She peeped up at him through shyly lowered lashes. She hoped he understood, that when something appealed to an artist, no other explanation was needed.

"Then those two it is. We just have to make one more stop." He guided her to the basement, which had brilliant white and walnut shelves with thousands of alcoholic beverages, all high end. Wes strode right past the aisles of expensive wine and went to a glass-enclosed room that held what Callie assumed were the most pricey items. He selected one of the cognacs. The little sign read "Cognac Louis XIII—Rare case." Callie's mouth dropped open as she saw the tiny price tag on the box. "18,060,20 €."

"Eighteen thousand euros?" she whispered in shock. *Oh my God.* That was twenty thousand dollars.

"Only the best. It's a century old. We'll taste it tonight, after the Louvre."

"You're going to let me taste what has to be the most expensive cognac on the planet?" She heard the squeak in her voice, but she couldn't stop it.

"Why not? And it is not the most expensive. There are others, but not easily available in Paris." Wes went off to pay for the chocolate and cognac. Callie just stared at his back.

What was she doing here? This was—hell, she didn't know what this was, but it was insane, of that she was positive. She'd come from a world where they couldn't afford cell phones, and now she was going to be drinking a hundred-year-old cognac just because she could, with a man who made his intention to sleep with her very clear. She had been so desperate to escape her breaking heart that she hadn't cared what the cost of escaping might be. Now she was beginning to see what it was.

Agreeing to go to Paris with Wes made her just one of his many collector items. Did he have some secret little black book with a checklist and her name under "innocent little ranch girls"? That was all she was, the latest conquest, a temporary fascination that he would taste and then move aside for the next fascination. The thought of this made the hollow place created by Fenn's upcoming marriage seem all the deeper, like an endless cavern with miles of despairing darkness. Would this fall into hopelessness ever stop?

Callie blinked away tears.

I'm such a fool.

Was she ever going to stop making mistakes?

Chapter 6

W hat's the matter?" Wes asked as he came back to her, the cognac and chocolate in a pink-and-black bag.

"Nothing." She flashed him a falsely bright smile.

He pursed his lips, thunderclouds gathering in his eyes. "When we return home, you will tell me what's bothering you."

"Sure," she lied and looked away, but not before she saw the dark retribution his gaze promised.

Neither of them spoke as they waited for Michel to drive them back to the hotel. She was grateful for Michel's timely arrival. Even after years of ranch labor, she was not used to five straight hours of shopping and walking around Paris. Concrete hurt her feet a lot more than the soft cushion of Colorado soil. There was so much she'd taken for granted. And she was overwhelmed. Drastically so. She missed the Broken Spur, missed the birds and the distant sounds of cattle. And missing that made her feel small and pitiful. All she'd ever wanted was to get away, to leave the ranch. She'd been gone three days and now she felt stranded and abandoned.

"Est-ce que la jeune dame se sent bien?" Michel queried. Wes, in the seat beside her, looked at Michel in the driver's seat.

"Oui. Je pense qu'elle a eu le mal du pays," Wes replied, telling Michel that Callie was probably homesick. He hoped Callie was only homesick and not regretting coming with him.

"Ahh, bien sûr. Je comprend." Michel turned in his seat while they paused at the red light and caught Callie's eye. "Do not be sad, mademoiselle. Embrace Paris," he encouraged.

Callie smiled but her heart wasn't in it.

When they arrived at the apartment she saw that all of the shopping had been delivered already. The endless site of bags and boxes made her run for her room. Wes was quick and just as she reached the curling stairs, he grabbed her waist from behind and dragged her back against him. She kicked out, trying to escape his hold.

"Stop," he growled in her ear.

She sagged, too weary to fight. When she went limp, he loosened his hold and turned her in his arms. He was a few steps lower on the stairs and they were face to face.

"Talk to me. I can't fix whatever it is if you don't talk to me."

Talk? He wanted her to talk? An unexpected streak of anger fueled her enough to respond.

"This is too much, Wes. I'm not the kind of girl you need, and I miss the ranch and…" She bit her lip. "And I know what you want. You made it clear with that whole bet in the barn. But I can't hide the truth. You *terrify* me. I've never been with a man before and—"

"What?" This time Wes was the one who looked dumbfounded. "You're a virgin?" The way he said "virgin," with a mixture of shock and dread were the final nails in her coffin. She burst into tears and fled up the stairs to her room. He didn't stop her this time. Collapsing onto her bed, she buried her face in one of the pillows and cried. She'd never felt more stupid in her life. What had she been thinking coming here with him? They were the least likely two people to be together in the history of the world. They had nothing in common. Nothing except art.

A few seconds later she heard footsteps and the bed sank as Wes sat down beside her. A hand touched her back, smoothing her hair and rubbing her tense shoulders.

"Why didn't you tell me?"

"Would it have mattered?" she asked, her voice muffled, but she refused to look at him.

"Darling," he murmured so tenderly that she wanted to cry harder. How could he do that? Be so dark and intense one minute and sweet the next?

"It matters. I would have done everything so differently." He rolled her onto her back and wiped tears from her cheeks.

"How?" she managed to ask.

He leaned down and kissed her. Slow, deep, that playful teasing. Before she could stop herself, her hands were in his hair, lightly tugging on the strands.

Stop fighting, a voice in her head whispered. *He's a gorgeous man and he wants you, and you want him.* The voice in her head was right. She was overthinking this for sure, but she wasn't ready to go all the way.

He did nothing else except kiss her. But the kiss was hot, wet, full of wicked desire that made her forget the world around her. It was a kiss full of promise and she knew she was accepting whatever would follow, even though it wouldn't be tonight.

When he stopped the kiss and drew back, he stroked her cheek. "Tonight you will sleep with me in my bed." He nuzzled her nose with his. "I know you miss home. Allow me to hold you and you won't be alone." He paused. "Tonight won't be about the bet. It's about comfort. All right?"

Callie nodded. The man could have talked angels into giving away their haloes without a second thought. Sleeping with him would lead to other things. Her body was completely on board with that plan already, and it was only a matter of time before the rest of her went along with it.

"You shouldn't be afraid of me. Do you understand? I won't hurt you." He paused as though debating with something inside himself. "Do you know what BDSM is?" he asked.

Callie nodded. She'd read plenty of romances over the last couple of years and had enjoyed the more erotic, edgy ones, the ones that made her physically react when she'd read them. But those were fantasy. You couldn't have that with a man in real life.

"Did Hayden tell you what sort of man I am? That my desires run along those lines?"

As he spoke, she saw nearly all the barriers between them crumble. This was a piece of his private life and he was sharing it with her.

"She didn't tell me," Callie replied. "Do you want to do that stuff with me?" Her breath seemed to catch in her throat and waver like a frightened bird.

"You want an honest answer?" He still stroked her face, as though the touch soothed him. The late afternoon sun hit his hair, making the red gleam and seem to burn with vibrant colors.

"Yes. I want an honest answer." She lifted herself into a sitting position, ready to face him as an equal but it only put her closer to him, making her feel his body heat. His presence was all consuming.

"I want to do many things to you. Some of them might seem frightening, but I know what I'm doing. However"—he paused as his fingers moved from her face to her hair and fisted gently but firmly in the strands—"you're a virgin. You don't need that sort of intensity. Not yet. And if you never want to try anything else you need only say so. The power to tell me no, that is and always will be yours, but until you say it, I will continue to come after you, Callie. Do you understand? I enjoy the chase and you've run me ragged these last few months. I haven't enjoyed anything this much in a very long time. So as long as you wish it, I'll continue to pursue you, however long it takes until you're mine."

His words raised a thousand questions. She wanted to know everything but she'd never discussed something so intimate before in her life.

"Ask me anything. I'll tell you," he promised, as though he could read the racing thoughts in her mind.

"Really?" She sat up a little more. His hand in her hair slid down to cup the back of her neck and he massaged her tense muscles.

"Yes."

"Do you…" She weighed her question carefully. "Like to hurt a woman in bed?" She'd read some books about men who were sadists, and that hadn't interested her at all. She wasn't a masochist.

"I've caused some pain, but always accompanied by pleasure and only because my bed partner has needed it. I prefer my hand, a paddle, or a light flogger for mild punishment or erotic punishment. You know the difference?"

She shook her head.

"Mild punishment is for when you've done something that's displeased me. Likely I'll spank you with a paddle or my hand. A few stinging blows, nothing that will leave a real mark and shouldn't bruise. Erotic punishment isn't done for behavior. It's done because you need it to heighten your climax. A bed partner on the verge of coming can sometimes have a more intense experience if there's a hint of pain or even just a new pattern of stimulation. A light flogger is best for this." He brushed teasing fingers over the side of her hip. "A master dominant can trail the strands of a flogger over a submissive's skin so delicately that she feels she's being kissed rather than flogged. It can warm her skin, rather than burn it. Stimulate her need for a faint sting, and then reward her with exquisite pleasure."

Callie's mouth was so dry she struggled to swallow. The idea of her naked, Wes wielding a flogger, just enough to make her come so hard she screamed…dear God.

"I see we have something to explore there, don't we?" he mused with a wicked glint in his eyes. She finally swallowed and he noticed, still grinning.

"And bondage?" she asked.

The smile flashed was all wolf. "So you *do* know a little about my world." The pride in his tone shouldn't have made her happy, but for some strange reason she was.

"Well? Do you do bondage?" she prodded.

He moved so fast she could only squeak in surprise. He had her pinned on her back on the bed, her wrists held in one of his hands, trapping them above her head. His other hand rubbed her waist, playing with the bottom of her shirt. Callie struggled against his hold, shocked by how alive she felt simply by his holding her captive. Her lower body thrummed with eager anticipation.

"Does that answer your question?" He was so close to her that she could feel the energy and excitement coiling in his body as he gazed at her mouth.

"Yes," she whispered, feeling like anything louder would destroy what was sizzling beneath her skin and his. She liked feeling on the edge with him. There was no denying that. She had been around him long enough to know that she enjoyed the way he scattered her senses, like riding through a field sending a flock of birds soaring into the sky. He shocked her, excited her, and the fear of his intensity was lessening. If she could ask questions and he'd give her honest answers, that was worth trusting.

"Anything else you want to ask?" He licked his lips, like a wolf eyeing a lone deer, but he didn't attack. He held back, and she could see that the effort to do so cost him.

"Maybe later, after I've had a drink. I can drink here, right?" She couldn't help but watch his lips as they quirked into a hint of a smile.

"I keep forgetting you're not even twenty-one. Yes, drinking here for you is legal." He grew serious again.

"Just because I'm young doesn't mean I'm a child," she said. If he wanted her, and she was finally accepting that he did, then he needed to treat her like an adult.

"Believe me, I don't think of you as a child. Young and innocent, but not a child."

She hadn't thought much of their age difference, but twelve years was a long time in some respects. He'd had scores of lovers, had lived on the earth that much longer and experienced so much more of everything. Would he find her youth and inexperience tiring?

"I've been honest with you. Now it's your turn. Something is bothering you and I want to know what it is."

Summoning up every bit of her courage, she met his stare evenly. "Does it bother you that I'm not experienced? That I'm a virgin?"

One corner of his mouth twitched. "You're very brave, Callie. I've never met a woman as brave as you."

"Brave? I'm not brave," she said and snorted. She got scared all the time. "You didn't answer my question."

His hand on her waist drifted upward, sliding underneath the loose shirt and cupping one breast over her bra. It was unexpected and she arched upwardly, instinctively pressing herself into his hand.

"I've always had women who were nothing like you," he murmured in that seductive, caressing tone that made her melt inside. His fingers caught her erect nipple through her bra and he lightly pinched it as he talked.

With a little hiss of breath at the pricking touch, she jolted, more than ever aware of where his hand was and what it was doing.

Wes continued to talk as he rolled her nipple between his thumb and forefinger. "You see everything differently. The world is new and shiny. Life holds so much of everything. I am fascinated by you and I want to do so much with you. I've never brought a woman to my apartment here in Paris before. I've never been with a virgin before." He chuckled. "You're a first for me in many ways."

She knew in that moment she was seeing a different Wes. This one was almost entirely unguarded. No games, no secrets, no hidden agendas. Only truth and desire existed between them. Her heart gave a sudden beat, as though it had been dead for centuries and was humming back to life, shaking dust off its tomb. Her body was already well on the way to its own decision. She would make love to him. Not right away, but soon. Fenn was gone. There was no childhood dream left to capture. She would make new dreams, ones with other men in them.

"We can go slow?" she asked. "I'm not ready tonight, but...I want to be with you." She didn't want to let him win the bet between them, but she knew now what was burning between them was inevitable. And he had known from the start. Maybe that's why he'd made the bet to begin with, because he'd known it would come down to this and she'd give in. A flicker of guilt moved through her, but she shoved it away. She refused to think of the bet, and her losing. Not right now.

Before she could say anything else, he was kissing her again. This time he shifted his whole body over hers, pinning her completely to the bed. He pressed one knee between hers, so that she could grind against his thigh. The hand at her breast slid down to her waist, then went back up under her shirt. He deftly tugged the bra cup down and then palmed her bare breast. Callie moaned against his lips, the intoxicating feel of his large hand covering her breast under her clothes was intense and erotic. She ground her jean-clad pelvis against his leg, her clit throbbing, almost stinging with the friction.

He seemed to sense her urgency and he moved his hand away from her breast to cup her mound, rubbing in just the right spot. She exploded inside like a bucket of firecrackers with sparks and burning heat. Panting, she went limp beneath him, legs trembling as little aftershocks of the sudden, unbelievable powerful climax rippled through her.

Wes moved his mouth down to her neck, teasing her skin with delicate nips and little licks. The hard press of his erection against her stomach was impossible to ignore.

"Do I…do I rub you?" she whispered nervously.

He lifted his head and she noticed his lips seemed fuller from their kisses. She'd marked him with her nibbling kisses. That subtle show of her effect on him pleased her and she couldn't stop smiling.

"Not now. If you get anywhere near my cock, I'll lose control." His voice was ragged.

She shivered at the way he'd said the word "cock." It made her want to purr and wriggle against him. A blush worked its way up her body as she wondered if dirty talk was something she liked. Was it?

"I love it when you blush." He sighed like a man lost in a favorite dream.

"That's good, because you make me blush all the time," she retorted a little grumpily. She'd like to see him blush for a change.

He bent and nipped her bottom lip before teasing her. "There's a little sass in you. I like it. Keep it up and I'll spank you." He winked and she nearly rolled her eyes. He was bluffing. He wouldn't spank her. The threat was made too often for him to really mean it.

"What time is dinner?" she asked between languid kisses. It was wonderful to lie on a bed with a man, one who was all hers in that moment. Her body was sated and she was simply enjoying the pleasure and intimacy of his kisses.

"Hmm…an hour and a half." He finished on a growl of delight as he rocked his hips against hers as though determined to excite himself like she had, but Callie sensed he was much better at mastering his body's responses than she was hers.

"Should we get dressed?"

He nuzzled her throat before he puffed out a sigh and pushed his body up so he could look down at her. "Unfortunately you're right. I don't want to be late meeting with Dimitri." He stole one more kiss from her before he got off the bed. Callie propped herself up on her elbows and watched him head for the bathroom. He paused, resting his palms on the frame of the door as he glanced over his shoulder at her.

"Wear the navy blue dress and the kitten heels that match. The yellow overcoat, too."

And just like that he was gone. Callie flopped down onto her bed, body still loose after that intense encounter. Everything had changed. One day in Paris and she was already giving herself to Wes, or at the least had agreed to at some future time. So much for her belief that she'd win in the wager they'd made. She was crumbling like the walls of Jericho. It wasn't like her, but then again, the girl she'd been before had been alone and unhappy. With Wes, she was someone new, someone sexy and exciting. She wanted to be this new woman, and while she was in Paris, she had the chance to and not worry about what anyone would think.

Her dreams were coming true and yet she was still nervous about tonight. She was going to meet one of Wes's clients and then she'd get to visit the Louvre. After that…well…she smiled. She would just have to wait and see. She glanced out the window at the distant Eiffel Tower. This was Paris, a land of dreams, a city of love…a world where she could be someone else. Someone she was meant to be.

Chapter 7

Wes leaned against the front door of his apartment, waiting for Callie to come down the stairs. He heard the soft click of her heels and then she came into view. The dark blue dress was cut conservatively but was sexy in a classy way, enhancing Callie's natural style. The bright yellow overcoat was a perfect counterpart to the dress, which flared out slightly at her knees to give her more mobility. The navy blue heels had gold buckles on the toes and had enough height to accept her shapely legs but were not too high that she'd be uncomfortable. He knew his little cowgirl well now. She'd rarely worn heels, if ever, and was a stranger to dresses and heels.

He waved a finger in a circle, indicating for her to twirl. Callie blushed but performed a graceful pirouette. She'd pulled her long blonde hair into a ponytail at the base of her neck with a thick navy blue ribbon. Wes fought off the wave of desire as his body jumped into overdrive. A few hours earlier he'd had her beneath him in a bed, kissing her, his hands exploring her full curves. He'd almost come right there when she had. The look of shock, of delight, as she climaxed had blown his mind apart with thoughts of what would come soon. She wanted to be with him, and so long as he could take it slow, he would have her in his bed. What he hadn't expected, however, was the series of strange emotions running through him like quicksilver. He shoved these soft emotions, ones of tenderness and sweetness, aside. They would not help him and he didn't need them as a weakness.

"How do I look?" she asked when she reached him at the door.

He caught her by the lapels of her coat and leaned down to nuzzle her cheek.

"More tasty than whatever I had planned to eat tonight," he growled softly and Callie made a tiny little noise between a whimper and a throaty purr. The sound went straight to his cock.

"Dinner, remember?"

He licked the shell of her ear and nibbled the lobe. She gripped his shoulders as he continued the sensual torture by kissing the sensitive spot just behind her ear. "We can be late." His hands dropped to her back, pulling her closer.

"Won't your client get upset?" Her husky tone made him momentarily forget everything besides her. It was so easy to lose himself when he was with her, like being pulled into the gravity of a bright sun.

"Wes, dinner," she reminded more sternly. That barely cut through the warm haze of desire cloaking him. Dimitri Razin wouldn't want to be kept waiting.

He exhaled, a little irritated that he couldn't keep kissing those delightful little spots on Callie's skin that made her shiver.

"Very well. There's just one thing missing before we go." He curled his hand in her ponytail and tugged slightly, forcing her head back so he could plant a lingering last kiss on her lips. Could he last a few hours without tasting her?

"What?"

He reached into his pocket and pulled out the leather box Jim Taylor had given him. He held it out to her.

"Wes, I don't want any more jewelry."

He curled her hands around the box. "You'll want this. Your father gave it to me to give to you before we left for Paris."

She opened the box and stared at the little seashell bracelet and then unfolded the small note. When she raised her gaze, her eyes were glimmering with tears.

"He says it was my mother's. She loved the sea, just like me." She removed the bracelet and tucked the note back in the box. "Can you put it around my wrist?" she asked.

Tucking the box into his pocket, he then took the bracelet and fastened it around her wrist.

When he was done, she brushed a fingertip over the little shells. "I never had much of my mother's things. She didn't have jewelry, or any heirlooms. She and my father were both poor and they put everything they had into the ranch. I never knew my father had this." She wiped away a stray tear. It destroyed Wes to see her cry.

"I think he was waiting for the right time to give you something this special."

She leaned into him, kissing him once more, sweet and light, but no less potent than any kiss they'd shared in the past. His chest burned with an inner warmth at the light kiss.

"Thank you, Wes."

He clasped her hand in his and they left the apartment. Michel was waiting to drive them to Fouquet's. It was a fairly trendy restaurant in many aspects, but the food was excellent and the atmosphere was pleasant enough for a business meeting. Merry lights of the restaurant illuminated the red canopy roof that covered the outdoor seating areas as they arrived. Tourists already filled the outdoor tables, chatting and dining. Wes escorted Callie straight to the main doors on the corner of the building. When they walked inside, Callie's eyes grew round and her lips parted in a little O. That didn't help Wes. He'd just gotten control of his body again and she was making him hard thinking about her lips wrapped around his shaft.

"It's so beautiful. I've never eaten at a fancy place like this before," she admitted.

Wes studied the restaurant, trying to see what had impressed her. Rows of white cloth-covered tables were surrounded by armless tall red chairs studded with gold pins along their frames. Chandeliers with more than a dozen electric candles each filled the room with a soft, warm glow that reflected off the light walnut wood-paneled walls.

A secluded table in the back had a lone man drinking wine.

"Ahh, there's Dimitri." Wes guided Callie toward the man and the table in the back.

"Wes," Dimitri said and chuckled as he stood and offered a hand in greeting. Wes shook it and nudged Callie forward. She'd been hanging behind, letting him shield her with his body. No doubt because Dimitri was intimidating. He was a tall, dark-haired, dark-eyed Russian, good-looking and far too confident when it came to women.

"Sorry, we're late. Dimitri, I would like you to meet Callie Taylor. Callie, this is Dimitri Razin."

Callie smiled and shook Dimitri's hand but he pressed a lingering kiss to her knuckles and she instinctively moved toward Wes. He was glad for two reasons. She was learning to trust him, and she preferred him to Dimitri. Wes was no fool. Dimitri was a natural womanizer. More than one beautiful lady in Paris hadn't been able to choose between Wes and Dimitri and they had taken her to bed together. But Wes had no intention of ever sharing Callie.

"You did not mention this was to be a mixture of business and pleasure, Wes." Dimitri winked rakishly at Callie.

Wes steered her to the nearest chair and helped her sit. Then he took the seat slightly closer to his friend.

"The pleasure is mine. *Only* mine." He shot Dimitri a warning look and the Russian nodded faintly, indicating he understood.

"I've had the best wine in the house brought down. The waiter will return to see to our order." He held out menus to Callie and Wes.

Callie thanked him and focused intently on her menu as though it contained the secrets of the universe. She was very shy, but he would make sure she wasn't shy with him when they were alone.

"So what is this piece you've had sent to the Louvre?" Wes asked.

Dimitri had connections with the President-Director of the Louvre and often had pieces stored there when he needed them to be authenticated.

His friend passed Wes a glass of wine and one to Callie. "It's a Sargent, one I've not seen on the market before. You know how much I like his work." He turned to Callie. "Do you know Sargent?"

She nodded, eyes brightening with interest.

"Callie's an artist," Wes informed his friend, feeling proud of Callie and her talent. It was one thing to show off a painting, but another thing to show off an artist, one who was living and breathing right next to him, one he'd kissed, one who tasted like sunshine and encouraged dreams he'd thought long lost to him. He wanted to shout his excitement from the rooftops, and then he wanted to closet himself away with her, taking her to bed for days.

Dimitri's gaze narrowed in sudden interest. "You are an artist? No wonder you have my friend so fascinated with you. Wes Thorne lives and breathes art."

Wes sipped his wine and raised the glass in a silent toast to his friend. "As do you, Dimitri."

"Not like you, my friend." Dimitri turned back to Callie, smiling and brushing his dark hair out of his eyes, as he seemed to realize he'd caught Callie's undivided attention. "Wes understands art, while the rest of us simply appreciate it. The patterns, the techniques, all the things that define that art, including an artist's heart and soul, that is what he sees that the rest of us do not."

Wes wanted to laugh, but deep down, he sensed Dimitri understood people the way he understood art.

"I can see what you mean," Callie said, shooting Wes one of those equally intelligent and curious looks.

Dimitri laughed in delight. "You are a perceptive lady. All good artists must be."

"The best artists see something for what it could be, not just what it is." Callie reached for her glass of wine and took a taste. Her hazel-green eyes settled on him and what he saw there heated his blood. The dewy-eyed innocence wasn't there, but an ancient knowing glint, as though there were things she saw and understood better than an average woman her age. It was a fleeting glimpse of the worldly artist she would someday become, the person he wanted her to be.

"I think, my friend"—Dimitri signaled their waiter with a little wave—"that you have found a most unique woman."

My masterpiece. Mine. He nodded at Callie. Well played, darling.

The waiter arrived and they placed their orders. Dimitri seemed fascinated by Callie and before long Callie was chatting with an ease and friendliness he hadn't seen before. Dimitri, ever a collector of human information, soon pried out such kernels of information like the fact that cobalt blue was her favorite color, the best night of her life was watching a meteor shower with her parents when she was four, just before her mother passed away. Wes's stomach had clenched at the thought of her so young, only four, and that a fuzzy memory tinted with the warmth of her mother's love had left such a lasting impression on her. He was glad she had that memory of her mother. Not all children were so lucky.

He for one was the product of two wretched examples of human nature. Grandpa Thorne was the only family member other than Hayden who Wes officially acknowledged. His own parents were a pair of polecats scratching, biting, clawing, with no thought or care as to those around them. When he'd left for college, he only came home to the island because he loved it, not because his parents were there. Someone had to keep an eye on his friends and, most important, his sister. If he had to run into his parents a few times a year at public events, it was something he would endure.

Callie pushed back her chair and both men rose to their feet as she stood. "If you'll excuse me, I need to use the ladies' room."

"What has you in such a black mood?" Dimitri asked when Callie was out of ear shot.

Wes shrugged. "Thoughts of the past, they turn me black." He rarely admitted weakness, but Dimitri was someone he trusted.

"There's no reason for that. You see the lovely lady who just left? She likes you. That has to erase all dark thoughts from a man when a woman like her wants you."

"Believe me, she is a hard one to get into bed. She's in love with my childhood friend. That's not an easy thing to erase from her mind."

Dimitri's dark brows rose. "Let me guess. She loves the man marrying your sister?"

"How did you know that?" Wes gulped down a large portion of his wine.

"The lovely Hayden Thorne no longer single? That news raced across continents quicker than you can imagine. I heard it in Moscow twelve hours before the news was officially announced."

"Amazing how news like that spreads." He glanced around the restaurant and then leaned closer to Dimitri. "What do you know of the black market for Goya paintings?"

"Goya?" Dimitri mused. "His sketches are the most popular items, smaller, easier to steal. Why do you ask?"

Wes pulled his phone out and showed a picture of the Goya forgery to his friend. "This is an unbelievable forgery of a piece I helped acquire for some friends on the island. They were robbed by a professional. I'm hoping to find it on the market and see it returned to the rightful owners."

The Russian laughed softly. "And you want me to get in touch with old contacts?"

"If you wouldn't mind."

"Let me have a night with your woman and I will do whatever you wish." There was a mischievous twinkle in his eyes.

"Anything but that." Wes kept his tone light, but his words were steel.

"I expected as much. Very well. You will owe me and I'll collect that favor when the time comes."

"Thank you."

If anyone could find something on the black market, Dimitri Razin could.

* * *

Callie left the bathroom and paused at the entryway back into the dining room. At the table she saw Wes lean over and show something to Dimitri on his phone. She couldn't help but wonder what that was about.

Secrets. Wes must have many. She had so few. He, as did Dimitri, saw through her so easily. But she was learning to see the world the way Wes did. Being around him was eye-opening. And being near him physically was changing her, too. Now that she'd come to the decision that she would be with him, she was both nervous and excited.

She wasn't going to think of Fenn. That was still a thorn in her heart. Thorne…in her heart. She almost laughed at the pun. Thorne indeed. It would be too dangerous to fall for a man like Wes. She would have bet her life that if she grabbed the nearest dictionary and looked up "heartbreaker" Wes would be there staring up at her from the page, brooding and too seductive.

And I've sworn off all men, so why am I letting him get too close to me? Because he's irresistible…

Pulling herself out of her thoughts, she walked back to the table. The two men straightened and stood as she took her seat. The waiter returned with their meals before she could try to come up with some way to ask them what they were talking about while she'd been gone. They likely wouldn't have told her. Dimitri was a man of secrets and a people reader. He was right about Wes, the way he viewed art. It was so obvious now, how he loved art because of its purity of expression. She sensed Wes preferred to avoid facing some of reality. Art was his escape. Callie was much the same.

After dinner, Dimitri volunteered drinks, but Wes said they should get to the Louvre. Michel was there, waiting to drive them to the museum. Dimitri took the passenger seat while Callie joined Wes in the back of the Porsche. Michel drove down the Rue de Rivoli and paused beside the large Louvre, where a pedestrian passageway opened up to the inner courtyard of the Louvre itself. They all got out and quickly walked through the passageway. When they entered the courtyard, the dark night gave birth to an amazing sight and Callie gasped.

The sky, a blue like Wes's eyes, made a vibrant rich backdrop behind the rising gold pyramid of glass and steel. A pool of water, black from the night, reflected the pyramid upside down. Beyond the pyramid, the Louvre's pale stones turned gold from lamps lit along the walkway facing the structure. The sight was breathtaking. Centuries of history were here. Inside the walls were some of the most famous works done by true geniuses. Her throat tightened as a wave of longing and awe swept through her. She was about to enter the hallowed halls of true masters. She, who knew so little of technique and had no formal training, rather than be daunted by facing these masters, felt invigorated. Tears of joy stung her eyes.

"Callie, are you crying?" Wes moved in front of her, concern filling his gaze. The golden lights of the Louvre's courtyard reflected in the dark pools of his eyes. "What's the matter, darling?" he asked again. "We haven't even gone inside yet."

She brushed away a tear. "I know. I just can't believe that I'm here."

"I promised to give you this," he reminded her. "There's so much more I want to offer you." He held out a hand, palm up. An invitation. A temptation. One she couldn't resist. She placed her hand in his and they entered the pyramid by climbing down the stairs into the underground entrance of the Louvre. The hall of the pyramid, the coat check rooms, and information and ticket windows were all dim now. A man stood waiting for them. He was a lean, dark-haired man in his fifties, good-looking in that way Frenchmen were as they aged.

"That is Pierre Monde, head of the administrative offices," Wes explained as they reached him.

"*Bonsoir, Monsieur Monde.*" Dimitri shook his hand and stepped back to allow Wes and Callie to meet him.

"This is Callie Taylor." Wes nodded at the man as he greeted Callie. "I understand we're here to view a Sargent. Could I show Ms. Taylor a few pieces from the collections before that?"

"Of course." Pierre lifted up a radio and called for a security guard. A man in a security uniform appeared and walked over to them.

"Monsieur Mignon can take you to any gallery you would like to see."

"Excellent." Wes looked at Callie and then back at the guard. "How about the Egyptian antiquities?"

Callie grinned. She loved Egyptian history but had never seen any artifacts in real life. Wes tightened his grip on her hand, and she looked up at him. He did that often, reached for her hand, and she knew every touch he gave meant something. It was as he'd told her a month ago in the tack room at the ranch. Every action he did had a distinct purpose. So what was the purpose for him to hold her hand?

"Come on." His eyes twinkled as he tugged her hand. The security guard was already moving down the hall.

"This is the crypt of the Sphinx," Mignon announced and waved a hand toward the next room just past him.

Callie walked past him and then froze at the entry, delight and awe stilling her in place. A sphinx statue sat in the center of the room. Lion paws stretched out, a stoic, mysterious expression on its face. The pale stone eyes appeared almost milky in the soft light of the exhibit and Callie instantly thought of a blind seer, seeing the future but unable to see what was before it. Hieroglyphs were carved into its chest and along the shoulders.

"26,000 BC," Wes murmured from behind her.

"Can you believe someone made this?" she asked Wes, and this time, she tugged him closer so they could look at the sphinx up close. She shot a glance over her shoulder. The guard wasn't watching.

"Do you think he'd let me touch it?" she asked in a whisper.

Wes followed her gaze to the guard, who wasn't looking and he grinned. "Go for it."

She reached out and touched the shoulder of the great pink granite creature. The stone was warm beneath her palm and she gasped. Without thinking, she took Wes's hand and placed it on the stone, holding his palm.

"Close your eyes," she told him, excitement fluttering through her.

He stared at her for a long second before he closed his eyes.

"Feel the heat. The granite heated by centuries in the sun. A dark-skinned man, eyes rimmed with kohl, working a chisel and hammer as he carved a magnificent mysterious gatekeeper who speaks in riddles to travelers."

As she spoke, the hardened lines around his eyes and mouth smoothed as he relaxed.

"Taste the sting of sand when the winds blow in from the south. Hear the rushes of the plants at the Nile's edge. Can you see the trio of the pyramids?"

Wes nodded faintly, then slowly opened his eyes and looked at where their hands were joined on the ancient stone.

"Tomorrow I want you to draw this. This moment right here." His voice was low and a little rough and his eyes were as bright as sapphires.

"I don't have any tools or paper." She reluctantly released his hand and their physical connection broke apart. Something inside her stirred, like a spring breeze rustling through the green grass outside the ranch. She had felt warm inside whenever they touched and she mourned the loss of it now.

Mignon coughed from the doorway. "We have time for one more artifact before Monsieur Razin will need you."

"Of course," Wes said. "What do you recommend?"

Mignon smiled broadly as though delighted to be consulted. "This way."

They walked down a short flight of steps into a crypt-like room containing a huge sarcophagus.

"The sarcophagus of King Ramses III," Mignon supplied.

Callie crept closer, in awe of the massive pink granite sarcophagus. The intricate hieroglyphs carved all around the surface of the tomb were stunning.

"What do you think he was like?" she asked Wes, thinking of the linen cloth wrapped body of a god-king inside his coffin.

Wes folded his arms over his chest, intently studying the carvings.

"He was a mortal man, one who wanted to build a life and leave an eternal legacy behind."

"Thousands of years later we still know his name and legacy. I'd say he managed it. Immortality. I couldn't imagine leaving behind something that would leave its mark on the world."

Wes slid his hands into his suit pocket. "You could, you know. You have talent, Callie, real talent."

Heat flooded her cheeks. "You're just saying that. There are a thousand artists out there just like me."

"No." His eyes darkened. "There aren't. I don't lie and I have no intention of fluffing your ego. I meant what I said. You could make an unbelievable artist. You see so much more than what others see. It sets you apart." He leaned close to her, and she found herself closing the gap between them, fascinated by the shape of his lips as he spoke.

"Tomorrow we'll buy the supplies you'll need." He took her hand and they left Ramses III to sleep in his granite tomb, to dream the dreams of a long-ago perished god-king.

Chapter 8

It was nearly midnight when Wes carried Callie from the car while Michel held the door. She had fallen asleep after leaving the Louvre. She'd been up for a day and a half with no real sleep and he had purposely kept her awake and engaged most of the day so she would adjust to the time change. He came to Paris every couple of months, so the change wasn't that difficult for him.

"You wore out the young lady?" Michel teased as he waited for Wes to go to the apartment elevators.

"Yes, poor thing." Wes chuckled. "Bonsoir, Monsieur."

"Bonsoir, Monsieur Thorne."

Wes nodded at the night guard who pressed the elevator button so Wes wouldn't have to put Callie down. He liked the way she felt in his arms, perfect. Caring for her soothed his dominant tendencies. Normally he didn't react so tenderly to a submissive, but Callie wasn't a submissive. She was something infinitely more important. She was *his* and he took care of what belonged to him.

When he got to the apartment door, however, he set her down on her feet, keeping one arm wrapped around her waist.

"What? We're home?" she mumbled sleepily, resting her head on his shoulder and leaning into him for support. That strange sense of fuzzy warmth inside him blossomed. Home. She felt at home here. That pleased him, and he was also pleased she was relying on him, trusting him physically. When he'd made the bet in the barn, he'd been thinking about his ego, his obsession, and his need to possess her, but the wager had taken on a new importance to him. He felt the strange need to prove to her that he could care for her, be the man she needed in order to get over Fenn.

"Yes, we're home. Hold on." He unlocked the door and got them both inside, then locked the door. After that, he picked her up again and carried her to her room. He placed her down on the bed and removed her shoes. Without thinking, he gripped one of her feet and rubbed the sole, massaging it. She sighed and stretched out on the bed still in her coat and dress. He rubbed her other foot and she giggled, jerking a little as though tickled.

"That feels so good," she said and moaned.

Wes couldn't stop the spreading smile on his face. There was something so erotic and intensely natural about Callie that he was endlessly fascinated by her. She was innocent in so many ways, yet she was also incredibly sensual. A rare combination in anyone, and it was something that wouldn't change, not so long as she had the right bed partner.

"Do you need help undressing?" he asked when he noticed she seemed content to lie on her back, almost asleep.

"Mmm…maybe." She giggled again and then flipped onto her stomach. "Can you unzip my dress?" She seemed to be waiting. He sighed. The woman was straining his control. He carefully removed her coat and then unzipped the back of her dress. The thin strip of a conservative black bra caught his attention. Unable to resist, he slid his fingers beneath the band between her shoulder blades and stroked her skin.

"That's nice…" She purred and nuzzled the comforter.

Wes blew out a measured breath, trying to ignore the male part of his body that came to life. She was such a temptation to him and she had no idea how much he wanted to strip her bare and press her deep into the bed and pound into her until they both nearly died from the pleasure. He needed to put some space between them or he'd lose control.

"I'll be in my room if you need anything." He got off her bed and walked back to his room. He stripped out of his suit coat, tossing it over the back of a chair and then he kicked off his shoes and pants and fetched a pair of cotton pajama pants from his dresser. He had a hard-on but there was no way he could deal with that right now. She'd hear him in the bathroom if he tried to see to his needs. Maybe with a little luck he could will it to go away.

He pulled back the covers of his bed and climbed in. Only a few minutes passed as he lay there and mastered his arousal before a quiet voice drifted to him from the doorway to his room and made him look up.

"Wes…" Callie stood in the doorway between his room and their shared bathroom. She wore a large t-shirt with a faded ranch logo and a pair of plaid boxers. Her hair was loose and tumbling around her shoulders.

He sat up and tossed his covers back, ready to get out of bed if she needed something.

"What is it?" he asked. Her eyes were round and the moonlight made them gleam with a reflected brightness.

She didn't immediately speak, but when she did, her voice was still soft and quiet, too shy.

"Can I stay with you tonight? You said I could." She took a hesitant step across the threshold, entering his domain. It took a lot of bravery on her end to do that.

He reached over to the empty side of his king-size bed and pulled back the covers in silent invitation. She needed him, his body heat, his presence, nothing more for now; he understood that. But the primal creature inside him growled in possessive pleasure as she padded over on bare feet and climbed into bed with him. She settled deep into the covers, her face angled toward the window. He lay behind her, fascinated by the moonlight that seemed to make her cheeks glow like alabaster with a hint of rose. A lock of her hair lay across her cheek and he delicately swept it behind her ear. She shivered a little and rolled on her back to stare up into his eyes.

"Wes…it still hurts." Thick tears pooled in her eyes and he used the pads of his fingers to brush them away. "Part of me still feels like…like I'm dying. How is that possible?"

He didn't want to talk about Fenn, especially not about her feelings for him, but it was unavoidable.

"First loves are often the hardest to forget. They cut deeper into a soul. You can't forget them overnight, but…" He stared back at her, solemn. "You can move on. Fill your days with other things, new things. You might wake up one day and realize what you felt was more a shadow of something greater you will feel someday for someone else." He wanted her to forget Fenn, but that wouldn't happen. She would someday find a man to love, a better man, but he didn't want to think of that, either. *He* wanted her, here, now, while she was just like this, a woman about to explore the world. He would be her first in many ways.

"Who was your first love?" she asked.

The question was so unexpected that he blinked. His first love? He'd never…he closed off his heart long ago. No woman had yet breached that impenetrable fortress around his heart. It was better this way. If you didn't love, you didn't hurt. So he lusted and desired. That was good enough.

Callie reached up and placed a hand on his bare shoulder, her skin soft and her touch light.

"You haven't loved," she guessed, a knowing shrewdness to her gaze that amazed him. She was so perceptive for one so young.

"I'm sorry," she whispered. The sincerity in her tone made him blush.

"Why?" he asked.

"Isn't loving the same as living? If you can't feel pain, you can't feel alive. And loving hurts sometimes." She nibbled her bottom lip, her eyes distant now, lost in her own pain.

Damn her observing nature. "You need to rest," he muttered and pulled the covers up tighter around their bodies. She watched him a moment longer before she turned back to the window. He shifted closer so he cocooned her from behind. Their bodies fit perfectly together and within a few minutes, every bit of tension in him seeped out and he settled into sleep. But the dreams that came were full of endless meadows, and Callie riding away, far out of his reach.

* * *

Callie woke to Paris birdsong. The happy chatter outside the windows was an endless delight and a comfort that reminded her of home, although the birds sounded different. Plump songbirds perched on the edge of the balcony railing, dancing on their tiny feet and fluttering their wings. Callie watched the little creatures flitter about for a few minutes. Behind her, Wes slept deeply, his breathing slow and even. The world seemed to slow to a stop, frozen like a golden ray of sunshine trapped in a jar, a memory preserved forever, just as perfect as anything could be. She was warm and safe, with a beautiful man in bed beside her.

She rolled over to face him. The hard lines around his eyes and mouth softened as he slept and she wondered what a man like him dreamed about. He had the world at his fingertips; anything he could ever want was within his reach. So what did a man who had everything dream about?

Well, not everything. He hadn't fallen in love. For some reason, he had kept his distance emotionally all these years from women. Why? A man like him had a distinct purpose for everything. Did love not fit into that equation?

The weight of his arm around her waist felt nice, more than nice. Their heads shared a large pillow and their noses were almost touching. She had never slept with a man before, but the last night she had been in bed with Wes. An intimacy was growing between them, which could only come from sharing a bed together through the night. Like invisible strands of a delicate tapestry weaving them together, tying them to one another.

Sleeping with someone was a gift of trust that lovers shared beyond their bodies. But she and Wes weren't lovers. Yet. A little smile curved her lips. Soon though. She wanted more, more of what he had promised in his kisses and his touches. There was an entire world out there that she wanted to know and experience. And if she had to let him win the bet, maybe it was worth it. She just had to keep her heart guarded and enjoy what passed between them purely on a physical level. It wouldn't be easy, but she'd made a promise to herself about never letting a man hurt her heart again and she wouldn't let anyone do that to her, not even Wes.

She had dreamed that Fenn would be the man to teach her the ways of passion, but that dream was shattered. In its place Wes had emerged. A dark knight who promised things she'd been afraid to wish for. She was no longer a young girl and there was a part of her, a deep secret part, that longed to explore these new sides of herself. Wes would help her with that. The question was, could she help him in return? A life without love was no life at all.

Maybe she could start small. Do little things. Yes. That could work.

Sliding out of bed, she tiptoed downstairs and went into the kitchen. Surely she could make some breakfast for him. He'd gotten them food yesterday, and now it was her turn. She studied the stove and was relieved to see she could decipher the heat levels without needing to know a lot of French.

The fridge had a dozen eggs and all of the ingredients she could want to make two omelets. The cupboards had flour and other items required for homemade biscuits. She was by no means a master chef, but some of the basics, like biscuits and omelets, were doable. After a few minutes of searching high and low in the drawers and cabinets, she found a few pans and a cookie sheet.

The next half hour passed in a whirlwind as she whipped up the biscuits. At one point she dropped the bag of flour. The second it hit the kitchen floor it exploded in a small white atomic cloud, coating her and most of the nearby flat surfaces.

"Shit," she cursed and picked up the flour bag, which was now considerably lighter. Maybe Wes wouldn't notice most of the contents were missing. She sneezed and a cloud of new flour whooshed into the air. With a little growl of frustration, she fetched some dishcloths and tried to wipe up most of the flour that dusted the counters like a light snowfall.

Having little luck with the mess, she decided that she'd clean up later and she focused on cutting biscuits out onto the cookie sheet. As she cooked she hummed a soft little song. There was nothing so delightful in life as losing herself to a task like cooking or cleaning.

Whether she was painting or doing work on the ranch, she never liked her hands to be idle. The activity let all of her worries and anxieties temporarily go as she created the meal. It wasn't fancy, but it tasted damn good. Anything you worked hard on seemed better because you worked for it.

The timer beeped and she searched the drawers for a mitt. She bent over the open oven door and inspected the biscuits. They were a warm golden brown. Perfect. Humming again, she pulled them out of the oven and turned it off. When she turned around to set them on the hot plates she'd put on the granite island earlier, she froze.

Wes stood in the doorway, wearing nothing but a pair of jeans. There was something undeniably sexy about him in suits, but in jeans…her body exploded with heat and desire. His bare chest displayed those perfect pectoral muscles and washboard abs. Callie blinked, trying to focus, but in a haze she realized she couldn't remember what she'd been trying to focus on.

"Busy morning?" he asked. His head tilted as his gaze slowly swept across the messy flour-strewn kitchen.

Was he mad? She'd pretty much made a hot mess of his kitchen and Wes seemed to never leave a thing out of place or messy.

"I'm so sorry. I was going to clean it up after I'd gotten a tray ready for you." She reached for a dish towel and wiped her white-powdered hands on it.

"A tray?" He raised one eyebrow. It felt like a challenge, but she didn't know why.

"Uh-huh, you know, when someone brings you breakfast in bed." God, she sounded like an idiot. She had wanted to do something nice for him, something that might make him smile. She loved his smiles. He had at least three of them. One when he was content, one when he was playful and when he was ready to pounce on her, and—

That third type of smile flashed over his face and it was her only warning. He stalked across the kitchen and before she could react, he'd gripped her by the waist and lifted her up. Her bottom hit the counter behind her as he set her down. And then he grasped her face, and with one long scorching look at her eyes, then her lips, he was kissing her. He nipped at her lips, bit her bottom lip, and teased her tongue in a wild type of play that drove her frantic. She clawed at his shoulders, his body, trying to get closer for more of this intoxicating rush of sensations. His skin was hot beneath her hands and his muscles jumped at her touch. She scraped his back with her nails, feeling an animal rise inside her.

"That's it," he growled. "Mark me, darling, *fuck*." He hissed and then he was embracing her again, hands sliding beneath the top of her boxers.

When he met the little cotton panties she wore, he traced the edges, then slid beneath them. His large hands on her bare bottom made her moan and she nipped his mouth, licked at him, feeling wild and playful. He massaged her ass, clenched it, and then his fingers traced that sensitive seam, exploring the hidden places no one had touched before. She jolted into him, surprised at the flare of awareness his touch created. He stroked, pressed, circled his fingers again and again on that one spot and she arched against him, rubbing her throbbing clit on the hard bulge in his jeans.

Then he pulled away and she whimpered in protest. She needed something… needed a release of the tension building inside her.

"Don't worry, I'll take care of it," he rasped as he lifted her off the counter and spun her around.

Before she even realized what was happening, he bent her face down over the granite island. She braced her head on her forearms, panting as he covered her from behind, kissing and nipping her neck. His hands were magic, one sliding around the front of her body, this time touching bare flesh as he cupped her sex. She gasped and jerked, but couldn't escape his touch. No man had ever touched her there and the fact that it was Wes was a little scary and exciting at the same time. He located that ultrasensitive bud. He pressed down hard, then eased up, then circled it lightly before pressing down again. He repeated the pattern over and over and she wriggled beneath him.

"You want more?" His harsh breath in her ear ratcheted up her arousal that much more.

"*Please*," she begged. She was near mindless. This building need for pleasure was the only thing that mattered now. It consumed her.

"All right, darling." The way he said darling made her burn inside.

He slid two fingers down into her sex and parted the slick folds. One long finger entered her, sliding in and out. She groaned at the strange feeling of that single penetration.

"So tight, Callie, so fucking tight." His hoarse words, the subtle dirtiness to them, undid her. She couldn't stop the orgasm when it hit her. He didn't let up on her. He tortured her by pushing a second finger inside her, stretching her, and her body reacted, clamping down on him, trying to keep him there.

"I can feel you," he groaned, burying his face in her neck, panting.

She pushed her hips back, grinding her ass against his groin, feeling the climax roll through her before she went limp. He cursed above her, his hips jerking hard against her, pinning her to the countertop and then he let out a little laugh.

"You okay?" He brushed back the hair from her neck and planted a soft lingering kiss.

Callie sucked in several ragged breaths. His fingers were still inside her. He turned them, curled them, and she whimpered, her inner muscles rippling around them before he withdrew his hand. He stood up and she tossed her hair back from her face and looked over her shoulders. He slid his two fingers into his mouth and sucked, a look of exquisite pleasure on his face.

"Do you have any idea how you taste?" He chuckled and helped her stand.

Her legs shook so he lifted her back up on the counter and then fisted his hand in her hair and slanted his mouth over hers. She tasted herself on him and the mere knowledge of that had her womb clenching with renewed hunger. Wes's kiss this time was sweet and slow, but rich and thorough as though sated with their mutual release and now he was basking in the afterglow along with her.

"You taste better than that cognac I bought...So much better." He nuzzled her cheek, breathing deeply, and she shivered in response and their lips brushed in a light kiss.

When their mouths broke apart again, he rested his forehead against hers. "You didn't answer my question. How are you feeling?" He massaged her neck, his eyes locked with hers.

"I'm good," she assured him. They hadn't actually had sex...well...they'd done something but she wasn't sure what to call it. "It felt amazing." The shy little smile she gave him wilted when she realized the breakfast was probably cold. "I'm sorry about all this. The food is cold."

"Sorry for what? It's my fault. I took one look at you covered in flour and tousled from bed and I couldn't resist you." He glanced around the kitchen. "What did you make?" His hands moved to her bare thighs and he rubbed her skin soothingly as he surveyed the room again.

"Omelets and biscuits," she replied and then she pressed a kiss to one of his bare shoulders, loving that she could do that and knowing he didn't mind. She could never have done that with Fenn. He hadn't been hers, hadn't been someone she could kiss whenever she'd wanted to. Callie's affectionate nature ran deep. Her father had told her that she was like her mother, and not being able to express that part of herself to a man had left her feeling cold. Now here she was with a hot, hungry man at her fingertips. She stifled a sigh of delight and pressed another tender kiss to his collarbone. Wes's hands on her back tightened a little and he released a long sigh, one of contentment.

"What a lovely way to wake up," he murmured in her hair. "Stay right here. I'll microwave the food and fetch some plates."

Callie gawked at him. They'd almost had sex in the kitchen and he seemed unaffected. Well...maybe more relaxed. She, however, felt...Well, it was hard to describe. More than one emotion churned inside her at that moment and it left her dazed and confused. She wanted to run and hide from embarrassment about how she'd just acted, like a cat in heat howling for more. But she also wanted to stay close to Wes, to inhale the scent of his skin and feel his body heat close to hers. They had shared another type of intimacy that couldn't be undone. It left her unsure of how to move forward. She wasn't a worldly woman. How was she supposed to act around a man she'd almost had sex with?

Chapter 9

With a sexy grin that made Callie's body hum with delight, Wes returned to her and handed her the plates. "You fill these and I'll pour some orange juice."

She did as he said, and once she had two platefuls, she followed him through the doorway.

"This way. We can eat on the couch in the sitting room."

Eat on the couch? He definitely didn't strike her as that relaxed of a man. It amazed her how much he had changed in the last few days. Paris Wes was more calm, more playful and easygoing. She wondered how many women had seen this side of him. How many others had slept with his body wrapped around hers as they kissed? The idea made her nauseous, but she forced it out of her mind. She had to focus on the here and now, not on what he'd done before or what he might do after they'd gone their separate ways.

The living room was another elegant space with an L-shaped brown leather couch and a massive sixty-five-inch flat-screen TV mounted to the wall. It was Wes's equivalent of what Fenn would have called a "man cave." Wes set the two glasses of orange juice on the table and turned the TV on. Callie realized she was still covered in flour and she froze midway crouched over the couch. Wes grinned as though reading her mind.

"I should change before I ruin your sofa." She set her plate down on the table, but Wes sat down on the couch and tugged her onto his lap.

"It's fine. It's just flour." He feathered a kiss on her lips, still smiling as though something amused him greatly. "Françoise will clean it up."

Callie curled her arms around his neck and gave him a light kiss, one full of affection and happiness. "Poor Françoise. I'll have to apologize to her."

Wes laughed and the hearty sound made her heart skip a few beats in delight. She loved his laugh. The sound was rare but rich and wonderful. It made her laugh, too.

"She won't mind, I promise. She'll be happy that I've used the kitchen for a change."

Callie's brows rose. "You don't cook a lot?"

He shrugged. "No. I tend to eat out and meet clients at restaurants."

"And what about your girlfriends?"

A frown marred his brows. "I don't have girlfriends. I have momentary relationships and those women never come here." He handed her a plate and a fork. "You are the first." This admission was quiet and full of introspection.

Did he mean the first girlfriend or the first girl to come to his apartment? How could she ask him in a way that would reveal what he meant?

"Why don't you have girlfriends?" It was the closest thing she could get to finding out answers. She lifted his plate from the table, handing it to him. He propped it on the couch next to them and took a few bites before replying, his tone a little cool.

"In my world, I pursue only limited relationships. I meet partners at BDSM clubs, temporary submissives, and we part ways at the end of the night. I've had more than one time where I have used the same submissive, but only inside the club."

Callie swallowed and set her half-eaten omelet down.

"Then why am I here, Wes? If this isn't your usual style, why change it for me? Do you think I need all this to be seduced? Is that it?" She was suddenly angry. Did he feel he had to play the romantic just to get her in bed? Was he really not so sweet and caring? Was the man she was starting to fall for just an act? That awful nausea was back with a vengeance and she swallowed an acidic taste in her mouth and slammed her plate down on the table, struggling to get off Wes's lap.

He set his own plate aside and gripped her chin, forcing her to meet his gaze.

"You aren't like other women. Yes, I want you and I'll admit I'd do anything required to get you in my bed. But I won't rush it. I won't rush *you*."

She didn't understand. He'd made a bet to do just that. Thirty days to get her into his bed. Was this his way of backing out or changing his mind? Logically his words shouldn't have hurt her, but she felt wounded all the same. Sure, she didn't want to give into him and have meaningless sex and let him win their wager, but she did still want him to *want* her. Maybe her lack of experience was still bothering him.

"It's because I'm a virgin. You think I need candles and romance. But you're not a romantic. Anything you try to give me would be a lie. So just do it. Sleep with me. Scratch your itch and send me home." The words she spat out were dripped with venom born of her wounds and he blinked, apparently startled.

"You think this is nothing but a quick fuck for me?" he growled, fury sparking in his gaze.

"Isn't it? Wasn't that the whole point of the bet we made?" she shot back, just as upset. Her chest was squeezing her heart so hard she was having trouble breathing.

"That's it," he snarled.

He shoved her onto her back on the couch and then flipped her over to her stomach. Only too late she realized she was flying across his lap, her bottom in the air. His hand came down hard on her ass. This was punishment. She was being punished!

She screeched and kicked, but he used one arm across the back of her knees to keep her legs down.

"Are you listening to me?" he demanded.

Smack!

It hurt, but it was more the sting of embarrassment that she hated than the edge of pain.

"Callie," he snarled.

She clenched her fists, beating the leather of the couch. "Yes, damn it!" She lashed out.

"Do you really think I see you as a quick fuck?" he demanded. "Because you aren't. If I have to redden your ass to drive that point home, I will. What's between us isn't as shallow as some bet we made. It's *always* been more than that and don't ever say otherwise again." His warning was followed by two more slaps to her burning ass.

Tears of anger and shame leaked down her face. She hurt, but the hurt was deep inside and not as much on her skin. The pent-up anxiety, the confusion, the agony of losing Fenn seemed to pool like a deep well within her, dark waters running deep. But his blows had ruptured the stones of that well and now the emotions were pouring out and she couldn't stop them. He turned her over and helped her sit up on his lap, then curled himself around her. One of his hands buried itself in her hair and he guided her head to rest in the crook of his neck.

"There's more to this, Callie. More to you." He stroked her hair, and she rested against his chest, her body shaking with the force of the emotions that drained out of her. All the tension leaked out of her and she finally stopped crying. She was empty. There was nothing left inside her, just a hollowness.

"I'm sorry. You aren't used to my world, to me. I'm not used to yours. It's going to take time. For now, I'm going to hold you, care for you, give you everything you need."

Through the fog of her emptiness she remembered the romances she'd read with BDSM and those dominants who'd held their submissives after they'd been punished. Aftercare. He was giving her aftercare. As a submissive, she could ask whatever she wanted now, do whatever she wanted in this brief moment where she was in control again. All she wanted was to be cuddled and to curl into him like a newborn kitten. She'd be a strong, independent woman again in a little while. For now, she wanted to absorb his confidence and strength into herself, let it fill the emptiness inside her and make her strong enough to face the world again.

After a few deep breaths, where she inhaled his scent like her own personal drug, she knew she had to speak.

"What are we doing?" She buried her face against his chest, clinging to him, loving that he let her grasp him like he was the last thing on earth that she could hold on to. "We're nothing alike. We're a disaster waiting to happen."

For a moment they clung to each other, suspended in time, just like that. Close, almost connected on a deeper level. His heartbeat was steady beneath her hand where it rested against his chest.

Thu-thump. Thu-thump. The beat was like her own, their pulses almost in sync.

"I've never met anyone like you, Callie. Never for a moment think you aren't unique. I want you here with me. Not just in my bed." He tugged gently on a loose strand of her hair, the act seeming to sooth him.

"Really? I thought this was all about the bet to sleep with me." She was too afraid to believe she meant something to him. All she'd ever wanted from Fenn was to be loved, to mean something. But she hadn't and it had nearly killed her. Yet...the idea of meaning something to Wes, it felt infinitely more powerful, more dangerous. She shivered at the thought. If this was Wes *not* in love, what would he be like when he did fall? It would be frightening as hell.

"You need an escape," he explained. "I need contentment. You make me content. I hope that I help you escape. When I made the bet, I wanted to give you a reason to get over Fenn, and yes, I want desperately to take you to my bed, but I knew you needed time. So I gave you a fighting chance, a purpose to strengthen your resistance. If you won, you'd get a way to live your dreams at art school. Either way, I win, darling. And no matter what, you will still end up in my bed. It's just a matter of when, not if."

She winced at his belief that she would just jump into his bed, but he'd been right about her need to fight. The bet had made her feel strong, powerful, and the desire to win so she could have a shot at art school with a good recommendation had given her a determination. Now, though, the bet didn't seem to matter, not when it came to sleeping with him because over the last several days she realized how much she wanted to be with him.

"How do we do this?" she asked. "Do you want me to be a submissive? Is that what you want to happen?" The idea frightened her. She didn't want anyone controlling her life.

Wes breathed deeply and met her gaze. "Look at me. I want to see your eyes." She stared back.

"If I told you to kneel at my feet in nothing but a collar and await my orders each day…" He spoke softly and the image he painted made her stomach clench in the worst way.

He nodded. "No. I can see that's not something that would interest you." He paused a beat, then continued. "If, after a day of doing whatever you wish, I capture you and tie you to my bed and torture you with pleasure at my command and mine alone…"

This time she couldn't help it. Her body heated with awareness, and she wriggled in his hold. He didn't release her or look away but continued.

"If I took a light flogger to your skin, warming it but never burning or stinging it, if I blindfolded you and kept you helpless and stimulated you to orgasm after orgasm, how would you feel?"

She started trembling all over again, every cell of her body aware of him and his words and desiring what he said to happen.

A slow smile touched his lips.

"Callie, your eyes are dilated and your cheeks are flushed. You are not a full-time submissive, but parts of you need domination and to be controlled, but only in the bedroom."

When she parted her lips ready to protest, he silenced her with a fingertip. "It doesn't mean you're weak or that you have no power. It means the opposite. You are strong in your ability to trust me as a dominant to give you the pleasure you need. Someone like me can give it to you. We'll start slow. Relationships between dominants and submissives must be built slowly and carefully if both parties wish to reach fulfillment. Do you understand?"

She nodded. It was a lot to take in, but she'd read BDSM romance novels and knew a little of what to expect. It was intimidating. *Really intimidating.*

"The most important part of doing this is setting limits. If I do anything that worries you or makes you feel too uncomfortable you say the word 'yellow.' That means we slow down and we talk about it. If you're still not ready, then we stop. And if I'm ever doing something that truly frightens you, you say the word 'red.' That is an immediate stop. We don't even have to talk about why it's a limit for you." He brushed a kiss over her lips and she leaned into him, wrapping her arms around his neck.

Red and yellow. She could handle that. She would have to trust that he would respect her decision if she had to use those words. It dawned on her then just how much trust she would have to give him in order for this to work.

"Today we'll spend some time exploring Paris. Anything you want to see, we'll see." He kept stroking her, pressing soothing kisses on her skin that sent frissons of pleasure through her. In his arms she felt safe and secure, almost content herself.

"Did you have enough to eat?" He reached for her plate and her stomach grumbled in response.

"Thanks." She took the plate and finished the last of her omelet and biscuits. Only after she was done did he eat the rest of his food and then he turned the TV to a news station. She shifted in his lap and her bottom singed with pain, but to her shock that zing of pain made her clit throb. Did pain turn her on?

Wes massaged her neck and leaned in to whisper in her ear.

"Pain and pleasure are often a fine line. That's why it's important to have safe words."

A very fine line indeed.

After she set her plate down, she got off his lap. "I'll go shower." Her legs shook a little and her bottom burned from his spanking, but she wasn't going to show any more weakness, not when she'd shown so much already. The sound of his soft chuckling didn't help her self-esteem one bit as she left the room.

* * *

Wes watched Callie flee. She was always running and more often than not she was running from him. He'd pushed too far too fast again, but her words had drawn out a dominant's anger in him. She thought she was a quick fuck and nothing more? It was an insult to both of them. He'd never worked so hard in his life to take his time with a woman because it was the right thing to do and she deserved it. It was as close to romantic as he got.

He leaned forward and covered his face with his hands and rubbed his eyes. For the first time in his life, he was feeling some measure of peace. Because of her. But there was so much more to it than that. He felt excited again, watching her fall in love with Paris as he had done all those years ago. The look on her face as she'd touched the sphinx, the way she'd handled Dimitri's subtle flirts at Fouquet's. She was coming into her own. A fierce, powerful artist who would take the world by storm if the right person guided her. And he was going to be that person.

A little chuckle escaped him as he bent to collect the plates. She had cooked for him. A little rustic meal of omelets and biscuits. In Paris, the land of fine cuisine. And it had rocked him to the core. To wake to the smell of something mouthwatering and to come down-stairs and find her covered in flour and adorably fuckable. He had lost his mind. No woman he'd ever been with had cooked for him. It was always a chef or a restaurant.

The women he'd dated in the past had expected that of him, and likely didn't know how to boil water themselves. But Callie had been cooking for years. She had to in order to feed two grown men working on the ranch. She was a fighter, his little cowgirl. And he planned to reward her for her sweetness. That simple act had meant so much more to him than he'd ever let on. And it turned him on, too. Bad. He'd come in his jeans just from dry-humping her sweet luscious ass. That had been a first for him.

There hadn't been a moment in his life since he'd left high school when he hadn't had total control over his body's responses around a woman. Living in the BDSM lifestyle had taught him how to use that control to bring a submissive to pleasure. If a dominant reached his fulfillment before his submissive because he had no control it hurt the sub. Subs deserved to have a dominant who had control.

Until this morning he'd never lost control with a sub before. But Callie was a firecracker in his hands. Kissing her was like celebrating the Fourth of July. Burning beautiful heat and passion. She set him ablaze with her responses to him. And there was so much she could still learn. Once she opened herself up to him fully, there would be no stopping either of them from embracing the greatest heights of pleasure.

Walking back to the messy kitchen made him smile and shake his head. He rinsed the plates and then scribbled a note for Françoise, apologizing for the mess. Then he headed upstairs to shower himself. He had a big day planned for Callie and he didn't want to waste any more time.

Chapter 10

The neighborhood of Montmartre was a place of colors and living dreams. Topped by the Byzantine-style white domes of the Sacré-Coeur, the Sacred Heart Basilica, the cathedral felt like a holy place both of the spirit and the heart. Artists were everywhere, their easels set up along the streets, their bohemian little stands full of life as they courted the tourists who flocked to the center of Paris's art district.

Callie stood next to Wes, taking in the main square, the Place du Tertre.

"Did you know that this square was a famous haunt of the artist Henri de Toulouse-Lautrec?" Wes waved at the eclectic mix of tourists and artists. It was easy to picture an artist haunting this place for inspiration.

"It's amazing." She wanted to study all of the sketches and the portraits around her.

"It's a bit busy with the bourgeois bohemian."

"What's that?"

Wes laughed. "Think of it as the French word for hipsters."

"Really?" She laughed, too.

"Yes. But this is your first time in Paris and you have to experience it. Especially from an artist's perspective." He curled his arm around her waist and guided her to the nearest row of artists.

Callie breathed in the air, which smelled of chalk dust. Wes had stayed close to her ever since they had left the apartment. He had actually relaxed in jeans and a light sweater, as though finally at ease enough to leave behind the suits. His dark masculine scent was heady and addictive.

They halted at the front row of artists and Wes spun her to face him, a possessive gleam in his eyes.

"You are getting your portrait done," he announced. "It's a rite of passage." He tucked a strand of hair behind her ear and they walked down the row of artists.

Wes paused behind each artist, examining their styles and examples of past works intently. He was in his element, like last night when he'd bent over the Sargent and examined its details for Dimitri. He was focused on the art, and she was focused on him. That itching in her right hand, the need to sketch, to channel that creative pulse which was humming like rich wine in her veins. She wanted to draw Wes, to put his likeness on paper, to own a part of him, how she saw him, in whatever small way she could. The temporary madness born of mutual passion would pass someday and they'd go their separate ways, but she knew now that he would be her first lover and she never wanted to forget him.

Artist after artist, Wes wasn't satisfied until he peered over the shoulder of the last man sketching at the end of the row. He was a man in his midforties, a pair of slender glasses resting on the bridge of his thin nose. His brown eyes studied Wes right back with the clarity reserved only to artists and the lovers of art.

"Monsieur, je voudrais un portrait de la jeune dame."

The man nodded. *"Bien sûr. Ça coûte soixante-dix euros."*

"Seventy euros?" Callie gasped. "Wes, that's way too expensive for a street portrait." She tugged at his sleeve, but Wes nudged her toward the small wooden stool.

"He's the best. I want only the best."

Callie sighed, seeing that an argument wouldn't get her anywhere. Wes played with her hair, settling it in a particular way over her shoulders that seemed to please him. He and the artist shared a knowing look and then the man lifted his hand in a universal gesture she understood and she responded by lifting her chin an inch and tilting her head to one side.

Over the next half hour the man worked at a steady pace with Wes directly behind him, observing the artist's progress. The serious expression on Wes's face made her feel a little silly and she couldn't stop it when she started to giggle.

"What?" Wes glanced around, as if expecting to discover the obvious source of amusement.

"I'm sorry," she said half giggling, half laughing. "You look so serious. Smile or something, otherwise I'll keep laughing."

Wes's solemn expression softened and a glint of wicked humor filled his gaze.

"Oh, I know plenty of ways to stop your laughing. Want to hear?" The scorching burn of his gaze showed her just how serious he was. Her breath caught in her throat and heat flooded her face.

"C'est fini, monsieur." The artist sat back, resting his hands on his charcoal-stained pants.

"Bon, c'est magnifique." Wes's gaze was rapt as he studied the sketch.

"Can I see?" She leaped up from the stool and hurried around the tall easel so she could see what the man had done.

Her heart stopped. It was only when Wes caught hold of her from behind, wrapping his arms around her waist and nuzzling her temple as they stared at the sketch together, that her heart finally jolted back into a steady beat.

The piece was done on gray paper. The man had used white charcoal to accent her cheeks and the flash in her eyes. He'd used the paper's darker color to let the shadows form rosy blushing cheeks and deepen the fall of her hair interspersed with light. It was done entirely in shadows of charcoal, yet rendered with such precision that she felt as though she was staring in a mirror. Yet what held her fascinated was the expression on her face he had somehow managed to capture. Slightly parted lips, slumberous eyes, a woman in the midst of lovemaking—that was how she appeared.

"He captured it," Wes murmured in her ear. "The most sensual expression I've ever seen. What were you thinking about, I wonder?" He asked the question almost rhetorically.

"Ice cream. I was thinking about ice cream."

He laughed. The vibration of his body behind hers was wonderful.

"You've spent way too much time around my sister. What were you really thinking about?"

The natural command in his tone was not loud but had just as much of an influence over her. She had to answer. There was no denying him what he wanted.

"You." The single word was breathless and he went rigid behind her, his warm breath making her shiver.

"You know how to torture a man, Callie." The warning was clear. From the way he pressed hard against her and pushed his fingers into her, she knew he was on the verge of losing control.

The artist, with his back to them, sprayed a finishing spray on the charcoal to protect it from smears. Then he placed a sheet of wax paper over it and rolled it up and slid it into a white cardboard tube.

Wes finally released her and pulled out a thick wad of money in a silver money clip and slipped seventy euros into the artist's hand.

"*Merci, monsieur. Vous avez une belle femme. Vous êtes un homme chanceux.*"

"*Je sais. C'est la chance en effet.*" Wes shook the artist's hand.

"What did he say?" Callie asked as they continued their walk along the street.

"He said you were beautiful."

Callie raised one eyebrow. "I understood that part. What did he say after that?"

Wes wrapped an arm around her shoulders and pulled her close. "He said I was a lucky man." His lips curved into a body-melting smile. "And I agreed with him."

Her heart fluttered a little with nervousness but she realized it was a happy fluttering. She'd never really felt that way before. With Fenn she was either happy or nervous. Never a mixture of both. This was new…and a little startling, but she liked how it felt. There was a warm buzz in her heart when she looked at Wes and let him cradle her against his side.

Yes…this was…nice. She liked nice.

"What's next? The Louvre or the Eiffel Tower?" he asked.

She was about to respond when she caught sight of a small corner shop with a dozen birdcages hanging just inside the shop window. An olive-skinned man with a colorful shirt was tending to the cages. The birds in the cages were colorful and chirping excitedly. Something about the sight enthralled Callie. The man seemed to notice her fascination and waved a hand for Callie to come closer for a better look.

"Callie, he's one of many Paris gypsies," Wes said, but he followed her as she crossed the street to get a closer look at the little shop full of birds. She walked through the open door and came over to the birdcages.

"Oh, Wes, they're beautiful. Look." She shot him an excited smile before gazing at the nearest cage, which had a pair of lovebirds. Their warm tropical-colored feathers and little curved beaks made them irresistible. Hopping from wooden bar to wooden bar in their cages, they fluttered and chirped, moving as a pair, always seemingly aware of each other. Like two sides of a perfect coin. Her heart squeezed in her chest as she watched them. Their sweet notes, the little coos and chirps, and the trills of their songs were enchanting.

"You like my birds?" The man's voice was heavily accented but he spoke English well.

Callie couldn't resist nodding eagerly and slipping one finger between the bars. One of the lovebirds gave a delicate exploring peck at her finger. The sensation tickled and she laughed.

"They're wonderful," Callie said. "Simply wonderful."

"Then they are yours." The man reached up to unhook the cage.

"Oh no! I couldn't, but thank you," Callie said and sighed. There was no way she could bring the birds home to Colorado.

Wes was watching her, a curious expression on his face. He held out a handful of euros and placed them in the man's palm.

"Thank you, Monsieur. We will take the birds." He helped her remove the cage from its hook on the stand and he handed it to Callie, who took it, mouth gaping open. The man had just bought her a pair of lovebirds in Paris. He must have written the book on seduction.

"Wes—"

"You want them. I want you to have them," he answered simply.

The gypsy man's dark eyes glinted with mischief and an ancient knowing.

"Mates for life." The gypsy patted her hand with a secretive smile.

Callie grinned and carried the birdcage outside. When she glanced behind her she saw Wes was still inside.

He lingered in the shop a moment longer, studying the jewelry and other odds and ends the gypsy was selling. A basket of bangle bracelets caught his eye. They were gold on the inside but the outside was dark blue with golden chain links painted into the blue. A little grin curved his lips. He slipped the gypsy a few euros to buy the bracelets, and then exited the shop. He caught up with Callie, who was only a few feet away, still focused on the lovebirds.

"Here." He slipped one bangle on each of her wrists. "There, those look beautiful against your skin." He stroked her flesh where it met the metal of the bangles.

Callie lifted one hand up to study the gilded bracelet on her right wrist, admiring the painted chain links. Something inside her shivered at the thought of Wes and chains together in the same sentence. They were just bracelets, yet the way he'd put them on her, the possessive gleam in his eyes. Heat blossomed in the pit of her belly and farther down. Was this a prelude to something else, a darker hint of what Wes wished to do to her? There was so much about him and his desires that were still a mystery to her.

"Let me call Michel. He'll take the birds back to the apartment and then take us to the Eiffel Tower."

Callie picked up the cage and followed him as he began to walk out of Montmartre to an easier spot for the car to pick them up.

"I can't believe you just bought me birds," she said. She had never made an impulsive buy in her life, except maybe one black bra that she never wore because it didn't belong on the ranch and she was always working.

Wes laughed. "If you had seen your face when you looked at those birds you would have bought them, too."

She tugged his sleeve, forcing him to stop. "Wes, you can't keep buying me everything I want."

"Why not?" He stroked the cardboard tube that held her portrait and focused a pensive stare on her.

"What?" His question completely confused her.

"Why can't I buy you everything you want?" His question came out as a challenge and for a second Callie just stared at him. She hadn't thought that far ahead about the point she was trying to make in this outlandish discussion.

"Because...because I don't deserve it. I like to pay my own way and if I can't afford it then I don't buy it."

Wes's lips slid into a sinful smile. "Darling, you deserve a lot more than you know. And I can do whatever I want with my money. If I want to buy a private island just for you, then I will."

Callie crossed her arms over her chest and glowered. "I wouldn't go to that island."

For some reason he burst out laughing. "Oh, you'd go. I'd carry you there over my shoulder if necessary."

"You'd have to catch me first," Callie muttered.

Her words lit a feral spark in his eyes that made her worried and aroused at the same time.

"Someday you and I will play a capture game. Do you know what that is?"

Callie's throat was suddenly dry and she shook her head.

Wes cupped her chin, then slid his fingers along the column of her throat, not even attempting to hide the blazing hunger in his eyes.

"A capture game is where I let you loose in a controlled space. You have to run from me, but when I catch you...I can do anything to you, except cross your hard limits."

Hard limits. She knew what that was. Anything she absolutely would not do. At least that was how hard limits were discussed in the novels she'd read. Maybe she should have Wes explain for clarity's sake.

"What are hard limits?" She inwardly cringed at how soft and husky her voice was. She was still mad at him for buying everything for her. They'd have to return to that subject soon.

"Hard limits are what a submissive absolutely refuses to do. These are serious things that are well beyond 'the red zone' we discussed. You will need to think about what your limits are. Things that aren't just uncomfortable, but unthinkable. Things that terrify you to the point of panic where you can't think. I never want you scared. Nervous anticipation is different and can be very rewarding later when you finally come apart in my arms." He continued to stroke her throat.

Hard limits. What were her hard limits?

"Think on it," he encouraged, and then he pulled his cell phone out to call Michel.

Callie was still pondering what her limits might be when Michel pulled up to the curb.

"Quick, let's take a photo of the birds," she begged. She wanted to make sure she captured this moment. She might as well use the expensive phone he'd given her. When she pulled out the phone and held her hand out so she could take a picture of herself, the birds, and Wes, he growled.

"I don't do selfies." He took the phone from her hand and passed it to Michel.

"*Pour moi, merci,*" he said to the grinning driver.

"Get close to Monsieur Wes, mademoiselle." Michel waved a hand to indicate they should get closer.

Callie lifted the small birdcage up and Wes put his arm around her shoulder. "I'm humoring you, darling." He leaned his head down to murmur in her ear. "I don't like photos of myself, so you will owe me."

Click-click. Michel took the photo and Callie turned her head to stare up at Wes.

"Owe you?" Why did he make that sound so good and yet so bad at the same time?

"Yes, you owe me for this. Payment comes tonight, no backing out." He brushed a thumb over her lips and a pulse beat hard in her as though nerves were connected to her entire body to whatever spot he touched.

"Bien." Michel gave the phone back to Callie. She wanted to look at the picture, but the storm clouds in Wes's eyes warned her that she had gone far enough for now. She gave the birdcage to Michel.

"I think we'll need supplies. I'm not sure exactly, since I've never had pet birds."

"I will buy all that is required, mademoiselle, do not worry." Michel was still grinning as he loaded the lovebirds into the back seat of his car. They chirped and chattered, huddling close. One bird ruffled the feathers of the other with obvious affection.

"See," Wes said and chuckled. "Your face is stunning." He held out his own phone, showing a quick snapshot he'd taken as she'd looked at the birds again. Her face had a peculiar look of wonder and love. This was what he saw when he looked at her? She wished more than anything that she could find a way to show him what he looked like to her. The time would come. She would get her art supplies and she would paint him in every way her hands longed to do.

Michel said a quick good-bye, took the birds with him and then he was gone. Wes then glanced around at the shops.

"You need art supplies. We can buy them here before we head for the tower." She took his hand when he offered and followed where he led. It was becoming so easy to follow him. It should have frightened her, but she still sensed there was something significant to this. She just hadn't figured it out yet.

* * *

The Eiffel Tower was not exactly what Callie had expected. Wes saw right away that she was less impressed by the tower and more interested in the sights below. They were on the middle deck because it was the highest he would agree to go. There was no way he'd go to the top.

"Wes, are you okay?" Callie was leaning against the railing with her back to the edge. Despite the metal mesh protecting the deck's inhabitants, a roll of nausea swept through him at seeing her so close to the edge. His vision spiraled slowly, dizzyingly.

"What?"

She left the edge and walked up to him. He was leaning back against the wall of the middle deck, relieved to feel the metal supporting him.

"You're really pale," she observed and reached up, placing the back of one hand to his forehead. Her brows were knit in concern. He shackled her wrists but didn't try to remove her hands from his face. He enjoyed her touch, perhaps too much. At that moment, holding on to her calmed him.

"Wes, you're scaring me." Her voice intruded through darkness and he realized at some point he'd closed his eyes. Her gentle fingers combed through his hair and his whole body shuddered. He rarely let women touch him. Intimacy was seldom allowed. Even after the sex was over…he kept his distance and made them keep theirs. With Callie though…he couldn't stay away from her. She was a drug. He was addicted to her in the worst way. If she touched him, he burned; if she kissed him, he became an inferno.

"Wes." Her lips touched his and the jolt of pleasure that rocketed through him momentarily dispelled the awful vertigo. When she moved back a few inches, he opened his eyes.

"Are you afraid of heights?" she asked. The girl was too smart, too observant. His weakness, the flaw he tried to hide, she'd exposed in just two days. There was no way he could deny it.

"Heights make me a little uneasy."

Callie gripped him by the arm. "One look over the edge. Do that with me. Then we go back down together right away. Deal?"

Wes blew out a shaking breath and forced every bit of testosterone he had to pump through his veins. Nearly blown to bits by a car bomb a month ago had been less frightening than this.

"One look and you'll owe me double tonight."

"Okay," she said and laughed. "Heights are a hard limit for you," she teased.

He gripped her by the waist and dragged her into his arms, letting every inch of their bodies touch. She shivered and her lashes fluttered, and that simple reaction had him tensing in hungry anticipation. How she made him ache! Never in his life had a woman made him burn like an unquenchable fire. He wanted to show her everything he could give her, and take everything she could offer, but only when she was ready. It had to be soon or he'd die.

"Darling, you haven't seen that side of me yet, but you will," he promised. She would get to know that side of him very well, and she would like it so much she'd scream his name in pleasure until she passed out.

Callie licked her lips and gave a little tug on his hold. "One look. You promised." Even in his grasp, dominated by him, she still challenged him, like any good little submissive who was looking for a sensual punishment from her dom. She was a natural and she just didn't know it yet.

He let her guide him to the edge.

"Now look down," she urged, her arm entwined with his, grounding him when he needed it the most.

His eyes took in the view. It was spectacular. Paris sprawled out around the base of the Eiffel Tower. The urban sprawl, the miles of monuments mixed with apartments, homes, shops, and museums. A city laid out from a bird's-eye view. It was an amazing sight, but the longer he looked, the more his stomach turned.

"Okay, we're good to go, aren't we?" Callie nudged him, getting him to move back to the inner wall toward the elevators.

It didn't escape his notice that he'd been able to trust her and rely on her. That was a first. The only other person he'd dared to rely on was his grandfather, but his grandfather had moved to London long ago to escape his parents. He missed the old bear. Wes couldn't hide his smile. Callie would like his grandfather and he'd like her. Perhaps he could take her to London next, as soon as the art theft was resolved.

The entire time they rode the elevator down he imagined how he'd make Callie pay her dues. He was torn between demanding she strip bare and get on her knees to ask for a spanking, or better yet, she'd have to spread her curvy legs so he could bury his face between her thighs. Yes... that image kept him hard the whole way down. But was she ready for that? She was close. Those barriers that kept her from opening herself up were slowly crumbling, and he, like a wolf prowling the perimeter, was ready to pounce. There was no denying it. The hunger for her, the all-consuming need to claim her, was winning out over rationality and good sense. But she had to come to him first. Willing and begging for him.

"We can do the Louvre tomorrow, right?" Callie asked, a little yawn escaping her.

Wes glanced at his watch. It was late afternoon.

"The Louvre can wait."

He'd already dialed Michel and the faithful driver was waiting near the base of the tower. When they met up with the driver, Callie climbed into the back and immediately inquired after the birds.

"They are fine, mademoiselle. I bought them a new cage and food," Michel assured her.

Callie relaxed and settled back in her seat. The late afternoon sun glinted off the bangle bracelets he'd bought for her. The golden bangles were a subtle sign that she belonged to him. The next step would be leather cuffs lined with the softest fur to keep her skin from chafing. These cuffs would be for bed play and he'd be able to do so many delicious things to her if she wore them. The thought of that nearly drove him out of his mind with lust. He clenched his hands into fists on his thighs.

As they entered the apartment, they ran into Françoise, who was just exiting. His housekeeper was in her late fifties, with raven black hair and light brown eyes that warmed with her smile as she held the door open for them.

"*Bonsoir, Monsieur Thorne,*" she greeted them.

Wes introduced Callie. The two women took to each other instantly.

"I bought the supplies you requested, mademoiselle," Françoise said.

"Supplies?" Wes darted his gaze between the two women.

Callie's cheeks pinkened. "I thought I would cook us a roast. Or rather, we could cook it together. Won't that be fun?"

He sensed that she was worried he wouldn't approve, but he did. The idea of her covered in flour again…He would have to take a cold shower before dinner or he wouldn't last through the meal.

"That sounds nice. Thank you, Françoise." He bid good night to the housekeeper as she collected her coat and slipped out the front door.

Callie set her bag of art supplies on the floor and started to pull off her coat. Wes moved quickly, coming up behind her to peel the slight coat from her shoulders. She smelled so good. The scent of the peppermint shampoo that lingered in her hair made her impossible to resist. He tossed her coat onto a chair nearby and gripped her from behind, holding her captive as he pressed against her and nuzzled her hair.

"You smell amazing," he whispered. A little shiver shot through her and he felt it vibrate through her and into him.

"Thank you," she replied breathlessly. "Do you want to make dinner? We could start now. It will take a while to cook."

"How long?" He brushed his lips over her ear.

"Four hours. It's a pot roast."

He didn't care how long it was if that meant four hours he could spend seducing her while it cooked.

"Sounds good." He stepped back and swatted her bottom. The little yelp she gave reminded him she was still sore from his last punishment.

"What was that for?" She smoothed a hand over her bottom, wincing before she shot him a scowl. The expression of her attempt to be mad at him was only sexy, too fucking sexy.

"I like to spank you as much as you like to be spanked. You'd better get used to it." He moved toward her again, but she darted into the kitchen, avoiding him. Tonight he was going to give her the opportunity to come to him and his bed. He wanted to end the bet once and for all. He didn't want the shadows of it between them any longer. Whatever it took, he would do. Seduce by touch, by look, by kiss. He would show no mercy this time for her broken heart. She needed someone new to make her whole, to give her everything she needed. The wait was over.

Chapter 11

Callie sensed the immediate change in Wes as he entered the kitchen. His eyes were dark like a winter sea during a mighty storm. It was not from anger, but from passion. She was learning his expressions, the subtle changes in his eyes that told her things when words could not. He was still an enigma, a tall, broad-shouldered, muscled mystery who stole her breath and her sanity. But tiny puzzle pieces were clicking into place.

He leaned against the counter, watching her like a wolf. She had to regain control and not think about how sexy and sinful he looked.

"Why don't you get out a roasting pan and turn the oven on," she suggested. Then she put her focus on the meat and the spices she needed. Françoise had acquired a tasty-looking three-pound chuck roast.

"Next?" Wes asked as he set a huge black roasting pan on the kitchen island.

"Wine? Cheap red. Nothing expensive."

"Cheap wine? What makes you think I would ever own a bottle of cheap wine?" The incredulous look on his face made her laugh.

"Yes. We're putting it in with the beef stock for the roast to soak in."

Grumbling, he retrieved a bottle from the wine rack by the pantry. "This is the cheapest I have. If we're using it, we might as well have a glass while we're cooking." He uncorked the bottle and poured two glasses for them before he handed the bottle to her.

For the next few minutes she prepared the roast in the pan and had Wes chopping baby carrots and potatoes. He worked quickly with his knife and deposited the vegetables into the pan around the meat. Then she handed him sage, rosemary, and celery salt, teaching him how to pinch the correct amount of each spice and sprinkle it over the pan. The intense look of concentration firming his lips into a hard line and knitting his brows together made her laugh.

"Cooking is supposed to be fun. It's half art, half science," she instructed and on sudden impulse she stood up on tiptoe and kissed the corner of his too-serious mouth. He relaxed and nearly dropped the spice bottles into the roaster, but he recovered himself and set them on the counter. Handing him the bottle of wine, she continued to smile at him, delighting in the fact she was teaching *him* how to do something.

"One cup of this and we're done. Then it's time to put it into the oven."

He splashed the wine over their creation, put it into the oven, and set the timer for four hours.

"Done," he announced as he spun around to face her, his eyes gleaming with pride, but she had a sense that half that gleam had less to do with the meal.

"Yeah," she echoed faintly, short of breath.

He placed a glass of wine into her hand.

"*Whatever* shall we do until it's ready?" The question sounded so innocent, but nothing about Wes was innocent.

She licked her lips nervously. The last two days…no, the last two months had been building to this. She could be with Wes, but it would mean letting go of that tiny fragment of her heart that was still carved with Fenn's name. And it would mean letting him win the bet. She'd lose her shot at getting an art school recommendation from his friend if she gave in. That wasn't something she wanted, but since she'd come here to Paris with him, her confidence had grown. She was considering applying for the scholarship program without a recommendation. Maybe she would be able to get in on her own merit.

"If…we do this, that means you win the bet." Holding her breath, she waited to see how he would react, to see if he would revel in his win, or if it had been like he'd said earlier and that everything between them wasn't just because of some silly bet.

"It does," he admitted. "But you know how I feel, that what I want from you isn't just because of some challenge, but because I've wanted you from the moment I saw you, because I have to have you. And if you agree to this, you won't be losing to me, Callie. We'll both win, of that I assure you. But we only do this if you're ready and willing."

The quicksilver flash of hesitation in his eyes was all she needed to see in order to trust him. He didn't want to rush her. His desire was tied to hers. She could trust him to be careful and gentle with her, but he needed something, too. He wouldn't ask her tonight, but she wanted to explore all the things he reveled in.

"Wes…I'm ready." The second the words were out of her mouth, she forgot to breathe for a few seconds and it was only when her chest was on fire that she sucked in precious air.

His eyes ignited and her own body flared, like a phoenix surging up from the ashes.

He finished his glass of wine and set it on the counter. Every move was slow and deliberate, as though he feared she'd bolt if he moved too fast. When he held out one hand to her, she knew that if she took it there would be no going back. Not for her body, but also not for her heart. She wasn't in love with Wes, but being with him would destroy that sliver of her young and foolish heart that still loved Fenn. It was time to let go. Sleeping with him might help cure her of the last bit of herself that believed in love and happily-ever-afters. She could prove to herself she could have sex with a man and enjoy it and not worry about falling in love and getting hurt.

She blew out a measured breath and placed her hand in his. He curled his fingers around hers and she was consumed by the flames of desire in his eyes. It never ceased to amaze her how he could do that, erase all sense of the world around them until all she saw was him, all she felt was him. That was all from one look, one touch. There was no going back now.

He led her out of the kitchen and down the hall. As they went through the library, the evening sun was a peach orange bleeding into a soft crimson and it illuminated the endless shelves of books and warmed the brown leather chairs near the staircase. Books had been portals to adventures for her and now she was actually living one.

They ascended the stairs together and when they reached his room he paused.

"Most women prefer their own bed. Mine or yours?"

She nibbled her lip, debating the choice. "Yours." *Mine* had been at the tip of her tongue, but for some reason she'd said his instead.

"You want to try something a little on the edge?" he asked as he went to the windows and let the curtains fall into place, dimming the room. He turned on one lonely lamp, letting shadows eat up the remaining light. Her skin burst into goose bumps and she rubbed her arms.

When he came back to stand in front of her, he had rolled up the sleeves of his sweater, exposing those strong, muscled forearms she ached to have wrapped around her.

"You mean BDSM?" Saying the word had her pulse racing.

"Yes. Do you remember my telling you about 'yellow' and 'red' and when to use them?"

She swallowed and nodded. Excitement skittered through her.

"I'm not going to let you hide. Do you understand? I plan to strip you bare in seconds and restrain you to my bed. If that is too much, tell me now."

"No…no intense pain," she whispered. "That is my hard limit."

He nodded once. "I agree. I would have not wished to do that, even if you'd begged me to. I may be a momentary sadist only with regard to spankings. Anything beyond that is too dark even for me." The conviction in his tone reassured her. Neither of them was into pain. That was a relief.

"Anything else?"

"No choking." That was the only other thing she knew for sure she couldn't handle.

Wes gently gripped her throat, but didn't squeeze. "What about gags? Any problems there?" he asked, his eyes fixed on her mouth, his thumb caressing the hollow spot in her throat.

Gags? Was she actually having this conversation? "What kind?" Her voice was church-mouse quiet.

"Something light, enough to slightly muffle any sound you make." His hand moved upward so his thumb could caress her lips, trace the seam of her mouth as though imagining what it would be like to gag her. "It's the muffled sounds I crave, nothing that restricts breathing. Just a slight softening of your pleasured cries."

The idea of her on a bed, slightly gagged, crying out, and him above her, slamming into her, hard and aroused into a state of wild abandon…Callie clamped her legs together. She liked the idea as much as he did. What the hell was wrong with her?

"If we use a gag, then I would provide you with something you can squeeze that will alert me to a red or yellow safe word."

Callie fingered her navy blue blouse, and then looked up at him. "I might be okay with that."

The flash of approval in his eyes made her belly quiver with renewed excitement.

"Are you really ready for this?" Wes asked one last time. "My rules?"

She nodded. "Your rules." She swallowed. "Just remember, I haven't done this before."

He stepped closer, tipped her chin up, and invaded her space until his heat radiated into her body, warming her, surrounding her.

"Don't worry, you'll do fine. That's the beauty of surrendering to me. I'm in charge and I'll tell you exactly what to do. You won't be able to disappoint me, only please me, and in pleasing me, I'll please you beyond all doubt. Now, one last important question. Are you on birth control? I am regularly tested and am clean."

Birth control? Right. That snapped her out of the hazy dreams of his body on top of hers.

"I have an IUD." She bit her lip, then added, "I'm clean." Which was obvious since she'd never been with anyone before.

"Good, because I plan to ride you bare," he growled, and then he was kissing her, hard, wild. She moaned against him, her hands coming up to rest on his chest. Seconds later, she heard a violent ripping sound and a sudden breeze cooled her upper body. She dropped her hands and pulled away in shock.

Her shirt hung off her arms in two swaths of cloth. Wes had ripped it clean in two.

"That was one of my new shirts! How about a new hard limit: no ripping of my blouses," she protested as she crossed her arms over her chest, trying to hide her breasts, even though they were concealed by her bra. A ripple of heat moved through her at the realization that the more he stripped her of her clothes, the more vulnerable she became.

"I'll buy you a dozen more." He unbuttoned her jeans, tugged the zipper down, and then peeled her jeans off her legs. She wobbled on her feet as the pants caught around her ankles and she gripped his shoulders for support.

"Hold on, darling," he warned.

With a little shriek, she was hoisted into the air and tossed onto the bed on her back. Jeans, socks, and shoes gone, she was left in nothing but her bra and panties. Covering herself instantly with her hands and crossing her legs, she jerked as he lunged for her. One hand fisted in her panties and he ripped them clear off. Callie's legs clamped together and she held fast to the bra.

"Callie, move your hands," he ordered.

Oh God. She dropped her hands and held her breath as he leaned over her and unbuttoned the front clasp at the center of her bra. The cups fell apart, exposing her completely to his view. He simply stared at them for a long moment, and then a dark, masculine smile of pride curved his lips. A little tremor wracked her as she fought off her desire to cover herself.

"There is no shame or embarrassment here. Only beauty. You are beautiful." He cupped one of her breasts, and then pinched her nipple, just enough that a zing of pleasure-pain shot straight through her. Instant wetness followed as he continued to play with her.

"I will play you, Callie, just like a Stradivarius violin. I'll figure out what makes you sing, sigh, and scream in pleasure."

His words burned her inside like the whiskey she'd stolen once from her father's liquor cabinet.

He removed his sweater, shoes, and socks and then crawled up on the bed in just his pants until he was beside her.

"Be brave for me," he murmured and then kissed her again.

She opened her mouth to him, losing herself in his taste. It was easier to forget that she was completely naked with him when he kissed her. His kisses turned from playful to deeply passionate, carnal. His hands were everywhere, stroking, exploring—rough, then tender. She couldn't adjust to the caresses but could only experience each sensation as it happened. She jolted upright when he suddenly slid his hand between her legs and teased the entrance of her folds.

"Easy, darling," he said between kisses as he thrust one finger inside her. She arched up and he bent his head to her breast, pressing soft kisses to the sensitive flesh before he sucked on her nipple. The feel of it was too good, too much but she still needed more. She hissed in pleasure as he bit the peak. Wes laughed softly, as though delighted by her reaction. She wrapped her arms around his neck, then slid her hands into his hair to hold him to her in silent encouragement.

"Ready for more?" he asked.

"Yes!" She gasped without thinking.

He got up off the bed so suddenly that she lay there in a daze of confused passion as he strode to his dresser and opened the top drawer. He dug around in the drawer before he turned and came back to her. In his hands he held a pair of leather cuffs lined with fur. Callie started to sit up and he froze her in place with one dark look.

"Wrists up," he instructed. "Spread eagle." He gestured to where he wanted her to reach, the posts of the bed by her head. She did as he commanded. The beating of her heart was hard enough that she could feel every pulse beneath every inch of her skin as she tried to catch her breath.

As he walked to the head of the bed, he trailed one lazy fingertip from her shin up her body to her chin and then he pushed slightly up so she tilted her head back to watch him.

"Good girl," he murmured and then he took hold of her right wrist, fastening the leather cuff around it. A silver link on one side folded out from the warm brown leather. The furry insides of the cuff were soft and she knew it would be hard to bruise herself in them. Wes bent and reached under the bed for something she couldn't see. It clinked as he removed it.

A small chain.

Her mouth dried and her thighs quivered with forbidden longing.

He clicked a hook to her right wrist's cuff and then chained it to the bedpost.

"Pull on the chain," he instructed.

Callie gave a little tentative tug. Satisfied, he moved around the room and secured her other wrist the same way. Then Wes returned to the side of the bed and cupped her cheek.

"Fight the cuffs and chains, give it everything you've got," he demanded. There was an almost frightening fire to his eyes and Callie panicked on pure animal instinct. She was his prey. Trapped.

Fighting, jerking, clawing, she thrashed for several seconds, but finally completely exhausted, she fell back onto the bed, panting, covered in a light sheen of sweet. Restrained. At his mercy.

Chapter 12

Y ou can't escape. There's no way out now." He caged her body beneath his as he leaned over the bed and kissed her. Biting her bottom lip, he sucked it into his mouth before ravaging her lips.

"Helpless, my sweet little Callie, so trusting, so brave. Now you are truly mine." Wes's words sounded like a promise of dark, erotic things to come as he gave her one more drugging kiss.

Her body trembled, fear and excitement taking over completely. What did he plan to do to her?

Wes straightened and walked to the edge of the bed. His hands snaked out, gripping her ankles. He was too strong, could easily control her now. Her breathing turned to soft pants as her desire for him and her excitement flowed through her.

"Keep them open or I'll paddle your ass a rich shade of red." It was her only warning. He bent over the bed and wedged his shoulders between her knees. She tensed. "Relax," he encouraged more gently.

Deep breath in, deep breath out. She could do this. His palms skated down her inner thighs and his warm breath fanned her exposed sex. A little shudder of vulnerability and awareness rippled through her. He lifted one eyebrow at her when her legs trembled beneath his hands. Her legs almost started to jerk closed, but he pressed harder on her, keeping them open as he held her still on the bed.

Callie lifted her head a little more so she could look down the length of her body. What she saw stole her breath.

Wes, poised above the most secret part of her where none had seen or touched her before. His disheveled hair fell across his eyes as he breathed deeply. His shoulder muscles tensed and moved with each small adjustment he made as he drew closer. His long dark brown lashes fanned up as he met her gaze. He was all masculine power, all raw lust and desire, like a sex god. Inescapable, completely consuming. And he wanted her. Whatever he saw in her own face seemed to encourage him because he bent his head and licked.

The gasp that escaped her was loud and shaky. The sensation was strange, warm, and soft, yet each lick shot her to a wild edge of need. He licked again, a different spot, a light thrusting of his tongue, a circular teasing and then a sucking on her tender bud. That was all it took. She burned to flames as a powerful orgasm swept through her, but he didn't stop. He added one finger, pushing it into her swollen channel, drawing out the ecstasy until she quivered helplessly around him, unable to think past his touch and the feel of his hands on her body.

Then he unfastened his jeans and lowered them down his hips, taking his black briefs off with them. Callie tensed at the sight of his cock. The man was hung. There was no way he'd fit inside her.

"Don't get scared now," he chuckled. "Too late for that." He held out a strip of cloth, a blindfold, and then climbed over her, sealing it over her eyes and knotting it behind her head. She felt like a horse with blinders on, not sure what was going on around her. The sudden surge of panic hit her like a freight train and she started panting.

"Wes...Wes I..."

A fingertip pressed her lips closed. "Deep breaths. I swore not to hurt you, except for the obvious part of taking your virginity. You must trust me, Callie. The loss of sight is to decrease your fear and heighten your senses." His voice was clear, almost in her ear, so rich and seductive that her body sagged back on the bed, much more relaxed by his assurances. She listened for sounds but couldn't make out what he was doing. Soft classical music began to play, which meant he must have turned on the sound system on the dresser. Rustling, like the sound of things being removed from plastic packages, was soon covered by the increasing volume of the music.

"Art is not always pencils on paper or paint on canvas. Art is any form of perfection." Wes's voice was close again and she felt his warm breath by her ear. "Listen to the music. Embrace every note, every melody and countermelody. Feel the soul of the music. What do you see when you hear it?" Something soft, like silk drifted down her neck, like a fingertip, but it didn't feel like skin to skin, but something softer.

"What is that?" she demanded.

Wes chuckled. "I'll allow that one question, but no more questions when I blindfold you. Answer with 'yes, sir.'"

"Y—yes, sir." The word "sir," a word of power and respect, made her feel a little nervous and excited at the same time. Not because she wanted to be subservient to him, but it was comforting to feel like he was in charge here and she only had to obey him to please him. It removed a lot of pressure from her as to what to do.

"Good girl. Now what you are feeling?" He paused, dragged the object in slow swirls on and around one of her nipples and it pebbled at the stimulation. "That is a paintbrush dipped in cold water." The sliver of the brush's tip swept over her nipple again, and she hissed at the coldness and how it made her come alive. "Now, tell me what you think. How does it feel?"

She waited a moment, trying to sort out what she felt. "It feels good, but in a sharp way," she whispered, a little shy for expressing what she felt sensually.

His chuckle rasped over her bare skin. "I may have no artistic talent, but I do enjoy this and I believe I do it quite well," he mused aloud and then his mouth left a trail of hot kisses up her throat, her chin, and then to her mouth.

The strings of the classical piece were bittersweet, a hint of sorrow and the promise of hope. Images filled her head and her heart as all she could do was listen, feel, and kiss Wes. There was a fluttering excitement of exploring Paris with Wes…exploring herself with him…

The bed shifted as Wes climbed over her and her thighs were nudged apart with gentle but firm hands. The blindfold was tugged from her eyes and she blinked dazedly. He was above her, arms braced on either side of her head and she felt him. A small nudge against her resistant flesh.

"Tell me what you can feel," he growled as he shifted inside her another inch. Callie moaned at the foreign sensation.

"I feel good…but I ache." It was all so—a swift thrust of his hips and she cried out at the stabbing pain. He silenced her with his lips, swallowing any noises she might have made.

"It'll be over soon," he murmured soothingly, coiling one hand in her hair as he held still inside her. "Focus on my mouth and the music," he urged and then slanted his mouth over hers again.

"So much pain," she whimpered against his lips. It was like a hot poker stabbing her inside.

"Shhhh." He kissed her. "Relax and kiss me."

She tried to do as he commanded. And then she heard it. The soft trill of birds. Her birds. The sweet little noises they made and the sound melted her, calmed her. Her knees clasped around Wes's narrow hips, but out of encouragement rather than pain.

"Better?" he asked. His blue eyes were electric, sparking with desire and yet shadowed with worry.

She gave a jerky little nod. "Better."

His body rocked back and then forward and the sensation stung a little but it was more comfortable now than painful. Wes slid a hand between their bodies and circled her clit with a fingertip. The added sensation kicked her body into a hungry need for more. A flood of wet heat eased his entrance into her body and he must have sensed it and he began to fuck her, slow, deep penetrations that made them both share moans each time he drove into the hilt.

"God," he groaned. "You feel like heaven."

Callie felt a blush heat her cheeks. "You feel good, too." She wasn't at all sure what a girl was supposed to say to a man making love to her, but she wanted him to know how good he felt. The weight of his body, the way her knees clutched his hips, the way he was in complete control. Every move he made ratcheted her pleasure higher and higher. She attempted to raise her hips a few times.

"I've dreamed about this, Callie," he confessed in a dark whisper, his face inches above hers. "Taking you to bed and fucking you in a thousand ways. I had no idea how good it would feel, how good *you* feel, wrapped so tight around me. God, it's incredible."

She squeezed her inner muscles in sheer reactive instinct to his word, and he cursed, but his face was taut with pleasure not anger.

"Do that again, when I'm all the way inside," he coached and rammed back into her. Their hips pressed pelvis to pelvis until no inch separated them, they were as close as two people could get. A strange emotion filled her chest and spread outward as she stared up at Wes. It was partly heat, but something softer, deeper, more lasting and more frightening because it would not easily fade. Being with him, not just physically, but here in Paris, touring, laughing, living…it was starting to hold a meaning for her, a purpose. Something she'd never thought she'd have outside the ranch in Colorado.

Wes had made that possible.

"What are you thinking about?" He withdrew from her and slid back in. The roll of his hips was leisurely as he nuzzled her cheek and then stole an openmouthed kiss before allowing her to answer.

"You, only you," she whispered as pleasure started to creep into her. A climax was close, like a shadow behind a thin curtain. She had but to pass through the filmy barrier. Just a little harder, a little rougher. "Don't be so gentle," she said, giving a little feminine growl.

Wes lost control. Her answer spurred him into a frenzy. He pinned her wrists to the bed, even though she was already chained. His hips pummeled against hers and she could only accept the pace and his power as he drove into her again and again. When the orgasm hit her, he came only a second later, both of them fighting for breath. The world around her shattered like a dying star, exploding with light and warmth. She almost swore her body floated back down to the bed from a place in the clouds. Above her Wes dropped heavily against her, barely able to hold himself up. His usually cool, seductive hardness was gone. In its place was a look of wonder and fascination tinged with wariness.

"Was I too rough? You never used your safe word." He seemed to be desperately trying to collect himself and regain control.

Callie couldn't speak, not right away, and this seemed to worry him because he hastily got out of bed and unchained her wrists, removing the cuffs. Then he cupped her face and forced her eyes to his.

"Are you all right, darling? Please say something."

She covered his wrists with her hands and smiled dreamily up at him. She felt...wonderful.

"I'm good. Better than good. Wonderful." She felt suddenly shy despite everything they'd done and she dropped her hands from his wrists and tried to pull away.

"Stay right there," he ordered and went to his closet where he fetched a shirt and a pair of boxers from his dresser. "Put these on." He assisted her, even though she tried to swat his hands away. Before she was done, he'd pulled back the sheets of his bed and settled her there.

"Wes, I'm fine—" He silenced her with a shake of his head.

"Rest. I put you through a lot. I'll go check on dinner and get you something to drink." He threw on a pair of jeans before she could stop him.

She stared at the empty doorway in shock. The last thing she wanted was to be left alone after...She glanced at the rumpled bed and shivered. She could sit here and mope or go after him.

With caution, she climbed out of the bed, wincing with each step as she entered the bathroom. She pulled Wes's boxers down and tended to the sore spot between her legs. She'd taken quite a pounding for her first time. A little bit of blood coated her thighs and she washed it off with her hands, trembling. After she pulled the boxers back up, she was disposing of the bloody towels when she realized she was being watched.

Wes stood at the entrance of the bathroom, a glass of water in hand. A scowl darkening his features more than his usual demeanor did.

"That's more blood than I thought..." He stared at the bloodied cloth, and then his eyes shot to hers. He set the water down on the counter next to her. "Maybe we should take you to a doctor."

Callie frowned right back at him and crossed her arms over her chest. "Don't be stupid, Wes. I'm fine. I figured there would be blood. It's not like I haven't bled down there before." Her sarcasm wasn't lost on him, but her flippant response didn't seem to amuse him, either.

"I'm serious, Callie. I might have hurt you. Damn, this was a bad idea. You aren't ready—"

Smack!

Her hand exploded with pain as she whacked him open palmed across the cheek. She barely bridled her anger and hurt at his insinuation that she wasn't ready.

He touched his reddening cheek in shock, dark red-brown brows lifting.

"I. Am. Fine," she snapped. "Stop trying to baby me and quit hurting me by suggesting I'm not ready. It's too late for that. We slept together. You can't give me my virginity back just because you're bored already. Don't try to hide that from me. I'm fully aware it took you only a few days to seduce me and get me into bed. Shame on me for making it easy for you to win that stupid bet."

Tears stung her eyes and carved cold paths down her cheeks. This wasn't how she'd pictured her first time. She hadn't been foolish enough to expect romance, candles, or declarations of love, but she wasn't expecting this, either. Not after Fenn had broken her heart and she'd vowed never to love again. The warmth in her chest hardened into stone and was on the verge of fracturing. She couldn't do this. Not again, not so soon after Fenn. Stifling a sob, she tried to run past Wes but he captured her by the waist and dragged her into his arms, fiercely holding her so she couldn't move. Her breath hitched and the anger churning inside her deflated, and all that was left was humiliation. She was bruised and battered on the inside.

Damn Wes and his beautiful life. I don't need it or him.

She struck out at his chest and he let her do it, but the blows weren't hard and she collapsed against him after only a moment of trying to get free. He made soft shushing noises, and as much as she hated it, the noise soothed her, as did the distant sounds of her love-birds.

"I'm sorry." The apology was gruff and awkward, as though those two words had never left his mouth before, which was probably true.

"You're the first virgin I've ever been with. I'm not sure what to do." His admission made her give a hiccupy laugh.

"What you should do is *not* run away from me. I want to be held, Wes. Held and talked to, that's all." She needed his physical closeness. Some primal urge inside her required his presence and his touch, as though that would reassure her all was well.

"That I can do." He let go of her and wiped the tears from her cheeks before he picked her up and carried her through his room and downstairs.

He settled her on the couch and tucked her in with a couple of thick blankets, then went into the kitchen. When he came back, he had another glass of water and he made her drink it all before he turned on the TV. He put in a movie without asking and it was a good one. An action movie with some comedy that distracted and entertained her.

Then Wes returned to the couch and settled in beside her, sliding her body over so that she was tucked into his side. For a minute, she didn't move, but then the temptation was too strong and she wrapped her arms around his chest, hugging him, letting herself fi-nally relax. This was what she had wanted all along, this right here. A warm, wonderful man to hold her after making love. She nuzzled his chest, inhaling his scent and she sighed.

"I'm learning, Callie. This is all new to me. I don't know how to be with you." The words were so quiet she thought for a moment she might have dreamed them.

"Just be, Wes. That's all you have to do," she murmured sleepily. After that, she was aware of nothing more than him holding her and the distant sounds of Paris outside.

Chapter 13

Fucking hell. This was not going according to any of his grand plans. Wes traced the fine blue veins on the back of one of Callie's hands where it lay on his chest. The plan had been to bed her, make her submit, then still be clearheaded enough to keep his distance. That wasn't what happened though.

He'd taken her body, her virginity, and something inside him had changed. Like mighty rivers carving canyons, it was unstoppable. What he couldn't see yet, no matter how he tried, was how was it changing him? What would he be like at the end of this? Satisfied? A damn mess? Who the hell knew. And the blood...He couldn't get the sight of it out of his head. He shuddered.

Pain. He'd hurt her, and not in the fun, erotic way he'd planned with a little spanking. No, this had been real pain. He should have prepared her body more for him, but the waiting had almost killed him. Yet she'd powered through it and climaxed like an angel beneath him. He was hopelessly addicted to the sight of her eyes as she came apart. The light of surprise, the slight lifting of her brows and the parted lips as she sucked in a shocked and delighted breath as her world splintered apart in dozens of overwhelming sensations and pleasures. It was like nothing he had ever seen. He, the man who had looked upon some of the most famous pieces of art, the most rare and stunning ones, could find none to compare to Callie when he made love to her.

Made love. She had made love, but Wes didn't know what he'd done, didn't know his own heart. Love wasn't for everyone. Love was a danger, a burden. He could do without it. But if Callie fell in love with him, that wouldn't be so bad. It might be nice, to be loved, even if he couldn't reciprocate, except physically.

Callie murmured something softly in her sleep. Her fingers on his chest curled into a fist, tightening, and her brows knotted as though worries carved those little lines. He didn't like to think that bad thoughts or concerns plagued her dreams. Wes lifted her hand and gently uncurled her fingers, pressing kisses to her knuckles. She relaxed again.

Her palm was a little wide and her fingers a little short and rough with calluses. The hands of a woman who worked hard, not the dainty and long manicured fingers of the women he'd been with in the past. Those women had never worked for anything, never had to fight to survive, or had to face losing their dreams because they'd had to make sacrifices. But Callie had. She'd done all of those things and she was only twenty. A sharp stab in his chest made him wince. He didn't like to think of everything she had missed out on in life while working, not when he had the ability to change her life.

A distant chime sounded and he tensed. The oven timer. The pot roast had cooked for four hours now. It had to be ready. But Callie was dead to the world. It took him nearly five minutes to cleverly maneuver himself off the couch without waking her. He draped a blanket over her and made sure a pillow rested beneath her head before he padded over to the kitchen. He wiped his palms on his jeans and searched the cabinets for oven mitts. When he found a pair, he slid them on and approached the oven.

This was easy. Right? Remove the item from the oven and voila!

He opened the oven and stumbled back at the wave of fierce heat. When he reached inside to grab the roaster's pan handles, he could feel beads of sweat breaking out on his chest and forehead. The side of the oven clipped his left forearm and he cursed as it seared his flesh.

"Damn it!" He nearly dropped the roaster onto the counter before he hastily ran his arm under cold water. How had Callie made this look so easy? Then again, he remembered flour covering every surface of his kitchen. Whoever said cooking was easy was lying through their teeth.

After seeing to the minor burn, he removed two plates from the shelf and started carving up the roast and loaded it onto the plates with vegetables. It didn't look all that impressive in giant lumps on the plate, but it smelled divine. He needed this to be perfect though, for Callie. Using his cell phone, he searched the Internet for plate arrangements of pot roast, and with a cocky little grin, he fixed the food in a pleasing way and dropped sprigs of fresh basil over the meat. It was a good thing he was a quick study and he was able to get it just right. It almost looked like it could have been prepared by a chef from Fouquet's. He chuckled, far too proud of himself, but he couldn't stop the smile from spreading.

"What's so funny?" Callie's amused, sleepy voice from behind him had him whipping around, using his body as a shield to hide the plates from her view.

"You should still be sleeping," he chastised, but he winked at her to show her he was only teasing.

She ran her hands through her tousled hair and smiled. "The

smell of a good pot roast could wake anyone out of a dead sleep, even Rip Van Winkle."

"Rip Van Winkle?" Wes asked, surprised she would reference an old classical short story.

"Yeah." Callie giggled, the sound pleasant and enticing. "Mom used to read me stories like *Rip Van Winkle* and *Sleepy Hollow* when I was a toddler."

"Really? That's not exactly light reading for a child, you know."

She shrugged and walked toward him. Her eyes were bedroom soft and her lips looked plump and kissable. God, the woman tested his control without even trying. He wanted to drag her into his arms and plant her on the nearest flat surface and take her again.

"Children remember magic. They remember tales that hold that magic. My mother read me the classics. Even though the deeper historical and political points made no sense to me at four years old, I will never forget the man who drank moonshine and fell asleep in the woods, only to wake twenty years later." She tapped the tip of her nose, winking at him. "Magic."

As she talked, he'd found he was enjoying this playful banter—light, yet personal conversation. It wasn't at all what he did with other women, and he certainly hadn't expected to like it so much. He took everything seriously because seriousness was the only way to stay in control. Yet Callie made him feel so light-hearted sometimes. It was nice.

"Now, quit hiding whatever is behind your back." She tried to reach around him but he caught her wrists and trapped them at the small of her back and grinned lazily down at her when she struggled uselessly to escape his hold. With his free hand, he fisted his fingers in her hair and lightly tugged her head back.

"I think you need a little kissing before dinner." He smiled against her lips as he teased her and she melted against him. Her dark gold lashes fluttered and the sight made his cock hard enough that he was uncomfortable in his jeans.

"Then kiss me, damn it!" she growled like a little puppy.

"Fuck, you make me so hot when you act like that," he said and laughed.

Confusion tinged her warm hazel eyes. "When I act like what?"

"Like a puppy, so young and sweet, with just a little bite to you." He trapped her in his arms and moved them back so he pinned her against the fridge. "Makes me want to wrestle you to the ground and fuck you senseless." He nipped her chin, then possessed her mouth, relishing the shock of her reaction to his words. Sometimes her natural sensuality and her innocence were an explosive combination.

"Don't worry. There's plenty of time to try that and a lot more," he teased between steamy, slow kisses. The way she responded to his kisses alone was beautiful. She put her whole heart and body into it, the flames of her hunger and the desire heating his own body until he swore he'd ignite.

Unable to resist, he cupped her between her legs, but she bit his lip hard and he stepped back.

"Sorry," she said and gasped. "I didn't mean to bite you. It's sore down there." She ducked her head but Wes refused to let her indulge in any more self-pity.

"You are right. Too soon to go at it again. But it is time for dinner." He gave her what he hoped looked like a reassuring smile. It was killing him to wait to have her again, but he would wait, so long as she needed him to. He, a man who swore never to wait for anything or anyone he wanted, had to bide his time. Callie was too precious a thing to risk. Too precious.

* * *

Dinner turned out perfect. Callie mentally gave herself a pat on the back. Of course, pot roast was easy so long as you had everything to throw into the pan in the right amounts. Wes had likely eaten much fancier and far more expensive meals than this, but she had a feeling it was the first time he'd actually helped cook. The look of pride in his eyes when he'd showed her the artfully arranged plates was obvious, and incredibly sweet. But hot too… There was nothing like a man who had worked hard on something and was proud of it. She knew Wes worked hard on his art consultations, but because of his wealth, everything else was too easy for him.

"I have to admit, this was an enjoyable experience." He set his fork and knife down on his plate and pushed it across the large dining room table.

"What was?" Did he mean the food or the sex they'd had earlier? She'd have to agree in either case. She felt different. Changed. Her virginity was gone and in its place was a secret knowledge of darker, more sinful pleasures and a knowledge of how things could be with a man like Wes. It was more than satisfaction. It was thrilling, a pure rush of excitement, anticipation, and then, at last, pleasure. So much pleasure.

"Both aspects of the evening," he clarified with a little twinkle in his eye. "Are you finished?" He gestured to the empty plate in front of her.

"Mm-hm." She nodded. Her stomach was pleasantly full and she wanted to take another nap. Was sex and good food going to overcome her years of natural work ethic? Probably. She almost giggled. It had been half a week away from the ranch now and she wasn't used to having so little to do. No horses to tend to, cattle to feed, fences to mend, men to cook for. Of course, when she went back, much of that would no longer be her duty, since Fenn had already hired fifteen able-bodied ranch hands to work full time on the Broken Spur.

Wes rose and collected their plates, setting them in the sink. The distant tinkling sound of porcelain and china assured her he wasn't planning on doing the dishes. She would have wanted to help if that was the case, and right now she didn't want to move at all. She leaned back in her chair and closed her eyes.

Seconds later they flew open again when she was being lifted up in Wes's arms.

"Wore you out, did I?" he said and chuckled. Callie was not the sort of woman who liked to be carried about, but she'd seen Fenn haul Hayden around over his shoulder. There was something feminine about it, and no doubt a silly part of her wanted a man to do that to her, to prove he was strong. Not to prove that she was weak. There was a difference.

"Not going to insist I put you down?" He seemed amused at her relaxed reaction to him carrying her.

"Nope. If you had any idea how tired I was, you wouldn't, either." She tightened her hold around his neck and buried her face in his shoulder, inhaling the rich scent of his skin. He didn't wear cologne, didn't need it. And she preferred a man's natural scent anyway. Men were supposed to smell like pines and winter and wild winds. Not like a bottle of rotted plants crushed and soaked in chemicals.

"Are you sniffing me?" Wes asked, a rough laugh escaping him when she ducked her head and blushed.

"I like how you smell, too," he said more softly, that rich seductive lilt in his voice like honey. "Makes me hungry for you, for your body, for your kiss. It makes me think that if dreams had a scent, they would smell like you."

She stared up at him, astonished at the almost bashful, poetic musings that slipped from his sensual lips. These were not words spent to entice or seduce, but rather confessed to her with a sense of curious wonder. There was so much about him she wanted to know. She didn't want to feel like he was a stranger, not after everything they'd shared so far.

"Wes, what's your favorite color?"

"Favorite color?" He climbed the stairs that led to their rooms and carried her into the bathroom.

"Yes. Color. What is it?"

He set her down on her feet and started to run a bath in the massive tub that was more like a hot tub than anything. Once he seemed satisfied with the water's temperature, he straightened.

"My favorite color." He crossed his arms, brows furrowed. "Yellow."

"What kind of yellow? There are a bunch." Callie thought of cadmium yellow, trying to ignore the wave of homesickness for the ranch.

Wes walked up to her and settled his hands on her hips, gazing down at her. "The yellow of a lantern's warm glow in summer."

There in his eyes, a secret shimmered effervescently and Callie ached to see it.

"Why that color?" she probed gently.

Wes sighed, the sound ancient and full of a century's worth of sorrow. "Before my ninth birthday, my life was rich in love, in color, in friends. I didn't know the darkness in men's hearts, didn't know the evil that drives people to hurt others to get what they want. I was just a boy. Innocent. I used to camp with my friends, Emery, Fenn, and Royce. The four of us were inseparable. And that last summer…" A man's rage and a boy's fear collided in his eyes and roughened his voice. "That summer our innocence perished. The lantern-glow yellow is the way back to those memories for me. It's a way to remind myself of what was, but is no longer." His hands were on her hips and they tightened slightly, as though he needed to root himself in place and holding her was the only way to do it.

Callie knew of the kidnapping of the Lockwood twins, had recently learned just how horrible things had been for Fenn and Emery. She could only imagine how hard it would be for Wes, as a little boy, to lose one friend and have another one come back emotionally damaged. Even though she had been only four, losing her mother had scarred her soul. There was an emptiness inside her that could never be filled, a void that could be filled only by the presence of a mother she would never have.

"Lantern yellow is a lovely color," she said. There was nothing else a person could say after a confession like his.

"And yours is cobalt blue. Why?" He seemed genuinely curious as to her answer and she felt compelled to tell him the truth.

"Your eyes. They're cobalt. It's such a rare shade of blue. No impurities, only endless depth." She reached up, unthinking as she touched his cheek and studied his eyes, this time from her artist's eyes. Sometimes the artist in her was its own being that woke like a sleeping goddess to wave her hand and create magic upon the page before slumbering again. Callie often teased that inner part of herself, calling it the reluctant muse. Around Wes there was no reluctance. If anything, he'd put her muse into overdrive.

"Keep talking about colors and you will end up in my bed, sore or not," he warned, his lips curling into a seductive smile that showed just how on edge he was while trying to maintain his control.

She wanted him. But her body still needed some time to recover before they made love again.

"Strip down and get in the bath," he ordered.

Still shy, she hesitated. The look he gave her promised a punishment, but she still wasn't ready to just whip off her clothes.

With a low laugh, he gripped her arm and turned her to face the counter. He pushed hard enough to keep her bent over, helpless, but not hurting.

"When I give you an order relating to the bedroom or the removal of clothes, you say 'yes, sir' and do as I ask."

Smack! The little slap to her bottom stung, but it was well away from her tender areas. He knew her body too well. Like how she would respond to a light pat at just the right spot on her backside, or the way to nibble her throat between kisses.

"Yes, sir," she hastily said, burying her face in her arm, a little turned on and more than humiliated by the fact that the spanking made her instantly wet.

"Good. One more for you to remember this lesson." *Smack!* This one was harder, but still nothing painful. The light sting always faded into a delicious heat a few seconds later. Wes kept her pinned down on the counter with one hand between her shoulder blades while his other hand massaged her ass, rubbing in the little reminder of her disobedience. Then he let her stand and he pointed at the floor by the bathtub.

"We'll try again. Strip now."

With trembling hands, she tugged the boxers down and kicked them away and then lifted the large t-shirt over her head. When she let the shirt flutter to the ground, she had to clench her hands in fists at her side so as to not cover her bare breasts. She was learning now that he'd punish her, deliciously so, if she tried to hide from him.

"Very good. I know you want to hide, Callie. But you are beautiful. Inside and out. I'll allow some modesty, because it's charming on you, but I want you to learn to accept your body and be comfortable sharing it with me."

"Yes, sir." Her fingers uncurled from their tight fists and she inhaled slowly, then exhaled. It helped.

I'm beautiful. She chanted the mantra a few times and was surprised that it made her feel beautiful standing bare before him.

"I don't expect or want you to adhere to most of the rules I would require of a submissive. We both know what's between us is more complicated." He stared only at her eyes as he spoke and she didn't feel like an object, but a person, and that made her relax.

"Wes, now that we've slept together…" She paused, terrified of how he might answer.

"Yes?" He was so patient, so calm, it was almost unnerving.

"Well, is that what you want? I mean you had me. Do you still…"

"Still want you?" He only continued once she'd nodded. "More than ever. Before I'd only had a taste of you. Now I'm not letting you go. You agreed to try to play by my rules and it will be so rewarding for us both. Tell me now if this isn't what you want. If you don't want me any longer then we can stop."

She shook her head. "I still want you, too."

"Good. When I have expectation or wishes, I will tell them to you so that you do not fear punishment. I will never really hurt you. What you've endured up to now is all that I'd ever put you through."

She nodded. That little reassurance made her feel better. The idea of doing something wrong without knowing made her uneasy.

"Now come here and kiss me." He waited like a lazy lion as she approached him. He didn't move to touch her but let her place her hands on his shoulders. He waited, so patiently, but she could see the barely banked fires in his deep blue eyes. Her naked body pressed to his clothed one, only their bare feet touched and for some reason that made her giggle. He moved fast, too fast, grabbing her and pulling her against him.

"What's so funny?" he demanded in a soft tone.

She shook her head and stood up on tiptoe, kissing his startled mouth. She'd managed to catch him by surprise and the knowledge of that turned her on. Knowing she'd caught him off guard only made her shake with silent laughter and he started laughing, too, even though she sensed he didn't want to.

"What's so funny?" he asked again.

"It's not something I can actually describe," she said and kissed the corner of his mouth, his jaw, then his cheek. *She was happy.* That was part of it. The rest was a sense of wholeness, of being complete and satisfied in a way she hadn't ever felt before.

"You are a confusing woman," he said and sighed, but it was accompanied by a soft smile that made her toes curl, especially when he followed it with a sweet, deep kiss. His hands cupped her bottom, clenched, and she jerked when he gave it a playful smack. Wetness pooled instantly between her thighs at that mix of pain and pleasure.

How did he know just what to do to her body to make it light up with inner fire?

"Go on and get in the bath, you minx." He tapped the tip of her nose and urged her to get into the tub that was nearly full by now. She did as he ordered, sighing as the hot water sizzled on her skin and soaked into her, melting away her stress and soreness.

"Feeling better?" Wes asked, watching her from beside the tub. Amusement danced in his eyes and she grinned sleepily up at him.

"I'm not going to last long with this. What's next, warm milk and cookies?"

He chuckled. "If you like." His rakish wink made her roll her eyes.

"Are you getting in with me? Plenty of room." She waved a hand at the expansive tub.

"I can't promise not to touch you again." He took a step back, as though the temptation was too great, but Callie had quick reflexes and she caught his hand, holding him still. Whenever he tried to pull away it made something inside her flutter with panic.

"*Please.*"

He pulled his hand free and she feared he'd walk away, but he stripped out of his jeans, sweater, and briefs and then climbed into the tub behind her. The water sloshed as he reached for her and pulled her onto his lap. She was too tired to fuss as he arranged her just the way he liked, her back to his chest. She leaned into him and rested her head on his shoulder, their cheeks touching as he held her close. It was oddly right, to feel and *be* this close to Wes. He'd seen part of her soul in the last few days and she was starting to see his. After the bearing of such secret parts of one's self there was no other need for barriers between them.

"Now that our bet is over, I have a serious matter to discuss with you, Callie. If you had the chance to go to art school, would you? If money was no object?" He added this last bit hastily.

Feeling a little bold, she stroked his forearm, which rested on her stomach. It was so nice to be able to touch him, like a lover. She'd never been able to do that with anyone else.

"I...If money wasn't a problem, then yes. I would. Assuming I could get in without a recommendation of course." She doubted she could do it. Art schools were incredibly competitive and she had no portfolio or any real experience besides her own self-taught techniques.

"That's good to hear. There's an excellent school on Long Island. I've spoken to Royce about applications for the spring semester and my friend has already written his recommendation based on the photos of the pictures I took of your art at the ranch. I've taken care of everything except for your entrance essay and three pieces of art you need to provide in three different mediums for your portfolio submission."

Callie stiffened. "What? I thought losing the bet meant I didn't get the recommendation..." That had been the only thing driving her to resist him and he'd made his seduction too irresistible. Now he was offering her the thing she'd wanted almost as much as she'd wanted him?

He chuckled. "My intention from the start when I made that wager with you was always to obtain the recommendation no matter whether you resisted me or not. Even if you succumbed, I planned to help you get into art school. Your application was filled out and ready before you ever boarded the plane with me in Walnut Springs."

He'd filled out an application for her? She wasn't sure whether she was angry or pleased…but she didn't like that he'd done it without talking to her. There was so much he hadn't considered though, like how far away Weston was from Colorado, from the ranch, and from her father.

"Wes, you can't just do things like that without first talking to me. Leaving my father and my life at the ranch for school is a huge decision that only I can make. That's a personal boundary you crossed."

His arms tightened around her waist, and his suddenly hard cock nudged her backside.

"I break down walls and leap over boundaries, darling. It's how I operate." His warm breath fanned over her cheeks and she shivered. Her temper and resistance apparently aroused him. The man was still a puzzle to her.

"You're not getting off that easily. You have to talk to me about decisions that affect my life." She tried to slide off his lap because this was definitely a face-to-face conversation. But he didn't let her move, even when she thrashed and water splashed over the tub's edge.

"Be still or I'm liable to fuck you into submission, so you'll listen to me." His harsh growl rumbled in her ear and she stilled. The most basic animal instincts deep inside her demanded she not fight him.

He was the alpha male and she'd resisted him. If she wanted to calm him down, she'd better not make any more sudden moves.

Dominants were a lot like predators in the wild. The romance novels she'd read hadn't been wrong about that. The question was how far would she dare to push him?

Chapter 14

When Callie went lax in his arms, Wes relaxed as well. She could feel the tension seep out of his limbs.

"Good. Now here's our discussion. You said if money was no object, you would go to art school. I'm paying your way so you're going. That's the end of the discussion."

The bristling inside her was barely containable, but she had to be careful. It also rankled her that he'd made some silly bet when he'd planned on giving her what she'd dreamed of all along. What had been the point of the bet then if there hadn't been any real stakes?

"Why did you even bet me if you were already going to get me the recommendation?"

His face grew serious. "Because you were drowning, Callie. Your heart was breaking and I couldn't stand to watch you suffer. I gave you a challenge, something to fight for. It kept your spirit from dying. Here you are, as feisty as the day I met you, recovering from your heartache. It's because you had the strength to fight back for the bet. It was never about winning, but about the challenge."

She was silent for a long moment. He was right. She'd been so focused on their wager, on his playful, intense seduction, that the pain in her heart from Fenn had eased and slowly started to fade. The unbearable pain of losing the first man she'd loved had begun to heal. Because of Wes. And now he was still helping her, offering to get her into art school.

"Wes, you are not going to pay for my art school." Taylors didn't like owing debts. If she was going to school, then she would pay.

Wes turned his head slightly and licked the inside of her ear. A bolt of desire so strong shot straight to her clit and she jolted in his tight hold. She arched her back, breasts jutting out, and he cupped them, squeezing them and kneading them with his elegant hands. They were strong looking but beautiful and Callie whimpered when he pinched her nipples.

"Wes, stop. We have to talk about this." She gripped his thighs, digging her fingers into his legs as a building wave of need whiplashed through her.

"I know you're sore, darling," he murmured in her ear. "Can you take me? I'll go nice and slow."

Could he keep that promise? Hell, did it matter? She wanted him so much…

"Okay…" She was barely coherent now. Trapped between Wes's hot body and the water, she could barely remember her own name. She ached for him. There was no other word for what she felt. Wes had to fill her, possess her, but it was the only way to ease the mind-numbing ache for him.

He lifted her up and placed her on her knees on the opposite seat in the large tub so that she faced the tub's edge and Wes stood behind her, knee deep in the water.

"Bend over and rest your head on your arms," he urged, his voice husky and soft.

She bent over, laying her hands on the marble platform that extended past the tub's edge and jerked in shock when Wes wedged a knee between her thighs from behind and parted her legs farther.

The soreness between her thighs stung a little as the blunt head of his cock nudged her entrance. He used one hand to guide himself into her and his other hand gripped her left shoulder. He rocked forward, pushing in a few inches. She tightened and twitched around him.

"Relax," he crooned. "Just relax."

She breathed deeply and let herself relax. This time when he pushed into her, her body accepted him, even though it was still tight.

"God, I thought I'd imagined how good you felt. But it's better than I remember."

A wicked surge of pride filled her. She loved knowing that he thought she felt good. Having no experience with sex, she was afraid she wouldn't know what to do to make sure he enjoyed himself, too.

"Does it hurt?" he asked.

"Not so much," she said, panting as he withdrew and waited. "I'm okay now. It feels better." It felt really good actually, once she relaxed and focused on how it felt to be full and stretched by him, connected at such an intimate place.

"Thank God," he groaned and began a leisurely but steady pace of thrusts. His hand on her shoulder tightened and his other hand slid down her belly to her clit. Fingering the sensitive pearl, he teased it, then pressed just hard enough that the stimulation with his penetrations was too much. The world blurred around her and a drugging fuzziness filled her head and the climax came but it was slow, drawn out, everlasting.

Ripples of pleasure, heat filling her, flushing her skin, her breath heavy. She'd never done drugs, wouldn't ever do them, but this was what they had to feel like…only infinitely better. Floating on ecstasy. Wes collapsed over her, bracing himself on one arm beside her shoulder as he nipped her ear and murmured soft sweet things.

It was something she would never forget as long as she lived. The way they felt together, bodies as close as physically possible, hearts beating wildly, his scent mixed with hers, and the way he spoke to her. Hushed endearments, things that made her heart clench, and something inside her unfurled, like the petals of a newly blooming flower stretching for the sun. He was opening her heart up, forcing light and heat into places she'd attempted to darken with shadows. Soon she wouldn't be able to keep him out. A man who could banish her inner darkness, make her feel alive again after her broken heart…There would be no stopping the love that would surely follow.

I'm falling for him. A man who keeps his women at a distance…And I promised myself I would never love anyone again…

It was her last coherent thought as she succumbed to exhaustion.

* * *

Wes realized Callie had fallen asleep seconds after he'd withdrawn from her body. She was worn out, the poor little thing. He shouldn't have taken her again so soon, but he hadn't been able to stop himself, not when she'd begged him to. He carefully cleaned her and then lifted her from the bath. She was wet, but he had a spare robe lying by the bathtub and he tucked her into the terry cloth folds before he carried her to his room. There had been only a brief thought that he should have taken her to her own bed. That had been his original intention all along. But now that he'd had her here in his arms, his bed was the only place he wanted her to be.

He was starting to learn that Callie disrupted every single plan he made. He knew now that she'd likely be upset if he left her alone in her room. But it wasn't just that. *He* wanted to be with her in his bed, too. Curling his body around hers each night had become a security he hadn't predicted he would need. The emptiness of his arms without her left a hollow feeling inside him.

He laid her down on his bed and pulled the sheets back. She didn't stir at all, not even when he shifted her beneath the comforter. The soft chatter of the birds from the other room distracted him. He strode back into her room and walked up to the elegant cage Michel had brought. The birds were tucked up in a preconstructed nest, something Michel no doubt thought was necessary.

Their little green beaks and peach-colored faces were attractive. The female lovebird was cuddled deep into the nest, eyes half closed as she chirped every now and then. Her protective mate hovered close by, singing softly as though to put her to sleep. Wes watched them in fascination. He'd never been allowed to have pets as a child, and over the years he'd locked that part of his dreams away. Even after moving out at eighteen, he'd never found an excuse to get a pet. Until he'd seen Callie's face. The whirlwind of color in the lovebirds' cage had caught her attention and the look of wonder on her face had been the most beautiful thing he'd ever seen. And he had looked upon some of the most beautiful women the world had ever seen.

None of them compare to her.

Every time he looked at her, everything around him seemed to slow and fade out until there was only her. She was young and innocent of the dark parts of the world, but her soul was old, wise beyond her twenty years. She understood people on a deeper level than he did. The artist inside her saw the world through a lens he'd never imagined possible. When she drew things, he was able to see into her mind and heart. She transported him beyond his own body and into a world she created. And that was only the beginning. Her potential was unbelievable. He knew she was going to fight him on art school, but he wasn't going to let her throw away her talent.

He lifted the cage stand and carried it into his room. The birds would need interaction with people. Since it seemed Callie would be spending more time in his room, the birds would need to be there as well. Michel had left a white cloth on a metal ring beneath the cage. Wes lifted it up and dropped it over the cage where it covered the bars fully. The birds quieted and Wes smiled, pleased that they would rest, too. He was responsible for the feathery little lovers now and he was growing fonder of them by the minute, and not just because they made Callie light up like the sun.

He started back toward his bed when his cell phone vibrated. He picked it up off the nightstand and answered quietly.

"Thorne here."

"Wes, I have news about your Goya. Can you meet me at the Quartier Pigalle in half an hour?" Dimitri Razin asked.

Wes checked his watch. It was 11:30 PM. "Sure. I'll be there soon." He hung up and walked over to his closet. Dressing in one of his least favorite suits, in case it got damaged, he walked back over to the bed. Callie looked darling, sweet, and so tempting that he hated to leave her. He pressed a kiss to her hair, a tender gesture that filled him with surprise. She stirred at his touch and her lashes fluttered up.

"Wes, are you going somewhere?" She reached up to touch his white dress shirt and the heat of her hand seared him like a physical brand.

Fuck. He didn't want to leave, but he had to see Dimitri.

"Sorry, darling. I've got to go out for a short while. Go back to sleep and I'll join you when I return."

That adorable little frown knit her brow and he brushed a fingertip over the little lines and smiled.

"Get some rest. We have a big day planned tomorrow." Unable to resist the allure of her lips, he stole one kiss that ended all too quick. Then he was striding away from the bed. If he looked back now, he'd never be able to leave.

He caught a taxi to the Quartier Pigalle, or Pig Alley to the non-locals. The quarter was located on the stretch of the Boulevard de Chichi from Place Blanche to Place Pigalle which was named after a famous sculptor from the eighteenth century named Jean-Baptiste Pigalle. In the past it was a den of inequity where wine was cheap and prostitutes freely roamed through the night. Now it was full of sex shops, peep shows, the Museum of Erotic Art, and, during the day, hot dog stands. At night it was different, almost like the red-light district in Amsterdam. It was an excellent place to meet Dimitri for a little talk, one he suspected could get interesting, given his friend's tone. He sensed there might be more to this than just a conversation.

The taxi driver pulled up in front of a black building with flashy red lights that said "peep show." Wes shook his head at the sight and slipped the driver his money before he climbed out of the car. A small alley split the two buildings, and Dimitri stood at the entrance, one shoulder propped against the stone building. He checked his watch, nodded at the alley where a car was parked. Wes followed Dimitri into the shadows.

"What did you find out?" he asked as he joined the other man at the back of the car. It was a nondescript sedan that held little attention for anyone who might pass by.

Dimitri smiled, but it was a grim expression. "I have discovered a most interesting connection to the Goya." He fished out a pair of car keys from his suit pocket and opened up the trunk of the car. In the dim light of the distant streetlamps, Wes could just make out the shape of a body. With anyone else he would have been surprised, but Dimitri could be a little cavalier.

"Umph!" A muffled shout echoed up from the deep confines of the trunk.

"This is a man named Rudolph Giennes. He deals in art, don't you, Mr. Giennes?" Dimitri shoved a small penlight into the man's face, allowing Wes to get a better look at the man. Beady eyes, a face made of all angles and planes, he silently snarled when Dimitri ripped a strip of gray duct tape off his mouth.

Wes crossed his arms and scowled down at Giennes.

"What's his connection to the Goya?" Wes asked his friend.

Dimitri laughed. "A fairly solid one. He had the piece hanging in his private gallery where he does back-door dealings. Wouldn't tell me his fence for the piece. I thought you wouldn't mind getting better acquainted with him on the subject." Dimitri flashed Wes a knowing grin and Wes could read the other man's mind.

"I'm not telling you a damn thing," Giennes snarled.

Dimitri struck fast, smacking Giennes across the face. Neither he nor Wes liked art thieves or those who associated with them.

"Mr. Giennes, please," Wes said, sighing heavily. "We can do this the easy way or the hard way. I wore my least favorite suit tonight and can burn it later if the blood gets too much for my dry cleaner to handle."

Giennes's eyes nearly popped out of his skull.

"No!" the bound man hissed. "You're not going to…" He stifled a yelp as Wes lunged for him, dragging him bodily from the car. Since Giennes's legs were free, he struggled to run away but Wes dug his hands in Giennes's shirt and spun him around, using the man's momentum to throw him against the nearest building. Giennes groaned in pain.

"Listen to me," Wes growled, shoving his face close to Giennes's. "I don't like to torture anyone for information, but my friend here, he's Russian. Old school. He'll cut you to pieces with a cigar cutter.

Do you want that? Because if you do, I'll stand by and watch."

"Why the fuck do you care so much about a painting?" Giennes gasped, his eyes near black in the dark alley, but they glittered with rage and greed.

"Because art matters. It matters more than you and me. More than anything in this world." Wes slammed the man back into the wall again. "I'm not letting some piece of shit like you steal and destroy something precious like that."

Giennes still didn't speak and that was it. Wes shot a glance over his shoulder at Dimitri, who was lounging back against his car, legs crossed at the ankles and looking bored.

"Dimitri, your cigar cutter please." Still gripping the thief with one hand, he held out his other hand, palm up, toward the Russian.

"Of course." Dimitri fished a small cigar cutter out of his trouser pocket. "Start with his fingers. He'll bleed a lot, but he won't die too fast."

"Duly noted." Wes took the cutter and jerked one of Giennes's hands toward it.

"Wait!" Giennes thrashed about. "Fuck! I'll talk!"

Wes relaxed, but only enough to pocket the cigar cutter. "Then talk."

"The Goya came from an American. Someone out of Long Island. That's all I know."

Wes's entire body went rigid. Someone from Long Island?

"Give me a name!" He let loose a shout and slammed his fist right into the wall beside Giennes's head. Pain exploded through his knuckles and shot up his arm, but he held on to his control, barely. If he didn't, he'd slam his fist into Giennes's face.

"It's a man, midthirties. He had a nickname, the Illusionist."

"The Illusionist?"

"Yes. He puts forgeries in the place of the paintings he steals. He creates an illusion that the real art was never taken. Most people never know they've been robbed. He's a right dangerous bastard. You'd never see him coming."

Dimitri burst out laughing. "The Illusionist? Oh, that's rich. We're dealing with a dramatic thief."

Wes didn't see the humor in this. This was serious. Someone from his island was stealing art and selling it on the black market. Art sold on the black market was mistreated, often ruined, and usually never seen again. There was no honor among thieves and no respect for masterpieces either.

"That's all I know," Giennes insisted. "He's rich, wore sunglasses the whole time we talked. Brown hair…" Giennes added these last few details, but that seemed to be the end of his usefulness.

"Dimitri, I trust you can assure me that Mr. Giennes finds a suitable way out of France in the next few hours? I'm sure he has friends in other countries to visit and that coming back to Paris wouldn't be wise."

"What?" Giennes stared at both of them, confused.

The Russian sauntered over and gripped Giennes by the throat, lightly squeezing. "My friend is much more polite than me. At home in Russia, I would have simply said, 'set foot in France ever again and I'll kill you.'"

"Kill?" Giennes's voice shot up an octave in pitch, whether from fear or from being deprived of oxygen Wes wasn't sure.

"A strong word, but an apt one. No one would ever find you when I'm through," Dimitri growled. He continued to squeeze until the thief's eyes rolled back in his head and he slumped forward unconscious.

"Don't worry. I'll take care of him." Dimitri dragged the limp body back to his car and shoved him into the trunk. Wes nodded. He didn't usually resort to such dark tactics, but he knew there was only one way to handle this and Dimitri had known best how to go about it. There was no sense in paying men like Giennes for information. He'd still hold back until the price was high enough. A little death threat was just as effective and a hell of a lot cheaper.

"Here, you don't want to forget this." Dimitri retrieved a white tube from the back seat of his car and placed it carefully into Wes's hands. "The Goya. Take care of her, my friend."

The relief at having such a piece back in his hands was intensely overwhelming, like he could breathe again.

"Thank you." He shook Dimitri's hand and left the alley, where he hailed a passing taxi. He didn't want to think about a traitor on his island or what that meant for his friends like the Mortons who collected pieces and were willing to share them with the world. Art was meant to be shared, but also protected. In the hands of thieves, it was only a matter of time before it was destroyed. Knowing that some fool calling himself the Illusionist was stealing paintings made a veil of red descend over Wes's vision. He would have to call the Mortons tomorrow and get hold of the FBI to let them know he'd recovered the painting.

Holding the tube with the rolled up Goya inside, he set it across his lap in the back of the taxi and gave the driver his address. The bed back in his apartment with a warm and willing woman was the place he wanted most to be in that moment. With Callie in his arms, he'd be able to touch her and soothe the raging fires inside him.

Chapter 15

Callie covered her mouth, stifling the scream that would have shattered the robust activity on the streets of the place the taxi driver called Pig Alley. She'd had him trail Wes's cab and she'd been afraid to get out and follow him on foot. This was stupid. She shouldn't have gone after him in a foreign city close to midnight. But she'd rationalized it by promising to stay in the taxi if things looked bad. She just had to know if he was meeting someone else. Part of her still believed she wasn't enough for Wes and he'd see other women. Logically, her mind told her Wes wasn't that kind of man, but late-night phone calls and leaving? What was she to think? That was how she'd ended up at Pig Alley.

The flashing lights and the questionable atmosphere had been one thing. Her father would have called this place a knife-fight magnet, since all manner of seedier things were going down. Sex shops, peep shows, toy shops, and women wearing very little and patrolling the streets with one goal in mind.

Clutching her coat around her, she remained in the back seat of the taxi, peering across to the street where she'd just witnessed Wes throw a man into a wall. The moonlight wasn't bright enough to see everything in the dark alley clearly, but there was no mistaking Wes and Dimitri accosting a man. A man who had been stuffed in a car trunk…A chill rippled through her and she shivered.

"Oh my God," Callie whispered. Fear sizzled like sharp electricity beneath her skin, frazzling her control until her body shook with the force of it.

Wes was a bad man. A very bad man. And she was all alone in Paris with him. This wasn't good. What could she do? If she ran, he'd follow her. He'd made that clear enough. But if she stayed, who knew what would happen.

Was he involved in the Russian mob with Dimitri? Was that how he'd accumulated all of his wealth? His love of art was likely a front. Her stomach became a hollow pit.

What the hell was she going to do? There wasn't an easy way to get home. She'd flown here on Wes's jet. While she and her father were now out of the woods financially, it didn't change the fact that she didn't have the money to buy a ticket home. Even if she did, there was no guarantee that Wes wouldn't come after her and stop her from boarding the plane. In fact, she was sure he would. The night's dinner worked its way up her throat. She had to get back to the apartment before Wes did. She didn't want to think about what he'd do if he found out she knew about his double life.

"Where to, mademoiselle?" the driver asked her.

"Back to my apartment." She told him the address in the Rue Cler neighborhood and he pulled out onto the street. Callie ducked down as they drove past Wes. In his hands he held a white tube. He hadn't had that when he left the house. Was he carrying drugs? Or money? Or something else? Callie didn't want to know. People who knew probably ended up dead.

By the time the taxi pulled up by the door, Callie swore she had aged a decade from the panic and stress. The doorman recognized her and he hit the button to let her in. She shot him a strained smile and ran straight for the elevators. There was no telling how soon Wes would get back. When she got into the elevator, she leaned back against the wood paneling and focused on slowing her breathing. Panting like a spent racehorse was a dead giveaway that she hadn't been sleeping. If he was heading back, too, he could be only minutes behind her and she couldn't take the chance he'd find out.

When she got inside the apartment she rushed into his bedroom and stripped out of her jeans, sweater, and shoes. The terry cloth robe lay across the rumpled sheets and she jerked the robe back on. She was just settling back into the bed when she heard the distant open and close of the front door of the apartment. The feel of the soft robe on her naked skin made her shudder. The last thing she wanted was to be bare skinned around a man who would likely kill her if he found out she knew his dirty secrets. But he'd sense something was off if she was suddenly wearing clothes.

The creak of the stairs from Wes's footsteps shot her heart into her throat. She couldn't breathe. Her head pounded hard against her skull and behind her eyes. Despite the cool sheets against her legs, her body was hot with building panic.

Please God, please, she silently prayed, her hands clenched into fists on the blankets and her eyes squeezed shut.

Relax, have to relax. She tried to calm down, focusing on counting her breaths, but knowing he was coming made her body rigid. Every muscle coiled tight and was ready to snap.

The bedroom door eased open with a slight squeak on the metal hinges. Wes entered the room as silent as a cat. Her ears strained to pick up on the sounds of him rustling as he kicked off his shoes and slid out of his clothes. The covers were pulled back and the bed dipped as he joined her. She flinched out of sheer instinct when he grabbed her, hauling her back against his body.

"Callie?" he whispered, voice full of concern. "Are you awake?"

She wanted to lie, but she couldn't. He sensed she was awake.

"I heard you come in." That was the truth. He tugged her so she lay flat on her back.

"You're trembling. Are you cold? I can warm you up." His voice was husky, soft, so perfectly seductive. So dangerous. One hand parted her robe a few inches, and he stroked a fingertip along her collarbone as he leaned over her, studying her.

"I couldn't sleep while you were gone." Not a lie.

"Well," he said, chuckling, "since we're both awake…" He trailed off as he dipped his head to kiss her.

She couldn't bear it. The second he touched her, she *wanted* him, even knowing the monster that he was. Her body betrayed her, warming up to him. *Have to get free, get away.* She flung herself off the bed, ducking from his reaching arms.

Her sudden flight from his arms apparently confused him. "Are you sore after sex in the bathtub?" He sat up and shoved the covers back. He'd put on a pair of black cotton pajama bottoms, but his chest was bare, smooth, and too enticing. If only he wasn't… She shuddered again.

"Yes, I'm sore." It took her a minute to remember what he'd asked. It was a lie though. She wasn't sore.

His eyes narrowed. "You can't lie to me, darling. I can read you like a book. Why are you running from me?" His tone was soft, seductive, but she heard the note of worry there. Why would he worry about her? Unless he was already guessing she'd found him out.

"I…uh…" Her mind blanked. She couldn't think of a darn thing, not when looking into his eyes and seeing that cobalt so dark now they seemed almost obsidian.

"Don't run. You won't like it when I catch you," he cautioned, but her instincts overrode everything else and she bolted for the door. She'd get a taxi, ride to a hotel, and call Fenn for help. He could wire her money. She'd pay him back if she could just get away.

She was fast. All those years of running on the ranch trails for exercise paid off. She was out of the apartment and sprinting to the elevator, hands clutching the robe tight about her body. When she got inside she slammed her finger onto the first-floor button and then hit the close button. Wes was running toward her, but the elevator was already closing. An instant before he reached her, the doors sealed shut. She held her thumb on the close button, praying it wouldn't open. For several seconds nothing happened.

Then the doors slid back open.

Callie opened her mouth to scream but Wes lunged inside and muffled her with a hand over her mouth as he shoved her back against the wall of the elevator. He didn't hurt her, but the impact knocked the wind out of her and he shoved one thigh between hers, using his full weight to pin her helpless. Immobilized and silenced, she watched as he let the doors close and then he pressed the emergency stop button.

She was sealed inside an enclosed space at midnight with a mad man…Tears blurred her vision and she blinked rapidly. Wes watched her eyes, studying the tears as they traveled down her cheeks and bumped into the hand he held over her mouth.

"What is the matter with you?" he growled. "Don't ever run from me like that. If you want to play that game, we do it my way. Not like this." He still looked confused, but angry, too.

Callie shut her eyes. Was he going to kill her now? How long would it take him to figure out that she'd seen his underworld dealings with Dimitri tonight?

The hand on her mouth dropped away and settled on her shoulder. "Darling, talk to me. You're scaring me," he said.

When she opened her eyes, she looked up at him. "Please don't kill me. I won't tell anyone what I saw, I swear."

"What? What are you talking about?" He fisted his other hand in her hair and tugged lightly, urging her to tilt her head back. His hips were still pressed to hers, keeping her prisoner against the elevator wall.

"I saw you and Dimitri," she confessed. There was no use hiding it now. He'd probably torture it out of her if she tried to stay quiet.

"You did?" His lips pursed into a tight line as he seemed to wait for her to say more.

"What exactly did you see?" he demanded.

Callie was ashamed of herself in that moment more than she'd ever been ashamed in her life. There was no way she could avoid telling him what she'd seen. She was terrified and there was no natural bravado in her to give her strength and defiance. She'd let this man into her body and her heart. Any damage, emotional or physical, was enough to scare her senseless.

"What did you see?" he repeated, surprisingly patient, and that only scared her more.

"I saw you beating up that man and taking something from him. It's drugs, isn't it? You're involved with the Russian mob or something, right?" She swallowed, but her throat was cracked because it was so dry.

To her horror Wes burst out laughing. "Oh, Callie, darling. I think I adore you. Drugs? Russian mob? I'll have to tell Dimitri that. He'll find it amusing, I'm sure." Wes pressed a kiss to her lips and she didn't fight him. Now she was the one confused. He wasn't acting like a man who'd been found out, or a man who was going to kill her for knowing about his drug involvement.

"But…that's what you were doing, right?" Her voice shook as the words came out clipped.

He stroked her throat, a devious smirk on his sensual lips. "Oh no. Nothing like that. I don't touch drugs and I have no mob involvement. You were really frightened of me, weren't you?" His fingers found her pulse, which still beat wildly. She licked her lips and nodded.

"I'm still scared. I don't know what you were doing. I know what I saw though. That man was in a trunk…and you punched him."

Wes raised one hand for her to see his bruised and bloodied knuckles. "I hit the wall next to him, not him. And he is the bad man, not me." As he spoke he slowly slid the bathrobe off her shoulders and pulled her forward a few inches to let the robe drop to the floor. Callie fisted her hands and smacked his chest, trying to push him away. She needed answers. But he had other ideas. His hands cupped her ass cheeks, giving them a hard squeeze. Callie hissed in outrage, but he silenced her with a deep, penetrating kiss.

Before she could even muster up a proper defense, he was jerking his pajama bottoms down and kicking her legs apart. His kiss was too potent. The erotic way his tongue played with her mouth, demanding surrender, made her wet and throbbing between her thighs. He grasped her right leg behind her knee and tucked her leg over his hip and began to work his way inside her. Through the haze of lust, she knew she needed him to explain what she'd seen…after they'd sated the wildness rising between them like an unstoppable force.

The blunt head of his erection parted her channel, driving in slowly, but filling her until she couldn't breathe. He hoisted her up, one hand under her ass as he pinned her against the elevator wall and fucked her. There was no other word for it. The movement of his hips changed from slow and gentle to hard and deep, almost punishing, but that thrilled her all the more. He wasn't gentle now, but purely animalistic. She cried out softly each time he slammed into her, not from pain but from the surprise at the pleasurable riot of sensations his possession created.

He was close to her, inside her, part of her. Wes's tongue taunted, teased, his cock ravaging her with the wicked thrusts. She'd never known something so dirty and rough could feel so good. He was fucking her in an elevator and she was completely naked. The whole idea made her skin flush with heat and her womb clench around him.

"Baby," he whispered raggedly against her throat, "you feel so good." He nipped her throat. He was losing that stiff formality, and he was just a man driven by lust and instinct. A man she couldn't resist.

The way he'd said "baby" made that delicious pressure inside her shoot that much higher and closer to that beautiful orgasm she knew was a breath away.

"Oh God, Wes!" She arched her back, and he seemed to plunge even deeper, and he responded with a guttural growl, slamming into her over and over. When he nuzzled her neck, then bit down on the sensitive spot where her neck met her shoulder, she exploded. Flames seemed to lick along her skin, singeing her with an overwhelming rush of pleasure. She swore he came at the same time she did, his body stiffening, his breathing harsh and ragged as he rode out both their climaxes with continued thrusts a few moments longer. She was weightless and shaking, her whole body out of control. If he put her down, she'd fall right on her ass.

"Fuck, that was…" He shook his head with a smile. "Callie, darling." He nuzzled her cheek and she started to almost purr, like a contented cat. The man had just destroyed her in the best way. She was completely and irrevocably his.

"Wes." She let his name escape her lips, but she couldn't seem to find the words for anything else.

"Come on, let's get you back into bed." He set her down on her feet and she clung to him, afraid she'd fall. With a quick jerk, he tugged his pajama bottoms back up over his lean hips and then retrieved the terry cloth robe from the floor and tucked her arms through the sleeves and secured it around her snuggly. He pressed the emergency button, turning it off, and the doors opened immediately, revealing the hall back to his apartment. She loosely held the robe closed and then squeaked in surprise as he lifted her into his arms and carried her back in.

"I can walk," she grumbled, albeit too drowsily as she tucked her head against his shoulder. She was getting used to being carried. It was nice. On the ranch, she was always carrying things, doing it herself, working until her muscles were sore and aching. Now she was being carried, and she felt so safe and secure.

"Sure you can. After an orgasm like that, darling, you'd fall right on your face, and I like your pert little nose far too much to see it bruised." His rumbling chuckle vibrated through her and she closed her eyes for a moment before the rush of memory of why she'd ran from him flooded back.

"Wes…are you going to tell me about what I saw tonight? I have to know what you were doing. It looked bad. To be honest, it scared me to death."

"I know." He sighed. "Enough that you ran from me in the middle of the night, naked as the day you were born. I won't forget that anytime soon." This time he was the one muttering. "But I promise, I'll explain everything. I'll even show you." They both remained silent all the way back to his bedroom, and despite the anxious flutter in her stomach, she couldn't get up the nerve to ask him again. Instead, she ran through every bad scenario in her head that could account for what she'd seen, but she couldn't think of any reason for what she'd seen him do.

When Wes set her down in the pile of rumpled sheets and blankets, he caught her chin in his head and tilted her head back.

"Move from this spot, and I'll chase you down again, and spank you. That's a promise," he warned. Then he left the room.

Callie regained her breath and pulled the robe close around her shoulders. Adrenaline still pumped through her, but it was wearing off and she would soon crash from exhaustion.

Wes returned to the bedroom, the white tube in his hands.

He eased down on the edge of the bed and removed the cap on the tube. Then he slid the contents free.

It wasn't drugs or money or anything else she might have expected. It was a painting. He spread it out carefully, as though he were handling a priceless artifact. She leaned forward to get a better look at the painting. A woman in deep concentration was standing and overlooking a cliff side.

"This is one of Goya's paintings. A rare one."

"It's so small." She touched the edge of the canvas, careful not to touch the oil. It was little bigger than a sheet of paper.

"The Mortons are friends of mine who live in Weston. I helped them procure this painting a few years ago through Sotheby's. A month ago it was stolen from their house during a party. It was the night before I flew out to see you and give you your party invitation. When you and I met Dimitri for dinner, I asked him to check into his contacts on the black market to track this painting down."

Callie tensed, shooting her gaze up to his. "Black market?"

Wes carefully rolled the Goya back up and put it into the tube. "Yes. The man you saw tonight, that was the man who bought the Goya from the thief. Dimitri and I were encouraging him to talk." He showed his bruised knuckles to her with a roguish grin. "I got a bit carried away. You shouldn't have witnessed it." When he brushed a lock of hair back from her face, she didn't flinch. She'd misjudged him and she hated how the guilt seemed to choke her.

"Are you still afraid of me?" His blue eyes seared her, plunging deep into her and shining a light in the hidden depths of his soul.

"I'm not scared anymore. I feel awful, Wes. I jumped to crazy conclusions." It sounded so childish to have been afraid of him, but she hoped he'd understand what she meant.

"I did haul a man out of a trunk and rough him up." He raised one eyebrow and then pounced on her before she could defend herself. Wes tugged her legs apart and she fell flat on her back, gasping when he pressed a kiss to her belly, then trailed his mouth down to her mound. She yelped in surprise at his sudden sensual assault, writhing beneath him as he licked her again and again, the torturous pleasure zinging straight to her clit. She clawed at the bedding, arching her back. He was relentless in his seduction, feathering light kisses on her mons, then flicking his tongue inside her until she was mindless and begging.

Then he lifted her legs up, throwing her ankles over his shoulders as he positioned himself at her entrance. He thrust inside her and they shared a soft moan as he filled her again. She was sensitive, so needing, that each inch he surged deeper felt too good and too much. Her head thrashed as he took his time entering her, slow and deep, his eyes locked on hers. That cobalt blue captivating her.

"That's it, baby," he growled. "I'm all bad and you've only had a taste of me."

Chapter 16

Wes's eyes were like the waters of Atlantis. They captivated and bewitched her with impossible dreams. Everything he did was for her, every smile, every kiss, every gift. All for her. A woman could fall in love with a man who courted with such perfection.

He was perfection. Each circle of his hips, striking that deep secret spot inside her that blacked out everything except the feel of him. His dark red hair was a crimson halo about his face. It was as if the goddess Diana gave him the ability to hunt down and seduce any woman into his bed.

Wes Thorne was a sex god. A god who at that moment was focused solely on her pleasure. He doubled his speed and the sensation of him fully merged with her was all it took to send her careening off the edge into bliss. The man could fuck her into unconsciousness.

Her lashes fluttered closed, and she lay limp and exhausted, letting him disentangle their bodies. He left the bed and she heard the faint sound of water running. She curled up in a ball on her side and started to drift to sleep. He joined her, pulling her body flush to his and he kissed her mouth, a slow, soft kiss with a surprising bit of tenderness. A lover exploring his love's mouth and tasting her like fine wine, sampling, drinking in. It was soft and full of emotions that were subtle and made her heart sing.

This was how she'd envisioned her first kiss. That kiss in the tack room had been an inferno. Was that how all great loves started? With a lightning strike upon the body followed by the tender warmth of a kiss tamed by sweetness and true affection? Both were perfect and exciting in their own ways and just as fulfilling. She'd never dreamed she'd ever experience both, and certainly not with a man like Wes.

"Darling, I'm sorry I scared you." He nuzzled her cheek and hugged her closer.

Callie felt so close to him that she surrendered to her desires and wrapped her arms about him, further connecting them. Invisible threads seemed to bind her to him and him to her. What was happening between them was past casual. They were beyond the point of no return.

Callie refused to let that scare her, not tonight. Everything felt right, felt wonderful. How often had she been this lucky? Never.

"Wes, in the morning I want you to tell me more about the art thief," she said when their mouths finally broke apart.

"Not tonight?" he said and chuckled, stroking a fingertip down the top of her nose.

"Just kiss me, damn it." She giggled and curled her fingers around his neck, urging his head back down to hers.

"As you wish," he murmured and stole her breath with a kiss of fire and passion. A kiss to defy all others in its perfection.

* * *

A black wraith crept along the property line of the Thorne estate on Long Island. Security guards and closed-circuit cameras had been played like fiddles to the shadow's tune.

"While the cat's away, the mice will play." The shadow laughed silently as it picked the lock on the balcony door of a first-floor bedroom.

Thorne was not in residence and his servants were lax in their duties, which was just the way the Illusionist liked it. Padding like a large jungle cat down the steps, he searched room by room.

No Monet, no Renoir…none of the most expensive pieces the shadow sought. He could steal the less expensive pieces, but that would spoil the plan, and Thorne would realize his defenses had been breached. Better to wait and find a means of getting access to wherever the real pieces were hidden away. He could wait. Thorne wouldn't get any warning. There would be no fun if he got wise and moved the priceless art off the island.

The Morton job had been perfectly executed right down to allowing a cracked frame to give away the fact that he'd stolen the painting. Just as he planned. Wes would rush to the rescue and offer one of his paintings as bait. It was only a matter of time. No one would ever suspect the shadow was so close to Wes. No one.

He passed in front of a handsome painting depicting the view of the Seine River. The colors used were lovely, the composition almost perfect. The artist's name was an unfamiliar scrawl of black paint in one corner. Why did Thorne have so many pieces created by unknown artists? It made little sense. Art only held value if the creator had value. A person who painted just like Monet was irrelevant if he wasn't actually Monet. So why did Thorne stock his collection with such items? The man touched the tip of the frame with one gloved fingertip, nudging a painting into a level-hanging position.

His eye for precision was what made him a master. He could

replicate any painting to perfection and, therefore, if the opportunity arose, steal original works and replace them with his forgeries, undetected. He'd stolen half a dozen pieces from the rich fat cats on Long Island already, and only the Mortons had realized their Goya was missing. That had sold quite well to one of his connections in France. A Brit named Giennes owned a back-door gallery close to Montmartre and buyers always paid well to get whatever Giennes had hanging on his walls. A Goya was easier to sell but less satisfying financially. A Monet or Renoir though…those would line his pockets for the next decade.

The Illusionist flashed a cocky little smile up at the security camera that had been wirelessly hacked. It was playing a looped feed of an empty hall while he took a look around. For all intents and purposes, he was a ghost, flitting unseen through Thorne's estate.

Uncatchable.

Unstoppable.

An illusion.

* * *

The sketchpad and its thick paper were crisp and white. A blank slate for Callie to create her dreams. Tucked up in a large armchair by Wes's bed, she sifted through the set of newly sharpened graphite pencils and picked a medium HB. Then she concentrated on her subject, a sexy, deliciously naked man in the king bed. Wes was asleep, sprawled out on his stomach, his face turned in her direction, one arm dangling off the bed. The blankets pooled at his lower back and exposed one muscled leg. He had the most amusing tendency to kick free of the sheets during the night so it was a good thing his large body was warm and it kept her from freezing.

She used the HB pencil to lightly sketch the bed frame, then the contours of his body. Tracing the way his arms bulged in places and the slopes of his shoulders down to his trim waist, she used shadows and patches of white to give his body definition and life. Using one of her lighter H pencils, she sketched the relaxed line of his brows, straight nose, strong chin, and the fall of his thick lashes against his cheeks. She sketched the slight upward curve of his lips and the sleepy look of satisfaction on his face.

What did a man like Wes Thorne dream about? Art? Women? Treasures from the basement of the Louvre?

The morning sun was that singular shade of buttery warm yellow as it slowly progressed across the room and climbed the bed frame to illuminate Wes. The sun, like a lover, caressed his lightly tanned skin, touching upon the tousled crown of red hair, revealing honey and bronze streaks amid the dark ruby strands. She'd had her hands buried in that hair, tugging on it as he'd tortured her with ecstasy last night. Nibbling her bottom lip, she sighed, a dreamy sense of contentment filling her to overflowing. Why couldn't every day be like this? Days full of art, adventure, and lovemaking.

Callie continued to sketch the rumpled bed scene, smiling more than once. She'd have to hide this one from him. He could never see it. He'd make fun of her. A few feet away, the lovebirds sat in their cage, puffing up their feathers and blinking sleepily. The female tucked her head close to her body, settling onto the bar closest to Callie. Her green-and-peach feathers were warm and seemed to glow with a faint glint on their tips as though they'd been dipped in liquid sunlight. The male lovebird jumped from the nest down to his mate and chirped excitedly. Callie shot a glance at Wes, but he didn't stir.

After finishing her sketch of Wes, she signed her initials and dated it before turning to a fresh page. The birds were difficult to capture. They weren't perfectly still but hopped and chattered. The

Parisian birds outside landed on the balcony and spoke in their own avian tongue, conversing with the lovebirds. Callie captured rough sketches of the birds, hasty sketches of their wings, their faces, their bright eyes and affectionate poses.

She would never be able to live somewhere without a lot of birds, whether in the wild or as pets. The sounds and the need to hear them were deep in her blood, just like her love of the mountains and the feel of herself on horseback. After only a handful of days in Paris, she knew she would have to come back here again someday. The city seemed to pulse with a quiet sort of creative energy, like the beating of an invisible heart made by the collective passions of a thousand artists, living and dead. She was connected to those other souls, joining them in a pursuit of the creation of true art.

As she worked on additional sketches, she contemplated her argument with Wes from the night before. He wanted to pay for her to go to art school. He'd already filled out the application. Callie knew she could get over the way he'd acted on her behalf, at least in this instance, but if he did that too often in other areas of her life, she was going to have problems with it.

Her real concern was the money. It was against everything in her to take a hefty financial handout like payment for art school. She would apply for scholarships of course, but if she couldn't qualify for any and Wes paid her tuition, it would be too much. She'd never be able to repay him. Never. So would he expect her to repay him in other ways? She was already sleeping with him. What else could he want? What else could she give?

Wes's cell phone buzzed on the table beside him. The rattling sound of the electronic device against the wood was loud and jarring. It set her lovebirds into a twittering rage. Wes groaned and fumbled for his phone.

"Not a morning person?" she asked sweetly when he studied the phone screen through one squinting eye and then hit the ignore button.

"And you are?" he asked with a sleepy chuckle as he rolled over onto his back.

"Yep. Farm work makes you a morning person whether you want to be one or not." She set down her light 2H pencil and picked up a dark 2B and shaded a portion of one of her lovebirds on the paper, fluffing the texture to show that the bird was preening its feathers. Pleased with the effect, she had the sudden urge to show it to Wes. She'd always kept her art fairly private. Her father and Fenn never really had time to look at it.

She flipped the pad in her arms and showed him the sketch. "What do you think?"

He sat up and immediately waved a hand, indicating she should come closer.

"Come over here." He scooted over so she could perch on the bed beside him as she handed him the pad. He took it with such obvious reverence, she started to blush. His keen gaze swept over the birds, not missing any detail. A wild flutter of nerves exploded in her stomach and her breath came a little shorter.

"You managed to capture them in motion. I always admire artists who can sketch a pose from memory when the subject is in constant motion." His gaze drifted to the birds in the cage. The two lovebirds were nestled together, watching him and Callie.

"You little rascals," he called out, then stroked Callie's back. "They stop moving the instant you're done. I bet they believe they're training you in the difficult act of capturing their likenesses."

Callie giggled, delighted that Wes was teasing her.

"I doubt that's their secret goal." She reached for her pad, but Wes moved it out of her reach.

"I'm not done looking." He flipped back a page before she could stop him, staring at the image she'd drawn of him in bed. Callie held her breath for so long her lungs burned. Would he be angry? Would he not like it? She didn't think she could bear either reaction.

"Callie." His voice was soft and low, his hand on her back stilled.

She shifted restlessly, worry and tension knotted painfully in her stomach.

"I'm sorry. I shouldn't have—"

"No," he said and set the pad down before he leaned in and kissed her soundly.

Dazed by the quick, passionate, and all too thorough kiss, she blinked up at him.

"You're not mad?"

"Mad? Of course not. I'm honored you drew me. You're incredibly talented." He traced her lips with his thumbs.

"No. I'm not. You don't have to flatter me, Wes. I'm already in your bed."

Dark clouds obscured the pure blue cobalt of his eyes.

"What we do in bed has nothing to do with this." He lifted the pad up. "If you were an old man with a bald head and completely unattractive, I would still tell you the truth about your art. You are talented. Luckily for me, you're a beautiful young woman who I happily seduced into my bed." He captured her chin. "Never for a moment think that I want to encourage your art simply to bed you. I wouldn't have cared about that if sex was the only thing I wanted. Do you understand?" His question seemed so earnest, as though he really did wish for her to understand.

"I think so," she replied. He liked her, and her art. He wasn't using her art as a way to sleep with her. He genuinely thought she had talent, and he genuinely desired her. That was a good thing.

When she smiled at him, the tension coiling in his body seemed to release.

"Good. Now why don't you join me in bed. I'm still a little tired." He set her pad safely out of the way and tugged her down beside him. She expected him to initiate sex and was surprised when he seemed content merely to hold her.

"This is nice," she whispered, nuzzling his throat and closing her eyes. She'd always wanted to have this sort of intimacy with a man, but hadn't, not until now. And the feel of her body with his nestled together like lovebirds made her chest nearly burst with a soft, sleepy warmth, like a glass of bourbon by a warm winter's fire.

Wes rubbed her back with one hand and rested his cheek on the crown of her hair.

"At the risk of ruining this pleasant moment," he said, laughing softly, "I want to talk to you about art school."

She stiffened but his arms tightened around her, keeping her from retreating.

"Historically," he continued, "artists with talent were financially supported by patrons. All I am proposing is that you allow me to be your patron."

Callie breathed in his warm masculine scent and relaxed. When he phrased his argument like that, it made it impossible to argue without sounding silly.

When she raised her head and faced him, she gazed at his mouth firmed into a solid line. She brushed a finger over his pursed lips, smiling a little.

"Patron, huh? I could agree to that."

His lips curved into a grin beneath her finger.

"Good. Then you don't have any objections to spending the next week receiving some private lessons at the Louvre?"

"Private lessons at the Louvre?" Callie blinked, staring at him. "Is that even possible? Who would give me these lessons?"

"Quite a few talented artists I know would happily volunteer." He seemed entirely serious.

"Okay...assuming you can get people to teach me, then I suppose I can't refuse."

"No." Wes touched the tip of his nose to hers. "You can't refuse, not any longer." The blue of his eyes was scorching and she knew he was right. Whatever he gave her, out of bed, in bed, she couldn't say no...and she didn't want to.

"Darling, when your eyes burn me like that it makes me hard." He lifted her onto his lap so she could straddle him. Then he fisted his hands in her hair and devoured her mouth. "Fuck, I want you wet for me."

"I am." She rubbed herself against the press of his erection through the thin layer of sheets that separated them, delighting at how comfortable she was becoming with her own sensuality.

"Not wet enough." He suddenly flipped her flat on her back and she squealed, laughing as he wrestled her out of her shirt and panties, despite her halfhearted attempts to escape him. When she was naked and flush beneath his lean muscled body, she finally stilled in her struggles and surrendered to him.

She gasped when he thrust into her without warning, but she was more than ready. He pumped his hips, wild and hard, gazing down at her as he claimed her. He kept her wrists pinned on either side of her head. No matter how she fought him, it was no use and that excited her all the more. The idea that he'd keep her beneath him, helpless, only to bring them both pleasure was what made the difference in her arousal. Being restrained by him only ever ended in pleasure, so much pleasure she would scream again and again if he didn't muffle her mouth with his. Wes groaned and sank deeper into her, the pressure of him filling her too much to bear for her to keep silent, either.

"Wes," she moaned, arching her back, her breasts aching for his attention.

With a little knowing smile, he swiveled his hips, striking a spot deep inside her. "Unable to get free, baby," he said and laughed darkly. "Makes you that much wetter for me, doesn't it?"

"Yes, God, yes." He'd reduced her to one-word expressions. The connection between them only deepened as he filled every part of her.

"Can you take more? Harder?" Wes growled out the questions, his focus on her face as if memorizing her reactions to his every move.

She nodded, out of breath. She could. She wanted more, harder. He slowed his pace but deepened his penetrations and at the same time making them harder. Throwing her head back, she arched with each jerk of his hips. Wes dropped his head toward her, nipping her chin, her throat, teasing her lips in ghostly kisses, making her desperate. Her fingers curled into fists as she panted and whimpered. Without mercy, he claimed her so completely, their union consuming her, burning her up until she had nothing left to give and all she could do was embrace the fine line of pain and pleasure.

"Let me see your eyes," he demanded, his voice rough.

She met his eyes and what she saw unmade her, like a star in the distant reaches of the galaxy, bursting in a brilliant flash of light. She saw desire and need beyond the physical in his face and that exploded her from the inside out. He needed her in a way no one ever had and it filled her with excitement and hope. She exploded with pleasure and his body shook above her as he shouted and then settled heavily upon her. Struggling to breathe, she sucked in breath after breath, hoping to ease the wild beating of her heart and the thundering blood in her ears.

Wes, panting and grinning, rolled their still-fused bodies so she lay on top. He pulled the blankets up around them and then lifted one of her hands to his lips. He kissed the tips of her fingers, then her knuckles, and then the inside of her palm. Wes's eyes were soft, and the tiny lines around his eyes showed as he smiled at her. Her heart squeezed and she took one of his hands and kissed the inside of his palm. His hands were an object of fascination to her. The fingers were strong, yet long and elegant. Hands that held her, hands that stroked and teased her until she forgot her name.

"Are you happy you came here with me?" he asked, his expression gravely serious.

It was hard to explain what she felt. Up until now, she'd ridden down one path, a path clear and open. But when Fenn had gotten engaged, she'd felt as skittish as a filly during a storm, and she'd run off her path and into the dark wooden glen of a place she'd never been. This new world was exciting but frightening at times. There were just as many shadows as there were pools of light cutting through the canopy of trees. Being with Wes didn't feel like a path to take, but rather like a glen, a place to simply exist. And that left her puzzled and unsure of herself.

"I'm happy," she finally said. It was the truth. Facing one's fears was sometimes the only way to fight for what mattered. Being happy mattered and if she had to get scared every now and then, she'd do it.

"What about you?" she asked him.

His fathomless eyes were tinged with sorrow. "I've never pursued happiness, but being with you…happiness comes so easily." His admission was full of confusion, as though he couldn't understand how that was possible.

"Everyone deserves to be happy," she noted.

Wes frowned. "Perhaps, but many don't look in the right places."

"Like your parents?" she prodded carefully. "You never talk about them, and from what Hayden says, they're not exactly easy to be around."

The bitter laugh that escaped him startled her. "Easy to be around? Callie, darling, you have no idea. Never were two people born who are so absorbed with themselves and their money and power. No one else matters to them. They manipulate everyone and demand everyone to fit within their rules. Hayden and I have been disowned to some degree for our failure to conform to their expectations."

"What did they expect of you?" She folded her arms on his chest and rested her chin on them.

His hands slid beneath the sheets to hold her hips, possessively gripping her. His cock still inside her made her body tingle with new awareness.

"Father wanted a Wall Street man. Mother wanted me to marry one of her friend's daughters to open social doors. Neither of those even remotely appealed to me."

Callie could sense that it made him feel trapped. His body tensed and his mouth formed a firm line.

"I'm sorry." She kissed his chest right above his heart. They made a strange pair. The man who had everything was trapped. She who had nothing and no way to really live was also in a way trapped. Yet they'd made Paris an escape for both of them. The only question was, how long could they both run?

Chapter 17

She's one of the most talented I've ever seen," Antoine Pichot said as he joined Wes in the observation room. They were in the bottom basement of the Louvre, in a private viewing room that had a window with a one-way mirror. For the last week Wes had brought Callie here and let her spend half the morning learning a new medium or style, with a new artist every day. Then he'd take her out to see the city in the afternoon and then home to bed, which happened to be his favorite part of the day.

The routine had been pleasant and oddly fulfilling. He couldn't imagine wanting anything more from his life in the past week than to be with Callie. While she took her lessons, he'd spent his time on commissions and at lunch he'd come to pick her up and take a few minutes to admire her work without her knowing.

"She's mastered watercolor, oil, acrylic, graphite, charcoal." Antoine ticked off the mediums on one hand. Antoine was one of the few painters who practiced old-style portraits with oil. Wes had made only one call and sent pictures of Callie's sketches before Antoine had agreed to coach her.

His beautiful Callie stole his complete focus. Perched on a stool before a large easel, she had her golden hair pulled back at the nape of her neck. An over-large white button-up shirt, one of his old ones, covered in splatters and smears of paint, hung around her full, luscious figure. She looked adorable and fuckable.

"I knew she would be brilliant." Wes smiled.

Antoine, a few years older than Wes, had expressed an interest in Callie—damned French men and their insatiable appetites. Then again he couldn't judge when it came to sexual hunger, but seeing Antoine's appreciative gaze sweep over Callie's body made him forcibly control his jealousy and his natural possessiveness when it came to his woman.

"Who is she? Where is she from?" Antoine braced his hands on the windowsill.

"Just a girl from a small town in Colorado. A true innocent." Wes checked his watch and then he and Antoine left the hidden room to join Callie.

"Wes!" She beamed at him. "I've almost got this imitation work down." She pointed proudly at a Degas ballerina she'd painted. It was perfect. He peered closely at the original piece next to hers, then back at hers. Brushstroke for brushstroke it was perfect. He couldn't tell them apart.

Antoine grinned. "She's a master. You want to know why?"

Wes nodded. He couldn't believe she'd come so far so fast.

"Most artists have egos. They refuse to mimic someone else's style. They always leave some little stylistic trait that gives them away under close scrutiny. Ms. Taylor doesn't do that."

A little chuckle escaped Callie as she set her brushes and palette down. "I think I'm supposed to take that as a compliment."

"You should," Antoine said, flashing her a winning smile that set Wes's teeth on edge.

"Hungry?" Wes said, forcing himself to swallow the rising tide of jealousy.

"Yeah." Callie kissed Antoine on the cheek before she left to see to the artwork and clean up her work station.

After she and Wes had said their good-byes to Antoine, they exited the Louvre's private artwork rooms. They were halfway out of the Louvre when his cell phone buzzed. Callie stopped walking when he did as he answered.

"Thorne here."

"Mr. Thorne, this is Agent Kostova from the FBI. The Mortons called to let me know the Goya had turned up on their doorstep via a private courier service this morning. They said it had a note from you explaining that you'd come across it in Paris. We're glad to see it returned."

"Good." Relief swept through Wes. He had trusted the courier service, but it was good to hear the Goya was officially back in its owners' protective hands. He hadn't wanted to let the painting out of his sight, but he'd had to in order to return it.

"Mr. Thorne, the reason I'm calling is that there has been another theft."

Wes's fingers tightened around his phone. "Another one?"

"Yes, during a party as well. We're keeping our men scarce on the ground to keep the thief feeling comfortable. The Mortons say you're still in Paris. We'd like for you to return to the Weston to give us a hand."

Another theft? He clenched his phone hard enough that the case creaked in his hand. He knew without a doubt who was behind this. The Illusionist.

"And what would you like me to do?" Wes asked Agent Kostova.

Callie moved closer as if sensing his tension, and she curled her fingers around his arm, leaning into him.

"I want you to help us arrange a sting. The last theft occurred at the private residence of Mr. Jaxon Barrington. He says you're friends."

"Jax?"

Jaxon Barrington was the owner of the exclusive BDSM club the Gilded Cuff, in Weston. Emery, Royce, and Wes were among the charter members.

Kostova laughed. "He said you'd be surprised. He was having an exclusive party and one of his smaller pieces went missing. He thought you might want to help him get the thief by using his club as a place to lure the thief. I can relay more details as soon as you return and we can meet in person."

Wes contemplated this. He wanted to stay in Paris with Callie, but this man had to be stopped. Art theft was the one thing he couldn't tolerate, especially when his friends were victims. This was exactly why he had a black room and kept it secret and undetectable. None of his valuable pieces could be found. To risk one of them so openly…it made every muscle in his body tense like coiled springs. But if it meant finding out who this thieving bastard was, he'd do it.

"I'll arrange a flight back tomorrow."

"Thank you, Mr. Thorne. We'll be in touch then." Kostova hung up.

"We're leaving Paris?" Callie's voice was soft but it echoed in the quiet, closed Renaissance gallery.

He glanced around, taking in the gazes of more than one Madonna clutching her infant Jesus to her bosom. Fuck, he didn't want to leave this place. Taking Callie back to Long Island meant she'd see Fenn again, and the very idea of that knotted Wes's stomach. She was finally surrendering to him. He could lose her if he brought her back too soon. One look at that damn cowboy and she'd be broken up inside again. It was the last thing he wanted.

"There's been another burglary of art. The FBI wants me to return and help them with a sting."

"Another one?" Her eyes widened as they started walking again.

"Yes. I'll get the details when we return to the island. I'm sorry, Callie." There was so much more he'd wanted to show her, but he wouldn't have the chance to do so.

She pulled on his arm, stopping him. Then she stood on tiptoe in front of the silent watchers, those Renaissance faces on cracked oil canvases, and she kissed him. Her little mouth was sweet and open, her tongue soft but exploring against his own. There was nothing in that moment he wanted except her. Only her. He'd give *everything* not to end this. A kiss had never felt so good before, so all-consuming that he didn't care to live a breath beyond that kiss.

He was a little foggy-headed when she broke the kiss and gazed up at him with those soulful, ancient eyes.

"You've given me something wonderful, Wes, something I can't ever repay. You've opened my eyes." Her long lashes fanned up as she blinked rapidly, eyes shining.

"Callie—"

She shook her head. "I was dying inside and you've rescued me. Thank you." When she kissed him again, he tasted a hint of salt and felt the wetness of tears upon her cheeks, and it crushed him. He never wanted to be the source of another tear for her, or let anything else make her cry for that matter.

"Name anything and I'll do it for you," he promised. Even if she demanded the moon, he'd get it for her. The need to make her happy filled him with a quiet desperation that he couldn't shake until he could make her smile again.

"We leave tomorrow?"

He nodded.

"Then dinner at home tonight." She grinned and that single smile hit him hard behind the knees. "Dessert in bed, too."

"Absolutely," he vowed. He would make this a night to remember. One he would never forget himself.

* * *

Callie finished her glass of merlot and followed Wes into the living room. The night was a little chilly, so he'd collected the softest blankets and put them on the couch by the TV. A night in with movies. Perfect. When she came fully into the room, she smiled in delighted surprise. Half a dozen candles littered the tables around them, their flames dancing in the breeze from the half-cracked window. Candlelight shimmered off the bottle of expensive cognac that sat on the coffee table along with a small dainty crimson box about the size of her hand. Wes stood by the couch, two glasses of cognac already poured.

"Take a seat." He inclined his head toward the sofa.

"What is all this?"

"The first part of dessert." His playful, devilish grin made her laugh. The sofa looked so cozy, all those blankets and the warmth of the nearby candles. How could a girl resist? Once she was settled on the couch, he joined her, sitting close enough that his body heat enveloped her in a delicious way. He pressed one of the glasses into her hand.

"Have you ever had a 'tasting' experience?"

"Tasting?" She'd never heard of that.

Wes lifted his glass in demonstration. "Tasting is when you sample drinks and food in a particular order and manner to show a contrast or an enhancement of flavors." He leaned forward and drew a fingertip down her nose. The touch made her tingle in secret places. "Our olfactory senses sometimes adjust too quickly to tastes and smells so we miss subtle, yet rich flavors. Tasting brings these flavors out." He stroked her lips. "It's about the aroma and the taste."

Callie watched him, transfixed, her body tingling with every little touch and scorching look he shot her way.

"So how does it work?" she asked.

"Raise your glass, take one sip, let the cognac coat your tongue, and then swallow it."

He waited until the rim of her glass touched her lips, and then they took a sip at the same time. The powerful taste of the cognac hit her a second later. The thick sweet taste was heavy on her tongue. Wes's throat worked as he swallowed and she couldn't help her fascination with the sight of him. Everything he did fascinated her, drew her in, made her hungry to be in bed with him and never leave. How could he have such a potent power over her like that?

"Your eyes are the same color as the cognac," he mused, as though hypnotized by her. "Makes a man realize how thirsty he is." He leaned down, his mouth inches from hers. His focus on her sent her stomach in dizzying spirals. It was impossible to ignore the feminine awareness of him. Her body came to life whenever he looked at her like that. She almost screamed in frustration when he pulled away without kissing her.

"Don't worry, darling. There will be *hours* of that tonight." His words wrapped a smoky haze of hunger around her for dark, delicious things. Her womb clenched in anticipation, but not being kissed woke her up enough from the daze to scowl.

"How many times does a girl have to ask to be kissed?" she demanded huskily, hoping he'd give in and kiss the hell out of her. It was what she wanted, what she needed.

Wes's wolfish grin created a little shiver inside her. "Patience, little tiger."

"Tiger?" She laughed, almost giddy, and took a hasty gulp of the cognac.

"Don't rush it." He *tsk*ed and lifted the small box from the table.

"What's that?" She reached for it, but he caught her wrist, holding it captive for a long second before he let it go with a kiss on her inner wrist.

"You are so impatient tonight."

Her smile faded. How could she explain the urgency to be with him? She couldn't confess her fear that tomorrow all of this wonderful passion would end. Her nose tingled as tears pricked her eyes.

His eyes narrowed and he cupped the nape of her neck. "What's wrong? Your eyes darkened," he noted.

She blinked away the sting of barely there tears. "What's in the box?" she asked, trying to be patient. The last week with him had been so incredible and wonderful that she was afraid to leave, to go back. For the first time in her life, she felt like she was the center of someone's universe and that someone was the center of hers, an unbroken circle rather than a one-way street. A feeling like that was hard to give up. *Wes* was hard to give up.

"I had these specially made." He lifted the lid and revealed a trio of chocolates. "There's a specialty chocolatier in Tulsa, Oklahoma, one of the best in the nation. They make unique flavors." He used a small fork to cut one of the chocolates in half and then to scrape out the insides. "The best way to taste chocolate is to sample the filling, let it linger on your tongue." He lifted the fork and she parted her lips, letting him feed her the delicious confection. It was rich, with a hint of orange, something that tasted like citrus, and warm milk chocolate. She moaned softly.

He cut into the next chocolate. "That is how you taste to me.

Fresh like spring with a hint of citrus." Scooting an inch closer, he held out his fork with the next chocolate's filling ready for her mouth. "Try this next."

She opened her mouth for the next bite. It was rich and dark, a hint of salt. "What's in that one?"

"Sea salt and the purest dark chocolate you can find on earth." One corner of his mouth tipped up in a devil-may-care grin.

Callie licked her lips. It tasted like him. A chocolate that tasted like her lover. *Her lover*. The word created a coiling of dark heat inside her.

When he cut into the third chocolate, her mouth was already watering. Wes's focus was intense. "This is what they call an oatmeal cookie." He fed her the last bit. Her eyes widened.

It actually tasted like an oatmeal cookie. "Now, drink your cognac, and when you're done swallowing, close your mouth and breathe slowly out through your nose."

She sipped the cognac, then shut her mouth and breathed out. New tastes exploded on her tongue. It was a thing of magic, the rush of maple syrup, brown sugar, nutmeg, cinnamon, each taste clear and distinct.

"Close your eyes and tell me what you see," he said. His hands were on her hips, their knees touching.

She did as he instructed. "I see…" She let the flavors speak to her. "A cabin at the base of a mountain. The leaves are red and gold. A warm fire in a stone fireplace, vermillion flames." She sighed, sinking into the heavenly vision. He was there with her in this fantasy cabin, his body and hers merging again and again, fingers entwined, whispers of pleasure and little gasps of ecstasy. No distance, only togetherness.

His lips touched hers, a real kiss, not part of her fantasy. She opened her mouth, seeking his tongue. He growled against her lips and suddenly she was being lifted up, her legs curling around his hips as he carried her to the floor and placed her on the thick carpet.

"Sorry, can't wait…" He gripped her shirt at the neck and ripped it clear down the middle. Buttons popped off, vanishing into the thick carpet as he bared her skin. She wore a sensible white cotton bra and he groaned, his hands shaking.

"Like a goddamn fantasy every time I see you." He slid between her thighs and feathered kisses on the swells of her breasts. Then he bit on the top of her bra with his teeth, tugging it down to allow her breasts to spill free. He licked and sucked on one nipple until it was erect and she whimpered. Then he turned to her other breast. Callie gripped his head, tugging the strands of his hair, urging him on. The cognac created a delicious buzz and she wanted nothing more than to make love to Wes all night and clear through tomorrow.

"Please, Wes. I *need* you," she begged. The ache between her thighs was sharp and demanding. Only he could erase the wild need in her to be taken, possessed. Fully and completely.

Wes sat back on his heels, tore his trousers open, and unzipped her jeans, tugging them down to her knees. After that, he removed her boots and socks. Then he laid her back on the carpet and covered her with his body, caging her in. He rolled his hips against hers, teasing her as he kissed her. Using one hand, he guided his shaft to her entrance. The sudden quick thrust up made her throw her head back and cry out. Wes nuzzled her neck and nipped the sensitive space between her neck and shoulder as he rode her.

Thrusting deep and hard, then slow and soft, he tortured her, teased her, until she was coming apart at the seams. She was dimly aware that she was begging him for more, harder. Her nails raked his back and her nipples rubbed his smooth chest, the sensation too much for her.

"Who do you belong to?" he demanded in a guttural growl against her ear.

She panted, unable to speak.

"Who?" He squeezed her bottom, lifting her up off the carpet a few inches to slap it. She yelped and groaned a moment later at the wave of wet heat inside her. Another slap to her ass, the slight bite making her frantic for more.

"Answer me."

"You!" She gasped. "God, only you, Wes. Please, fuck me," she pleaded.

That was all it took. He pounded into her, rolling his hips in different, unpredictable angles. When he bit down on her neck, gently but firmly, she blew apart. Blood roared in her ears and she struggled to remember who she was, where she was. Precious air filled her lungs and she sucked it in greedily, resting her head on the floor. The beautiful ceiling moldings spun above her as she welcomed the dizziness that accompanied the aftershocks of her pleasure. Wes's body weight was welcome over hers, his hot skin feeling good against her own.

Everywhere they touched burned in all the right ways. He lowered his head, kissing her, then rested his forehead against hers. She had never felt so close to anyone as she did in that moment. She didn't need words, nor did he. When he pulled away, she had only a few seconds to miss him before he was lifting her up and carrying her completely naked through the hall and toward the stairs. A lazy smile curled her lips. She liked it when he went all caveman and carried her about. It was nice to feel small and delicate in his arms. He didn't go to his room, but hers.

"Why here?" she asked as he set her down on her back on the bed.

He stood there, fully bare and suddenly erect again. "I want to have you on every flat surface, starting with this one." He crawled on the bed to lean over her limp, sated body.

"Okay, I won't argue with that." She arched beneath him, letting her breasts brush his chest.

"Did you know"—he chuckled between his kisses—"that this bed belonged to a French princess?"

Callie arched a brow. "Really? Which one?"

His hand slid down her body, parting her legs wider before he positioned himself and thrust home. They moved together.

"Does it matter?" he gritted out as she clenched her inner walls around him. "Fuck, that feels good."

"You're making that up," she said, laughing, and she then groaned as he twisted his hips and hit a new spot inside her that made her see stars. "Oh, right there," she begged, digging her nails into his shoulders.

He growled low in triumph and started driving into her again, hitting that spot over and over. She tugged his head to hers, hungry for his kiss, needing them to be connected in as many ways as possible. He pinned her hands down, lacing his fingers through hers. One more connection, one more way that they fused their bodies into one being. The thought, the sheer swell of joy at thinking about that was all it took to send Callie over the edge. The way he shuddered above her showed her that he was coming apart at exactly the same time. Chests pressed together, his heartbeat fast and wild against hers, beating at the same pace, as though one heart, not two. Wes continued to kiss her, even though they were both starved for air and shaking like newborn foals.

"Is it always like this?" she asked between lingering kisses, smiling inside and out as her entire body quaked with the aftershocks of pleasure.

The startled look in his eyes confused her. "No. It's not," he said quietly, his gaze searing her.

"Was it good for you, too?" She nibbled her lip worriedly. Even though she was sore and too many sensations still pulsed through her, she felt him twitch inside her.

"It was better," he said this with such sincerity and seriousness that she blushed. "I mean that. No one else has ever felt this good." He rocked his hips and her body vibrated like a string on a violin, a single note of pleasure resonating deep inside her. She didn't want to go back to Long Island. There was so much to lose if she went home.

"Don't worry about tomorrow." He squeezed her hands in his. "I'm not letting you go."

His words should have frightened her but they had the opposite effect. It was exactly what she needed to hear. They didn't love each other, but what they had was good, too good to give up.

"Good." She smiled at him, and then kissed him, letting her lips linger against his. There were a few more precious hours before they had to leave paradise.

Chapter 18

W es, have a seat," Jaxon Barrington said as he gestured for Wes to sit. They were in the executive office of the Gilded Cuff. Jaxon, the owner, Wes's long-time friend and the most recent victim of the Illusionist, was pacing. Another man, thin, muscled, in a navy blue suit, leaned back against the desk, arms folded. FBI, if Wes had to guess.

"Agent Kostova said we should meet here." Jaxon raked a hand through his dark hair and finally forced himself to sit down behind his desk, but his grim expression remained.

Kostova pushed away from the desk and held out a hand to Wes, who took it. Kostova looked young, probably late twenties.

"Mr. Thorne, glad to meet you. We definitely need your help. Whoever is behind the thefts is starting to piss me off. His ego is unrivaled. Mr. Barrington was explaining to me how secure his club is and yet one of his paintings was removed during a party. I want to catch this guy. The bureau wants to catch him. I suspect he'll take his trade somewhere else soon and we might lose our chance to find him." Kostova glanced at Jaxon, then at Wes.

"Barrington said your collection is the only thing expensive enough to draw this man's attention. Is it true you have a Monet and a Renoir?"

After Wes answered with a curt nod, the agent continued. "What we'd like to do is host a party here at the club and have you put the Monet and Renoir on display. He won't be able to resist the challenge. We'll have to find a way to spread the word, of course, and he'll need time to see the piece and replicate it."

Wes twisted the silver signet ring with his family's crest on it, debating silently. Was he willing to risk one of his priceless works to catch the arrogant bastard who was stealing from his friends? Sure, an auction house could put a dollar price on his collection, but for him, those paintings weren't measured by money. They brought him peace and looking at them filled him with a quiet, irresistible joy. Nothing else had made him feel like that, nothing except Callie.

He thought of the Mortons, and how happy and relieved they'd been when he'd shipped the Goya home. Daniel had called him to thank him, and the warmth in his chest at getting that call helped. Whoever was stealing the art was risking the art itself and that was enough for him to step in.

"We can use the Monet. I won't risk both," Wes said after a long moment of consideration. If he used one to lure the thief, he wouldn't risk the other. "I can have it brought to the club whenever you want."

"Good." Agent Kostova nodded. "Now to get the word out, I'd suggest you attend a couple of social functions, go to those types of parties where the thief has been showing up at. Drop hints about the Monet in casual conversation. Since we're positive he's a local man, word should get to him quickly."

"Wes, the annual polo match is scheduled for tomorrow, and Emery has a gala tonight. We could go to the gala and if we still need to spread the word, we could play polo," Jaxon suggested. "You know how quickly word spreads beneath the tents."

"Very well." He rose and shook Jaxon and Agent Kostova's hands. It was time to go home.

He'd hated to leave Callie all alone at the house. After leaving Paris yesterday she'd been quiet. He didn't like it. He wanted her laughing, smiling, playful. Not guarded and secretive. She'd been too tired from the flight last night and he'd left her to sleep while he'd busied himself with calls and plans. Hours had passed quickly in his black room as he caught up on business. He hadn't gone back to his own room, knowing he'd want to go to Callie and make love to her. It had been better to exile himself to the king-size bed in the black room for the night.

After he left Jaxon's club, he drove home to seek out his little masterpiece. He'd had an art room prepared for her and wanted to show it to her. When he pulled into the main drive of his house, there were several cars out front. With a scowl, he recognized two of them. He left his Hennessey out front and strode inside the large door. His trusted butler, Bradley, seemed too relieved to see him.

"Mr. Thorne, we have a situation," Bradley murmured delicately as he kept up with Wes's long strides.

"What sort of trouble?"

A frown deepened on his butler's face. "Your parents are in the Winter Garden with your sister and her fiancé. Ms. Taylor is there as well." Bradley's fists clenched.

"And what is the trouble?" He was almost afraid to ask. He'd never seen his butler's feathers ruffled before.

"Well…your parents have been behaving a little indelicately. They brought Ms. Vanderholt with them. It seems they have allowed Ms. Taylor to believe that…" Bradley glanced away nervously and then looked back. "That you and Ms. Vanderholt are engaged."

"What?" The comment stopped him cold. His parents were bold enough to try a move like that? Corrine knew very well he wouldn't be seeing her again in any capacity. Well, that was going to be dealt with immediately.

He stormed into the Winter Garden and despite the fact that it was actually a hothouse for flowers, the room was full of a winter chill. Callie was standing off to one corner, biting her bottom lip as Hayden and Fenn watched Corrine and his parents with narrowed eyes.

"Yes, this will have to be remodeled of course," his mother was saying to Corrine.

"I agree." Corrine's cold gaze swept across the room, then hit him. "Wes!" She rose and started toward him. He didn't even look her way. His legs ate up the ground as he brushed right past her to reach Callie.

Her lips parted in surprise as he grasped her face in his hands and kissed her. He did it thoroughly, letting himself go as he embraced her fully. It didn't matter how many people were here watching him. Callie belonged to him and he didn't want Corrine thinking she could slither her way in between them. Callie's hands dug into his arms as her tongue shyly touched his, and only when she fully melted for him did he let her go. She wavered on her feet and he turned around to face everyone.

"Mother, what are you doing here?" He didn't bother with the pretense of civilities. There was no point. On more than one occasion, he'd made it quite clear that his parents weren't welcome at his house.

"Now, wait a minute." His father was on his feet in an instant, blustering, his face ruddy with his displeasure.

"Father, I'm in no mood for you today. Take mother, Corrine, and yourself and get out of my house." His tone was tipped with icy venom, but he held Callie against him, absorbing the faint trembling of her body.

Corrine's eyes, so deadly wild, were the opposite of her cool, collected face.

"Mrs. Thorne, we should leave," Corrine said in a soothing, silky tone, but her eyes were murderous, not at him but at Callie.

I warned you, Corrine. He wanted to say it out loud, but now was not the time. That woman would be leaving. She knew where he stood now, or more accurately who he stood with. The room remained as silent as a tomb while his parents and Corrine left. Only when the door to the Winter Garden had closed behind him did he let out a slow breath.

"What the hell, Wes?" Fenn growled as he and Hayden walked over to him. Callie tried to extricate herself from his hold, but he dug his fingers into her hips, keeping her close.

"I'm sorry you witnessed that," Wes replied. "They knew they weren't welcome."

What bothered him was why they had come, and why with Corrine? He knew his mother thought Corrine was a perfect wife for him, but he'd rather die than shackle himself to her. How he had ever been attracted to her in the first place was a mystery.

"I'm just glad they're gone," Callie said. "I didn't like them. No offense, Wes," she said quietly, as though disturbed she'd spoken openly against his family. Her eyes were dark with concern and her brows knit with faint worry lines. He cupped her face and leaned down to kiss away her tears.

"No one likes them," he assured her. "Least of all me."

She relaxed at his reassurance and without a word tucked herself into his arms. He held her a long moment, enjoying the simple connection of their embrace.

When they broke apart he realized their audience was watching with no small amount of curiosity and astonishment. Hayden looked amused, her eyes twinkling and her mouth twisting into a secretive smile. Fenn, however, looked…well…Wes saw the tempest brewing in him. Fenn had asked him at the engagement party to watch out for Callie, to take care of her. He'd done that and more.

"I want a word with you," Fenn said. "Outside." He jerked his head toward the door.

"Very well." Wes patted Callie's back before he released her and then followed his friend as they departed the room. The second they were outside, Fenn curled his hands into Wes's collar and slammed him into the wall so hard the breath was knocked from his lungs.

"What the hell are you doing?" Fenn demanded, crashing him against the wall again.

Wes's head collided with the wood-paneled walls and little black dots spotted his vision for a few seconds.

"What are you talking about?" He shoved at Fenn, but the other man had the advantage as he used his body to pin Wes to the wall.

"Callie. Are you sleeping with her?"

Wes's own anger boiled to the surface. "If I am, it's not your concern."

"Like hell it isn't!" Fenn spat.

Wes used Fenn's distraction to punch the cowboy square in the jaw. He grunted and stumbled back, clutching his mouth.

"You broke her heart, Fenn," Wes reminded him quietly. "I picked up the pieces and am protecting what's mine."

"She isn't yours!" Fenn clenched his fists and licked his bleeding lip.

"She came to me and wanted me. I wanted her. We've been happy together." He never thought he'd say that about any relationship with a woman, but he *was* happy.

"How long?" Fenn began to pace the hall, like a caged tiger.

"How long until you lose interest and drop her? She's not enough for you."

Not enough? A ruby veil seemed to descend in front of his eyes and he tackled the other man. They crashed to the ground, knocking a vase off a nearby end table. The cacophony of noises that followed barely intruded on Wes and Fenn as they kicked and punched. Clothes ripped and blood splattered.

A booming voice cut through the din and hands grabbed him, throwing him off Fenn. "Enough!"

It took a few seconds for Wes to find himself again through the rage. Royce stood there, feet braced apart, his body an obstacle between them. In the garden doorway, Hayden and Callie stood there, gaping.

"What the fuck, guys?" Royce snapped as he glowered between Wes and Fenn.

Wes got to his feet, but stumbled and threw out a hand to catch himself against the wall as his vision cartwheeled. One too many blows to the head, he guessed. Dragging the back of his hand across his mouth, it came away streaked with blood from a split lip. If he hadn't been so mad, he might have laughed. He and Fenn were fighting again, now about Callie.

Hayden helped Fenn to his feet but he growled at her when she tried to drag him away.

"We're not done with this discussion, Thorne," Fenn warned.

"You're done." Royce faced him, but his tone was low and cold. It was a dangerous side of Royce, one rarely seen. "Whatever is between you, deal with it. We've been through too much to put up with any more of this bullshit." Royce fixed them both with a stare before he gestured to Fenn. "I need to talk to you."

Wes didn't linger. He needed to cool off and get away from Fenn. He stumbled more as he walked down the hall, picking one of the nearest rooms where he'd have a bit of privacy. The room he chose was a rarely used study, one that had become a graveyard for objects Royce had bought as gifts over the years from his exotic travels for digs.

An old leather sofa against one wall called his name. With a groan he eased onto the couch and wiped at his split lip again. The bitter taste of his blood made him wince, more from the acrid taste than the pain. The fight had been a mistake—he'd be the first to admit it—if necessary, but every time Fenn was around, Callie got hurt and Wes just couldn't take it. She was his woman, and if he had to pummel his friend to protect her, then he'd do it. The study door creaked open and Callie peered around the edge.

"Can I come in?" She raised a small medical box.

Wes almost grinned. How could she always find first-aid kits?

"Please." He waved her inside and placed a hand on the couch beside him. Her eyes flicked to the spot and a delicate blush bloomed on her cheeks. His breath caught as he panicked, thinking she'd deny the little command he'd issued. She'd become so perfectly submissive in bed, freeing herself with him, but he hadn't pushed her.

When she took that first step toward him, he exhaled in relief. Closing the study doors, she joined him on the couch and then unclasped the latch on the first-aid kit. A little grin suddenly curved her lips.

"What?" he asked, smiling back at her. It was so easy to smile around her.

Callie raised her head and she smiled even brighter. "It's like when we first met. You and Fenn were knocking each other's lights out and I had to patch you up."

Wes laughed, holding her gaze. "Only this time, we fought over you, not my sister."

"You were fighting over me?" The genuine surprise on her face was irritating.

"Callie, you are worth fighting for." If only she'd understand he meant more than a bout of fisticuffs.

"You have to stop saying things like that," she murmured as she raised an antiseptic cloth to his bleeding lip.

It stung like a lash of a whip to skin. He knew that particular sensation only too well because he'd had to spend a year learning how to operate a whip before the other doms had deemed him safe to use it on a sub. There had been plenty of mishaps and the pain he'd given himself was a sharp reminder that a dom must know his instruments in and out before he could use them on a sub.

"Don't be such a baby," she chastised and reached for his knuckles, which were covered in scrapes and red marks that would likely turn purple in a few hours.

"Me? A baby? Why you little—" He stole the first-aid kit from her lap and dropped it to the ground and then tackled her back on the soft leather couch, pinning her wrists on either side of her head. Her wheat-gold hair gleamed in tantalizing waves around her face.

"I missed you last night," she whispered, a shy glimmer in her eyes as she ducked her head, seeming too embarrassed to admit this and face him at the same time.

Her comment pleased him. She missed him. There had been plenty of women in his life who had uttered such words, but none had meant them, none but Callie. Deception and mind games were not in her nature, and he loved that about her. As much as he liked games, he preferred them in bed. Being with Callie, however, was freeing. He could be himself, a person he'd spent so many years trying to protect from his parents and others who would try to use him.

"I'm sorry, darling. I had something important to work on.

Tonight I promise I'll come to bed." He grinned and dipped his head and stole a kiss. Despite his best intentions to keep it brief, Callie melted beneath him, raising her hips and using her knees to grip his waist and draw him down on top of her. He groaned against her lips, bucking his pelvis on instinct, needing to be inside her, but clothes were in the way.

"Hang on," he growled and leaped up from the couch and hastily stalked over to the study door to lock it before returning to the couch.

He lifted her up and sat back down on the couch, her body straddling his. With a swift rip, he tore open her flannel button-up shirt, baring her bra-clad breasts. She jolted when he tugged the cups down and sealed one mouth over her nipple and sucked on the tip. Callie threaded her hands through his hair and tugged on the strands, the slight edge of pain on his scalp raising his explosive lust that much more. As he continued to play with her breasts, his hands unbuttoned her jeans, but he knew he'd have to rearrange them if he wanted to get inside her.

"Damn, Callie. I'm sorry, I can't wait." His need was too strong.

He shifted her off his lap, pushed her stomach first against the back cushion of the couch, then unzipped his trousers and freed his erection. When he braced his knees on either side of her from behind, she dropped her head forward onto her folded arms. Wes didn't wait. He yanked her jeans down past her thighs and ripped her cotton panties clean off her body. A quick brush of his fingers between her slit came back wet. She was ready for him. More than ready. He reached around, holding her still by the waist while his other hand guided his shaft to her entrance. When he thrust deep and hard, she hissed and threw her head back.

"Wes!" she said and whimpered, but the way she shoved her hips back told him it was from pleasure not pain.

"Fuck, that's good," he growled against her neck as he gave into his need to possess her.

Have to mark her, show her and the world she's mine. Only mine. He sank his teeth into the back of her neck in a gentle but firm love bite, leaving a mark on her skin as he sucked on the tender flesh. Soon he would put a collar on her neck, a permanent mark of his ownership, a chain to bind her to him. What a surprise it would be! He would have laughed but the little sounds of pleasure she was making drove him over the edge and he pinned her to the couch and fucked her hard until she came screaming. He only had a second to clamp a hand over her mouth to muffle the delicious noise of her pleasure before his body went rigid, his balls drawing tight as he shot deep inside her. The world blew out around him, his vision almost blacking out as he shouted and then relaxed, his chest pressing against her back.

"Holy hell," Callie said and breathed out after he'd removed his hand. She dropped her chin onto the top of the couch, and he could see her face in profile as she tried to catch her breath. A kittenish smile, drowsy, sexy, and adorable, curved her lips and he twitched inside her. Her inner muscles clamped around it in response and little waves of aftershocks rippled through her and into him.

"Hell? More like heaven," Wes corrected as he curled his arms around her, embracing her from behind, and rolled his hips, coaxing a little moan and a husky laugh from her.

"You're gonna kill me if you keep this up." Her sensual tone said she wouldn't mind dying that way and he swelled with pride.

There had never been such a strong sense of pleasure with any other woman before. When he was with Callie, it was like his past encounters were shades, mere flickering shadows or echoes of this wild, explosive, all-consuming need to be with Callie and no other.

What he couldn't understand was why? Why her? Not that he was complaining, but he always knew his own motives, and this obsession with Callie was puzzling. Wanting her was dangerous on more than one front.

Her emotions, so easily turned to love, could deepen and he'd run the risk of hurting her when this affair ended. Not that he wanted it to end, but all things ended at some point, didn't they? Lust didn't last forever. His parents' desire for each other hadn't. That dark thought brought him up short. His parents had been passionate with each other, but things had turned south quickly. How did that old poem go? Nothing gold can stay?

He hugged Callie tight for a moment longer, hating the fact that someday they'd go their separate ways and some other man would touch her, kiss her, take her to all the places he wouldn't get the chance to.

"Come on," he urged gently as he withdrew from her. He pulled a handkerchief from his trousers and cleaned them up before they straightened their clothes.

"You destroyed my underwear?" The ripped cotton panties dangled from one of her elegant fingertips and a mocking scowl twitched into a quick smile.

"A hazard of being sexy, darling. None of your panties are safe." He raised his hands into a mock monster pose as though he had claws and he gnashed his teeth together in an audible bite.

Callie burst out laughing, just as he desired. He didn't know where the urge to be silly came from, but she brought out a soft, funny side to him he hadn't thought he possessed. She stuffed the ripped underwear into her jeans pocket and then threw her arms around his neck, covering his cheek with little kisses. He gripped her waist, surprised and delighted at the display of affection from her. Normally he wasn't interested in the small, tender touches or kisses after sex, but something about Callie made her irresistible. He couldn't get enough.

"Are you up for a polo match tomorrow morning?"

Callie nodded. "Yes, definitely." Her eyes glittered with a new life he hadn't seen since he'd first met her in Colorado. The woman loved horses, belonged on the back of one. He'd almost forgotten that when they'd been in Paris. She must miss her ranch and her horse. He knew she'd been homesick but she had seemed to recover. That didn't mean she didn't still miss riding. It didn't sit well with him that she might be unhappy. He'd have to change that first thing tomorrow.

"Good, polo it is. I'll take you riding tomorrow before the match." He patted her bottom and she snuggled into him.

"Sounds perfect." She sighed and the sound flooded him with a soft cottony warmth starting in his chest.

"I have a surprise for you, too. Something for tonight."

"Oh?" she replied in a low husky tone that made him grin.

"Yes, and you can't seduce any answers out of me," he vowed.

She wrinkled her nose. "Me seduce? That's *your* area of expertise."

He gave her a harrumph to show her just how wrong she was. He was beginning to figure out that she had some power of manipulation over him, but he'd better hide that or he'd be in trouble. He'd be the butt of every joke if it ever got out that a sweet little innocent woman like Callie had him wrapped around her little finger. It was his own fault. Staying distant from her emotionally was nearly impossible, especially when he spent half the time buried in her hot little body.

"What are you thinking about?" She'd fixed her clothes and was watching him with avid interest. For one so young, who had seen so little of life, she had an uncanny way of reading him and people in general. His grandfather would call her an old soul. Wes didn't believe in things like that, but damn it, her soft warm hazel green eyes did seem to reveal a century of understanding.

"Polo, I most certainly am thinking about polo." He winked at her, but she flashed a look of barely concealed disappointment. She'd admitted to thinking about him. He knew that, but he didn't want to admit she had such an effect on him. As the dom, he had to stay in control of himself and this relationship.

"Oh." That one syllable was so broken and soft that he cursed inwardly.

"Why don't you go find Bradley. He has a present for you."

The sadness was quickly buried beneath a smile and a shrug. "Why would Bradley give me a present?"

Wes caught her by the waist and held her still so he could swat her delectable ass in a light punishment for her sarcasm.

"You know damn well it's from me. Now off you go. It should keep you busy for a few hours. I have some work to do but will find you later."

Callie nibbled her lip, watching him a moment longer. "Okay." She turned on her heel and headed for the door. She had to unlock it, but she didn't look at him again as she left. How could she make him feel so villainous? He'd never cared before about a woman's feelings outside of a submissive's needs during a moment of passion and the recovery period afterward. This was new territory for him.

Wes waited, counting the seconds before he straightened his own clothes and checked his hair in the mirror. Callie's hands had mussed it up. Raking his fingers through his hair to put it back in place, he nodded at his reflection in the little hanging mirror by the door before he exited the room. The unstoppable force that was his little sister stood right in front of him, hands on her hips, eyes spitting sparks.

"You're really sleeping with her?" Hayden accused in a low feminine growl of warning.

"It's none of your business." He straightened his tie and smoothed it down the front of his coat as he buttoned it closed.

"Oh, that's rich. You're all for beating Fenn to a pulp for touching me, but when he returns the favor, suddenly it's none of our business?"

"Hayden, she's an adult and she can make her own choices." He tried to nudge her aside but she slapped a hand on his chest, halting him.

"Sure she is. I'll give you that, but she's not a sub for you to play spank and fuck with. She's a real person with a heart that was recently broken. She's not a toy."

Wes's irritation flared to real anger. He removed his sister's hand and responded as coldly as he felt in that moment.

"I know she's not a toy, but she doesn't seem to mind the 'spank and fuck' as you call it, and as long as she wants me and that, she has me." This time he didn't bother to be gentle as he forcibly moved Hayden from his path. That didn't stop her from delivering a parting shot at him, however.

"She's too innocent for you, Wes. You'd be better off with that bitch Corrine if you plan on acting like such an asshole."

He didn't deign to reply to such a remark, no matter how true it might be. Callie was innocent, and far too good for a man like him. But he couldn't stay away from her. He couldn't let her go.

Chapter 19

It was the most amazing thing she'd ever done. One painting on an 18" x 24" canvas in just eight hours. After Callie had located Mr. Bradley, he'd taken her to a bedroom that had been turned into an art studio. It was obvious Wes had planned the room with her in mind. It was full of blank canvases on easels, fresh palettes, and an assortment of brushes and paints. Callie had chosen acrylics for this piece because it needed fewer layers of colors.

The oversized dress shirt she'd gotten accustomed to wearing was covered in smatters of paint. The rich scent that was uniquely Wes's clung to the fabric and deepened her longing for him. It was a growing sense inside her that she hadn't felt for anyone else, not even Fenn. The need to see Wes, to be near him, to belong to him was overpowering. Even when she was lost in her painting, she still felt that pull toward him.

But it's not love. I won't let it be love. It was a promise she had to keep. She had to stay safe, keep her heart out of the picture.

A sigh broke from her lips and she studied the canvas, her finished work. *The Lantern's Glow* she called it. The entire background was black, fading only to a dark forest green around the center where she'd painted a lantern. Inside the lantern a scene of four little boys around a campfire glowed like a memory trapped in a fortune-teller's crystal ball. She'd turned the lantern into the object that showed the past.

The circular green-yellow light pooled outward in a luminous glow around the lantern and in that glow she'd painted four adult, masculine faces. Wes, Royce, Emery, and Fenn. Each of their somber gazes was turned toward the lantern and the image of the innocent children they'd been. In a way, their faces, half shadowed, were not unlike the boys before the campfire, a reflection within a reflection. Ever since Wes had told her about the lantern-yellow color, she'd had a haunting image in her head. She wanted to show it to Wes, but she was nervous about his reaction. Would he understand that she meant it as a tribute? Not a way to remind him of the pain of his past.

Soft booted steps behind had her spinning around on the stool. "Wes!"

Only it wasn't Wes, but Royce. He wore jeans and a leather motorcycle jacket and black boots. He'd snuck in through the partially open door and was staring straight at her painting, not her.

"That's me," he murmured, his voice low and rough with emotion. "Why did you paint this?" A flash of fire in his eyes warned her she was on dangerous ground.

"I…" She swallowed hard. "It's a gift for Wes. He told me about how you used to go camping."

Royce's intense features softened slightly. "He told you about that?" With slow steps, he reached the painting and studied it. One of his hands raised as though to touch the lantern but he stopped a mere inch from the canvas. His brown eyes were dark, like burnt umber.

"He said you were talented, but this…you've painted our souls."
Royce finally turned his gaze toward her.

"Really?" The idea that she'd touched him that deeply, and that
Wes would have such faith in her talent to tell one of his closest
friends, made her light-headed and excited.

"Yes."

A collection of emotions fluttered through her like a rush of
doves from a tree.

Royce slid his hands back into his pockets and gazed at the painting. This hardened seducer, a dom, a professor, instantly trans-
formed. The boy from the photographs Bradley had collected for
her to study shone through. But it wasn't the innocent child she
glimpsed now. It was a boy ravaged with horror and tragedy. Even
knowing Fenn was alive hadn't erased the monstrous taint of
twenty-five years of believing he'd been murdered. Only time could
ease such a deep wound. It lingered, like shadows late in the fall.

"Do you think Wes will like it?" Callie asked. Her hands
clenched in her lap as she waited with bated breath for Royce's reply.

The man stepped back and shook his head, as though waking
from a dark dream.

"I think he won't like it, but he will see it for what it is, a beautiful
tragedy. A work of genius done by the woman he loves."

"Loves?" Callie barely got the one word out.

The sadness in Royce's eyes faded.

"He beat the shit out of Fenn over you. Wes *doesn't* lose control,
not like that, not unless his heart is involved. He always keeps his
cool, stays distant. But with you, he's broken every one of his rules.
Trust me, I know him better than he knows himself. He loves you."

He loves you. The words settled so deep into her heart that she
knew that hope would grow from those words. If only it were true
that Wes loved her, because in that moment, sitting on her stool,

having painted one of Wes's tragic secrets, she realized she loved him.

No. I can't love him. I swore never to fall for another man again. But she had fallen, so slowly, so softly, she'd never seen it coming. Like rolling down a gentle sloping hill covered in wild flowers. She'd been distracted by the beauty, the scent, the colors, the wonder of the rolling sensation and never realized that she had been falling.

She loved Wes. Not in the way she loved Fenn. The two emotions were worlds apart. How had she ever thought she'd been in love with Fenn? Sure, she loved him, but she hadn't been in love. The vast difference was startling. Wes had been so right about love, even though he'd never been in love himself. He said she'd learn the difference someday. It had just come sooner than she'd expected.

Royce chuckled. "You think he isn't in love with you? Fine. How about a little wager, cowgirl?"

She couldn't help but laugh. What was it with these billionaires and their wagers? First Wes, now Royce? "Only if you stop calling me that. What kind of wager?"

"Whether Wes loves you or not." He crossed his arms over his chest and leaned back against the wall close to her.

"You want to bet on something like that?" She hopped off the stool and turned away from Royce to quickly clean her brushes in a water-filled jar.

"Honey, I'm the king of bets. So, are you in?"

When she turned back around, she noticed he was eyeing her ass.

"Ahem," she said, coughing pointedly. "Do you want Wes to punch you, too?"

He continued to appraise her body with open appreciation for a moment longer than he should have before his eyes met hers.

"So, honey, what will it be?"

Callie raised a brow, a habit she was inheriting from Wes, but she grinned, too.

"What sort of wager? Because I think I'll win." There was no way Wes was in love with her, and while that made her smile a little bitter, she would enjoy putting this playboy professor in his place.

"Your painting." He inclined his head toward *The Lantern's Glow*. "If Wes isn't in love with you, I get the painting. If he is, you give the painting to Wes."

"But I thought you thought he loved me. Wouldn't you want a bet that favors your opinion if you want the painting?"

Royce, the devil, only laughed. "That's the point of bets. They're more fun when you have something to lose."

"Okay. Deal then." She held out a hand and Royce, rather than shake it, raised it to his lips. He winked at her, and then headed for the door. He paused and turned back, tossing something at her.

She caught the small metallic object in her hand. It was a silver key.

"What's this?"

"Belongs to Wes's black room. The door is behind the Seine River painting in the hall by the kitchen. You should check it out, when he's not around, of course." Royce grinned and waved before he left.

Callie stared at the key, then curled her fingers around it. A black room? What the heck was that? Knowing that Royce had suggested she check the room out gave her pause. He was trouble, and from what she'd learned of him from Wes's conversations, Royce was a prankster. It wouldn't be too far of a stretch for her to believe he'd set her up to get caught by Wes, and she'd likely end up with a sore, well-spanked ass.

Still…her curiosity was piqued and she slipped the key into her jeans pocket. Then she covered the canvas of *The Lantern's Glow* and lifted it off the easel. She wanted this to be a surprise, so she slid it under the bed. After she'd carefully secured the painting, she cleaned up her supplies and was in the process of pocketing her phone when Wes came in through the door of the studio.

"There you are." He strode over to her and caught her by the waist, dragging her into his embrace. After a ruthless, almost bruising kiss that left her lips swollen and her head foggy from weak-kneed desire she realized he was speaking to her.

"We have to attend a gala tonight. Emery is hosting, so we'll be among friends."

"A gala?" That was a fancy party…Damn, she wasn't ready for something like that. She barely had made it through the small dinner party a few weeks ago.

"Yes, a fund-raiser for the local university, the one you are applying to for art school. Royce invited the head of their art school to meet you." Wes's smug grin vanished after a moment. "What's the matter?"

Callie sucked in a pained breath. Her stomach pitched straight south to her feet.

"Head of the art school? Oh my God, I'm not ready, Wes. I can't—"

He gripped her face in his palms, his eyes mesmerizing her until she calmed down.

"You're going to be fine, darling." His hypnotic, silky tone did actually soothe her, but a permanent fleet of butterflies seemed to be living in her stomach.

"Wes, I have no clue what to do or say if he talks to me." She tried to take a deep breath but her chest was tight.

He rubbed his thumbs across her cheek bones and she leaned into him. In that single week she'd been with him in Paris, they'd gone from practically strangers to the most intimate of lovers. Not in all of her wildest dreams would she have thought she'd be craving his touch and needing to hear his opinions on things that mattered to her. She was so used to carrying her burdens alone and taking care of herself, her father, and Fenn. Between them and the ranch, it was exhausting and draining. But with Wes, it was so different. She learned to lean on him for support, for advice, for emotional and physical comfort...and that wasn't including the sex.

There weren't enough words in the world to describe Wes's love-making. He rocked her to the core each time he kissed her. Each time he even looked at her she could feel that build up of passion in her lower body. She didn't want to think about what would happen when this thing between them ended. Her heart couldn't take it.

"Talk about art. You know art. You've studied under some of the best masters in the last week. It will impress him." He held onto her a minute longer and when he let her go he was smiling that bad-boy grin of his.

"Now, remember that red gown with the train and the bow on the back? I want you to wear that tonight. I'll be back in two hours with some jewelry."

"Wes, I don't like it when you buy me expensive jewelry." She crossed her arms over her chest. In the last week, she'd gotten braver at putting her foot down on his insatiable purchasing habits. It didn't seem to stop him, but she liked putting up a fight, even if it was a token one.

"I know." He smirked. "But this isn't just jewelry. It's your collar." He wasn't smiling anymore. A dark intensity had replaced his charming grin. Was he teasing? She couldn't tell.

"My collar?" She swallowed hard as he raised one hand to her throat. He didn't grip her by the neck, but rather he ran the backs of his fingers over the sensitive hollow of her throat.

"You are mine, Callie. I warned you of that a month ago." Wes's silky words sank into her slowly, almost as seductive as the delicate caress against her skin.

"Wes, I don't just want to belong to someone. I want someone to belong to me." She met his stare, hoping he'd understand. If he wanted to own her, she wanted to own him right back. If he thought this thing between them was one way, he was wrong. Anger sparked underneath her skin.

"You are the submissive. That's how it works. You belong to me." He captured her mouth with his. The kiss was potent, a raw domination of his lips over hers. Their tongues touched and then dueled and she moaned against him. She was mad at him for controlling her at a moment like this. Here she was melting with his kiss, when she should have been smacking him. A little voice in the back of her head told her she should shut up and enjoy this and fight him later.

When their lips parted a long while later, Callie leaned into him and Wes curled his arms around her, holding her close. One of his hands stroked her back and when she tucked her head under his chin it fit perfectly. She was starting to love that he was so much taller than her. It had been intimidating at first, but now she had to admit she liked it when he seemed to completely encompass her in his embrace.

"I'll be back in a little while," he murmured in her ear and dropped his arms.

Callie's shoulders slumped as he walked away. As an independent young woman she'd never felt this way before. The bone-deep ache each time Wes left her even for a short while seemed to be soul crushing. If only he loved her, the sense of loss wouldn't seem so deep. But he didn't love her. Had never loved any woman. How was she supposed to deal with that? It was too late for her. She was already in love despite every vow she'd made to herself to not fall again.

She wrung her hands and tried to stop the burn of tears in her eyes.

I'm doomed.

* * *

Wes checked his tie in the mirror. The dark blue strip of silk cut a nice contrast to his white dress shirt. He was used to suits, and tonight's gala would be a standard event for him, but he knew Callie was on edge. The small dinner party had frightened her. A two-hundred-person party would likely send her running for the hills. But tonight was important. He and Jaxon would start inviting Cuff members to the club. That was the one thing Wes had pieced together when he'd met with Jaxon and Agent Kostova. The theft from Barrington's house during an exclusive club-member-only event meant it had to be a club member who was behind the theft.

He picked up the red velvet box from his bed and flipped it open. The collar he'd had designed for Callie was a thing of beauty. It was a delicate chain made of diamond-studded links, with a flat silver pendant engraved with his family's crest. The design matched his signet ring and his favorite pair of cuff links, which was a letter "T" with a thorny vine curling around the letter. A collaring ceremony was normally a very involved affair at the Gilded Cuff, but he knew Callie wasn't ready for that type of intensity. He would have to settle for a simple ceremony at the club sometime in the future. His hand trembled a brief instant as he closed the case and headed for the connecting door to Callie's room. He had never collared someone before and an unfamiliar nervousness created a tightness in his chest.

When he reached the door to her room, he slid it open quietly enough to not alert her. The evening sun's warm colors lit the bed and made the room glow. But it was Callie, seated at the vanity table, pulling up her hair in long curls with silver diamond-studded pins who caught his breath.

For a few seconds, she didn't see him, and he had the exquisite pleasure of gazing upon her. The red evening gown hugged her body at the waist and flared out at the hips. A large red bow at her lower back acted like a modern style of a bustle, giving the gown a pleasant shape before it flowed out at the legs in wide pleats for a full-bodied skirt. The heart-shaped bodice cupped her luscious breasts, putting them on perfect display. She was so beautiful it hurt, but for the first time, it wasn't a woman's body but the look on her face that held him enraptured. Her lips curved in a small smile.

"Are you going to tell me why we're really going to this gala tonight?"

She turned in her chair to face him, the halo of gold-blonde hair shining in the light from her window. He didn't want to worry her with the details, but he didn't want to lie, either.

"It's the thief again. I've figured out he's a member of the Gilded Cuff. That's the BDSM club here in Weston that I belong to. I plan to lure him out. I need to spread the word at this party tonight and see if I can convince him my Monet is worth stealing."

"Your Monet?" Callie slid out of her chair, lifting up her skirts as she approached him.

"Yes. It's one of the most valuable pieces of art still within the thief's immediate striking range. We need to catch him before he moves his operation off Long Island. The Monet is the only way to do it. It's big enough to draw him out. At least that's what the FBI is hoping. Now, for something more important." He held up the velvet box and she blinked at him, then at it, confused.

"What's that?"

"Your collar." He set the box down on the desk in the corner and opened it, removing the chain necklace.

"Oh no. You're not distracting me with that. Finish telling me about the thief. How do you plan to catch him?"

"Turn around," he ordered.

Callie had the audacity to huff like a stubborn pony and tap her foot.

"Callie, I don't care if you're wearing a seven-thousand-dollar dress. I'll wrinkle it if you need your ass reddened."

"You jerk," she muttered and gave him her back. She lifted her hair and he carefully laid the chain necklace against her collarbone and fastened the clasp. Her breathing hitched as he nuzzled her ear from behind. The rapid rise and fall of her breasts against the tight bodice was an arresting sight.

"Do you like it?" he asked, steering her over to the full-body mirror.

Her fingers brushed the chain links and then touched the pendant.

"It's lovely. What does it mean to have a collar?" Her eyes were large and she gazed at him through the reflection of the mirror.

His heart skipped a few beats. How could he put it into words? All submissives who were in the lifestyle knew what it meant. It was practically the equivalent of an engagement ring.

"A collar is a sign of possession, a sign of commitment. By collaring you, it's a more permanent way of staking my claim. No other dominant may touch you without my permission, no other can claim you."

"Do you belong to me in the same way?" Her lovely eyes lit with a warm fire, but they reflected with a responding challenge. It made his blood burn.

"Some doms will be with other submissives even if they've collared someone, but that's not the general rule. It's certainly not how I do things. While you're mine, I will be with only you." He knew what she needed him to say, and this was the closest reassurance he could give her.

Her lashes fanned down as she studied the pendant more closely.

"It's your crest," she noted, her voice husky and low. The rich sound went straight to his cock. He wanted to be inside her, to take her to bed, not have her parade around at the gala tonight. But maybe...after...He grinned.

"Of course. I want to make it clear who you belong to, not just that you're taken but that you're mine." He was still smiling.

"What?" she demanded. "It makes me nervous when you smile like that."

"Really? Why?" He raised a brow, his hands resting on her hips now, holding her close.

"I usually end up tied down to your bed, that's why." His little cowgirl wrinkled her nose.

"You don't like it when I tie you down and fuck you?" He purred the words in her ear and relished the way her lashes fluttered closed and a little sigh escaped her lips.

"You're trying to distract me, Wes. Don't. I want to know what you're planning to do about the thief. I didn't press you when we were in Paris, but you owe me an explanation."

She was right. He didn't want to admit it but she was.

"I am going to put my Monet on display at the club. Jaxon Barrington, the owner, will host another party. We've got a week to give the thief time to forge the painting that he'll attempt to replace the original with."

"You're not taking the real one to the club, are you? That's too risky."

"We have to," he said.

"Not if I paint a forgery, too." She spun in his arms and curled her hands around his neck. "Think about it. You can take the forgery to the club and he won't see the difference."

Wes was shocked he hadn't thought of that first. Callie was exceptional at that. The question was whether the thief would fall for it.

"Do you think you could create a forgery in a few days? We'd need to put it in the club soon."

Smiling, Callie nodded. "Yes, I can. I'll start first thing tomorrow." She nearly bounced like an excited puppy and pressed a quick kiss to his lips.

"You ready for tonight?" he asked.

Like a soldier ready for a battle, she squared her shoulders and nodded curtly.

"Callie, darling, relax. It's a gala, not the inquisition." He crooked one elbow and offered her his arm.

She flashed him a mock scowl. "There had better be champagne. I'm going to need a drink." She took his offered arm and he helped her from the room. He knew she might not like the party, but she would certainly like what he planned to do later. After the gala it would be time to take her to his black room. He wanted no secrets between them, not anymore.

Chapter 20

Hang in there, you're doing great," Hayden whispered into Callie's ear. Callie exhaled in relief and put a hand to her stomach. The little fleet of butterflies were starting to settle down. Finally.

"Little devils," she muttered.

"What's that?" Hayden asked before she took a sip of her champagne.

"Oh, nothing," Callie covered quickly.

Both she and Hayden were clinging to the outskirts of the party. The large gilded ballroom was full of people, all dressed exquisitely. A jazz band played at the back of the ballroom, but no one was dancing. Everyone was mingling and talking. Callie's feet hurt and she was hungry. If she ate more than a few finger sandwiches she'd bust out of the dress, which would not be a good thing.

Across the room, Wes was engaged in conversation with a few men who appeared to be in their thirties, or perhaps forties. He leaned in, whispered something, and one man nodded eagerly and shook Wes's hand. Callie wondered if he was spreading word of the painting. As though he sensed her gaze, he looked in her direction. Those cobalt blue eyes cut deep into her and she felt raw, exposed. How could he do that all the way from across the room? Make her feel naked and vulnerable? Her skin tingled with awareness.

"Callie, you're blushing." Hayden's gentle cautionary tone reminded her she wasn't alone.

"Sorry." She tore her focus away from Wes and tried to look at Hayden. "So how's the wedding planning going? We didn't get a chance to talk yesterday before your parents and that awful woman showed up." Callie grimaced at the mere memory of Wes's parents and Corrine. Three of the most unpleasant people she'd ever met.

"You mean Corrine? Yeah." Hayden brushed a lock of her red hair over her shoulder. "Total bitch. And I don't use that word except in rare circumstances. She's been panting after Wes for years but he doesn't like her."

"He doesn't?" For some stupid reason, she really needed to hear Hayden say Wes didn't like Corrine. She picked up on the fact that Corrine and Wes had a past, but she didn't know how serious it was.

"Corrine wants the Thorne name, and the family money, but not really him. He knows that. I think he let her join the Gilded Cuff as a joke. I hate to say it but he used her."

"Used?" The idea that Wes used Corrine left a bad taste in her mouth.

Hayden snorted. "No one ever said Wes was a saint." Then she sobered. "You can't let him use you either." She set the champagne down on a passing tray and clasped Callie's hand in hers. "I know my brother. He's not the kind of man you settle down with."

A little stab of pain shot through her chest but she forced a smile. "I never thought Fenn would settle down, but you're marrying him." Callie didn't mean for her comment to come out like a barb, but Hayden winced.

"I guess men can surprise us. I know Wes likes you. I just want you to be careful. Promise you won't let him break your heart."

Callie shrugged, trying to hide the rapid fire of emotions that tore through her. She was in love with Wes, and it was up to him not to break her heart. He did own her. The weight of the chain necklace felt permanent, like a branding iron had been pressed to her skin and Wes's ownership was irrevocable. Her heart was his, her soul was his, and her body longed for his. She couldn't just go back to being the woman she was. Too much had changed. The life she'd always longed for, one of beauty and art, was so close to being hers, and at its center was the man who'd made her dreams come true.

His eyes were focused on her again and she grinned at him, unable to stop herself. A faint smile flirted with his lips and he raised his glass of champagne in a silent toast from where he stood. His red hair had been combed back and his elegant suit made him the most attractive man in the room. He was the only man in the room. When he looked at her, everything else faded away.

A masculine voice interrupted her thoughts. "Excuse me."

Blinking, Callie recovered herself and found that Hayden had wandered off while she'd been day dreaming. In her place, an attractive man with raven black hair and light toffee-brown eyes was watching her. His lips curved in an apologetic smile as he held out a hand.

"I didn't mean to startle you. We haven't met. I'm Stephen Vain. I'm a friend of Wes's."

"It's nice to meet you, Mr. Vain. I'm Callie Taylor." She released his hand and her gaze darted around the crowd again. Wes was gone, probably somewhere spreading the painting news.

"I hate these parties," Vain said and chuckled. "I saw you hiding out here in this spot and had to see if I could join you for a few minutes."

Callie laughed, knowing exactly how he felt. It would be nice to have someone to talk to while she hid in an alcove for a little while longer.

"So you and Wes are friends?" she asked.

Vain nodded, leaning one shoulder against the wall, his back to the room as he faced her.

"I've known him since we were ten years old. Did the whole prep school thing together."

"What do you do? If you don't mind me asking." Callie wasn't one for small talk, but Vain was friendly and his smile genuine.

"I work at the Long Island Art Museum as the curator."

"Really?" She couldn't believe it. An actual curator! It would have been a dream job for her.

"I heard from Hayden you are quite the artist. I'd love to see some of your work." He reached into his pocket and pulled out a silver engraved card case and handed her a crisp white business card.

"Thank you." She slipped the card into her small black clutch purse.

"Do you mind if I ask a personal question?" Vain prompted, his eyes darkening with a slight seriousness.

"Uh…sure, I guess." Callie wasn't really sure what someone like him would want to know about her.

"Are you and Wes together?" His gaze dropped to somewhere below her chin and she realized he must be looking at her collar with the clearly visible pendant with Wes's family crest.

"Well, sort of. I don't know," she confessed, her cheeks heating.

Vain took pity on her and smiled. "It's okay. I didn't mean to pry. I'm a member of the Gilded Cuff. I'm sure Wes has mentioned it."

"Yes." She nodded, cleared her throat, and continued. "You're a member?"

"I am. Wes was my sponsor membership. He provided my recommendation when I submitted an application a few years back. It's also why I know the significance of your necklace. It's a collar with his family crest. A claim that runs very deep for a dominant. He must really care about you to collar you."

His words made her blush furiously, but she didn't dare ask him more about how much Wes might care about her.

"So you're a dom like Wes?" She couldn't picture it. Vain had such an easygoing smile, none of the brooding seductiveness that Wes had, which frightened and excited her in all the right ways.

Vain grinned. "I am. But I keep that part of myself hidden. Wes loves to flaunt that side much more than me. I like my secrets to be kept secret." He winked at her. An irresistible giggle escaped her.

"Well, I've bothered you enough for the evening. I wouldn't want to make Wes jealous. Maybe I'll see you at the club soon. I hear Wes is finally going to show off his Monet in a few days. You should ask Wes to bring you."

"I don't think he'd take me to the club." Callie sighed. Wes had been closed-lipped about the Gilded Cuff, but her curiosity was piqued.

"He's a dom. All you have to do is act real sweet and beg him. No dom would be able to resist a lovely woman like you if you begged." Vain snickered. "I'd pay good money to see Wes refuse anything you asked. I bet he couldn't say no."

"Bet?" a new voice said, interrupting. Royce joined them. "Vain, you'd better not be corrupting Wes's sweet little cowgirl." He shook Vain's hand and turned to face Callie. "Wes is looking for you, sweetheart. He's ready to leave."

"Thanks, Royce." Callie said good-bye to Vain and started weaving through the crowd of people. Once she'd gotten out of the ballroom, she went in search of her coat. A butler had taken it to a library near the front door and hung it on a portable rack. The hall was empty and the sounds of the gala were muted now that the doors had closed again. She didn't have too much trouble locating the library. The door had been cracked open, and gold light spilled out in a bright slim shaft through the opening. She caught a glimpse of books just beyond it.

Gripping her skirts in one hand, she nudged the heavy oak door open and slipped inside. The library was lit with several lamps on reading tables, making the room warm and welcoming. Two long metal coat racks were at the back of the library near the stone fireplace. Callie hunted for her coat, searching through the expensive furs and designer-label jackets. She nearly laughed as she remembered her own coat was an expensive black velvet wrap.

Suddenly a hand brushed against her waist and the hiss of an angry breath caressed her ear. The thick cloying scent of brandy was overpowering.

"So you're Thorne's flavor of the month?" a man sneered and jerked her back against his body.

"Let go of me!" Callie dropped her coat and rammed an elbow into the man's stomach on pure instinct.

"Why you little…"

Pain exploded against the back of her head as fingers dug into her hair and jerked. A scream worked its way to her lips, but he clasped a hand around her throat, squeezing that cry for help into a strangled whimper.

"Shut up, we're just gonna have a little talk," the man growled while keeping pressure on her throat hard enough that her vision began to spot. The strong alcoholic fumes suggested he was drunk.

She dug her nails into his arm, trying to claw and scratch but as her lungs burned, panic took over.

"Here's what I want to know. How come Thorne always gets everything I want? My jobs, my school, anything I wanted, he took from me. I should be the premier art expert in North America, not him. It should have been me." His grip squeezed tighter and her hands dropped as all fight in her began to die. She couldn't breathe. She expected her life to flash before her eyes, but all she saw was Wes. A distant roar of rage chased her into the fast approaching blackness.

Callie hit the floor with a thud and air rushed into her. The world came back into focus. She was lying on the library floor in a crumpled heap, throat sharp with pain. Raising herself up on her hands she saw Wes grappling with a man, the one who'd been choking her.

"Stonecypher, you piece of shit!" Wes snarled so viciously that Callie tensed. Cool, calm Wes was gone. In his place was a warrior, a bloodthirsty creature who scared her, but he was fighting for her. Wes threw a punch. The other man flew back, hitting a table and crashing to the ground. He groaned but didn't rise. Wes's predatory gaze stayed on the fallen man a second longer before he looked about the room. When he caught sight of her, he rushed over, his breathing hard as he bent and scooped her up in his arms.

"Oh darling," he murmured. He pressed his forehead to hers, his eyes closing briefly. "Are you all right?"

She managed a nod, then winced at the stab of pain in her throat. "Who was that?" She croaked out.

"Thomas Stonecypher. An old schoolmate. Not a friend." Wes's menacing glare frightened her enough that she trembled in his arms, even though she knew logically it had nothing to do with her. Stonecypher stayed limp on the floor.

"Is he dead?"

"No. I just knocked him out. He's got a thick skull. He'll just have a headache when he wakes up."

"That's a pity," she grumbled. Painful shards dug into her throat and she rubbed it. Wes's necklace had pressed into her skin and left dents in the shape of chain links. He noticed, and with a gentle touch, he removed the necklace and slipped it into his coat pocket before his fingers returned to her neck and massaged gently.

"Let's go home." Wes lifted her up but she pressed against his chest.

"I can walk. I don't want anyone to see you carrying me."

"Very well, but once we're home, it's my rules and I'm going to make sure you're okay." Wes wrapped an arm about her waist and escorted her to the front door. After he handed a valet his card, he helped Callie into her coat.

"He just squeezed my throat a little and yanked my hair." Her hand touched her scalp and the flash of pain made her cringe. *Yikes. That's going to hurt tomorrow.*

When she glanced up at Wes, his face was stony, his lovely blue eyes full of winter fire.

"I'm so sorry." He kissed her lips and rubbed her back with his hands, warming her up.

"It's not your fault. That man's insane."

"Thomas is…well, he's always been the jealous type. We were friends as boys, but he didn't have as keen an eye as I do for art and didn't handle it when I came out on top. Not every man can handle being second. Thomas is one of them."

Callie didn't speak for several long moments. She wanted to change the subject.

"Did you tell everyone about the Monet like you planned?"

Wes sighed. "Yes. All the prominent members know, even Thomas."

"What?" Callie froze. "He's a dom at the club, too?" Something about that bothered her.

"He is. He doesn't come that often. Usually when I'm out of town. We tend to avoid each other."

Wes led her down the steps as the valet pulled up in Wes's Hennessey Venom GT. He slipped the valet a twenty dollar bill and then opened Callie's door for her.

"You don't think he's the art thief, do you?" Callie asked. It made sense. The man who was jealous of Wes was the one who could do the most damage. She buckled herself in and waited for Wes to get inside the car.

"I hadn't considered that," he admitted. "You think he might be?"

Callie shrugged and then ticked off the evidence on her fingers.

"He's an art specialist like you, he has a serious jealous streak, he has all the same connections as you do, and he's a dom at the club. Seems like he should be added to your list of suspects."

"You could be right. I'll call the FBI and have them alerted. They can probably dig into his financials and put a surveillance team on him. If he does go for the Monet, then he'll get caught."

"Good." Callie settled back in her seat and neither of them said a word until they were back at his house.

"Wes, can I see the Monet?" she asked, tugging on his arm.

"I'd be happy to bring it tomorrow morning for you to look at while you work."

"Why not now?" she demanded.

His eyes narrowed speculatively. "It's somewhere safe and I don't want to jeopardize its location." He was shutting her out, closing down. The stab of pain at seeing him build barriers spurred her to action.

She reached her hand into his coat pocket, stealing back her collar and showed it to him.

"You claimed me as yours, Wes. If you 'own' me, then there can't be any secrets, not between us. That's a hard limit for me. I'll walk away. Do you understand? Don't shut me out." Her edgy tone softened as she gripped his hands and squeezed.

"I *want* to belong to you, but secrets would wound me and I know you don't want to hurt me."

His eyes softened and he grasped her hands back, squeezing lightly as he leaned down to kiss her lips. The gentle pressure of his mouth against hers made her feel light enough that a spring breeze could have blown her away like the fluffy white seeds of a dandelion. She'd never understood how women could talk about a man sweeping them off their feet. Yet, now, with Wes's gentle, sensual kiss, and the way it scattered her senses and destroyed her resistance, she knew what it meant to be swept away.

When he drew back from her, he nodded as though to himself.

"If you want no more secrets, then you need to trust me completely. There's a part of me that's dark, Callie. I can't hide that once you've seen it." He studied her face, apparently waiting for her to protest or turn back. But she wouldn't. She loved him, all of him. Even his secrets.

Chapter 21

Very well." He took her by the hand and led her down the hall. They stopped in front of a wall with a lovely painting of the Seine River. He used a small key from his pocket, not connected to his other keys, to unlock a hidden door behind the painting. Callie carefully memorized how he found the key hole and opened the door. As she followed him into the darkness behind the painting, she shivered. This must be what Royce had called the black room.

A sudden bloom of gold light filled the room and illuminated the black, sleek furniture. There was a black leather couch, a dark grenadilla wood desk, and a massive four-poster bed with a black silk comforter. The walls weren't black but painted a storm-cloud gray and decorated with art. Her gaze jumped from piece to piece. A Monet, a Renoir, her sketch of him in bed asleep, the gypsy lovebirds, and her portrait that the artist had drawn of her in Montmartre.

There was nothing particularly shocking about the room, except for the deep sense that everything in this room was only for him, and he wouldn't have to share it with the rest of the world. She understood that need for a private sacred place. This was his private world and he was sharing it with her, a room no one else, save Royce, had seen. In a way he was sharing himself with her.

"I was wondering where the sketches went." She grinned at him. The tension in his body eased and his shoulders lowered.

"This is my black room." He waved a hand around it. "Some of my most treasured possessions are kept here."

"Why call it the black room?" Callie wondered if the name came from the decorations or for some other reason.

"It's not a room listed on any blueprint. You can't find it unless you know exactly where to look. No one else knows about it."

Callie nearly confessed that Royce knew, but she kept her mouth shut. Somehow her gut told her that that wouldn't be a good idea.

She lifted her skirts and walked over to the Monet. She got within a foot of it and the painting drew her in. The cool palette of blues, purples, and greens, not a hint of warm color was unique. The scene depicted the bank of a river, just after dawn when mist crept along the shore and clung to the thick copse of trees on the left side of the bank. The perfect brush strokes and the way the water and mist melded together was true mastery. It was one of the most beautiful things she'd ever seen. *True art*. Her throat worked and her nose burned as she tried not to cry. She never thought something could be so lovely.

The heat of Wes's body warmed her from behind.

"This piece soothes me," he whispered in her ear. His hands peeled her coat from her shoulders. "Ever since Emery and Fenn were kidnapped as children, something inside me has been…broken. No, that's not the right word." He let her coat drop to the floor.

Callie lifted her head and stared at him over her shoulder. He was gazing at her back and then reached for the zipper of her dress.

"Scarred. That is the right word. Everything about my life was shattered by their loss and when Emery was found, he wasn't the same. Some bonds go soul deep. Royce and I...we took his pain into our hearts and his scars became our own."

The zipper slid down to her lower back and she shivered as the cool air kissed the skin he bared as he parted her gown and let it fall to the ground in a pool of crimson at her ankles. She wore no bra and only a pair of red lacy bikini-cut panties. Not her usual style of sensible cottons, but the dress seemed to demand sexiness. Still, being bare, she had to fight the urge to cover her breasts, but she knew better now. Wes liked her body, especially when he was stripping her of expensive clothes.

"You are so lucky not to have scars." He embraced her from behind, wrapping her arms around her waist and nuzzling her neck as he spoke. She tilted her head to the side, giving him more room to lick and nibble his way to her ear. The hard press of his erection against her bottom showed he was as turned on as she was. His hands slid up her stomach and cupped her breasts, kneading them. Wetness pooled between her thighs, and her clit pulsed to life. Callie squirmed against him unable to stop herself. He chuckled and stepped back, dropping his hands.

"You want me, Callie. All of me. Well, you've got me. Even the darkest parts." He moved over to his desk and opened one of the drawers. He pulled out two leather cuffs lined with fur inside and a strip of black cloth. When he came toward her, Callie stared at the items in his hands and then with a slow breath held out her wrists.

"Good girl. From now until we leave this room, I am Master. You will call me that. Do you understand?"

Callie tried to swallow but her throat was dry, so she nodded. He brushed his knuckles over her cheek, an approving gleam in his eyes. She leaned into his touch and he kissed her. The gentle claiming turned rough, the moist softness of his mouth turning wild, as it sent spirals of desire coiling deep into her belly, burning low and hungry.

Then he fastened the cuffs around her wrists. The leather was soft and the fur against her skin even more so. He slid a finger between her wrist and the cuff, testing to make sure it wasn't too tight. Then he lifted the black cloth. She expected him to blindfold her, but instead he parted her lips and stretched the cloth across her mouth and tied it snuggly behind her head. It was an effective gag, but not one that affected her breathing in any way. Just like he promised when they'd talked about this in Paris.

Wes hooked her cuffs together with a small chain and then he hit a small red button on the wall by the foot of the bed and a silver hook lowered from the ceiling. He raised her arms and when her wrists were level with the hook, he secured the chain on the tip of the hook, and then raised the hook one inch. Just enough to keep her from standing on tiptoes to unhook herself.

Helpless. She was completely helpless, in a room that couldn't be found with a man who warned her of his inner darkness. A little panicked whimper escaped her, muffled by the gag.

Wes walked around from behind her and cupped her chin, his eyes fathomless, except for the heady lust gleaming there.

"Breathe, Callie. It's just us. And pleasure, so much pleasure." He leaned in and nuzzled her cheek. She jerked against the cuffs and chains, struggling to get closer to him, but couldn't.

He was in complete control.

Wes tilted her chin back, exposing the column of her throat, and then he licked and nipped a path down to her collarbone, worshipping each inch of flesh he encountered. Each kiss and nip lit a fire in her blood and she prayed he wouldn't stop this sweet torture. Callie dropped her head back. Every part of her was focused on his mouth. She panted against the gag and her back arched.

"So impatient," he said and chuckled as he stepped back, his gaze raking down her naked body so heavily that she could feel invisible hands on her. She huffed against the gag as he walked over to the dresser by the bed. The rasp of wood opening and Wes's broad back before he turned around to face her was all she could see. In his hand was a long leather-wrapped stick about two feet long with several ribbons of leather dangling from one end.

A flogger.

Every muscle in her body tensed and she gasped against the gag. He was going to flog her.

She tried to calm down, but fear and excitement chased each other through her veins until she was dizzy from the rushing blood.

"This is a light flogger," Wes explained as he drew the ribbons along the palm of his left hand, and then with a quick flick of his right hand, he snapped the ribbons down over his left palm. No trace of pain crossed his features. Maybe it didn't hurt…or he had a really high pain tolerance. Callie gulped.

"You remember in Paris, when we talked about this? How I can make you burn and your skin heat up, but without real pain?"

She managed a shaky nod. She did remember.

"We are going to try that." He reached back into the drawer and pulled out a golf-ball-size silver bell. "This is what you will use to give me your safe word while you're gagged. Clench it in your fist like this and the sound is muffled. I will know you are fine. If you need me to stop, open your palm more and shake the bell." He approached her again and settled the bell in her right hand.

"Go ahead, shake it for practice."

The bell jingled as she shook it. There was plenty of wrist flexibility for her to easily shake it. That made her relax. She had part of her control back. He'd respect her if she used that. She trusted her feelings for him and relied on that to feel safe with him.

"Remember, Callie," Wes spoke softly in her ear as he settled one hand on her waist. "Trust me. I will stop if you use the bell, but know that my goal is not to hurt, only to arouse you. Do you trust me?"

She nodded. As insane as it was, she did trust him. The initial wave of panic had faded and she was calm again, as calm as she could be considering that she was chained and strung up for Wes's pleasure. A little thrill rippled through her.

Wes set the flogger down and he plucked the silver cuff links out of his dress shirt and set them on the dresser. Then he removed his expensive suit coat. As he rolled up his shirt sleeves he exposed his muscled forearms. There was something disturbingly beautiful about the way Wes looked half-undressed. His dark red hair fell across his eyes and he brushed it back with one hand before he retrieved the flogger and walked behind her.

"Relax into the blows," he instructed. It was her only warning.

The first blow landed on her upper back. She gasped loudly, but more from shock than pain. She had a few seconds to realize it didn't hurt. More like a slightly heated stroke of leather upon skin. How many times had she smacked a set of leather reins against her thigh while riding? This was exactly the same sensation. No pain. Another strike hit her lower back, then her ass. Her body, once a little chilly, heated up beneath the flogger's caress.

It seemed to go on for hours, the light blows, the delicate slaps of soft leather to bare flesh. She closed her eyes, surrendering to the anticipation and the following release of tension after each strike. She clutched the bell, loosely, no need to shake it. She was safe here in this blackness, with Wes, her dark protector, setting her free with each delicious kiss of leather to hot skin. Her mind slipped into a strange place, half euphoria, half heighted awareness.

The touch of the flogger disappeared, and strong hands clutched her hips. The gag was tugged down from her mouth and suddenly Wes was embracing her. She still hung from the hook, but he'd opened his trousers and freed his cock, clearly intending to make love to her standing. His hands cupped her ass, lifted, and her legs curled around his hips. He cupped the back of her neck and kissed her hard while he positioned himself to enter her with his other hand.

Then he thrust up, hard and fast, but she was so wet that he entered smoothly. Callie cried out at the feel of him filling her, stretching her to the point of almost painful tightness. He could fuck her like this, pulling her down on his shaft as hard and fast as he liked. An orgasm exploded through her. The flogging had primed her so well that she hadn't been aware of how on edge she'd been until he'd pushed into her.

Wes's lips claimed hers as he rocked against her body. Her nipples, so achingly sensitive, scraped against his fine dress shirt and Callie moaned. A second orgasm rolled through her, so brutal it left her shaking and struggling to breathe. She was limp and boneless but Wes kept driving into her, seeking his own pleasure. There was something wild and raw about him, the way he stared into her eyes as he pumped into her over and over. One of his hands held her up by her ass, and the other still held the back of her neck, keeping her still. When he finally came, he shouted, hoarse and guttural.

Her skin burned lightly as he stroked her back, up and down with one hand. He wrapped one arm around her waist and his other hand slid down to caress her bottom. The touch almost hurt, in a good kind of way, like after a hard day's work on the ranch, when every muscle was exhausted, and she collapsed into bed. Two mind-numbing body-exploding orgasms at Wes's hands had that same effect on her.

"How do you feel, darling?" he asked in a faint whisper against her ear. His warm breath made her shiver and the light sheen of sweat from their lovemaking cooled her skin.

"Like I died and went to heaven." Her words were almost slurred with exhaustion and she dropped her head to rest on his shoulder. It was hard to think beyond the fuzzy sense of safety and the warmth of his touch.

"Stay strong enough for a moment longer." He released her body and she sagged in her restraints. The faint whir of chains from the ceiling lasted a few seconds before she slumped. His strong arms caught her, like a ragdoll. She let him unhook her and remove her cuffs. Then he lifted her into the cradle of his arms and carried her over to the king-size bed.

She used the last bit of her energy to crawl beneath the blankets and snuggle into the pillow. Her entire body was sensitive at his touch, but she had no energy left to show it.

"Wes, you won't leave me?" She yawned and tried to open her eyes. When she managed to find him, he was stripping out of his clothes. The sight of his sun-kissed muscular body sent little aftershocks through her. Her inner walls fluttered in an echo of an orgasm as he climbed into bed beside her and curled his body around her. The lights dimmed and she let herself drift away. Her last memory of that night was the ghostly faint murmur of his response.

"God help me, Callie. I can't ever let you go."

* * *

It took only a few minutes for Callie to fall asleep in Wes's arms. He held his breath, counting the seconds before he left the bed and quickly returned with a small lotion bottle. She snuggled right up against him again and he warmed a drop of lotion on his palm before he slipped it beneath the sheets and rubbed it over her back in slow circles. It would help her skin to soften and heal. Not that he'd marked her, a few red lines that would fade in a day. No welts, no pain. That was what she needed, just a hint of darkness, a hint of something close to the edge. And giving it to her had been euphoric. She had given him what no other woman had been able to give him before. Complete trust and surrender.

He'd done much harsher things to other submissives depending on their needs, but nothing had fulfilled him like tonight with Callie. That shadow in his soul, the scars he hid from the world, seemed to burn away whenever he touched her. She was a light, shining clear through him and obliterating that darkness he warned her about. It scared the fucking hell out of him. She had the power to save him. He didn't want someone to have that strength over him, but he couldn't pull back. He was in too deep. Callie belonged to him, and he wouldn't give her up, even if it meant losing himself to her in return.

A soft sigh whispered against his bare chest as her lips parted and she murmured his name. He tightened his hold on her. Was she dreaming about him? The thought made his lips curve into a genuine smile. Dreams were a sacred realm, and if he owned her there, she was his. Forever.

Chapter 22

Callie had lied to Wes. And she hated it. But something in her gut told her it was necessary. He'd given her access to the Monet painting and in the last two days she'd done as he asked and forged the painting. Stroke for stroke. It was perfect. Even she, someone who was constantly doubting her own skill, had to admit it was a remarkable replica. She'd made the piece Wes needed and it would be bait for the art thief. But that wasn't what made her tense with shame.

Her secret wasn't technically a lie, not really. The guilt at concealing something from him was strong. If she dared to share it with Wes, it might jeopardize her own plan to catch the thief. She knew Wes was doing what he thought was best, but Callie had ranch instincts. That sense of when a storm is coming, even if you can't see a cloud for miles. She was convinced the thief was still one step ahead of Wes and the FBI, as sure as she could smell rain on the horizon.

After Thomas Stonecypher's attack on her in the library, Callie was convinced he was the thief. He'd snuck up on her and she wasn't going to let him do that again. If he had some scheme to steal the Monet, she was going to do everything in her power to stop him.

"Callie?" Wes stood in the doorway of the studio, dressed in dark brown riding pants and a navy blue polo shirt. His riding boots gleamed from fresh polish and looked new except for the slight scuffing on the toes. His red hair was swept back carelessly as though he'd combed it with his fingers. The man looked like a walking personification of sin. Why did he have to look so good? She swallowed her guilt and smiled. It was only temporary. She'd be able to tell him everything once all of this was over.

"Is it time?" She glanced at the small delicate wristwatch with a mother-of-pearl face and a brown leather band on her left wrist. Wes had bought it for her in Paris after he'd taken one look at her old digital watch. She'd lost track of time this morning, but painting seemed to have that effect on her. His lips twitched as he walked over to her and reached for her.

"No! I'm covered in paint. You'll ruin your clothes." She protested, but couldn't escape when he captured her in his arms. His soft lips brushed against her cheek and everything inside her warmed up and she wanted to purr like a contented cat. Every time he held her, it was like coming home, taking that first step inside her front door after a long day's hard work.

"I'd much rather ride you than any polo pony today, but it's important to go. Agent Kostova will see that the forgery makes it to the Gilded Cuff tonight."

She stiffened in his arms and raised her head to meet his eyes. "You're not going with them to make sure it's secured there?"

Wes shook his head. "Jax will be there to make sure it's handled, and Stephen Vain said he'd help out. He heard we were featuring the Monet at the upcoming party and as a curator he makes art preservation his priority."

"Mr. Vain?" She remembered him from the gala. Another dom.

"Yes. Good man, Vain. He used to be on the Camden Auction House Board, but Camden underwent a few board changes in the last year and he resigned two months ago. I helped him secure the curator position he has now."

Callie didn't know anything about auction houses or boards. "Why would someone resign from a board position? Isn't that supposed to be a good job to have?"

Wes curled an arm around her waist as they left the art studio and walked back to her room where she could change for the polo match.

"He and the newly elected board chairman, Peter Wells, didn't see eye to eye on pretty much everything. I'd never tell Stephen, but Wells might be the better choice. He's all about trimming costs and maximizing auction efficiency so Camden can sell more pieces a day than it has been doing in the last few years. Several of the current board members came to me and asked me about adding Wells to the board, and I agreed that he would be a good choice." Wes leaned one shoulder against the bedpost while she dug through her clothes in the walk-in closet, trying to figure out what she would wear.

"So when Wells took over, how did he make Vain resign?" Callie plucked a rose-red dress with a flowing skirt that reached the tops of her knees and held it out so Wes could see. His gaze drifted over the dress and he nodded, an approving light in his blue eyes that made her flush.

"From what I heard"—Wes's voice grew louder and she turned to see him walking into the closet with her—"Wells waged a bit of a campaign against Vain. It got nasty. Vain bowed out within just a few months of Wells starting." Wes watched as she unbuttoned the large paint-covered dress shirt and let it drop to the floor. He made no move to help her undress, and she knew why. He loved to watch her strip. She had figured out that in Paris. He would order her in that deep dom voice and she'd peel off one article of clothing at a time, letting his gaze devour her.

When she stripped out of her pants and threw them at him, he caught the jeans, dropped them to the floor, and then lunged for her. Callie shrieked and darted out of the closet, laughing as she evaded Wes. The low, playful growl behind her made her shiver and then gasp as he pinned her to the side of her bed. She bent over, and he followed her, whispering in her ear.

"After the polo match, you and I will have a little time to our-selves." He rubbed one palm over her ass and smacked it lightly. Heat flared in the wake of his touch and she let out a throaty purr.

The erection pressing into her bottom was a clear sign she wasn't the only one affected by their position and her reaction.

"You are killing me, Callie." He kissed her cheek, and with a re-luctant sigh, let her go. "Get dressed before I change my mind and make us late to the match."

After flashing him what she hoped was a saucy grin, to which he rolled his eyes, she ran back to the closet and got dressed. When she came back out, she noticed the tip of a canvas tucked under her bed close to Wes's boots. She forced her gaze up to his, hoping he wouldn't notice where her eyes had focused seconds before. The lie, the deception ate away at her stomach again, and she prayed he wouldn't sense anything was amiss.

"You ready?" He held out a hand and she took it, grateful to have a reason to touch him.

"Ready." She smiled and followed him to the door. She didn't dare cast a glance at the bed and what she'd hidden underneath. One lie. That was it, but God it felt so huge. She never wanted to hide anything from Wes, but she had to go with her gut.

* * *

Wes mounted his polo pony named Vengeance and trotted behind Royce, Emery, and Fenn. As a team of four, they were perfect to go up against the opposing team of four players. Stephen Vain III, Thomas Stonecypher, Gerald Parker, and Samuel Cross were on the opposing team, all men his age who he'd grown up with. Whenever a charity needed money, polo was an easy way to raise support. The ladies dressed in their best clothes and mingled by the field, drinking mimosas while the players waged war on the turf. Gossip ran rampant among the tents, which was just what the FBI needed for the plan to work. The unveiling of the Monet would be quite a topic for the members of the Gilded Cuff who would be attending the match.

"Ready for some fun?" Royce nudged Fenn in the ribs and their horses nipped at each other as the two men bumped shoulders. Fenn chuckled and slapped the neck of his horse.

"I haven't played since I was eight. What do you think?" Fenn retorted.

"I think," Emery said as he joined his brother, "it's like riding a bike. You played well on those tiny polo ponies we had as kids. You'll be fine."

Wes grinned as the Lockwood twins ribbed each other. It was a sight he'd never expected to see again, all four of them together. Something in his chest squeezed painfully and he checked his reins and then gripped his mallet. Vengeance shifted restlessly beneath him. He was a bit wild for a polo pony, but Wes took the risk because the horse had speed.

"Easy, Ven," he soothed with a pat. Vengeance was a retired racehorse, a thoroughbred with an excellent bloodline. Built for bursts of speed, stamina, and agility, he was every polo player's dream. Wes had trained Vengeance after he turned three years old, and the horse could read Wes's cues by the slightest pressure of his legs or by weight cues whenever Wes adjusted his body. Wes always had a few other mounts as backup because they often needed to change rides during each seven-and-a-half-minute chukker period.

Wes followed his friends out onto the field where the announcer was discussing the players' bios and their statistics. It wasn't something he ever listened to, but he wondered what Callie had to be thinking of all of this. He sat up on his horse and glanced over his shoulder at the large tent full of tables where ladies and gentlemen were seated or walking about. The flare of the rose-colored dress made Callie jump out in his line of sight. She was deep in discussion with Hayden and Sophie, Emery Lockwood's fiancée. Callie was smiling and laughing, too, which made him smile.

"What's with the goofy grin?" Emery asked Wes. He reined back his pony and was checking his chin strap on his helmet.

Wes just shook his head. "None of your business."

His best friend laughed, the sound carrying. "If I had to guess, it has to do with the reason my brother has a black eye and split lip."

"Maybe, but he deserved it," Wes growled. Fenn may be one of his best friends, but he wouldn't hesitate to blacken his other eye if Fenn ever mentioned Callie again in a way that pissed him off.

"Okay. You win. I won't ask any more questions." Emery raised his hand to imitate a whipping noise. "Happens to the best of us." Then he laughed hard and the pony jumped forward.

Wes was too distracted to play much of an aggressive game. Every thought seemed to be focused on Callie. If he could catch the art thief, he'd be able to take her back to Paris. In the short time there, he'd only been able to scratch the surface of what the city had to offer. The idea of how much he still wanted to experience with her left him feeling oddly excited. The little tremors in his stomach were foreign, but not unwelcome.

Royce shouted as he chased the white plastic ball down the line, which was an invisible path the ball took that defined the play of the game. Players were restricted by the path of the ball. Wes's black pony huffed and darted after the ball but Stonecypher drew up alongside Royce, mallet lowered. Royce, as the hitter, had the natural right of way, but Stonecypher could approach alongside and hook the ball away. Wes kicked Ven's side and sprinted toward his friend. But Stonecypher smacked the white ball away, changing the play.

Stephen Vain galloped past him, a grin twisting his lips as he waved his mallet in a mock salute.

"Bastard," Wes said, laughing. Game on.

The next two chukker periods went by quickly, the play rough. More than one risky play and almost illegal moves happened on both sides. Wes changed horses twice and now sat astride one of the chestnut ponies, a gelding named Lord Nelson. Nelson wasn't nearly as quick as Vengeance but was more agile. With a tied score, a horse with agility was better.

Fenn raced up ahead, mallet swinging for a blow. Suddenly, Stonecypher's horse rushed at Fenn.

"Fenn! On your right!" Wes shouted out the warning but there wasn't enough time for Fenn to react. Their horses were on a collision course. Wes reacted on pure instinct. That little boy inside him, the one who remembered Fenn gone all those years, took over. He dug his heels into Nelson's flanks and the horse leaped forward, closing the distance and Stonecypher's mount smashed Nelson shoulder to shoulder just as Stonecypher swung his mallet, striking Wes in the solar plexus.

Air whooshed out of his lungs and he went limp. Nelson screamed and reared back. When he thrashed his head, Wes's weak grip on the reins slackened and the strips of leather slipped free of his hold.

There had only been three other times in his life when a horse had thrown him, but that spark of panic in his chest, the clawing agony of his lungs struggling to breathe and the weightless free fall, were unforgettable. He struck the ground hard, the impact knocking the last bit of air from his lungs before his head snapped back and a sharp pain followed him into darkness.

Chapter 23

A panicked shout and the screaming of hooves jerked Callie's focus back to the field. Fenn had the ball, but Stonecypher was rushing at him, mallet raised dangerously. Wes was only a yard behind and then in a blink he and his horse were wedged between Fenn and Stonecypher. The mallet swung and Callie leaped to her feet, trying to see what happened. Wes's horse reared, his muscles gleaming, mouth frothing, as it screamed. Wes slipped off the back of the horse and hit the ground. A sickening fear gripped her in its jaws. The horse stumbled and rolled over Wes before it got back up onto its feet.

"Wes!" Callie screamed and kicked off her heels so she could run across the field faster. All she could think about was getting to him. She had to. Tears blurred her eyes and she choked down sobs. He was only fifty feet away and not moving. Stonecypher, Fenn, and the other riders had dismounted and were on the ground beside him.

"I swear, Lockwood, I didn't mean to—" Stonecypher's face was ashen as he stared at Wes's body.

Callie lunged forward, but when she got close, strong arms caught her and held her back.

"Hey, kid, hold on." Fenn's voice was distant, almost muffled beneath the blood roaring in her ears.

"Let go of me!" She struggled, arms flailing and legs thrashing against Fenn's body. A muttered curse reached her ears and then she was free. She shoved past him and dropped by Wes's side. Emery and Stephen Vain were examining him.

"Doesn't look like any bones were broken," Vain observed. His eyes met hers before he focused on Wes again.

Callie gripped one of Wes's hands and squeezed.

"Wes, please, wake up." She felt so helpless, like the little girl whose mother would never come home. Some memories were so deep that even a young child couldn't forget them.

His dark lashes fluttered and then he finally opened his eyes. With a low moan, he lifted his head, only to drop it back to the ground.

"Easy." Emery patted his shoulder and glanced at Callie.

"What happened?" Wes tried to raise himself up again and this time succeeded.

"You fell," she explained, her voice breaking. "We should call an ambulance."

He cursed. "I don't need an ambulance." He struggled to get up, wavered only a few steps before he seemed to regain control, and he started off in the direction that his horse had run, which was back to the stables.

When she tried to go after him and grab his arm, Wes growled at her. She retreated a step and they all watched him stalk off toward the stables. The ambulance crew had apparently been waiting behind the tents in case of emergencies and when Emery spoke to them, he told them Wes was headed for the stables.

Callie was rooted to the ground. Her whole body shook and she was a little dizzy, and also hurt by Wes's brush-off. He didn't want her to check on him and that stung. More than stung, it created a heavy ache in her chest. She rubbed the spot over her heart, trying to ease a pain she knew full well wouldn't ease until she'd taken care of Wes.

"Are you okay?" Fenn wrapped his arm around her shoulders, shaking her a little and she focused on him.

"Huh? Oh, I'm fine. Just a little shook up. I was so afraid…" Her sentence died in a breathless whisper.

Fenn cupped her cheek and met her gaze. "Pretty scary to see someone you love get hurt, huh?"

"Yeah," she agreed, and when he chuckled she scowled. "What?"

"You love Wes. You didn't deny that just now." Fine lines around his eyes creased as he smiled. "I guess it was worth a few punches to get him to admit he loves you, too."

"He doesn't." She rubbed at her eyes, brushing away tears, but she gasped as Fenn caught her by the shoulders.

"I was wrong about him, kid. So you listen to me. A man like Wes does not get into fights over a woman, not unless he loves her. Hell, he got mad when I suggested it was only desire for you. He was pissed. He may not be ready to tell you he loves you, but it sure shows."

She wanted to cry. If he loved her, he wouldn't have walked off after the accident, and she told Fenn as much.

He unclipped his riding helmet and shook his head. "You think he wants you to see him hurt? A man likes to be strong and protect his woman, not frighten her by getting hurt. His pride is injured and he's probably scared that you'll lose faith in his ability to take care of you."

"But that's ridiculous."

Fenn laughed. "As I recall, you once told me, men never make sense."

He had her there and she couldn't argue.

"So what can I do?"

A serious expression lined his face as he considered this. "He needs to get his sense of power and strength back. Find a way to make him feel comfortable again and he'll be okay." With a brotherly pat on her head, Fenn walked away.

Callie remained on the field a few minutes longer, the grass cool beneath her feet as she watched the crowds disperse. One person caught her attention.

Corrine Vanderholt was standing next to the edge of the large party tent, her attention on the stables where Wes had gone. A smug smile curved her lips as she glanced around and then slipped back into the vanishing crowds. A little shiver of dread tiptoed down Callie's spine. Was Corrine happy that Wes had been hurt? Would she try to get back with Wes and was she heading off to find him at that very moment? Jealousy crawled beneath her skin and she despised admitting she was worried Wes would be tempted by Corrine.

The questions had no ready answer, but Callie would be watching her closely from now on. Something wasn't right. Every instinct she had screamed that Corrine had liked Wes getting hurt.

Callie collected her shoes and slipped them on before she headed to the stables. Wes hadn't come back out yet, so he might still be inside. As she reached the stables' main entrance, two paramedics walked past her. Emery was right behind them, looking bemused.

"Where is Wes?" she asked.

Emery waved a hand back down the long dim hall of the stalls.

"He's brooding, but fine. A bump on the head is all." Emery's assurance didn't soothe her. She needed to see Wes, to make sure he was, in fact, all right.

The stalls were full of polo ponies who stuck their faces over the edges of the doors to eye her curiously. The heavy warm scent of hay and grain made her feel safe. It would always remind her of the ranch. A large tack room bore glossy English-style saddles, and a rack behind them was laden with large cup trophies. Fat ribbons in a dozen colors hung from pegs on the rack, their forked ends gleaming in the soft gold glow of the ceiling lights.

Wes was at the end of the row of fifteen stalls. She saw his dark silhouette against the daylight behind him from the rear entrance of the barn. His tall, lean, booted legs, narrow hips, wide shoulders, all of him focused as he held a horse's face in his hands, his forehead pressed to the beast's in a sign of gentle endearment that tugged at her heart. He was so sexy, so alive, and at that moment completely ignorant of her presence.

She loved him so much it hurt. It wasn't the same as she'd felt with Fenn. That had been a shallow cut to her soul when he'd rejected her. With Wes, it was like nothing else she could ever have imagined. Everything she someday hoped to be was tied to him, like an ocean to the shore. Always crashing back to each other, pulled by an invisible force like gravity. A love that was built into the fabric of the universe. It couldn't be explained or ignored. Only embraced and cherished.

I will love you for the rest of my life, Wes Thorne. Even if you break my heart, it will be yours.

The horse he was stroking shifted and bumped its nose against Wes's chest and Wes chuckled. The sound was rich and low. It made her entire body explode with heated memories of their nights in Paris. Without a word, she walked right up to him and put her arms around him, hugging him. If he was startled, she couldn't tell. Her face was buried against his chest.

"Hello, darling." He kissed her temple and curled his arms around her body.

"Don't ever push me away like that again. *Ever*." She rubbed her cheek against the soft cotton of his polo jersey. His scent, mixed with a little sweat and hay, made him enticing and irresistible.

A hand patted her lower back and then he eased her away a few inches so their gazes could meet. Around them, the silent equine witnesses huffed and pawed their hooves against hay-covered stone.

"Keep coming after me." His eyes were heavy with a solemnity she hadn't expected. "Don't let me shut you out. Whatever you ask of me, I can't refuse you. You know that, don't you?"

Her heart skidded to a stop as hope sprung forth. Could he mean what she hoped? That he belonged to her just as she belonged to him? She was too afraid to ask if he meant that.

"How's your head?" She touched his cheek gently.

One corner of his mouth rose in a crooked grin. "Just a small bump." He reached behind his head, but she caught his wrist.

"Don't touch it if it hurts. Did the paramedics tend to it?"

He nodded. "Are you hoping to patch me up again?" It was meant as a tease, but she didn't find it funny.

"I don't want to make that a hobby, stitching you back up or bandaging your wounds. I'm serious, Wes. Be careful for me."

"You were really worried?" His brows arched and his lips softened in a tender half-smile.

"Of course I was. A horse practically fell on you. You weren't moving…" She couldn't finish the thought.

"I'm sorry I scared you." His earnestness made the knot of panic in her chest ease a little. He held her a long moment, neither of them brave enough to speak.

"Are you ready to go home?" he finally asked.

"Yes." She still had her arms around him and she tilted her head back. "Wes, will you take me to the club tonight? I know you plan to go watch over the forged Monet. I want to go with you."

His eyes narrowed. "You want to go to the Gilded Cuff with me?"

She nodded.

"No."

"But—"

"Callie, that's a full BDSM club. You wouldn't know what to do, and you are far too shy. Besides, I'd have to collar you in front of everyone just to keep the other doms from approaching you."

She nibbled her bottom lip, considering how brave she might be to go to the club and play by his rules. She didn't know if she could succeed but she wanted to try.

"Wes, this is important to me. I want to do this." Going to the club was part of his life and she knew that if she ever wanted to convince him they could be together, then she had to prove she could survive in his dark world.

"You're serious about the club?" A flicker of consideration in his eyes showed she might have a chance to convince him.

"Please," she begged, staring at his lips, then his eyes. She stood on tiptoes and curled her fingers around the back of his neck to pull his face down for a kiss.

This time she was the aggressor and used her lips to convince him how much she deserved him and wanted to please him. He growled softly against her mouth, his hands spanning her waist and pulling her against him. The kiss deepened and this time she lost her control. Clinging to him, she sighed and moaned as he assaulted her senses.

When they finally broke apart, she was pinned back against the wall next to Vengeance's stall and Wes was stroking her bare arms, his eyes bedroom soft, his lashes at half-mast as he gazed intently at her kiss-swollen lips.

"All right. You can come tonight, but I'll need to keep you close in order to make sure you don't anger any of the doms. I love your fire, but not all masters like their submissives spirited." He threaded his fingers through her hair and the caress was soothing.

"I can do this, Wes. I promise." She had faith that she would be brave enough to survive a night at one of the most exclusive BDSM clubs on the East Coast.

"We'll be there together." His assurance warmed her.

Together. What a difference one small word could make.

* * *

Corrine Vanderholt lingered in the tack room, eavesdropping on Wes's conversation with the little blonde-haired twit. It still infuriated her that Wes had broken off their relationship for a girl like that. A small-town nobody. Corrine had connections to the Kennedys, for God's sake. Any man should want to marry her. Lucky for her, though, she didn't actually like Wes. Sure, she played submissive, because that was the only way a woman could get any time with him. And that had been her goal. To get time with him, to get him to propose to her.

She had no interest in his love or his money. She wanted his art. For the last few years she'd been watching him as he purchased several rare, near priceless pieces. The Monet, the Renoir, they would all be hers. There was just one problem. He kept these rare pieces well hidden. Her partner had cased Wes's house and hadn't found them anywhere. But Corrine knew they had to be there somewhere. Paranoid Wes had just hidden them and they needed a way to trick him into showing the paintings' location.

Her partner had developed a plan to steal art from Wes's friends and clients. When Wes learned of the thefts he would want to get involved, and just as her partner had predicted, Wes would use his own art as bait to draw out the illusive thief. A little smile curled her lips. Wes had it all wrong. He was the mouse in this game and she was the cat.

It was a good thing she'd thought to follow him to the barn. That little nobody in the rose dress had revealed an unexpected twist. Wes wasn't planning to hang the real Monet in the club. He was going to hang a fake. That meant her plan to steal it had to be changed. A wicked sense of glee filled her. Oh, it would be too easy to get Wes to hand over the real Monet and anything else Corrine desired.

"There you are." A deep masculine chuckle came from the back door of the tack room that led to the other row of stalls on the other side of the stables.

Corrine turned to see her partner. He called himself the Illusionist, but she didn't care about the nickname. She only cared about him and the art they would steal.

"Hey, baby," she purred and wrapped her arms around his neck.

His brown eyes burned through her. He was the only man who ever made her *feel* before. She didn't have to playact any certain way when she was around him. She could just be herself.

"What's Thorne up to?" He settled his hands on her lower back and tugged her close.

"Changing the game, that's what. He put a forgery in the club this afternoon. The real Monet is still hidden."

Her partner frowned. "Damn."

Corrine stroked her fingertips along the nape of his neck, teasing with the edge of his polo jersey. "It's okay. I know what we can do."

"Do you?" He bent his head, kissing her until she was breathless.

"Yes," she replied. She had the perfect plan. And it would cost Wes that sweet girl he'd dared to fall for.

Chapter 24

Remember to breathe."

Callie had to repeat Wes's suggestion a few times as he parked his Hennessey in a lot outside an old warehouse building. Her hands were shaking as she climbed out of the car and glanced around. It was eight o'clock and the lack of buildings around this isolated warehouse was a little eerie in the dark.

"Ready?" Wes held out a hand and she took it, grateful to have him to hold on to.

He looked good in his black wool suit. His clothes and his demeanor screamed that he was a powerful dom. She wore only jeans, a t-shirt, and a pair of soft leather cuffs with a fur lining. When she'd asked earlier that evening what to wear, he'd told her to dress comfortably because she'd change at the club and he'd taken care of her outfit, which he'd put in the submissive locker room earlier that day.

She had no idea what to expect. Would Wes want to do a public scene with her? Sure, she'd read plenty of romance novels, but what was this like in real life? What she did with Wes in private was wonderful, explosive, but she was afraid she couldn't do something in public, not something incredibly intimate. What if he wanted her to be naked in front of his friends or the other doms? They hadn't talked about that, but she was feeling right now like those might be close to her hard limits.

"Darling, are you all right? You've got a death grip on my hand." Wes gave her a reassuring squeeze.

"I'm good," Callie lied. He frowned and that look made her instantly regret lying.

"Callie, once we're inside the club. No lying. That's important. I won't be mad at you, even if you tell me you're terrified. All you have to do is use your safe words. 'Yellow' to slow down if you're uncomfortable and 'red' to stop immediately."

She nodded, relief flooding her. Wes would protect her. All she had to do was rely on him to guide her through the night.

Callie followed Wes as they reached the warehouse. He opened the large wooden door to the inside of the club lobby. Craggy rock walls and sconces with warm gold lights gave the castle a medieval ambiance. There was one red-painted door at the end of the lobby, and a man in a black suit with a red armband stood by the door, checking IDs of the men and women passing into a dark interior beyond. A few people stood in a line in front of a desk where a woman in a pantsuit and black-framed glasses was checking names off a list.

Wes guided Callie straight to the desk as the last couple of people walked away.

"Evening, Aria. I've brought Ms. Callie Taylor. She is my submissive tonight. She's the one I called you about."

The woman, Aria, was a tall brunette, with powerful but lovely features. With a warm smile at Callie, she shook Wes's offered hand.

"Ms. Taylor, welcome! It's about time Wes collared someone."

Callie shot a glance at Wes. He'd mentioned he would collar her, but hadn't explained much about doing it at the club. Clearly it was a bigger deal than he'd let on if he was telling people about it.

"Hi, Aria," Callie said, trying to remain calm, even though her entire body vibrated with nervous energy.

"Call her Mistress Aria," Wes intoned in that dom voice of his, but he did it low enough that only she could hear.

"Mistress Aria," she hastily corrected, then squeezed Wes's hand.

Aria winked at Wes. "She's cute. I like her. Much better than your previous sub."

It took everything in Callie not to ask who that previous sub had been, but her gut told her not to.

Corrine. That venomous woman was everywhere.

"She's all cuffed, I see," Aria noted and gestured toward the door. "Why don't you take her to the submissive locker room."

"Thank you." Wes and Callie approached the big red door and the bouncer's eyes swept over her before he spoke to Wes.

"Have a lovely evening, Mr. Thorne."

Wes chuckled. "I intend to."

As they passed through into the dim club's interior, Callie gripped his hand even harder. The massive room was dark but she could still see everything clearly. The brocaded couches, the luscious, old Victorian boudoir feel to the room. The heavy red velvet curtains with gold cords that hid smaller rooms from view in a large circle around the main room. There was a bar off to one side with two men in black leather pants and black t-shirts pouring drinks.

Couches and chairs were placed in various groupings on thick carpets. Music boomed from hidden speakers and people were lounging about, some heavily kissing, others doing a lot more than that. Callie ducked her head, completely embarrassed to see such open sexual activity.

"This way." Wes led her to a room that had a door with a wooden sign with the words "Submissive Chambers" painted in a flowing gold script. He handed her a gold key on a red satin string.

"Go in there and open locker number eighteen. Strip down out of your clothes and put on what I left in there for you. Then come back out here. I'll be waiting for you." The intense look in his eyes sent little shivers of panic and excitement through her. She recognized that look, the one that scorched her like hot lust. He was fully the dominant tonight and yet it didn't frighten her.

With a little gulp and a flutter of nerves, Callie let go of his hand and pushed the door open. The locker room was not at all what she'd expected. There were benches of dark wood and polished wooden lockers with silver numbers nailed to the front of each locker. Showers and changing rooms lined one wall. There were about ten women inside already chatting excitedly as they casually stripped out of their clothes.

"Hi!" A vivacious dark blonde-haired woman walked over to her. "You're Callie, right?" the woman spoke as she finished fastening her garter belts to her stockings. She wore a bra and panty set that looked like it came out of a Victoria's Secret catalog and she had a model-perfect body.

Oh boy. I can do this.

"Yeah, I'm Callie Taylor."

The woman smiled. "I'm Katrina. I'm here with Royce tonight. He asked me to help you if you need it. I'm his sub, but he said you should stick with us if Wes has to leave you for a while. This is your first time at the club, right?"

"Yeah. This is pretty intimidating." Her mouth was dry and she swallowed hard. It was one thing for her to be intimate with Wes in private, but maybe she really wasn't ready to do something so public with him…

"You'll be fine," Katrina assured her and then introduced her to the other subs, who were all friendly. Callie wasn't sure if she'd re-member their names. Everything was overwhelming, but it was a relief to know she'd be out there with people who were nice.

"Wes said I'm supposed to use locker eighteen?" Callie glanced around at the numbers and Katrina pointed to the one she needed.

"That's it. Let's see what your master left you to wear. It's lingerie night." Katrina giggled and snapped the band of one of her garters. "Royce likes this stuff. My last master only let me wear panties, noth-ing else. I didn't really like that so much. I'm glad Royce likes to leave some of my body to the imagination of the other doms." The other subs around them chuckled.

But Callie wasn't laughing. What if Wes hadn't left her anything to wear?

Katrina took the key from her and opened the locker, pulling out a lacy black-and-crème-colored bra and bikini panties.

"Classy, yet sexy." Katrina handed her the items. Callie took them, her hands shaking. She was only going to wear this? Nothing else? Her ears started to ring and she had trouble swallowing.

I can't do this.

The idea of total strangers seeing her in this…only this? No. She wasn't sexy like Katrina or the others. She wouldn't look good in this, and she certainly didn't want a bunch of intim-idating, gorgeous dominants outside to see how pathetic she looked in comparison to the other women. A dumpy girl from a ranch…Yeah, she would stand out in the worst way and Wes would come to his senses and realize she wasn't the kind of girl he would want to be with. Her stomach clenched and she swal-lowed down a wave of nausea.

She grabbed Katrina's hand. "Get Wes, please. He's outside."

She leaned against the row of lockers, clutching the items, her legs shaking hard enough that her knees knocked together.

The door to the locker room opened and Wes strode in, Katrina on his heels.

"What's the matter?" he asked, cupping Callie's face the second he reached her. Concern darkened his eyes as he studied her face. She wanted to burrow into him, lose herself in his warmth and the protectiveness of his arms. In that moment she would have given anything to be back with him in Paris, just the two of them, or to be locked away with him in the black room. She liked his dark side but didn't want to have to share herself with anyone but him.

"I can't wear this," she breathed, showing him the underwear. "Those other men will see me. I'm not…" She trailed off, unable to voice how she felt. He would be the gentleman and disagree with her about her body, but she knew better. She was no supermodel or wafer-thin socialite. She had curves and muscles and a tiny bit of plumpness.

He sighed heavily, disapproval layering that single utterance of her name. "Callie—"

"Please, Wes."

As they talked, Katrina ushered the other subs out of the room, leaving them alone.

"All right. Let me go grab something else. Put these things on and I'll bring something to put over them." He brushed a kiss on her forehead and left.

With trembling hands, she peeled off her shirt and jeans. Then she put her clothes in the locker and slipped on the panties and bra. They were lovely, but she couldn't let other men she didn't know see her like this. A metallic taste filled her mouth as panic struck again.

"Here." Wes came back into the room and handed her a large white dress shirt. "You may wear this over the outfit I selected, but that is the only concession I will allow." His tone was dark and she knew she couldn't argue out of this.

"Thank you," she said. As soon as she slipped his shirt over her body, she relaxed. This she could live with. It dropped to her upper thighs and hinted at her curves rather than flaunted them.

His palm smacked her ass and she jumped. "Thank you, Master," he corrected. "Now come along. It's time to collar you."

* * *

Wes's heart was beating fast. Callie looked so delicious, so perfect in his shirt and nothing else. Her curvy legs and bare feet showed just how sexy she was. He was going to be the envy of every dom in the Cuff tonight. As he led her into the main room, every dom's focus turned their way. Even the subs dared to raise their eyes curiously. Royce was reclining in an armchair, hands behind his head. Katrina, his sub, was seated at his feet on a large pillow to keep her knees from bruising.

Wes pointed to the floor by Royce, who tossed a pillow down where his friend pointed.

"Kneel, sub."

As soon as he spoke the words, the doms gathered around them, all their submissives kneeling. Callie tried to mimic their pose as she sank to her knees next to Katrina and kept her head bowed. The cushion made the kneeling pose quite comfortable.

Pride filled him as he gazed down at her. She was his every fantasy.

"Tonight, I claim Callie Taylor as my submissive. She will be my responsibility, and I her master. Any punishments to her must be dealt through me as she now belongs to me." He removed the collar from his suit pocket and leaned down over Callie.

"Lift your hair, little sub," he instructed gently.

Her hands lifted and she caught her long honey-gold hair away from her neck. As he fastened the collar around her neck, a little shiver rippled along her skin when he touched her. Seeing his collar on her before had been a thrill, but now it meant so much more. She was his in the most permanent way he knew how to claim her. Normally, during a collaring, a submissive would endure an erotic punishment but it was up to their master.

"Stand, Callie."

She rose and folded her cuffed hands in front of her and kept her head bent in respect. For a woman new to the lifestyle, she had good instincts.

He tilted her chin up and relished watching the little spark of surprise in her eyes.

"You are mine." The words were soft, but he knew she heard them by the way a delicate blush pinked her cheeks. The vow he made had come true. He could see in her lovely eyes that she belonged to him in every way.

He couldn't resist not taking what he wanted any longer. With little effort, he picked her up off the floor and carried her to a nearby couch. Reclining, he settled her onto his lap and curled his arms around her waist, grinning as he kissed away her squeal of surprise. Her lips parted beneath his and he delved inside with his tongue. She tasted sweet, like fruit and something uniquely her own. She melted against him and he let go of his control. He took her mouth, and his hands roamed her body, slipping up beneath the large shirt she wore, exploring her body freely as he staked his claim. The laughter and cat calls from the other doms were distant. His sole focus was on Callie and the way he could imprint her taste in his mouth.

There was a strange thrill at having a woman here at the club who was truly his, one he owned in a way he'd never had before. She was his, no man could touch her, and he could show all the other doms just what they were missing. Her little purrs, her kittenish sighs, and the wicked way she learned how to kiss him back that caused his trousers to tighten painfully as his body went rigid with need.

"Unless you plan on taking her to one of the private rooms, you'd better slow it down." Royce's loud jibe cut through the haze of lust in Wes's brain.

Fuck. Why couldn't he enjoy his little submissive?

"Don't forget the plan," Royce muttered as he leaned forward in his chair, eyeing Wes seriously. He then flicked his gaze to the Monet painting that hung on a wall ten feet away from them.

Royce was right. He needed to focus on the Monet, not on Callie. She was supposed to be his outward distraction to any in the club who might question him if he came alone.

With a sigh of regret, he got up from the chair and set Callie down on the couch beside Royce. She touched her kiss-swollen lips and smiled foolishly up at him. He loved that about her, the way she lost herself to passion and to him so easily and embraced every wonderful second of each kiss.

The sooner I catch the Illusionist, the sooner Callie and I can go back to Paris.

He stole one more little kiss and made sure he captured her complete attention.

"Remain with Royce. Do not speak to anyone unless they speak to you first. Remember to address doms as 'sir.' The subs have cuffs and collars and less clothes so you should be able to tell them apart. I'll be back in a moment."

He whispered quietly in Royce's ear to watch over her before he headed to the back office.

Jaxon was seated at his desk, but then got up when Wes entered.

"Did you see the Monet?" Jaxon said as he gestured for Wes to go back into the main club room. Once there, Jax pointed to a wall across the room. Illuminated by a small horizontal light overhead, the Monet forgery was visible to anyone walking by.

"Yes, I saw it when I came in. I trust Vain helped to transport it here without any issues?"

Jaxon nodded. "Yes, he was extremely helpful. Kept an eye on it the whole time for me while we moved it here and set it up. I have my cameras on it. Anyone who gets close to it will be watched carefully."

"Good." He relaxed. This was the first night. They would give the thief a week to forge the painting in an attempt to make a switch.

"I hope this works," Jaxon growled. "I want my Sargent painting back and once we find this thief, the FBI assured me they would get to the bottom of it and track down the other paintings this man sold."

"Don't worry, Jax. It's my priority." Wes noticed Stephen Vain approach Royce. Royce laughed at something Vain said and then waved a hand at Callie and Katrina. Both women got to their feet and walked to the bar together.

Knowing Royce, he'd sent them to get some water. It was important to keep a submissive well cared for. A healthy sub was a happy one, and a happy sub was more pleasing to bed, at least in his opinion.

A man entered the club's main room through the door and Wes's entire body went rigid.

Thomas Stonecypher. The man just didn't know when to stay away. Between the incident at the gala and that attack at the polo match…

"Wes," Jaxon cautioned, but Wes was already striding toward the other man.

"Wes, don't." Jax grabbed his arm, forcing Wes to halt. He spun to glare at Jax.

"What? I owe that bastard a crushed windpipe."

"Everyone here is a suspect. Even Stonecypher. Let him be. We need to watch him and the others, or else we'll scare off the thief and this will be pointless."

Wes jerked free of Jax's grip and snarled. "Fine."

"Come on, I need you to help me watch some of the newer doms. You have a sharp eye. I don't know them that well, and it could be that our thief is a new member."

"Very well." He glanced toward the bar again, where Callie was standing with Katrina. With a glass of water in her hand, she was chatting with the woman and smiling. Her other hand touched her collar every now and then, as though to check to see if it was still there. Seeing that made him smile. She would get used to wearing it. He wanted to see it around her neck often.

Yes, darling. I own you. Knowing that made him pleased more than he'd ever felt when he'd brought a submissive to the club. Tonight he'd take her home and prove that. He would strip her bare without a care for her shyness since he'd have her all to himself.

You are mine.

Chapter 25

Well, well," an acidic feminine voice said, cutting through Callie's conversation with Katrina.

"Uh-oh, bitch alert," Katrina muttered.

When Callie glanced over her shoulder, she winced. Corrine was standing there, in a knockout lacy lingerie outfit. Her long skinny legs went on for miles and she could have been a supermodel, except for the sour look on her face.

"Get lost, kitty cat," Corrine spat. "I have to talk to Wes's new toy."

Fury sparked the tinder inside Callie but she held off reacting. This was Wes's world and she didn't want to embarrass him. But she still needed to deal with this woman. Her bullying couldn't go on forever.

"It's fine, Katrina. Please tell Royce I'll be back in a moment."

"Okay." Katrina touched her shoulder in a silent show of support.

Corrine seemed to wait for Katrina to be out of earshot before she went into her verbal assault.

"How does it feel, *Callie*?" She emphasized her name like it was a bad taste. "He brought you into my world, where he fucked me for months. Did he tell you? He screwed me on every flat surface in this club. I was here first. It's my territory. You are just a sad, sorry replacement." She glanced around with a cruel smile. "The doms are already betting on how long it takes him to tire of you. I'm betting a few weeks. You can't give him what he needs." Corrine placed perfectly manicured hands with bloodred nails on her hips as she swept her gaze over the room.

"You are nothing but a temporary amusement. You weren't the first little innocent creature he's brought here and you won't be the last."

Callie was so furious that she acted before she could think. Gripping her glass of water she tossed it right in Corrine's face. She let out an earsplitting shriek and lunged for Callie, but suddenly Stephen Vain was there, dragging Corrine away.

"Enough!" Vain snarled and shoved Corrine back and held up a warning hand. "Go back to your master and tell him you deserve ten lashings at the St. Andrew's Cross."

Corrine hissed like a wet alley cat, stalked away, dripping water behind her.

"Oh God." Callie was torn between mortification and the desire to laugh. "I shouldn't have done that, but she's—"

"A crazy bitch." Vain's raspy chuckle put her at ease.

"Yes, exactly." Callie sighed in relief. Maybe that was the worst that could happen tonight. She'd faced Corrine and survived.

"Having a good time so far?" Vain asked.

She nodded. "Yes. Oh yes, sir!" She had completely forgotten she was talking to a dom.

He waved a hand. "It's fine. I'm not that strict. Here, let me get you a new drink, something a little stronger than water. You'll need it if she decides to come back later when I'm not around." He leaned over the bar and grabbed one of the bottles of scotch and an empty glass.

"Thank you, sir." Callie turned her focus back to the room, watching the doms and subs curiously while Vain prepared her a drink.

"Here, drink it up." He pressed a glass with amber liquid in it into her hand.

She raised it to her lips and downed the whole glass. Then coughed. The drink burned like fire.

"Whoa, easy." He patted her back.

"Sorry." She gasped and set the glass on the counter.

"A beautiful woman should never apologize." He chuckled and walked away.

Callie left the bar and headed back to Katrina and Royce.

"Hanging in there, little cowgirl?" Royce teased. He had put Katrina on his lap and she was kissing his neck and licking his ear. Royce groaned and palmed Katrina's ass.

Callie ducked her head, too embarrassed to look. She was a little tired and wanted Wes to come back. She knew he was busy keeping his eye on the Monet, though, the real reason they were there tonight.

"Feeling tired?" Royce asked her.

"Yeah, I guess it's been a long day. Do you think Wes would get mad if I just took a quick nap here on the couch?" She tucked her knees up and curled into the soft, warm sofa cushions.

"No, he won't. Go ahead, I'll keep an eye on you," Royce promised.

"Thanks." She folded her arms on the armrest and then put her chin on her arms and closed her eyes. Just a short nap, that's all she needed...

She sensed him before she heard him. The warm breath on her face and the heat of his body as he leaned over her. It was a struggle to open her eyes. She was still tired, but his voice stirred her awake. Her skin tingled where he touched her, his palm brushing her hair as he whispered her name.

"Callie, darling, time to wake up." Wes stroked a hand over her hair.

"What? How long was I asleep?" She blinked rapidly, slowly trying to bring Wes into focus. Her stomach gave a strange little twist, almost like a cramp, and her head felt a little fuzzy.

Wes was leaning over her. He'd removed his suit coat and his sleeves were rolled up. Her throat went dry and a pulse began to beat between her thighs. He looked sexy as hell and seeing him so informal only reminded her of the pleasure in his arms. Wes was an addiction, one that would never be cured.

"You've been asleep for an hour. Royce didn't want to wake you. The club is closing soon."

Brushing her hair back from her face, she sighed. "I'm sorry, Wes." When she sat up, the world spun around her in dizzying circles.

"Are you okay?" He picked her up off the couch and set her on her feet. That only made it worse. Everything spun around her even faster and a wave of nausea made her buckle over.

"Wes…I don't feel so good." She clutched at her stomach, moaning. Everything seemed to be spinning and she couldn't catch her breath.

"You have had a stressful day. Let me take you home." He caught her behind her knees and back to lift her into the cradle of his arms.

The jarring movement of his steps made her sick, so she closed her eyes again, hoping to quell the sudden sickness. Her blood pounded hard in her ears and the entire world swayed around her like she was the one off balance. It was hard to think. Panic swept through her as she fought to stay awake.

"Just rest." Wes's distant voice came to her through a dark tunnel thick with fog.

"Wes, I can't…move." The last word was barely a whisper, one she could barely breathe. He hadn't heard her. She was…fading into darkness.

* * *

The tires of the Hennessey Venom GT screeched to a halt inside his garage as Wes threw the car into park and launched himself out of the driver's side. He shouted for his butler as he wrenched the passenger-side door open and bent over Callie. She was unconscious and had been for a while—how long, he wasn't sure. Her exhaustion and disorientation in the club were a warning he'd almost ignored. When she'd passed out completely in the car and became unresponsive, his trepidation had increased.

Arms around her limp body, he lifted her into his embrace and called for Bradley again, his voice ragged as he clutched her tighter to him. His legs moved of their own volition until he found himself in the room they'd made love in earlier that week. The warmth of that memory was overridden by a blind panic he couldn't quell.

Callie didn't stir as he carried her. No murmur from her soft lips to tell him she was still here, still with him—just silence that was swallowed by a wave of pure fear.

"Bradley!" he shouted. His butler didn't answer. That was unusual. Where the fuck was Bradley? He had the uncanny ability of always being present whenever Wes came home, but not tonight.

Wes settled Callie on the couch and put a pillow under her head, then brushed his hand over her face. Her forehead was cool to the touch and a fine sheen of perspiration coated her skin. Something was wrong with her…He headed for the intercom and pressed the button.

"Bradley, I'm in the old study. I need you straight away. Callie is sick."

Sweat coated his palms and blood pounded in his ears. He turned back to Callie and pulled his cellphone out of his pocket. He was going to call an ambulance. She could have food poisoning or the flu. She needed immediate medical attention.

A familiar clicking noise from behind him froze him in place. He knew that noise, heard it in his nightmares.

A gun being cocked. Then there was only that roaring silence, broken only by the uneven breath escaping his lips.

"Put the phone down," a cold voice instructed.

Wes slowly lowered the phone, his heartbeat racing. Each beat hit him as hard as a cannon. He'd been caught off guard. Every single lesson Hans had taught him didn't matter now. It was too late. He'd sworn twenty-five years ago that he'd never be careless, never let his enemies find a way to get to him. But he'd grown careless. He'd been lost in his obsession with Callie and hadn't seen the danger until it was too late. A metallic taste filled his mouth as he struggled to fight off the panic. Callie needed him to survive this so he could save her.

"Here's how this is going to go. You give me the real Monet and I'll tell you what she's been poisoned with so you might be able to save her."

"Poisoned?" The word escaped his lips through gritted teeth.

"Yes. I thought you might need the proper motivation to cooperate. Slipping her something in her drink while I was at the club was an easy solution. How does the saying go? Only fools fall in love? Consider yourself a fool."

The confirmation that Callie had been poisoned hit Wes in the stomach, a quick jerk of his body involuntarily loosened his grip on the phone and it crashed to the floor with a dull thud. He didn't care about the phone. All he cared about was Callie—his one darting glance down showed her unmoving body on the couch, pulling at his insides like a black hole. He would do anything to save her.

"Turn around and face me." The voice, so dead and cold, was almost silky, like the skin of a snake.

He did as he was told and faced the man who'd threatened the only one who truly mattered in his life.

"It's you?" He couldn't believe it. It wasn't Thomas Stonecypher. He'd thought it had to be. No one else had a grudge against Wes like he did. No one, except… *God, I'm a fool. How did I not see what was right in front of me?*

Stephen Vain III stood in the doorway and held a Beretta, aiming at Wes's chest. He wore all black and his hands were gloved.

"Hello, Wes." He flashed a crooked smile and leaned against the doorjamb, relaxing now that Wes was facing him.

"Vain, what are you doing?" Wes asked.

"Getting revenge." Vain shrugged. "I lost the Camden board position because of you. The auction house was perfect to clean the money—after all, who would suspect a world-class auction house was trafficking stolen goods? After you recommended Peter Wells to the board, he got appointed and convinced the other members to make me resign. I couldn't maintain the lifestyle I'd grown accustomed to, not when fencing the art became that much harder. I lost my advantage—and that means I lost a lot of money. Someone has to pay for that. What a shame for you to have to get so close to her, eh?" Vain waved the gun toward Callie's prone form, his cocky attitude riling every violent instinct inside Wes to attack, but he held still. Saving Callie was his priority and he couldn't do that if he didn't know what Vain had given her. "But if it hadn't been her, it would have been someone else you loved, like that sister of yours."

Wes's fists clenched at his side. "Tell me what poison you gave Callie."

Vain ignored him and suddenly glanced down the hall. "I'm here." He spoke to someone outside the study.

Wes tensed, prepared for another man with a gun. But it was Corrine. She joined Vain and kissed his cheek before looking at Wes.

"What? Don't tell me you're surprised." She smirked, and the iciness of her eyes sliced him to the bone. "I never really wanted you. It was only your art. Speaking of which, where is the Monet, Wes?"

"Back at the club." He clenched his hands into fists, afraid to move. He shot a glance at Callie on the couch. "Go back to the Cuff and take it. I don't care. Now tell me what you gave Callie."

"She doesn't have much time left," Corrine added gleefully as she studied her watch. "Now stop lying to us. I heard you talking in the barn today. I know the real Monet is not the one you sent to the club."

"The clock is ticking, Wes. The Monet or your woman. You can save only one." Vain flicked his gun barrel at Callie.

Only one? The one piece of art he'd protect at all costs. It was an easy choice. Callie was the only masterpiece that mattered. Everything else he owned could be given away in an instant, so long as Callie was still his, and still alive. Needing her above all else was deeper than an instinct, deeper than any basic urge to have her. Like a light shining through heavy storm clouds, he understood that now. She didn't exist to complete his soul, to make him a better man. No, he existed to complete her, to give her everything in her life and make her dreams come true. It was his true purpose, the direction his life had meant to go and Vain would not rob Callie of her future.

He was going to kill Vain and Corrine if anything happened to her.

"I have to take you to the Monet." He reached slowly into his coat pocket for the keys and pointed across the hallway where the black room was. "It's in there." He shoved past them and fished out his keys, his hands strangely steady as he moved the painting of the river aside and then triggered the hidden lock. If he could get them the painting quickly, he could call an ambulance. As he opened the black room door and led them inside, Vain stayed close, but not too close that Wes could have pulled the gun from him. Of course, he wouldn't have risked doing that. He needed to know what poison Vain had used.

"There. Take it." He pointed at the Monet. "The real one."

Vain handed Corrine the gun and she trained it on Wes while Vain walked up to the painting and studied it closely.

The colors, once so subtle and rich, had been a visual lullaby to him, easing an ache inside him he'd never known how to heal. That was before he'd met Callie. From the moment he'd seen her, she was like waking up from a dream and seeing reality for what it was. Brilliant smiles, tender kisses, warm bodies cuddled close by winter fires. And love. So much love that it hurt to imagine one second of a life without her. A Monet couldn't compare to that.

"He's right. It's the real one." Vain lifted the Monet off the wall hook and headed for the door. "Corrine, meet me at the car in two minutes. Only tell him about the poison after I'm out of the room."

After Vain departed, Corrine kept her eye on her watch. When two minutes had passed, she began to back out of the room.

"Corrine!" Wes shouted, his voice breaking. "Tell me what he gave her." He took one step forward, fear choking him. Callie was across the hall. *Dying*. Because he'd been a fool to underestimate the thief.

Corrine stopped at the door's threshold, her cold eyes softening only a second.

"You really care about her. The mighty, impenetrable heart of Wesley Thorne can break after all." She laughed. The cold sound raked over his ears.

"Please." He would get on his knees if he needed to. He would do anything for Callie. "I love her more than anything in my entire life." The words came out and he didn't regret them. It took losing her to see that. He *loved* her. Not only that, but he belonged to her. She owned him as much as he owned her. He could never give another woman his heart.

"Jimsonweed. That's what he slipped into her drink. She'll need Valium if she starts to convulse. Have the doctors give her a purgative like magnesium sulfate." Corrine backed out into the hall and then she bolted down it and out of sight.

Wes ran straight to the study and grabbed his phone. He dialed 911 and told the dispatcher to have the hospital send him a helicopter life flight. Then he wrapped a blanket around Callie and carried her from the study. He passed Bradley as he reached the front door. His butler was slowly getting up from the floor.

"Sir?" he said, voice shaky. "I think…someone is in the house. Someone came up behind me and knocked me out…I can't remember."

"Bradley, come with me. Callie's been poisoned. The hospital is sending a chopper to get us. I want you checked out as well."

Bradley opened the doors so Wes could carry Callie outside. A distant roar of a chopper gave him the barest glimmer of hope.

Callie's lashes fluttered and for a second he saw her eyes. The pupils were dilated.

"Wes." She lifted one hand as though to touch his cheek, but her hand fell limp into her lap and her head rolled back.

"No, baby, please hang on." Tears cut like knives across his eyes as he held on to her. This was all his fault.

"Callie, listen to me. I can't live without you. Do you hear me?" His voice broke as he clutched her tighter. A helicopter rose up over the trees and came overhead, slowly lowering to the ground.

Wes, with Callie in his arms, rushed to the paramedics who opened the doors and lifted a medical stretcher out. Bradley stepped back as the medics got to work strapping Callie in before they loaded her into the chopper. Then Wes and Bradley climbed inside.

The paramedics began to work on her and Wes shouted over the roar of the helicopter's rotating blades what poison Callie had been drugged with. He watched as they inserted an IV into Callie's arm to get fluids into her.

"Sir." Bradley held out Wes's phone. "You had better call her father. He should be flown in from Colorado immediately, just in case…"

Tears blotted out Wes's vision, making it hard to see the numbers on his phone. He finally dialed. It was hard to hear, but he pressed one hand over his other ear.

"Hello?" Jim Taylor answered on the second ring.

"Jim, it's Wes. There's been a situation…" How could he tell the man that he might lose his daughter just like he'd lost his wife?

"Callie?" Jim's voice was breathless, as though shock hit him hard. "What's wrong?"

"Jim, you need to get to the airport. I'll pay for a private charter to get you in twenty minutes."

"God damn it." The older man's voice broke. "What happened to my baby girl?"

For a long second Wes struggled to find words.

"It's a long story, Jim. I can't tell you now. She's been poisoned. We are on a life flight to the hospital." Unable to speak anymore, he shoved the phone at Bradley who continued to speak to Jim.

Wes took Callie's left hand and laced his fingers through hers, squeezing.

"Please stay strong, Callie. I need you. You can't teach me to love and then abandon me." He swiped a hand across his face and it came back wet with tears. He had lived a charmed life, everything at his fingertips.

Everything except love.

Love had found him and now he would lose it.

Chapter 26

Out of the darkness a gold light blossomed before Callie's eyes. It grew from a tiny pinprick into an expanding horizon of glorious color. A shape loomed ahead. A sphinx. The warm stone was carved with familiar symbols. She reached out to touch it. Invisible fingers covered hers, squeezing lightly, then tighter. A breeze ruffled against her face, reminding her of the downy soft feathers of a bird.

"I can't live without you." The words were uttered so frantically, and were so wonderful.

"Can't live without you," she repeated, smiling deep inside. Why did she like those words? Who said them? Strange questions bounced through her mind, like a dozen bright tennis balls…bouncing away…The green court beneath them changed, deepened to a forest and the tennis balls shrunk to flashing fireflies. The thick scent of summer filled her lungs. She drew a deep breath, then looked about. Another pale yellow-green light shone through the gloom.

A lantern.

Four boys sat around the lantern. Small tents were erected behind them. They laughed and sang, roasting marshmallows over a tiny sputtering fire.

"I know you!" she cried out excitedly. The memories were so close, she could almost touch them. She ran toward them, but as she reached them, the boys were swallowed by the shadows. The small flames licking at the logs spit and crackled before the fire died. Gray smoke drifted up in serpentine coils before it vanished.

A loud roar, so loud. The sphinx was angry. It shook its head and clawed its paws in the desert sands. She tried to find it, but it was gone and the golden horizon was gone, too. She could still feel that invisible pressure on her hand as everything threatened to fade back into darkness.

"You can't teach me to love, then abandon me."

That voice. Dark, rich, seductive, yet full of anguish.

She knew that voice. It dropped into her like a stone into a deep well, striking a part of her that awakened at that sound. That voice belonged to a man, a man she belonged to.

"Please, find me!" she screamed out, hoping he could hear. Where was he? Why couldn't he find her?

"Please," she begged. "I don't want to go."

Go. There it was, a strange pull by something inside her, trying to force her into a deeper darkness, one where there would be no more light.

She focused on the darkness around her and then down at her hand. The pressure was there. It hadn't left. She poured every bit of her strength into it and squeezed back. The invisible pressure tightened around her hand in return. Vibrations rolled through her, like deep notes of cellos humming and dying, then striking again.

"She's responding," a new voice said. *"Sir, please let go of her hand. We need to—"*

"No. I'm not letting go."

"Never let go," she tried to say, but her tongue was thick and wouldn't move. The world around her was a fuzzy gray, like a heavy fog had dropped down from the mountains by her home.

Home. She missed the mountains, the silver birch trees with leaves that turned a bright yellow each fall. Leaves burst into a view before her, swirling in circles, caught up by the wind and into a whirling fire around her. Crisp air stinging her eyes and nose as she rode up winding trails.

"Callie, open your eyes."

It was him. Her lifeline. The one she belonged to. Light sparked across her eyelids as they fluttered weakly. She needed to see him, the man who owned her heart.

Bright light burst through as she finally got her eyes open and she whimpered as her entire body quivered and then went very still from weakness.

A face leaned over her, blotting out the fluorescent lights above.

Wes. The name finally came back to her, and as he stared at her so grimly, she frowned back. Flashes of another Wes, one laughing, smiling, seductive, so full of fire and life, almost hurt to remember. The man gazing down at her was gaunt, his eyes lined with fatigue and a shadow of a beard tinting his jaw with a ruddy brown shade.

"What's wrong?" The words were barely above a whisper, but he exhaled in relief and stroked her cheek with the back of his hand. She wanted him to smile, to see that man she'd fallen in love with and not this ashen-faced ghost.

"Thank God." Tears coated the tips of his lashes.

"Wes," she repeated, a tad stronger. In bits and pieces the night of the club came back to her but everything beyond her fight with Corrine was a terrifying blank slate.

"Hush, just rest. You've been through a lot, darling." Wes's hand gripping hers shook faintly.

"What happened? The Monet…"

He bent to press a kiss to her forehead. "It was Stephen Vain. He was the thief. He and Corrine were partners. He poisoned you with Jimsonweed at the club and waited for me to bring you home. Then he blackmailed me into giving him the real Monet in the black room before he would tell me what poison he gave you."

Callie had to focus on what he said, but once she processed it all, she squeezed his hand again. She had been a pawn for Corrine and Vain to use to get the Monet?

"He got away with the Monet in the black room?"

Wes nodded. "The FBI is working with Interpol to track him and Corrine. I know it's a matter of time before they're found, but there's no guarantee that we'll recover any of the paintings."

Despite her weakness, she laughed a little, then winced.

"What's the matter?" Wes smoothed her hair back from her face. He seemed to think she was in pain.

"It's okay, Wes." She managed to smile at him. "The real Monet is safe." Thank God she could finally tell him the secret she'd been hiding the last few days. Her plan had worked and she'd outwitted the thief. Even though she'd been wrong about Thomas Stonecypher, she hadn't been wrong about how the thief had been one step ahead of them.

Wes started to shake his head.

"I painted a second forgery of the Monet. Royce gave me a spare key to the black room. I switched the real one out and put the second fake Monet in your black room."

His lips parted and his eyes widened. "What? Where's the real painting?"

She giggled, but it was breathless. "The real one is under the bed in my studio. I didn't think anyone would think to check all the beds in your mansion."

"Callie, my God!" Wes's fists clenched and he looked like he wanted to punch a wall.

"You're mad?"

"Mad? Mad is not a strong enough word for what I'm feeling right now," he growled as he shoved his chair back from the hospital bed and got to his feet to pace.

"What if Vain had realized the other one was a fake, too? I wouldn't have known where to find the real one. You were unconscious and I could have lost you since I didn't know you'd switched them."

"Please, Wes. I'm sorry. I thought I was doing the right thing. I just wanted to protect the Monet. I know how much you loved it." Hot tears leaked out of her eyes and rolled down her cheeks.

When he noticed, he strode back over to her and leaned over to hug her. His lips were soft against her ear.

"You are the only thing that matters to me, Callie. Nothing is worth your life. Do you understand? *You* are the only thing I love." He lifted his head so their faces were inches apart, eyes locked.

"You love me?" Her bottom lip quivered and she couldn't seem to control it. She bit it to keep from crying. She was so happy. How was it possible to contain everything she was feeling?

"Shh…there will be plenty of time for me to tell you how much I adore you later. I want you to rest now. Your father will be here in a few hours. I want you rested so when he arrives, you'll be well enough that he won't want to kill me."

"He's coming here?"

"Yes, he's going to take you home to Colorado. I have to fix some things here while you recover." Wes caressed the back of her hand with his thumb.

"But I don't want to go back to Colorado without you."

A little smile curved his lips. "You're saying you can't last a few weeks without me?"

A few weeks? She didn't want to go five minutes without him. She shook her head and the movement hurt.

"I'm making another bet with you, darling. Make it, say, three weeks without me and I promise you'll be rewarded."

"No, I want you. Now. Don't you dare leave me, Wes." She squeezed his hand.

"I'm not leaving you, but I do need to send you home because it's the best place for you to heal while I get things settled here. Can you please try to be brave for me and give me some time? Can you do that?"

She nodded, but didn't release his hand. "Don't let go." She was afraid of that darkness coming back. If he held on to her, she wouldn't slip away.

He eased back into the chair by her bed and kept a grip on her hand.

"Never. You are mine. I made a promise to keep you."

As her lashes fell, she finally relaxed.

"You are mine, too," she whispered, then drifted away.

* * *

Three weeks. It seemed like he counted the days whenever Callie wasn't with him. Of course, this hell was of his own making. He'd sent her home to Walnut Springs with her father as soon as she'd gotten out of the hospital. The poison had weakened her body and the doctors had urged her to rest in a place where she was most comfortable with the least amount of stress. That wasn't his home in Weston. The mansion was a flurry of activity as he changed everything in the house he could think of to make it ready for Callie. He finished her art applications, spoke with her soon-to-be professors, arranged for a real studio to be built for her by the Winter Garden.

Everything was going to be perfect.

But it didn't change the fact that he missed her. It was almost like she haunted him, a living ghost, her voice teasing his ears to where he'd turn, thinking she'd be there, only to remember he'd sent her away. The look of betrayal and hurt in her tired eyes had wounded him, but she'd been too exhausted and on medication when Jim had taken Wes's jet to fly her home.

Jim had made it clear that if Wes came for Callie, he'd better be ready to ask for her hand in marriage. Wes agreed. If that was what it took to have Callie in his life, a ring and a ceremony, he'd do it. What's more…he *wanted* to do it.

Wes stood in the old bedroom that had been Callie's temporary studio, his hands tucked into his trouser pockets as he took in the easels full of art. He couldn't wait to see her tomorrow. She had no idea he was coming, so it would be a surprise. A wonderful one, he hoped.

A light rap of knuckles had him turning toward the door. Royce was leaning against the frame, smirking.

"So you love the little cowgirl, don't you?" He rolled his eyes.

Wes shrugged. "No point in denying it."

Royce pushed away from the door frame and walked over to the bed and knelt down.

"Well that's good to hear, because I had a friendly little bet with Callie about whether you did in fact love her. I won, you see, because I knew you loved her. She didn't believe me."

Wes stiffened. "A bet with Callie?" He knew Royce too well, and his bets often had unorthodox payments. "What were the terms?"

His friend slid something out from under the bed, a canvas covered with cloth. He carried it over to an easel and set it up.

"Because I won, she was supposed to give you this. I figured she must have forgotten, what with nearly dying and all." Royce chuckled but there was no real humor in his tone.

"What is it?" Wes joined him as he faced the covered canvas.

"Take a look." Royce nodded at it.

With one hand, Wes carefully let the white cloth drop from the painting and then sucked in a breath.

His soul was there, in the dark green forest, bathed in the lantern-yellow color that had always been a siren call for him. Four little boys…camping. Four men's faces, like dark gods watching over their younger incarnations. Callie knew his deepest secrets now, had painted them on this canvas. The loss of his innocence. She'd shown him that she understood what he mourned and couldn't reclaim, but she reminded him, too, that he wasn't scarred anymore, not in the way he'd believed all these years. She'd painted a light to show him the way out of the darkness, to show him the way home.

"A woman like that…is worth keeping," Royce noted in a thoughtful, almost quiet tone.

Wes's throat constricted and it took him a second longer to answer.

"A woman like that is worth loving."

* * *

Callie leaned against a wooden beam on the Broken Spur ranch's front porch and watched the snow fall. The flakes were thick and large, drifting in the light breeze, catching in swirls and eddies as wind danced down from the mountains. A few brave horses had left the shelter of the barn to plod about in the thickening snow, their panting breaths and soft whinnies a comfort Callie had missed more than she'd realized.

It was finally here. Winter had come. The scent of wood fires burning from the newly built ranch cabins close to the house smelled good. She shivered and tugged her flannel-lined coat closer. Three long weeks had passed since Wes had insisted she fly home to Colorado with her father. She had been too tired and still recovering from the Jimsonweed to argue with Wes when he put her on his plane and sent her home. He'd tried to make it all about another silly bet. Could she last three weeks without him? Yes, she had, but she didn't want to go another day past today without him. If she wasn't so afraid he'd changed his mind about her, she would have asked her father for the money to fly out there to see him. But that little part of her deep inside still doubted he loved her, at least enough for it to last.

She had almost begun to fear her time with Wes had been but a strange and wondrous dream. If it hadn't been for her lovebirds, the ones she'd brought home to Colorado, who chirped each morning and night before she went to sleep she would have thought Paris was a dream. All she had to do was look at them and she remembered each detail of Paris, and the way it felt to be in love with Wes. A grand adventure that now had ended. If only she could accept that.

As the days passed, he hadn't called and she'd lost hope that what he'd said in the hospital about loving her had been true. He'd promised to never let her go. But he had. She'd given him everything and it hadn't been enough.

A screen door opened behind her and her father walked out onto the porch. He looked pleased.

"What are you so happy about?" she asked.

"That damn boy is finally coming." Jim rubbed his hands together and watched the distant road that led to the highway.

Hope surged through her, but she buried it. Her heart wasn't strong enough to survive any more hope.

"What boy?" She stared at her father, afraid of his answer.

Jim held up his cell phone. "Wes. He's pulling onto our road and should be at the ranch in a few minutes. He just called."

"What?" Her heart shuddered and she felt that weak bit of hope blossom. "Why is he coming now?" She knew her father didn't have an explanation.

"He promised to explain when he gets here."

A black Range Rover appeared from the woods and crunched over the falling snow as it drove toward them. Callie was strangely nervous. She hadn't spoken to him in so many days and it felt like years.

The SUV parked in front of the house and Wes climbed out. He looked…sexy. In jeans and a knee-length black wool coat and a charcoal gray sweater. His hair was combed back.

Holding her breath, she watched him. He closed the car door and walked across the snow and up to the steps of the porch. It took everything in her not to run to him, to throw herself into his arms. He looked at her, just an all too quick glance before he focused on Jim.

"Jim," he said, greeting and nodding at her father.

Jim cleared his throat. "Remember what I told you. I better see you on one knee or I might not give you a second chance." Then her father turned and went back inside, the screen door slamming behind him.

Wes walked up the steps until they were nose to nose. They simply stared at one another for a long moment. Callie held her breath, every muscle tense, her entire body craving his warmth and his touch. He reached for her, but Callie flinched, so afraid she'd do something stupid, like beg him to kiss her. His eyes darkened and his lips parted in a soft exhale before he spoke.

"God, I've missed you." His voice was rough and low.

"Why did you send me away? You promised to keep me, Wes! But you sent me away and I haven't seen or heard from you in three weeks! You and your stupid bets!" She hit her balled fists against his chest as a sob caught in her throat, betraying just how hurt she'd felt at his abandonment.

His eyes softened. "My darling, my sweet darling," he murmured and tucked her into his arms, kissing her roughly as though starved for her. She was lost for a long wonderful moment in that kiss that seemed to go on for years. He was tasting her like he would a fine cognac or pure dark chocolate, savoring her taste, and she did the same to him. Going too long without him had been one hell of a withdrawal without her sweet addiction of his kiss.

"I'm sorry I didn't call you. I didn't think you would see it as me leaving you. I wanted you to rest and get better. That couldn't happen if I was here. I'd lose control and take you to bed and that could hurt you if you were too weak. You almost died…" He stopped, took a deep breath, and pressed his forehead to hers. She could feel his hands shaking as they cupped her face.

"And?" she pressed.

"Callie. I love you. I've never loved any woman before. I'm sure I'm going about this all wrong. I wanted to surprise you and bring you home to Long Island, where I've made everything perfect for the rest of our lives together. The last three weeks I've been making changes to my homes both in Weston and in Paris so that you would have everything you could ever want or need. I wanted it to be a surprise."

"Wes, I don't need perfect. I need you." She curled her arms around his neck and brushed her fingertips into his hair at the nape of his neck. His lashes dropped to half-mast.

"I want to be with you. To stay wherever you are, the ranch or the mansion in Weston."

"That's good. Because I've spoken to your father and a ranch cabin is all ours for the winter holidays, on one condition." He reached into his pocket and then got down on one knee. "Callie, you're the center of my world. A life without you isn't living. You were right all along. I've never been in love. I couldn't have imagined what that meant, not until you. I need you in my life. Do you understand? There will be no walking away. You're mine and I'm yours. Forever. I'll do anything, give you anything, just to make you happy. I'm begging you. Marry me."

He was the most powerful, dominant man she'd ever met, and yet he was on his knees begging her to marry him. Warmth blossomed in her chest and she started to nod, tears blinding her eyes. A future with Wes, one full of life, love, art, adventure, someday even children. It was a future she would fight to keep every day of the rest of her life.

"Yes," she gasped. "Yes." She couldn't get out any other words, but it didn't matter. She was in his arms again and he enveloped her with his warmth.

"I never had dreams before I met you." His rough whisper in her ear made her heart clench. His blue eyes were so brilliant and she saw love shining in their depths. "*You* are my dream," he said. "I will do everything in my power to make you happy."

She pressed a finger to his lips. "You only have to love me. It's the only thing I want. To love you and to be loved in return." She peeled back the collar of her coat and showed him the chain necklace she wore. His necklace.

His sweet smile turned wonderfully wicked. "Then you will be the most loved woman in the world." He lowered his voice to a whisper. "Once we're alone, I'll show you just how much I can give you."

"Alone?"

He nodded his head at something behind her. When she turned, she found her father standing in the doorway, his arms crossed over his chest, but he seemed satisfied.

"That will do, boy. You have my blessing. Welcome to the family."

"Thank you, Jim."

"Why don't you both come inside and warm up." Jim held the door open.

Callie turned to Wes, hoping he wouldn't mind being around her father. Emotions flashed across his face and he hugged Callie close.

"What are you thinking about?" she whispered.

He smiled down at her.

"I'm thinking I'm the luckiest man alive. I have a woman to love and a real family. I thought I had everything I wanted. And then I met you." He nuzzled her cheek, then placed a tender kiss on her lips, and she felt his heart there, beating in time with her own.

"You're burned into my soul, Callie." He placed her hand to his chest above his heart.

She leaned into him, hugging him. "From the moment I met you, you've always been in mine. Even before I knew that I loved you, my heart loved you. Just promise me one thing, no more wagers. I don't think I'd survive another bet." This time she kissed him, pushing him against the wooden porch beam. He chuckled against her lips.

"No more bets," he promised.

"Good. Now get over here and make me blush." She tugged at the lapels of his coat.

"Easy, little sub, I owe you plenty of spankings." He murmured seductively.

"Mmm, sounds tempting. Maybe later though. Now, I want you to kiss me, damn it."

"For you?" He raised a brow, trailing one hand down her back. "Anything."

Their lips melted and their hearts merged. She'd never imagined that kissing anyone would feel like this, as though their two souls were touching. Yet, from the moment she'd met Wes Thorne, they'd been connected by something deeper, purer than she could have imagined and a single kiss was but a beautiful drop in a vast sea. This kiss was its own work of art.

A true masterpiece.

Epilogue

Royce Devereaux leaned back against the bar, grinning lazily, as Katrina Evans blew him a kiss good-bye. She sauntered away in those killer heels and black lace lingerie. He was still fully clothed in his jeans and a black t-shirt. They'd only done a minor scene tonight, a light spanking and a little more. He'd been too distracted to get into it tonight, not when they were alone. Half the rush was taking a woman to unbelievable heights of pleasure, knowing others could see her come apart screaming his name.

That hadn't happened tonight. It had been a nice evening. Nice. He grimaced. His nights used to be explosive, mind-blowing, but never *nice*. He was born to be bad. Born to be wicked, and he hadn't yet found a woman who could keep up with him.

He studied the other doms in the Gilded Cuff. Many of them were preoccupied with their own subs, unaware of his scrutiny. They were immersed in their own love affairs, bodies entwined. Royce felt a momentary flare of nostalgia he couldn't quite place, causing him to give in to an uncharacteristic sigh. It used to be fun. He, Emery, and Wes breaking in new submissives with games and using wicked sex toys. Their world had seemed limitless. Until now.

Now it's just me. The sharp pang of anger and jealousy shot through him, leaving a sour taste in his mouth.

His phone vibrated in his jeans pocket and when he checked the screen, he saw a text from Wes.

"She said yes."

That was it. Royce growled softly, his fist clenching around the phone before he shoved it back into his pocket. Wes had flown out to Colorado that day to propose to Callie Taylor.

Royce spun to face the bar and reached over the edge to grab a nearby bottle of bourbon and a shot glass. Tonight was not his night. He was totally alone since Kat's departure, and now he was completely fucked and not in the way he wanted, because the last of his best friends had just gotten engaged.

To Wes and Callie, he thought, as he downed the first of what promised to be a series of shots. The liquid burned his throat and he savored it, tilting his head back to the ceiling and letting it wash through him.

"Royce?" Aria Lexington, the Gilded Cuff's top domme and gatekeeper of membership check-ins, walked up to him. Wearing her usual dark suit and black glasses with her hair in a sleek yet sexy chignon, she was a man's perfect librarian fantasy. Not his though…He liked a submissive woman in bed, one he could spank, not one who'd rather spank him.

"What do you want?" he replied as he turned to face her, filling his glass of bourbon as he met her gaze.

"There's a young woman in the lobby. She says she has to talk to you. Her name is Mackenzie Martin."

Royce froze, the bourbon spilling over the edges of his glass and onto his fingers before he recovered and hastily set the bottle on the bar. It thunked hard against the wood surface and drew the attention of the bartender, who quirked a brow in concern.

"I was going to turn her away, per our privacy policy, but she seemed earnest and she's not dressed for the club, if you get my meaning. She actually seems a bit frightened, and well…it looks like she's been roughed up by someone."

Kenzie was here? For a moment Royce's brain short-circuited. His teacher's assistant was standing in the lobby of *his* club? The club she wasn't supposed to know about. And she was roughed up. Someone had hurt her…

"Let her in," he told Aria. "She's one of my graduate students. My TA."

Aria straightened her glasses and blinked. "Are you sure? We had a ban of all students from the university at your request."

"Aria," Royce growled low. Even though the woman was a domme, she responded to his alpha dominance and lowered her head a few inches.

"Very well. You should come with me. She seems a bit skittish and insisted she speak to no one but you."

Every muscle in Royce's body tensed. What had happened to his TA? They rarely shared a civil word to one another and for her to seek him out was…abnormal. Adding to that what Aria had said about her being skittish, that wasn't good.

Aria led Royce through the main club floor. When she opened the door to the lobby, one of the club monitors, Bruce, stood just outside watching something in the corner of the room far away from him.

"Where is she?" Royce asked him, glancing about the partially dim lobby.

Bruce gave a little nod indicating a bench on the far wall by the door. There, dripping wet, her eyes wide, hands clenched into fists, was Kenzie Martin. Royce took in her posture, the way her arms curled around her chest, her cable-knit sweater hanging limp about her body. She looked like a half-drowned kitten. Her jeans were dark with water and soaked with mud on one side as though she'd fallen. A small tear of her jeans on one knee caught his eye because of the bright crimson slash of blood. A bruise marred her cheek on the left side. Her head was bowed as though she was tired and attempting to hide or make herself appear smaller. They were the actions of a creature who'd been recently attacked.

His blood boiled and he clenched his fists. She'd been hurt and he was going to kill whoever had touched her.

"Dr. Devereaux?" She sat up when she saw him, her chocolate-brown eyes darting from him to Aria and then to Bruce.

"Kenzie, what's happened?" He left Aria and Bruce as he strode over to her and knelt down on one knee so he was level with her. He cupped her cheeks and turned her face, inspecting the damage. Her long lashes fluttered and a single tear trickled down her bruised cheek. It glistened beneath the muted lamplight from the wall sconces and he brushed it away with the pad of his thumb.

"Can I speak with you privately?" she whispered, her gaze flicking to Bruce and Aria, who were still in the lobby, watching them intently.

"Okay, sure. There's a room in the club where we can have some privacy." He offered her a hand.

Normally he avoided touching her because she was so tempting. There was too much fire in her, too much sass, and he wanted to dominate her right into his bed…spank the sass right out of her until she was begging for him to take her. But she was off-limits. He'd never slept with a student at his college and he never would. It was a line he wouldn't cross. And Kenzie had made it clear what she thought of him romantically, which was nothing. Rather than blush at his mildly inappropriate remarks that sometimes slipped out while they worked late on grading assignments, she just fired right back at him with some remark that put him in his place. Namely as her professor and not as a potential lover. Now, when her frightened gaze and trembling lips set off every instinct in him to protect her, she was more off-limits than ever.

She slipped her hand into his without questioning him. He led her past Aria and Bruce and into the club. Most of the subs and doms were getting up to leave for the night, but a few couples still lingering in the club eyed them with interest. Kenzie shifted closer to him, an almost unconscious move as he took her back to one of the private rooms.

She followed him inside but skidded to a halt when she saw the massive bed in the center of the room. Her almond-shaped eyes widened.

"What—"

"Relax, Kenzie. It's just a bed. Sit down and tell me what happened." He guided her over and gently pushed on her shoulders until she sat. Then he walked over to a dresser and opened the top drawer. Every private room kept a first-aid kit handy just in case the play got a little rough. He flipped the case open and dug through its contents until he found some antiseptic pads and a couple of Band-Aids. Tearing the packet open, he walked back to her and lifted one of her legs onto the bed so it was easier to reach. Her knee was scraped, the cut was not deep, but still bloody.

"This may sting," he warned softly. The cool cloth wiped away the dirt and blood as he rubbed gently at the cut.

Kenzie bit her lip, but made no sound. After he cleaned the cut and covered it with a Band-Aid he treated her scraped hands the same way. Once that was done, he cupped her chin and tilted her head to look up at him.

"Tell me what happened."

She swallowed hard and nodded.

"I was in your office finishing up putting the exam scores into your database." Kenzie paused, licked her chapped, split bottom lip, and then continued. "Three men broke into your office while I was there."

His blood began to pound a steady, fast rhythm deep inside his head. Flashes of the past, of old fears, threatened to resurface. No, this wasn't twenty-five years ago. He wasn't a little boy whose friends were taken by masked men.

"And?" he prompted, burying his dark thoughts of his past.

"They were looking for you, Dr. Devereaux. They attacked me before I could act. One hit me a few times." She touched her cheek and then met his gaze. It was all steel and courage in her eyes.

Damn, what a woman Kenzie was.

"I pretended to be unconscious and overheard them talking to someone on the phone. When they weren't looking, I jumped out of the office window behind your desk."

"What? That's a second-story window!"

Kenzie's responding chuckle was full of pain. "Yeah. One hell of a drop. It's how I got so banged up. I sort of scaled down the drain pipe until it broke. I'm just glad I had my car keys in my jeans and not my purse. I drove straight here."

"Why didn't you go to the police or go home?"

Two red spots colored her cheeks. "I thought they might check my wallet. It has my driver's license in there with my apartment address on it."

"You should have gone to the police." He turned his back on her as he walked over to a trash bin to dispose of the cleansing wipes and Band-Aid wrappings.

"They said something on the phone that had me worried and

made me afraid to get the police involved. I think they have an inside connection to the police department here. And they seemed to want to talk to you about illegal trafficking. I didn't want to get you in the middle of something…" She trailed off and he understood what she meant. She thought he was involved in something illicit and didn't want to bring that to the police. Talk about TA loyalty.

Royce faced her again as he considered everything she'd told him. He didn't have any enemies that he was aware of. He didn't owe money, and he certainly hadn't crossed anyone to the point that they would hire thugs to break into his office.

"Illegal trafficking…" he mused aloud. "I have no idea what they're talking about." He hoped that would reassure her. She didn't look that convinced.

"Dr. Devereaux, I'm afraid to go back to my apartment."

He knew for Kenzie to admit her fear of anything meant it was serious. He was responsible for her injuries and he needed to protect her. To do that, he had to figure out what the hell was going on.

"I'll take you somewhere safe tonight." He knew just where to bring her.

Kenzie let her bandaged leg drop off the bed. "Where?"

"My home."

Her lips parted but he silenced her with one of his dom scowls. It had cowered many a rebellious submissive in the club before.

"Until I figure out what's going on, I want you near me. Allow me to protect you. Understood?"

She nodded, eyes wide.

"Good. Now, let's get out of here. The quicker we figure this out, the better."

If he didn't resolve this issue soon, he'd be in deep shit. Kenzie under his roof was going to drive him insane with lust. He knew the moment her natural sass returned he'd be tempted to bend her over the nearest flat surface, spank her, and then fuck her until they both couldn't walk. And that was bad. Really bad.

If he couldn't maintain his control, she'd end up in his bed, and his most important rule would be broken.

Every passion has its price…

See the next page for an excerpt from THE GILDED CUFF by Lauren Smith.

AVAILABLE NOW

Chapter 1

Emery Lockwood and Fenn Lockwood,
eight-year-old twin sons of Elliot and Miranda
Lockwood, were abducted from their family
residence on Long Island between seven and
eight p.m. The kidnapping occurred during a
summer party hosted by the Lockwoods.

—*New York Times,* June 10, 1990

Long Island, New York

T his is absolutely the stupidest thing I've ever done.

Sophie Ryder tugged the hem of her short skirt down over her legs a few more inches. It was still way too high. But she couldn't have worn something modest, per her usual style. Not at an elite underground BDSM club on Long Island's Gold Coast. Sophie had never been to any club before, let alone one like this. She'd had to borrow the black mini-skirt and the red lace-up corset from her friend Hayden Thorne, who was a member of the club and knew what she should wear.

The Gilded Cuff. It was *the* place for those who enjoyed their kink and could afford to pay.

Sophie sighed. A journalist's salary wasn't enough to afford anything like what the people around her wore, and she was definitely feeling less sexy in her practical black flats with a bit of sparkle on the tips. Sensuality rippled off every person in the room as they brushed against her in their Armani suits and Dior gowns, and she was wary of getting too close. Their cultured voices echoed off the craggy gray stone walls as they chatted and gossiped. Although she was uneasy with the frank way the people around her touched and teased each other with looks and light caresses, even while patiently waiting in line, a stirring of nervousness skittered through her chest and her abdomen. Half of it had to do with the sexual chemistry of her surroundings, and the rest of it had to do with the story that would make her career, if she could only find who she was looking for and save his life in time. Her editor at the Kansas newspaper she wrote for had given her one week to break the story. What she didn't know was how long she had to save the life of a man who at this very moment was in the club somewhere. She swallowed hard and tried to focus her thoughts.

Following the crowd, she joined the line leading up to a single walnut wood desk with gilt edges. A woman in a tailored gray suit over a red silk blouse stood there checking names off a list with a feather pen. Sophie fought to restrain her frantic pulse and the flutter of rebellious butterflies in her stomach as she finally reached the desk.

"Name, please?" The woman peered over wide, black-rimmed glasses. She looked a cross between a sexy librarian and a no-nonsense lawyer.

A flicker of panic darted through Sophie. She hoped her inside source would come through. Not just anyone could get into the club. You had to be referred by an existing member as a guest.

"My name's Sophie Ryder. I'm Hayden Thorne's guest." At the mention of her new friend's name the other woman instantly smiled, warmth filling her gaze.

"Yes, of course. She called and mentioned you'd be coming. Welcome to the Gilded Cuff, Sophie." She reached for a small glossy pamphlet and handed it over. "These are the club rules. Read over them carefully before you go inside. Come to me if you have any questions. You can also go to anyone wearing a red armband. They are our club monitors. If you get in too deep and you get panicked, say the word "red" and that will make the game or the scene stop. It's the common safe word. Any doms inside should respect that. If they don't, they face our monitors."

"Okay," Sophie sucked in a breath, trying not to think about what sort of scene would make her use a safe word. This really was the most stupid thing she'd ever done. Her heart drummed a staccato beat as a wave of dread swept through her. She should leave…No. She had to stay at least a few more minutes. A life could hang in the balance, a life she could save.

"There's just one more thing. I need to know if you are a domme or a sub." The woman trailed the feather tip end of her pen under the tip of her chin, considering Sophie, measuring her.

"A domme or sub?" Sophie knew the words. Dominant and submissive. Just another part of the BDSM world, a lifestyle she knew so little about. Sophie definitely wasn't a domme. Dommes were the feminine dominants in a D/s relationship. She certainly had no urge to whip her bed partner.

She liked control, yes, but only when it came to her life and doing what she needed to do. In bed? Well…she'd always liked to think of an aggressive man as one who took what he wanted, gave her what she needed. Not that she'd ever had a man like that before. Until now, every bedroom encounter had been a stunning lesson in disappointment.

The woman suddenly smiled again, as though she'd been privy to Sophie's inner thoughts. "You're definitely not a domme." Amusement twitched the corners of her mouth. "I sense you would enjoy an *aggressive* partner."

How in the hell? Sophie quivered. The flash of a teasing image, a man pinning her to the mattress, ruthlessly pumping into her until she exploded with pleasure. Heat flooded her face.

"Ahh, there's the sub. Here, take these." The woman captured Sophie's wrists and clamped a pair of supple leather cuffs around each wrist. Sewn into the leather, a red satin ribbon ran the length of each cuff. The woman at the desk didn't secure Sophie's wrists together, but merely ensured she had cuffs ready to be cinched together should she find a partner inside. The feel of the cuffs around her wrists sent a ripple of excitement through her. How was it possible to feel already bound and trapped? They constrained her, but didn't cut off her circulation, like wearing a choker necklace. She wanted to tug at the cuffs the way she would a tight necklace, because she was unused to the restriction.

"These tell the doms inside that you're a sub, but you're unclaimed and new to the lifestyle. Other subs will be wearing cuffs; some won't. It depends on if they are currently connected with a particular dom and whether that dom wishes to show an ownership. Since you're not with anyone, the red ribbons tell everyone you're new and learning the lifestyle. They'll know to go easy on you and to ask permission before doing or trying anything with you. The monitors will keep a close eye on you."

Relief coursed through Sophie. Thank heavens. She was only here to pursue a story. Part of the job was to get information however she could, do whatever it took. But she wasn't sure she would be ready to do the things she guessed went on behind the heavy oak doors. Still, for the story, she would probably have to do something out of her comfort zone. It was the nature of writing about criminal stories. Of course, tonight wasn't about a crime, but rather a victim—and this victim was the answer to everything she'd spent years hoping to learn. And she was positive he was in danger.

When she'd gone to the local police with her suspicions, they'd turned a blind eye and run her off with the usual assurances that they kept a close eye on their community. But they didn't see patterns like she did. They hadn't read thousands of articles about crimes and noticed what she did. Somewhere inside this club, a man's life was hanging by a thread and she would save him and get the story of the century.

"Cuffs please." A heavily muscled man reached for her wrists as she approached the door that led deeper into the club. He wore an expensive suit with a red armband on his bicep, but his sheer brawny power was actually accented, rather than hidden, by his attire. It surprised her. She'd expected men to be running around in black leather and women fully naked, surrounded by chains, whips, and the whole shebang.

The man looked at her wrists, then up at her face. "You know the safe word, little sub?"

"Red."

"Good girl. Go on in and have a good time." The man's mouth broke into a wide smile, but it vanished just as quickly. She smiled back, and bowed her head slightly in a nod as she passed by him.

She moved through the open door into another world. Instead of a dungeon with walls fitted with iron chains, Sophie found the Gilded Cuff was the opposite of what she'd anticipated.

Music and darkness ruled the landscape of the club, engulfing her senses. She halted abruptly, her heart skittering in a brief flare of panic at not being able to see anything around her.

The dungeons and screams she'd expected weren't there. Was this typical for a BDSM atmosphere? Her initial research had clearly led her astray. It wasn't like her to be unprepared and The Gilded Cuff certainly surprised her. Every scenario she'd planned for in her head now seemed silly and ineffective. This place and these people weren't anything like what'd she'd imagined they would be and that frightened her more than the cuffs did. Being unprepared could get you killed. It was a lesson she'd learned the hard way and she had the scars to prove it. The club's rule pamphlet the woman at the desk had given her was still in her hands and a slight layer of sweat marked the glossy paper's surface.

I probably should have glanced at it. What if I break a rule by accident?

The last thing she needed to do was end up in trouble or worse, get kicked out and not have a chance to do what she'd come to do. It might be her *only* chance to save the man who'd become her obsession.

Sophie made her way through an expansive room bordered with rope-tied crimson velvet drapes that kept prying eyes away from the large beds beyond them when the curtains were untied. Only the sounds coming from behind the draperies hinted at what was happening there. Her body reacted to the sounds, and she became aroused despite her intention to remain aloof. Around here, people lounged on gothic-style, brocade-upholstered couches. Old portraits hung along the walls, imperious images of beautiful men and women from ages past watching coldly from their frames. Sophie had the feeling that she'd stepped into another time and place entirely removed from the cozy streets of the small town of Weston, on the north shore of Long Island.

The slow pulse of a bass beat and a singer's husky crooning wrapped around Sophie like an erotic blanket. As if she were in a dark dream, moving shadows and music filled her, and she breathed deeply, teased by hints of sex and expensive perfume. Awareness of the world outside wavered, rippling in her mind like a mirage. Someone bumped into her from behind, trying to pass by her to go deeper into the club. The sudden movement jerked her back to herself and out of the club's dark spell.

"Sorry!" she gasped and stepped out of the way.

As her eyes adjusted to the dim light, bodies manifested in twisting shapes. The sounds of sexual exploration were an odd compliment to the song being played. A heavy blush flooded Sophie's cheeks, heating her entire face. Her own sexual experiences had been awkward and brief. The memories of those nights were unwanted, uncomfortable, and passionless. Merely reliving them in her mind made her feel like a stranger in her own skin. She raised her chin and focused on her goal again.

The cuffs on her wrists made her feel vulnerable. At any moment a dom could come and clip her wrists together and haul her into a dark corner to show her true passion at his hands. The idea made her body hum to life in a way she hadn't thought possible. Every cell in her seemed to yearn now toward an encounter with a stranger in this place of sins and secrets. She trailed her fingertips over the backs of velveteen couches and the slightly rough texture of the fabric made her wonder how it would feel against her bare skin as she was stretched out beneath a hard masculine body.

The oppressive sensual darkness that slithered around the edges of her own control was too much. There was a low-lit lamp not too far away, and Sophie headed for it, drawn by the promise of its comfort. Light was safe; you could see what was happening. It was the dark that set her on edge. If she couldn't see what was going on around her, she was vulnerable. There was barely enough light for her to see where she was headed. She needed to calm down, regain her composure and remind herself why she was here.

Her heart trampled a wild beat against her ribs as she realized it would be so easy for any one of the strong, muscular doms in the club to slide a hand inside her bodice and discover the thing she'd hidden there, an object that had become precious to her over the last few years.

Her hand came to rest on the copy of an old photograph. She knew taking it out would be a risk, but she couldn't fight the need to steal the quick glance the dim light would allow her.

Unfolding the picture gently, her lips pursed as she studied the face of the eight-year-old boy in the picture. This was the childhood photo of the man she'd come to meet tonight.

The black and white photo had been on the front page of the *New York Times* twenty-five years ago. The boy was dressed in rags, and bruises marred his angelic face; his haunted eyes gazed at the camera. A bloody cut traced the line of his jaw from chin to neck. Eyes wide, he clasped a thick woolen blanket to his body as a policeman held out a hand to him.

Emery Lockwood. The sole survivor of the most notorious child abduction in American history since that of the Lindbergh baby. And he was somewhere in the Gilded Cuff tonight.

Over the last year she'd become obsessed with the photo and had taken to looking at it when she needed reassurance. Its subject had been kidnapped but survived and escaped, when so many children like him over the years had not been so lucky. Sophie's throat constricted, and shards of invisible glass dug into her throat as she tried to shrug off her own awful memories. Her best friend Rachel, the playground, that man with the gray van…

The photo was creased in places and its edges were worn. The defiance in Emery's face compelled her in a way nothing else in her life had. Compelled with an intensity that scared her. She had to see him, had to talk to him and understand him and the tragedy he'd survived. She was afraid he might be the target of another attempt on his life and she had to warn him. It wouldn't be fair for him to die, not after everything he'd survived. She had to help him. But it wasn't just that. It was the only way she could ease the guilt she'd felt at not being able to help catch the man who'd taken her friend. She had to talk to Emery. Even though she knew it wouldn't bring Rachel back, something inside her felt like meeting him would bring closure.

With a forced shrug of her shoulders, she relaxed and focused on Emery's face. After years of studying kidnapping cases she'd noticed something crucial in a certain style of kidnappings, a tendency by the predators to repeat patterns of behavior. When she'd started digging through Emery's case and read the hundreds of articles and police reports, she'd sensed it. That prickling sensation at the back of her mind that warned her that what had been started twenty-five years ago wasn't over yet. She hadn't been able to save Rachel, but she would save Emery.

I have to. She owed it to Rachel, owed it to herself and to everyone who'd lost someone to the darkness, to evil. Guilt stained her deep inside but when she saw Emery's face in that photograph, it reminded her that not every stolen child died. A part of her, one she knowingly buried in her heart, was convinced that talking to him, hearing his story, would ease the old wounds from her own past that never seemed to heal. And in return, she might be the one to solve his kidnapping and rescue him from a threat she was convinced still existed.

She wasn't the boldest woman—at least not naturally—but the quest for truth always gave her that added level of bravery. Sometimes she felt, when in the grips of pursuing a story, that she became the person she ought to be, someone brave enough to fight the evil in the world. Not the tortured girl from Kansas who'd lost her best friend to a pedophile when she was seven years old.

Sophie would have preferred to conduct an interview somewhere less intimate, preferably wearing more clothing. But Emery was nearly impossible to reach—he avoided the press, apparently despising their efforts to get him to tell his story. She didn't blame him. Retelling his story could be traumatic for him, but she didn't have a choice. If what she suspected was true, she needed the details she was sure he'd kept from the police because they might be the keys to figuring out who'd kidnapped him and why.

She'd made calls to his company, but the front desk there had refused to transfer her to his line, probably because of his "no press" rule. Thanks to Hayden she knew Emery rarely left the Lockwood estate but he came to the Gilded Cuff a few times a month. This was the only opportunity she might have to reach him.

Emery ran his father's company from a vast mansion on the Lockwood estate, nestled in the thick woods of Long Island's Gold Coast. No visitors were permitted and he left the house only when in the company of private guards.

Sophie tucked the photo back into her corset and looked around, peering at the faces of the doms walking past her. More than once their gazes dropped to the cuffs on her wrists, possessively assessing her body. Her face scorched with an irremovable blush at their perusal. Whenever she made eye contact with a dom, he would frown and she'd instantly drop her gaze.

Respect; must remember to respect the doms and not make eye contact unless they command it. Otherwise she might end up bent over a spanking bench. Her corset seemed to shrink, making it hard to breathe, and heat flashed from her head to her toes.

Men and women—submissives judging by the cuffs they bore on their wrists—were wearing even less than she was as they walked around with drink trays, carrying glasses to doms on couches. Several doms had subs kneeling at their feet, heads bowed. A man sitting on a nearby love seat was watching her with hooded eyes.

He had a sub at his feet, his hand stroking her long blond hair. The woman's eyes were half closed, cheeks flushed with pleasure. The dom's cobalt blue eyes measured her—not with sexual interest, but seemingly with mere curiosity—the way a sated mountain lion might watch a plump rabbit crossing its path.

Sophie pulled her eyes away from the redheaded dom and his ensnaring gaze. The club was almost too much to take in. Collars, leashes, the occasional pole with chains hanging from it, and a giant cross were all there, part of the fantasy world created amid the glitz and old world décor.

Sliding past entwined bodies and expensive furniture, she saw more that intrigued her. The club itself was this one large room with several halls splitting off the main room. Hayden had explained earlier that morning the layout of the club. She had pointed out that no matter which hall you went down you had to come back to the main room to exit the club. A handy safety feature. A little exhalation of relief escaped her lips. How deep did a man like Emery Lockwood live this lifestyle? Would she find him in one of the private rooms or would he be part of a public scene like the ones she was witnessing now?

She was nearly halfway across the room when a man caught her by her arm and spun her to face him. Her lips parted, ready to scream the word "red", but when she met his gaze she froze, the shout dying at the back of her throat. He raised her wrists, fingering the red ribbon around her leather cuffs. His gray eyes were as silver as moonlight, and openly interested. Sophie tried to jerk free of his hold. He held tight. The arousal that had been slowly building in her body flashed cold and sharp. She could use the safe word. She knew that. But after one deep breath, she forced herself to relax. Part of the job tonight was to blend in, to find Emery. She couldn't do that if she ran off and cried for help at the first contact. It would be smarter to let this play out a bit; maybe she could squeeze the dom for information about Emery later if she didn't find him soon. For Sophie, not being able to get to Emery was more frightening than anything this man might try to do to her.

"I see your cuffs, little sub. I'm not going to hurt you."

His russet hair fell across his eyes and he flicked his head: power, possession, dominance. He was raw masculinity. A natural dom. He was the sort of good-looking man that she would have mooned over when she was a teenager. Hell, even now at twenty-four she should have been melting into a puddle at this man's feet. His gaze bit into her. A stab of sudden apprehension made her stomach pitch, but she needed to find Emery and going along with this guy might be the best way to get information. He tugged her wrists, jerking her body against his as he regarded her hungrily. "I need an unclaimed sub for a contest. Tonight is your lucky night, sweetheart."

ABOUT THE AUTHOR

LAUREN SMITH was born and raised in Tulsa. She attended Oklahoma State University, where she earned a B.A. in both history and political science. Drawn to paintings and museums, Lauren is obsessed with antiques and satisfies her fascination with history by writing and exploring exotic, ancient lands.